FACE OF AN ANGEL

DENISE CHÁVEZ

D0036869

WARNER BOOKS

A Time Warner Company

Warner Books Edition
Copyright © 1994 by Denise Chávez
All rights reserved.

This Warner Books edition is published by arrangement with Farrar, Straus and Giroux, 19 Union Square West, New York, NY 10003

Warner Books, Inc., 1271 Avenue of the Americas, New York, NY 10020

⦿ A Time Warner Company

Printed in the United States of America

First Warner Books Printing: November 1995

10 9 8 7 6 5 4 3 2 1

Library of Congress Cataloging-in-Publication Data

Chávez, Denise
    Face of an angel / Denise Chávez.
    p. cm
    ISBN 0-446-67185-1 (pbk.)
    1. Mexican American women—Southwestern States—Fiction.
2. Mexican American families—Southwestern States—Fiction. 3. Mexican Americans—Southwestern States—Fiction. 4. Restaurants—Southwestern States—Fiction. 5. Waitresses—Southwestern States—Fiction 6. Family—Southwestern States—Fiction. 7. Southwestern States—Fiction.
I. Title.
       [PS3553.H346F34   1995]
       813'.54—dc20   95-21094
                                 CIP

Cover design by Diane Luger
Cover illustration by Amy Cordova

For my father, E. E. Chávez

For all the women, criadas and ayudantes, who have taught me the meaning of the word service: Teresita, Esperanza, Celia, Cata I, Cata II, Concha, Ninfa, Regina, Cuca, Isa, Belsora, Berta, Lina, Socorro, Emilia, Delfina, Toña

For Katy, Carolyn, Minda, Celia, Nellie, Maggie, for all my sisters likewise who have waited, will wait. ¡Buen provecho! And don't forget to ring up the bar!

My grandmother's voice was rarely heard, it was a whisper, a moan. Who heard?

My mother's voice cried out in rage and pain. Who heard?

My voice is strong. It is breath. New Life. Song. Who hears?

Dosamantes Family Tree

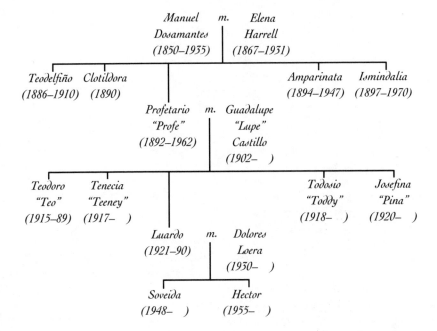

Manuel Dosamantes (1850–1935) m. Elena Harrell (1867–1931)

Teodelfiño (1886–1910)

Clotildora (1890)

Profetario "Profe" (1892–1962) m. Guadalupe "Lupe" Castillo (1902–)

Amparinata (1894–1947)

Ismindalia (1897–1970)

Teodoro "Teo" (1915–89)

Tenecia "Teeney" (1917–)

Luardo (1921–90) m. Dolores Loera (1930–)

Todosio "Toddy" (1918–)

Josefina "Pina" (1920–)

Soveida (1948–)

Hector (1955–)

Angels

1

A Long Story

Luardo my father. Dolores my mother. Hector my brother. Mara my cousin. Fathers. Mothers. Brothers. Sisters. Cousins. The concept of naming gets in the way. Now that I am older I can allow myself to look at my family as people. People like myself with hunger and hope. People with failings.

Luardo was once Dad, and as I grew older Dolores became Dolly. I was always Soveida. The Soveida who sat in other rooms.

What kind of name is that?

It's the name of a dead woman. The other Soveida was a pregnant woman with two small children. She was only twenty-seven years old when she was killed instantly in a car accident. Dolores read about it in the obituary column. She liked the name. It stuck. I, Soveida Dosamantes, am her namesake. Husbandless. Childless. Daughter of. Sister of. Wife of. Mother of no one except herself. A helpless child who would never have chosen that name.

I am also almost parentless. My mother, Dolly, is more like a sister to me now than a mother. My father, Luardo, was never a real father, more like an unpleasant uncle. My real family is my grandmother, Mamá Lupita, and my cousin, Mara.

I never knew the face of the real Soveida, but I have imagined her often in my dreams. I see her proud fertile nakedness, a vision of life dancing in a nearby room, her long dark hair flowing. In my dreams she is forever young, not as she would be now: seventy-two years old, white-haired, belly-bloated, a babysitter sucking on the past like a mint.

I don't want to call them by those names. Mother. Father. Brother. Sister. Cousin.

The longer I live, the more I see that it is the same life, the same story, the same characters. All of them with the same face.

The more I think about it, it had to happen.

My grandmother Lupita says, "Soveida, you like to read. What you're reading is the story of the world. Everyone has a story, your mamá has a story, your daddy has a story, even *you* have a story to tell. Tell it while you can, while you have the strength, because when you get to be my age, the telling gets harder. The memories are the clothes in your closet that you never wear and are afraid to throw out because you'll hurt someone. But then you realize one long day, m'jita, that there's no one left to hurt except yourself. All of a sudden you get old. You love your life. You sing. You dance. You laugh. You love. You cry. It had to happen. Don't you see? You lie down. And then you wake up suddenly with a mouthful of cenizas, nothing but ash. A memory of sweetness buried in the ground. M'jita, everyone has to die."

I speak for them now. Mother. Father. Brother. Sister. Cousin. Uncle. Aunt. Husband. Lover.

Their memories are mine. That sweet telling mine. Mine the ash.

It's a long story.

2

The Sleepwalker

Manuel Dosamantes Iturbide, my great-grandfather on my father's side, was born in Guanajuato, México. He came to the U.S. through Nuevo Laredo and worked for a while in Texas. His destination was California, but he never made it.

Manuel was a jack-of-all-trades, working at times as a carpenter, farmer, and cowboy. A man of natural talent, keen ingenuity, and cleverness, he was good at whatever he did. He was a hard worker as well, honest and forthright. Wherever he went, his bosses begged him to stay on, promising him a home, and good pay.

At the last job in Fort Davis, he was offered a partnership in a cattle ranch. The ranch came with a price tag, however: the owner's dark-skinned, flat-chested daughter, Tobarda Acosta. Tobarda was well past her prime, like a piece of meat with all its natural juices gone. Manuel knew it was time to move on when Tobarda herself sought him out, flowers in her wispy hair, offering herself to him in the long summer darkness, no moon to be seen. Manuel wished that Tobarda was a woman he could love, for already that magic, soul-sinking pull of West Texas had affected him. He longed to stay awhile, maybe a long time, in that place that had almost brought him peace. Damn! If it weren't for that woman sidling up to him like a hungry cat, the one that was always ignored. He could not look at her without feeling some kind of pity, and that was very bad. So he turned away, leaving everything behind: his clothes, his horse, his gear.

Walking away from Tobarda that immense, still night was one of the hardest things he ever did, he told his son Profetario years later. Manuel knew that he could never love Tobarda the way he wanted to love a woman, and he was mad at himself for not wanting to love her.

He was mad at himself as well for abandoning Don Severio, her father, an old man with a bad stomach who knew he didn't have long to live. Don Severio had offered Manuel his beloved children: Tobarda and the ranch, La Esperanza, named after his mother.

Manuel knew he would break the old man's heart, as well as the daughter's. He'd done it already, as he walked into that solid night: no stars, no light, no prayers. Nothing but a desperate, almost hopeful darkness, the darkness of a sleepwalker who must and will get away. His actions that night were just as automatic and deep-rooted.

Earlier, Tobarda had come to him in the small room near the stables, "his room." It was full of the smell of horse and man. Leather harnesses and saddles hung on the walls. Manuel's small bed faced an open window that looked out onto an exercise yard where he gently broke the new horses, asking only as much as the horse could give. Likewise, he took Tobarda that night. What else could he do? He felt sorry for her.

She came in brazenly, as he was reading by the kerosene lamp. He felt a presence, took his gun out, then lowered it, seeing the once shy woman standing there, in a dark robe, with her stringy, longish hair draped over her bony shoulders. He stood there as she took off the robe, then the nightgown, and lay on top of his bed. Her body was like that of a fifteen-year-old boy's: very thin, with no muscle tone, her legs long as a newborn calf's. Her arms were crossed over her breasts, which were more like a cow's reddish teats.

Manuel Dosamantes approached her, sat on the edge of the bed, and embraced her nakedness. She cried softly, and then with a deep breath placed her arms around him and drew him near. He felt like running but he was unable to. She had him, a demon lover, and she pulled him to her. And he, a mere man, caressed her as he would a dying tree, with outstretched hands, feeling a deep compassion, an overwhelming, nostalgic emptiness. Dry, bumpy, uncharted, her body lay there, unmoving, as he took off his clothes and got on top of her. His actions were heavy, like an underwater swimmer, and when she opened her legs, he awoke. She was dry, and nothing could unloosen her. He struggled, she was silent; he moaned, she bit her lip. Exhausted, he slid off her, his own sweat the only wetness he'd felt. Dios mío, what have I done, what am I doing, he thought to himself as he arose, startled from his nocturnal walk toward hell, or freedom, he didn't know which. What have I done? What am I trying to do?

Tobarda lay there stiffly, hands clenched, eyes closed.

Quickly, Manuel moved away from her and threw on his clothes. It was then that Tobarda opened her eyes and stared at him, wide-eyed, slightly sad. He looked at her, and again a wave of pity and unrest came upon him. But before it washed over him completely, he was gone from the room.

He left behind all his memories: the picture of his mother, Galardita, in her high-collared dress, her braided hair wrapped around her head like a halo; his father, Pacífico, with his white beard, seated next to his mother, she standing over him, ever watchful, stern; his brothers, Juan María and Evaristo, as children, in long, white dresses; and himself, as a boy, standing next to a dried tree, in a nowhere land on the outskirts of his colonial hometown, Guanajuato. He had lived in poverty and hope there, full of parched dreams from all the heat. Now that hope for water, for green, for lushness was dead. It had died in the mountains near Fort Davis with a thirsty woman whom he could not love. Ever.

Manuel ran toward the heat and the desert, toward the mesquite and the scrub brush. When he tired of running, he found a town of five hundred in Natividad county, New Mexico. Agua Oscura—dark water—it was called.

He would work here and make his money here. He knew how to farm, to build, to handle animals. He had all the experience anyone needed to survive in this harsh land. Its severity suited him. He responded to this land as a hearty, hungry woman does to lovemaking. He found it gave him what he needed: a response. He was able to see the change, dramatically. Water was this land's lover, and this love affair, the push and pull of nature with man, a man with his spirit, was what drew him to Agua Oscura. It allowed him to feel, at last, at home.

Tobarda was a parched memory. If Don Severio had ever looked for him, he never knew. What became of Tobarda and his photographs, he didn't know either. After he lost his photographs, he lost contact with the world of his birth: Guanajuato, that celebrated place where the clay in the earth preserved its buried corpses. Yes, he was far away from those human mummies that were later dug up and displayed for the tourists: leering men, defiled women, and pathetic children, with leathery, caked limbs, dusty, sparse hair, flaccid breasts and crumbling penises that reminded him of who he was, where he was always going.

He would never again see those mountains, those valleys. The view was now of another land, a land where his children would grow and flourish.

When he first moved to Agua Oscura, Manuel had nightmares, of walking down a long dark tunnel leading to a large room where the walls were cluttered with glass-enclosed coffins. Wandering through that unpleasant maze, he would stop and come up to someone familiar. He peered through the dusty glass, where he saw the naked form of the long-dead Tobarda. He tried to get away, and he would wake with a small cry, engulfed in a lingering mustiness and the scent of decay. Even as an old man, he could summon up that smell at will; it had pervaded his life and permeated his clothes. It was the smell of resentment from the dead, a bitter scent of the spirits who were angry at what had been done to them. It was the smell of Tobarda.

Sometimes it caught him unawares, and he would be back again in Guanajuato or Fort Davis, or in the grave, or all those places at once, with all those he'd loved, the living and the dead.

It was enough to make a man go mad.

But Manuel Dosamantes was not weak; he was convinced he could overcome the haunting aroma of the past. And so, when he got to Agua Oscura, he found a job, right off, on a farm belonging to Jorge Campos. In time he became the foreman, and then the manager. But Jorge died and so did his wife, quickly, of a broken heart. Manuel bought the farm, named it De los Campos in memory of Jorge, and determined it was time to find a wife. But who?

In Agua Oscura, there was no one he could love. If he was to love anyone, it would have to be someone from far away, someone who would come to him out of the vast unknown. Someone sent by God.

He could either go searching for that person or wait until she came to him. Manuel was tired of always running, so this time he decided the woman he would love would come along, eventually.

He waited ten years. At age thirty-five Manuel Dosamantes was in the prime of his manhood. He was tall, with a large chest and slim hips. A quiet man, he worked hard and ran a successful farm with various employees. He owned a great deal of land in Agua Oscura as well, and could have retired at his young age, if he had so wished. Everyone wondered why he had not married or moved someplace else, to a larger city.

Agua Oscura now had a population of nearly two thousand. There were years of drought, some years of abundance, and Manuel Dosamantes had held firm and prospered. He still looked out of the corner of his eye for that woman he'd always waited for: someone to ease his tormented dreams, someone to give him children and make him feel as if all his expended energy and sweat hadn't been for nothing.

In the summer of 1885, Elena Harrell came from Chihuahua to Agua Oscura to visit her father's sister, Jewel Harrell. She was eighteen years old, a radiant young woman with blond hair, blue eyes, and a lovely face. She was tall, stately, thin, but substantial. Her father, Bartel Harrell, was a miner and speculator and spoke impeccable Spanish. He had married Estrella de las Casas, daughter of Enrique Palomar de las Casas, from Chihuahua, México, scion of one of the wealthiest families in the state of Chihuahua. Their daughter, Elena, had grown up in luxury but, despite that, was a simple, selfless girl. She taught in a small community school for people who couldn't afford private schooling. This caused her father, Bartel, and her mother much consternation.

The summer of 1885 was hot and dry. The year before, Agua Oscura had witnessed devastating floods: the Río Grande jumped its banks and caused the town to shift its boundaries. Manuel Dosamantes lost most of his crops, but was able to sell what he was able to salvage at a premium price. No matter what—floods, droughts, earthquakes, influenza outbreaks—Manuel survived them all.

Jewel Harrell welcomed her niece, Elena, with open arms. It was time, Bartel had told her, for his daughter to learn her father's language. Perhaps while she was away her notions of running the charitable school would dissipate. Possible, thought her father. Probable, thought her mother. Doubtful, thought Elena.

Once Elena Harrell came to Agua Oscura in the summer of 1885, she never left. She did learn some English; that had been her father's real concern. Her mother got her wish, as well: she never went back to the dusty adobe classroom on the outskirts of Chihuahua. Instead, she became Mrs. Manuel Dosamantes.

It was inevitable that Manuel and Elena should be drawn to each other: both were Mexicans hungry for a preservation of language and custom. Both were loners with keen intellects. Both were young, hardworking, physically rooted people in full flower. Both had eyes that constantly looked inward.

They met at la tía Harrell's, at a welcoming party for Elena in early June. It was a delicious night, a slight breeze fanning Jewel's long patio.

"Mr. Dosamantes, I want you to meet my niece, Elena Harrell. Elena, dear, this is Mr. Dosamantes."

"Good evening, Señorita Harrell."

"Buenas noches, I mean, good evening, Mr. Dosamantes. Tía, do you mind if I speak Spanish?"

"Now, Elena, remember what your father said!"

"Sí, tía, I remember. But please, tía, I'm sure Mr. Dosamantes won't mind, will you? Oh, all right, now you go on, I promise to speak only English."

"Very well, Elena. Mr. Dosamantes, I'll leave you now, as I see Reverend Prithley coming this way. Excuse me, won't you?"

Manuel and Elena talked all night long, in Spanish. She felt as if she'd known Manuel all her life. She felt so comfortable with him she didn't have to be Elena Harrell, American citizen. In her heart, she was Elena Harrell, a Mexican whose father was an Anglo. He was a good man; it wasn't his fault he was a güero. Everyone loved Bartel Harrell—her mother, especially. It was Estrella who had taught him his beautiful Spanish. She had taught it to him lovingly, carefully, not at all with any sign of impatience, so common among relatives or married people who try to teach something to each other.

Manuel taught Elena what correct English he knew in the same patient way. It did not matter—not then or later—that Elena never mastered English fully; she spoke in a delightfully broken, colorful way.

The night of tía Jewel's party was the beginning of a new life for Manuel Dosamantes. He knew that evening that he had, at last, met the woman for whom he had waited so many years. He began a committed courtship the very next day. Elena, for her part, reciprocated his attention. She was taken with this gentleman farmer she'd met in this small, out-of-the-way town. When he asked her to marry him, she said yes.

The night they were married, his nightmares stopped.

Manuel told Elena everything about himself, save the story of Tobarda Acosta, the woman whose husband he felt he should have been. Elena would have understood, he thought, but why tell her, what for? To deepen his guilt? Besides, he had only now begun to live. Why stunt himself further with the retelling of what might have been?

They married in August. It was a big wedding. Everyone came from Chihuahua; no one from Guanajuato. Manuel had lost or forgotten all the addresses of his family. He could not remember his brothers' faces; no doubt his parents were long dead, Don Severio too. Tobarda was probably still alone, childless, with a womb tight as a walnut, her once red teats now brown, small dry outcroppings on a dying cottonwood —far away in a forgotten field.

Manuel and Elena named their first child Teodelfiño. Elena made up the name Teodelfiño—she liked to do that—as she made up the names of their other children: Clotildora, Amparinata, Ismindalia, and Profetario. If they were real names, she'd never heard them. Elena Harrell de Dosamantes would give her children a fighting chance with names like that, names even the demons would have trouble pronouncing, names like Reina María del Cielo, Rosa Elena Perfecta, María del Carmen Graciela, or Canutino Jesús Salvador, names with a ring to them of paradise. Manuel, too, had never seen or heard of names like these in his many wanderings, or in his dreams of that large room off the long tunnel, names that had been tacked on the bottoms of glass-covered coffins.

Manuel was very happy. All the rest of his life, until he died at the age of eighty-five, he thanked God he had awakened in time to leave that darkened room in Fort Davis, Texas, Tobarda Acosta burning there, in her private, inextinguishable hell. With Elena, he had long, light nights of liquid dreams.

I never knew my great-grandfather Manuel Dosamantes. Nor did I really know my grandfather Profetario very well. To me he was a blustery man, big as the sky, always yelling at my grandmother Lupe. He was a man who lived under the yoke of his father Manuel's perfectly balanced life. Profetario was a rascal, living with two wives, two families. The Dosamantes name fit him, eternally split between two lovers. My father, Luardo, was like his own father, a divided man, unable to ever come together within himself.

What stories I know about these people I will share with you. The stories begin with the men and always end with the women; that's the way it is in our family.

3

Insurance

Luardo Dosamantes, my father, believed in insurance. The more
the better. He was always buying it, or jotting down information about
insurance he'd heard about on television. He had five basic insurance
policies from different companies, one each for fire, flood, earthquake,
accidental death, and dismemberment. Recently he'd picked up a cancer packet. Just in case. Not that there was a chance, but—you never
know. He was a believer in vitamins and aloe-vera juice, which he
drank with milk as he swabbed himself briskly with jojoba oil. Oh, he
was prepared—for disease, damage, mutilation, and even death. What
he wasn't prepared for was life.

I tried to teach him, several years before his death, to use a washing
machine. I was the one who had helped him move from that last
apartment, his third move in one year. I had collected seven large
garbage bags full of dirty laundry, most of which probably should have
been burned, and carried them to a nearby dumpster.

Later, Luardo watched me put the so-called whites in the washer,
saw me pull out and then fill the empty quarter receptacle holder,
observed me measure out the cup of extra-duty laundry detergent with
bleach. After all this, he walked away. "To get hamburgers." When
he came back several hours later, with a cold sack of hamburgers and
watery drinks, I had already washed, rewashed, dried, and folded his
clothes. There was an unspoken agreement between us: he would help
me out when I was low on cash, or needed to borrow his car, and I
would help him move. Again. And again.

This time he returned to find the stove scrubbed, the rug sham-
pooed, and the green tiles on the sideboards scraped clean with a sharp
knife. The large efficiency apartment was nearly perfect. I was in the

bathroom portion of the room, working on the brown ring in the toilet bowl. Luardo beamed. The toilet gleamed. He would get his deposit back.

I wasn't hungry. I would eat later, in another setting. I told him to lay the food down. He left quickly, quietly, with another promise to return soon. My work was almost done. Luardo had felt he was in the way. Women's work, that's what it was. Men were in the way. Cleaning, scrubbing, all those cleansers. Knowledge of vacuum cleaners, washers, electrical appliances, household gadgets, anything having to do with house or yard or animal, anything living or non-living that required attention, care, and maintenance, was of no concern to Luardo Dosamantes. What mattered was his dream.

I'd like to move to México and live with a sixteen-year-old girl. There. That was it. A dream.

In his sweetest dreams Luardo Dosamantes was making love. He had the capacity of knowing he was both asleep and awake to ecstasy at these times. In his recurring dream that went on for what seemed years, he was always in the stage of either sucking a nipple or taking as much as he could of a breast in his mouth. If he wasn't doing that, he was aware of a growing tension in his groin, a burning, throbbing pulsation in his penis that felt ready to explode. He would be on the verge of delight and then he would sink back into gray sleep, without sensation. When he awoke, he would pull down his shorts, rub himself excitedly, stretch his balls with one hand as he pumped with the other.

The sweetest part of the dream was where he suckled the offered breasts. Breasts of all kinds. At times the breasts were voluptuous and dark. Sometimes they were the small, childlike buds of a little girl who was unafraid of him.

Lately the breasts had been those of an old woman, sometimes deformed, or flaccid, or, most recently, enormous, misshapen, bruised. They were an offering he could not, would not take. Somehow he kept finding himself up against that aged, leathered chest, suckling happily like a small warm animal. There was something horrible about it, nonetheless, as he was reminded of a familiar and very old woman's breasts. He wondered whose they were. His mother's? His grandmother's?

Luardo Dosamantes began to suckle these old dream teats early in 1978. It was quite a disturbing thing for him. Was this aberration of dreaming to persist? Was it a portent of things to come? Up until then, the breasts had been young or ample—always delicious. He looked forward to this nighttime passion of his, the daily enjoyment and employment of his mouth on the breasts of women who offered themselves to him without question, like Alicia, the office secretary, with her pert and tiny nipples as delicate as flowers. Or Minerva, the woman he'd met at the Dew Drop Inn, with her chichis pointed high up to the sky. Hell, her chichis saluted the sky in that tight little dress of hers! Minerva's nipples were circled by fine soft hairs Luardo liked to lick and swirl with his long, impatient tongue. Minerva wore her "levanta chichis," as he called her push-up bras. Her imposing breasts were braced in metal and lifted higher and higher like birds in a tall tree. Once Luardo's dream woman had three breasts and he spent his time going from one to another to another and then back again, lapping and then tonguing all those nipples in one giant lick. In his waking life, Minerva's breasts were his and so were Alicia's and so were Dolores's and so were Mara's. And so were the countless other breasts he suckled and chewed and tongued and squeezed and gummed and pinched and licked. They were the breasts of all the women he had made love to in his fifty-going-on-sixty years.

The first breasts he ever saw up close belonged to Valentina Duarte, the daughter of old man Duarte, the silversmith who lived down the street in Chiva Town. Valentina would let the neighborhood boys chew on her without having to pay anything. Not like the girls over at Doña Felicia's, the East Side's house of prostitution. Long 'Dobe it was called. Long 'Dobe, because the adobe building was long and stretched out like a train, each room a stop for some weary traveler. Luardo had grown up with all the boys and men snickering about the Long 'Dobe, but he was too young then to frequent the place. But he saw people coming and going from there often, men of all types—young, old, farmers, bankers, rich, famous, never his own father, even if the neighborhood boys said they'd seen him there. It wasn't true. His father, Papá Profe, Profetario Dosamantes, had his own 'dobe. There lived his mistress of many years, María Mejía. Profe didn't need the services of the women at the Long 'Dobe, he had his own houses to attend to.

Luardo had chewed on Valentina Duarte a little. She'd invited him herself because she liked him, she said. But Luardo only did it several times. Valentina wasn't very clean. And she wasn't even pretty. Her nipples were dark and large like thumbs. The left breast was bigger than the right. That was the one she liked the boys to chew. The other one, she said, was for herself. She had long breasts like young puppies and it was possible that she could chew on them, everyone said. No one had actually seen her do it, but it was reputed to be true. Frankly, Luardo didn't want anything to do with a girl who chewed on herself like Valentina did; it wasn't nice. But Valentina was memorable in the fact that her breasts were the first ones he'd ever seen.

A handsome boy, Luardo never lacked for female companionship. He was a bright boy, and popular. His father owned a thriving grocery store, and much was expected of him in the business world. He wanted to go to college after high school to major in business. No telling what young Dosamantes could be. His grandfather had been a great man. People still spoke of Don Manuel Dosamantes in reverential terms. Not so of his father, Profetario, who lost almost everything for a woman. But, no matter, Luardo Dosamantes was destined for greatness. What that greatness was, no one knew. Not even Luardo himself. He was bright, he knew that he never needed to study much, and it was a good thing, because he wasn't inclined that way. He had a natural charm, was a pleasant man to be around, and always had a joke or an anecdote to tell. Tall, with a full head of dark, wavy hair, Luardo just couldn't fail.

"If it hadn't been for his two loves—drinking and screwing—Luardo Dosamantes would probably have been a great man, even governor of New Mexico, maybe even a senator," said the old man Angel Contreras. He sat on a bench in the plaza talking to Fernandito Lotuche, an aged Spaniard who somehow found himself spending his twilight years in the New World.

Cando Cantú, a retired janitor who sat nearby and overheard the conversation, mumbled, "Yes, compadre, you tell the truth. No matter what history does to romanticize the tale, Luardo Dosamantes will always be nothing more than what he was."

"What's that, compadre?" Cando called out. "A civil servant? He is a job counselor for the city. Is that what you mean, compadre Angel?"

"No, for everything that's said and done, he'll just be a pendejo. Plain and simple. Like his father."

"Pues sí," said Fernandito with that Castilian lisp of his.

There was nothing fancy about Luardo's job, even if he was the office boss. What he did was interview people for possible employment and then go through the files, marking down what jobs were taken and which were not. Many came through the small office on West Hidalgo Street, day laborers from Juárez, nervous secretaries, former home-makers who were now widowed, girls fresh out of high school. Many women, especially, passed through. He even helped a few. The young girls were the ones he tried to help the most, encouraging all of them to "study typing, you can always use that skill, you'll always be assured of a job, honey." He invited the young ones to lunch; the attractive, more mature women for a drink after work. He found time to help these women who were unemployed, finding them what jobs he could, usually at minimum wage. He was well liked by his secretaries, in-cluding Alicia. "Ay, Mr. Dosamantes, you shouldn't tease like that" was often heard. Oh, he was a joker, very funny, always ready for a few laughs. He did the best he could at that job for over thirty-five years and when he retired he was given an award for service to Agua Oscura. His co-workers bought him a watch mounted in silver and turquoise. The inscription on the back read: "We'll miss you, Mr. D."

When the breast dreams turned ugly back in 1978, Luardo got very worried. He wondered if his sexual prowess was waning at last. What else could that dream mean? Luardo decided to retire the following year. He wouldn't be eligible for full pension, but it was worth his virility. He was getting tired and it was beginning to show. With the decision to retire came a great lethargy. He found himself truly un-happy for the first time in his life. Not just unhappy inside. Unhappy out loud. He and Dolores were having problems—when didn't they?—but this was to be the year he finally left Dolores and moved to Mamá's. He stayed there briefly and then found an apartment on the other side of town. He thought of moving away, to another part of the state, yes, of maybe even moving to México to see if he liked it. If he did, he might decide to stay there permanently. Luardo wasn't exactly sure of where he'd end up—Los Mochis, Cozumel, some beach town probably. He'd find a cheap place to live and hire someone to clean house and cook for him. She'd be young, yeah, around sixteen years old, and after a while the girl, let's nickname her Chica, Chica would move in with him.

The best thing about all this would be that Chica couldn't ever get enough of his lovemaking. Yes, that would be it! She would be a mature sixteen; they grew up faster down there in México, and she'd have no family. And get this, this was even better, she was a virgin when she started working for her patrón. He, Luardo Dosamantes, would teach his Chica how to keep house. He didn't want kids, he'd already had two, a girl he loved but never understood, and a son he couldn't stand. No, he didn't want any kids ruining whatever he and Chica had going. He'd have to get her fixed. It was easy down there and she'd be home before you could say Saskatchewan. Luardo would never move back to the not-so-good U.S.A., because, you see, in México you could live on a hundred dollars a month, just like the advertisements said. I'll live the life of a king. Yes, that's it.

If it weren't for the bad dreams. First, it started with the breasts, the old, mutilated ones, and then before he knew it he was moving down to the withered thighs and the hairless vagina and inside to the dried womb. He would be loving Chica when suddenly a face would turn to him or he would feel a wrinkled hand on his erect penis. The old crone would touch herself lasciviously while licking her dried lips and then would laugh in his face. Worse yet, sometimes she would stoop down to take his still stiff organ in her toothless mouth. A nightmare, surely! Before 1978 Luardo had never seen the face of the woman to whom the breasts belonged. Never! Always the breasts had been beautiful, and flawless! What aberration of nature was this now? What was happening to his happiest dreams? For hours, or what seemed like hours, he had once suckled phantom breasts, breasts he so loved. But now—what was he to do—stop dreaming? He might as well die.

With these horrible nightmares came desperation and depression. Eventually, Luardo quit his job, got his watch, and began to amass insurance. Any kind. He owned his five basic policies as well as his cancer policy, and he was thinking about purchasing several others. Luardo Dosamantes had become, in a relatively short time, a great believer and authority in insurance. The more the better.

"You never know what's going to happen," he'd say. "You could walk outside the door and that could be it, you never know. You damn well better be prepared."

He and Dolores were finally divorced in 1979. He celebrated by reassigning the beneficiaries on all his policies. Whereas once they had read Dolores Loera, wife, they now read Soveida Dosamantes, daughter, followed by Lupita Dosamantes, mother. Not that Mamá would outlast Soveida. But you never knew. As for Hector, let him buy his own insurance. He certainly needed it. No son was ever more ungrateful. Hector didn't deserve to be anyone's beneficiary. Someday that boy would end up in prison after having killed someone. Luardo's only wish was that he would take his own life first. Either scenario was inevitable.

Luardo went out and bought a metal safety box and promptly showed me where the key was kept. "I'm leaving the key. Also the car. I'm putting the insurance in that little brown box. I'm locking it. You know your mother, Soveida, she still tries to get into my things. Here's where the key is, so that if anything happens to me, you'll know where to look."

Luardo felt better.

If only it weren't for the dreams. Dammit.

4

Are You Wearing a Bra?

Dolores Loera, my mother, grew up harnessed. As a child, she'd been swaddled in rags; as a young girl, she was confined to dark Victorian blouses with high necklines and long sleeves; as a young woman, she was bound in softened cloth. Her mother, Doña Trancha, was old-fashioned. She thought that every respectable young woman should have her breasts taped down. But it was a losing battle and finally Doña Trancha had to acquiesce when Dolores turned twelve. It was hopeless. Dolores needed a brassière.

Every few months Dolores had increased a notch: from an AA to an A, from a 34 to a 36, from a B to a C, from 38 to 40, and on to a D. "My harness," that's what she always called her brassière. She wouldn't call it a bra. The diminutive wasn't for her. What she wore was a *brassière*, with a harsh *z* sound. She was large-busted, uncomfortable. The straps cut into her shoulders, leaving reddened, indented areas. She was prone to headaches, as well as back and neck problems. Sleep was a dilemma. Dolores could never rest on her chest or sides. From the age of twelve, she slept fully on her back, without a pillow.

Luardo liked her from the beginning. She was thirteen when he met her, thin, but with the breasts of a mature woman. He liked women with what he called "two strong points." That was his joke, anyway. "She's a *sharp* woman, get it?"

But what a man thinks and a woman knows is another matter.

Dolores often talked to me about breasts. Hers and mine.

"My breasts have been like misbehaving children, unmanageable and in the way. I've never wished my curse on any other living woman. Now you, Soveida, you have a good-sized bust, with the promise of getting larger, just let you have a child. You've always had the nipples of a married woman. I hate to think why. First they were silver-dollar size. Then small-pancake size. It isn't nice to have nipples so large."

Dolores was not happy with the way I turned out. Physically, I was a precocious girl, just as she had been. By age fifteen I was eager and ready for some man to come along. But no one did, Dolores saw to that.

"No dating until you're eighteen, Soveida!"

"Eighteen!!" I screeched. "But Mara got to go out when she was seventeen."

"Well, Mara. It must have been a mistake on Mamá's part. You know as well as I do that Mamá wouldn't let her date at all. She must have sneaked out at seventeen, maybe even before that. But that was Mara, Soveida, that isn't you. You may look like a woman, you may have the *nipples* of a woman, but you aren't a woman. Breasts doesn't mean you have brains. I was hoping you wouldn't grow up so fast. God knows I know what it's like having some man pinching and punching away at your breasts and wanting to get inside your blouse and your skirt. I was just hoping you'd stay a little girl longer, without having to worry about all that stuff."

When Dolores spoke about "all that stuff," she meant anything having to do with the bodily functions or necessities of being female— from top to bottom and back around. There was a lot of ground to cover in that phrase, "all that stuff."

"Dolores, who ever thought of that phrase 'sanitary napkin'? It had to have been a man, because no woman in her right mind would refer to them as 'sanitary.' They aren't a bandage to swab up something dirty. The blood that comes out of me is beautiful! Have you ever tasted it?"

"Ay, Soveida! Cochina, you dirty thing! Shut your mouth!"

"Only a man with his head in the dirt would think of calling them 'sanitary napkins,' thank you, wipe up your mess. Once I was in these sand dunes, and it was during my period. It got so I had trained myself to go bleed only when I went to the bathroom, and there I was, alone, on some high windswept dune, when I had the urge. I just dug a hole in the sand. I squatted there and the blood came out of me. Clean, pure. That's the way it should be, a good bleeding outdoors, natural, unfettered, in full moonlight. But no, we have 'sanitary napkins,' and worse yet, little deodorized pellets to plug us up, keep the dirty stuff inside. Later we pull out the pellet and flush it away."

"Escandalosa! Soveida, don't talk about all that stuff! They're things we shouldn't talk about, not now, not ever. Don't even think about them."

"Maybe we'll forget we have bodies that bleed. I don't want to forget I have a body, maybe you do. I don't!"

"Oh, Soveida! I know I have a body. Wait until you're older. Then you'll want to forget when your man's still stuck to your nipples and you gave up nursing thirty years before."

"Dolores! You're talking about all that stuff again!"

"No, I'm not. I'm just talking about life. How about when you just want to go to sleep and your entire backside is wet and your man is angry with you and won't talk to you during the day but at night he's all smiles and 'let me rub your legs.' Just wait, Soveida. Someday my words will come back to haunt you. You'll remember. You're young still, even if you have the nipples of a married woman."

"Dolores!"

"You can't lie to me. You never could. All those cuchispetes, as Mamá Lupita calls them, aren't the same thing as being married to the same man for forty years. And I am *still* married to your father even if we *are* divorced. When you take a man on, you take a man on. Mark my words. After all these years, I still have to answer to others for your father."

"You do *not* have to answer for Luardo. When are you going to remember that?"

"Soveida, you never lived with a man a full number of years. And him not altered in the place that matters. Imagine how it is when all a man wants to do is stay in bed and he's almost retirement age. If I'd known I was going to eventually divorce your father, I would have done it a lot sooner. Learn from my mistakes."

"Is that true? Would you really have divorced Luardo?"

"Why can't you just call us Mom and Dad?"

"I just can't. You know that."

"I tried to keep you a girl as long as I could, just as my mother, Trancha, did with me. May she rest in peace. I wouldn't listen to her. I started having dreams about what I thought love was when I was only thirteen. Your dad had already been sniffing around me. Three years later we were married. Yes, I was happy with him in the beginning. Maybe if it weren't for all the other women. But it wasn't only the women. When he was with those women, at least there was peace and rest. It was too many other things."

"Do you still love Luardo?"

"Why do you ask? No. Yes. Sometimes. Not often."

"Is this what you meant by 'all that stuff,' Dolores?"

"I'm trying to talk to you, Soveida, but you're not listening to me."

"I'm listening."

"You got your breasts from me. No one else. Your grandmother had teats like a dog's. Maybe that's why she lost all her children when they were still little. Pobrecita mamá, she didn't have any nourishment to give any of us. I never felt bad about Dad being gone all the time. I could never blame him. She was so hard to live with. That's why I married your dad."

"You were sixteen? It's hard to believe."

"I loved him, Soveida. I did love him! When I loved him, the nights were never long enough. Your brother, Hector, looks so much like Luardo. Maybe that's why they hate each other so much. Why don't you make up with your brother, Soveida? You never talk about him, you never see him. He just became the assistant manager at that car-parts place, Dyno-Car."

"Let's not talk about Hector. Or Luardo. Have you ever noticed that when we start talking about ourselves we always end up talking about them?"

"I can truthfully say that the happiest times of my life have been when I've been sleeping. And here all those years I thought *I* was the problem. But it was your father, Soveida. He'd leave the house early and would come back later, smelling of another woman or his own vomit. I should have locked the door and never let him come back in. His absences got longer and my tears got harder until one day they just dried up. It's a good story. Somebody should write about it. But it won't be me. I'd rather write about mi tía Adelaida and the day she got paralyzed. I could never tell all the stories even if I tried. And I don't want to try. Who would believe them? You just tell me who. And if I've gone on too long about all that stuff, Soveida, it's because I wanted you to have a different life."

Dolores dabbed the inside of her wrist with cologne and then behind her ears. She then patted the front of her bra straps, discolored by countless applications of cologne. "My harness," she said out loud as she carefully tapped the cologne under each armpit and then in the cleavage between her ponderous breasts and then lifted the finger to her nose. "My Sin."

5

Y tú, ¿qué?
And What About You?

Home is coming back when you've been away, messing up the covers and lying underneath them in darkness without anyone to demand anything of you: no food, no sex, no errands of service, no talk, no noise, no smells, no thought. When I was a child, everything was so quiet. People talked without talking. There was no need for words, for all the business words entail: emotions, arguments, misunderstandings. Mother, my mother, was never one for words. Anything that could be stated could just as well be conveyed with a look, a raised eyebrow, a curled lip.

My mother's parents weren't born deaf but you might have thought they were. She grew up in a house of silent innuendo. Mother, my mother's name was Trancha. She was a cold woman. When I see what she had to endure, I understand her coldness.

My father, Primitivo, was a

The Dolores I first met was wild, eager, spirited. Everything was miraculous to her. Men. The way men were. The way they smelled.

Pressing her small fingers into my flesh, she would touch me as if she were deciphering some ancient language, some mysterious and lost culture blessedly removed from her own. When she made love to me she called out to the woman who had created her, to all the other women who had existed before her, women whose life it was to love. She told them that she loved me. Me! That was how it was then.

Dolores was filled with a hunger men love to see, to know, a hunger that makes men desirous and headstrong and committed. She would be mine. All of her. That little girl with the large brown eyes, the small, delicate hands, the great burning heart.

It's hard for me to talk. It's been

miner. He lived with us so little I often wondered if I really did have a father. Often we didn't have enough food or heat. Mother, my mother, was not a good cook. Her cooking got worse and eventually it stopped altogether. If we needed to eat, my older sister, Lina, usually cooked. Home was Lina baking pies or empanaditas de camote or her flat bread made of tortilla dough, with the fork marks evenly spaced to let the air escape. Home was the three of us women in a house of women, each doing something different. Mother sitting at the window staring out into that great vast darkness, me reading something while chewing on a piece of Lina's bread, and Lina at the stove, cooking.

"Spanish rice. It's all in the guiso, Dolores. Brown your onions with the rice. That's the secret, and then, when they're done, brown, not burnt, quickly put in the tomato sauce, but not the water, not just yet, and let it all simmer. When that's ready, it's time for the water, hot, the hottest from the tap, or boiled, better."

Lina's rice. Lina's bread. Mother staring out the window near the door, as close to the darkness as she could get without getting lost in it. Waiting for my father to come home from the mine. His life was one long errand for someone other than his family.

so long since I've felt this way for her. After that first year I never saw the woman I loved again. These last two years we've been two strangers cohabiting the same space, nodding and holding mumbled conversations, not knowing or caring if the other heard. We listen to each other abstractedly, halfheartedly, ignoring the occasional spontaneous bursts of truth that sputter out like bubbles of saliva and are swallowed.

"Maybe it would be best if I went away, Dolores."

"Do as you please."

"You're choking me! I'm suffocating!"

"Don't let your mother hear you. When you yell, it upsets her. You know she can hear everything from the Blue House."

"You leave my mother out of this. I have to go away! All of you are killing me."

"Mamá Lupita can hear you!"

"It's not good, it never was. And now you suspect me of *that*. I never did *that*, not *that*. Not to my own child!"

"Mara wasn't your child! She was my dead sister's child!"

"You expected too much!"

"I was your wife!"

"You make me tired! You talk too much."

"*I* talk too much? You don't talk at all. Your silence is driving me mad!"

"How can I talk when there isn't

When he came home, it was to die.

It's no wonder my mother never cooked. Who was there to cook for? Her parents were both deaf and she grew up without childish rhymes, with an unsure alphabet. She was the last child, with several other brothers and sisters, all of them gone. She was the baby, her parents' tongue.

She met a man, Primitivo, also of few words. Their courtship was one of nods, unspoken agreement. There was the comfort of his solidity. Never bother with the words. What can words do but lie?

Mother knew the warmth of him those early mornings of their first year as she knew his face, his strong back and his hands, working. She knew his breath as light in the long, intractable obscurity of night. What she didn't know was that one day he would be gone and that she would become the mother, father, lover to herself. It's not surprising that Mother grew old that way, sitting by the door, waiting. Waiting for that warmth. It had been so glorious.

Every time my father would come back home he'd leave his hurried seed. And when he returned again, Mother had lost another child, usually a boy. Out of the twelve, only Emanuelina and I survived. My father, Primitivo Loera, was an unfortunate vagabond. All it got him in the end

anything to say, when the saying time is gone . . ."

"She'll hear you!"

"Let her, goddammit! So she'll know you're killing me and why I have to go."

"Luardo! Don't!"

"Stop crying! Don't you ever get tired of crying?"

When I first met Dolores she was a child, she couldn't be touched enough. She was Don Primitivo Loera's little girl, María Dolores, the quiet one, the one who lived across from the cemetery. She tracked me down and sought me out and begged for loving.

All the girls wanted me. I'm not lying. Everyone's secrets were revealed in el Padre Cantucci's confessional. He was a greasy, corpulent loafer who loved to gossip and who delighted in directing lives. My objective then was to break away from all that hypocrisy.

Dolores was thirteen and I was twenty-two. I had moved away from home long before, and had lived alone, and with women, working wherever I could. I didn't want to run my father's store. I wanted to work for the government. My best friend, Chante, had a cousin who was a plumber. He said the plumber's life was good, occasional shit, get it done, and get paid. I didn't know what I was going to do, but I was going was that curse of illness that plagued him, aged him, broke him, covered him at last.

"Out there," he said, "that's where I want to be buried. Where a man can breathe fresh air." So, when he died, Mother buried him in San Pedro Cemetery, across the street from her house, a place where he had never spent much time. Never mind the fresh air. He had already had his share of it. Mother knew where he was, at last. Near the little cactus Juanita Archibeque had put up in memory of her husband, Antonio, near the Camuñezes' little baby girl, Nefrida, who had died when she was only two months old, near old Padre Faustino, the priest who had choked to death eating menudo for supper, near her mother and father, close to all her sons and Zoraida, her other daughter, and near where she, too, would be buried someday. From her window Mother could see the statue of San Pedro holding his simulated gold-leaf keys. He and Primitivo Loera were out of the wind, sheltered under some leafy trees, facing the mountains, in the shade.

I can understand Mother, my mother's coldness. Our house was a house of women. Women waiting. Lina baking, me reading. Mother, my mother, sitting in the darkness. Me trying to escape my mother's hunger and the to do something. To make something of my life.

Dolores was thin but she was full-breasted. She was pale then, face like an angel's. Her hair was long. She wore it braided around her head, a black halo with white ribbons that kept slipping off. She had to keep undoing and redoing it again and again.

What I desired most in her was her desire. She was so eager to love. She gave me wonderful pleasure then. Not full pleasure like Mauricia, my girlfriend, who was a woman and felt things fully, but a tumultuous pleasure I had never experienced.

Chante told me, "Leave the kid alone, she'll drive you mad or get you married." But I always liked them young. Soft like that. Waiting for me to tell them what to do. Little girls. He was right. Funny!

After my daughter, Soveida, was born, Dolores's body came to life. She became a woman. Dolores was twenty-five when Hector came along, seven years after Soveida. At thirty Dolores was lovely, but then all the loving stopped.

Before I knew Dolores, I couldn't love. After I loved her she became a stranger. Damn el Padre Cantucci's predictions!

Dolores spread: hips, thighs, stomach. She was never fat, she looked good, her breasts large, smell of food, once hot, now cold.

"Mother! I'm hungry!"

"María Dolores Loera! Enough! We'll wait for your father, he should be here soon!"

"You and your women killed me."

"Them? They were a replacement."

"Hell, yes, for the space in your chest where a heart should be. You can't feel anything."

"*I* can't feel. That's good, a cold stone talking about feeling."

"Yes!"

"You can't feel."

"Stop it! She'll hear you!"

"That's all you wanted me for, to escape your mother—that old woman. She couldn't feel either, that's why you are the way you are."

"Yes, I wanted to escape. Y tú, ¿qué?"

"I have to leave. You don't understand, do you?"

"*She'll hear you!*"

"Chante was right, little girl. Have my balls on a spit, roast them, serve them cooked in your sex. Christ, it's been my hell."

"Whodoyouthinkyouarethe world'sgreatestloverallthegirls followyoutotheendsoftheearth throwthemselvesdowncryforyou dieforyouLuardo?"

"Y tú, ¿qué? What about you?"

not saggy. She would go to bed early and undress when I was out of the room. When I got to her, she would be asleep with a rosary in her hand.

"You and your women killed me."

"Them? They were a replacement."

"Hell, yes, for the space in your chest where a heart should be. You can't feel anything."

"*I* can't feel? That's good, a cold stone talking about feeling."

"Yes!"

"You can't feel."

"Stop it! She'll hear you."

"That's all you wanted me for, to escape your mother—that old woman. She couldn't feel either, that's why you are the way you are."

"Yes, I wanted to escape. Y tú, ¿qué?"

"I have to leave. You don't understand, do you?"

"*She'll hear you!*"

"Chante was right, little girl. Have my balls on a spit, roast them, serve them cooked in your sex. Christ, it's been my hell."

"Whodoyouthinkyouarethe world'sgreatestloverallthegirls followyoutotheendsoftheearth throwthemselvesdowncryforyou dieforyouLuardo?"

"Y tú, ¿qué? What about you?"

6

Family

Don Primitivo Loera loved children. Other people's, and especially if they were small and could be held by someone else. To his own daughter, Dolores, he was always absent. He had dreams of finding gold in the hills, and striking it rich.

He was once a farmer, and could have remained one all his life. But he was too good-hearted, too loyal. Especially toward relatives. That was his biggest problem: he believed in family. With him, it was a duty to help his kin, even if they extended his debts and lost his land forever. Because of this, he was a firm believer in the axiom: Just because they're your relatives doesn't mean you have to like them. He may not have liked them, but he deeply loved them. That's what the Bible taught. So he believed in them, even if they robbed him blind.

Family was a double-edged knife, Primitivo often thought. On the one hand, it was good to be connected to people, to share the common bonds of land and birth, an extended history of one's own, to enjoy laughter without explanation, or to hug without reason, to know that, no matter what, these familiar faces—a permutation of your own—would be part of you for all life and into death. On the other hand, most of these faces were really the faces of strangers, even as they put on softened, borrowed white gloves and rolled you down the church aisle toward that last blessing this side of paradise.

Yes, one of these rheumy-eyed, baba-faced, yapping nephews that earlier laughed at you during a Thanksgiving dinner with food in his mouth would later grimly and thin-lipped say the prayers for the dead in your memory and then wonder what kind of food would be served for lunch. This same nephew would lay his white gloves in the shape of a cross on a gray coffin under a tent at San Pedro Cemetery some blustery winter day, the tumbleweeds blowing over the hard ground, skimming the scrub brush and mesquite, here and there popping up like surprised witnesses in your eternal passage.

Even in the best of times, there was a double-edged reality to family. Forget the funerals. Then everything was patched up, or dismissed, forgotten, or reconstructed. Primitivo knew that; he'd done it himself so many times, with his own uncles and aunts, people he mourned, but also remembered for their cruelty to him or his brothers, sisters, and mother. At his own father Biterbo's memorial service (the body was never found), he'd cried loudly as he thought of the leather strap across his backside the time his father had whipped him mercilessly for asking too many questions. Primitivo remembered why his father Biterbo Loera had punished him so brutally: it had to do with his father's other family in Chihuahua, México, which no one, except Biterbo, and now his son, Primitivo, knew about.

"This will teach you to ask questions!"

"Papá!"

"Don't call me that! You're no son of mine! You've disgraced me in front of everyone. What do you know about anything? Just leave it alone."

Biterbo had whipped him until he couldn't stand up and then one of his father's other children—there were five of them—came to clean him up. Her name was Lucinda and she smelled of soap and herbs. Some herb he couldn't name. It was a smell that stayed with him all his life. And sometimes when he was alone, far away from any other human being, in the campo with his sheep, or in the deepest part of the mine looking for gold, he smelled that scent again. Lucinda!

It was on that fateful stopover in Chihuahua, at the house on the outskirts of town, that Primitivo first learned about his father's other family. As they entered the house, a small girl called out, "Papá, you're home!"

Primitivo stared incredulously at his father, but Biterbo's face was buried in the girl's dark curls.

Other young people of various ages came up and embraced Biterbo, and from the shadows appeared a tall, thin woman with a face like a polished wooden mask. Her name was Marvela and she was the mother of these children.

It *was* possible for his father to have a mistress and another family, Primitivo argued to himself in bed late that night. Biterbo was a trader and traveled often, sometimes as far as the capital, México. Much of his business, Primitivo knew, was based in Chihuahua.

At twelve, nearly the size of a man, Primitivo felt confused about his father's other life: he shared a secret delight in knowing he had other brothers and sisters, and yet he felt shame for his mother, a woman who had never known shame.

Alta Gracia knew nothing about Marvela, the various birthings etched into her dark, burnished, sphinx-like face. And what about the children: Cristerna, the oldest; Lucinda, who smelled of herbs; Mariac, a tall boy, older than Primitivo; Zeñio, the family clown; Gildardo, a shy boy; the twins, Lorencita and Doroteo; and, last, the baby, Rosella, near his sister Maclovia's age.

Why had his father beat him so mercilessly into a bitter silence, a silence he would willingly have carried with him to the grave? In that beating Primitivo became an accomplice to all his father's lies. If he ever did tell the truth, no one would ever believe it. He couldn't. Alta Gracia never did find out about Marvela, nor did Marvela find out about Alta Gracia. When Biterbo was in his late forties he disappeared from Agua Oscura forever. Some said he'd been abducted and later killed by bandits. Others said illness had taken hold of him on the road. So many things were said. But no one ever imagined that Biterbo Loera was alive and well until the age of seventy-six in Chihuahua, México, tucked away in the shade of trees with his other family. No one would ever have recognized him, either. He was so altered by loving.

To have known paradise was possible for only one man. And that man was Biterbo Loera.

Primitivo was consigned to the dust, to the wild land of eternal reckoning with what was and what might have been.

Primitivo's was a life that once held promise. Until that fateful pilgrimage to La Sierra de las Uvas in honor of Our Lady of Guadalupe's feast day.

That was the day he met and fell in love with Trancha Cádiz.

Primitivo had come to the sierra with a petition, a request for healing for his mother, who was beginning seriously to decline.

"There's nothing to be done, m'ijo," she'd said, "but rest as much as I can so I'll be ready to die." Primitivo never realized the truth of his mother's words.

The pilgrimage was Primitivo's last resort. What medicine there was had failed long ago, what rest there might have been was finished, and each day Alta Gracia lifted her head slightly from her narrow bed only to stare at the air in front of her, the gray light of her eyes already in that spiraling tunnel that led to that other world.

"I'm tired. Bless me, son, and let me rest."

"I'm going on the climb, Mamá. It's my manda, my promise to the Virgencita."

"Go with God, son, and la Virgencita. She will heal us all."

The day was cold and the climb took hours. Not like last year, everyone said, when the pilgrimage had been like a picnic. This year the clouds hung low and everyone was afraid of snow.

Primitivo followed a group of women who sang and said rosary after rosary. One girl answered all the prayers softly, her voice trailing behind the others, as if she were continually trying to catch up. Her name was Trancha Cádiz.

Primitivo climbed La Sierra de las Uvas in the early morning hours, begging for his mother's life, and descended that evening at sunset a man in love. He would marry the Girl of the Trailing Prayers.

Alta Gracia Loera lived until the spring. By the following December, Primitivo had married Trancha and she was pregnant with their child.

That fateful pilgrimage had brought rest to Alta Gracia Loera but not to her son. Nor to his long-suffering wife, Trancha. Every year for years to come she was with child. And every year that child died. Out of all those children, only three survived for any length of time. The death of his son, Eluid, had been Primitivo's greatest loss.

It was as if each dead child yanked Trancha's womb and made her blood colder and more bitter.

She gave him no peace.

Vuelta la burra en el maíz, he thought each time she began her endless litany of complaints. Here we go again.

"My children never had a father. Maybe they'd still be alive if you weren't always gone so long. You killed them with your neglect. Look what's left you, two sickly girls, and one worse than the other."

"Ya, mujer, ya," Primitivo would say in desperation. "Stop your nagging!"

"May the Virgencita protect me, I'm always waiting. One day your corpse will come back to me."

And then I'll have peace from your womb, Primitivo thought. And the ghosts that came from that womb. Two daughters were enough to multiply an everlasting sorrow.

Primitivo Loera walked down the street. He was an old man now, stooped and unsteady. He had his children, the dead, the living. Better the name Loera end with him as he wandered through the streets of Agua Oscura with this bag of Popsicles for his granddaughters, Mara and Soveida, two daughters from two daughters. He knew what awaited these little girls. He wished there was something he could do. But there was nothing.

"¿Dónde están las niñas? Hello, babies, come to Granpa. Come on, babies, Granpa's here," he called out weakly as he entered his daughter Dolores's house, carrying his precious gifts. He had lung cancer and was dying.

Why was it, Primitivo thought as he sat down wearily to rest, that family was a double-edged knife?

7

The Ideal

Dolores and Luardo had always been at odds. In Luardo's case, he was the baby and Mamá Lupita's favorite child. That put a tremendous burden on him to have an opinion. As a result, he rarely did. If he did have an opinion, it was wrestled from him after much prodding, prolonged debate, and confrontation.

"What do you think?"

"I don't know."

"What are you thinking?"

"I don't know."

"What do you want for dinner?"

"I don't care."

Luardo had never assumed full responsibility for himself. First his mother, Mamá Lupita, had coddled and pampered him. He was breech-born. He always did things slowly or a little backwards. At age three and a half he was still suckling. At age four he still hadn't walked and was carried everywhere. It annoyed his father, Papá Profe, that his nieces Amelia and Sara combed his long blond curls and played with him as if he were a baby doll. Lupita delighted in seeing him so loved. He was the prettiest baby she'd had, no doubt about it. Teodoro, the oldest son, was already a little old man when he was born. Teodoro never needed anything, he never cried. The oldest daughter was Tenecia. She was also the ugliest, born dark and hairy, with soft fur all over her face and body. It took all of Lupita's strength for her to touch the little girl. Even as a baby, Teeney was unusual. Despite her growing ugliness (the fur fell off eventually), Tenecia, or Teeney, was always the brightest, happiest, and most loving of all Lupita's children. Teeney was also the most popular, the best loved, the one who always won school awards for congeniality. Poor child, thought Mamá Lupita many times, she had to overcome her ugliness somehow.

That somehow was personality. It was no surprise that when she was of marriageable age Teeney Dosamantes turned the eye of the handsomest young man in town, Adrino Talamantes. Teeney wasn't much to look at as a young woman—her face was slightly pock-marked—but she had a stunning figure for a few years, with a high bust and good legs. Adrino married Teeney because he loved her laugh, Lupita told everyone. It was true. To hear Teeney's infectious, sonorous laughter made you feel whole and good, a happy part of life. Teeney gave Adrino something all the other thin-waisted, small-hipped, burning-eyed girls never could: joy.

"Oh, she was an ugly baby! The ugliest I ever saw," Oralia, Mamá's elderly maid, said, "but she was special, very special. I could see that. There was a certain mark on her forehead."

Then there was Todosio, Toddy. The moody one. Always crying as a baby. The one who always had a sty or colic or gas or diarrhea. As a child he went from one illness to another, from one crisis to another. At age five he fell into a ditch behind the church. At age eight he had influenza and nearly died. At age ten a bee bit him and he went into shock. At age twelve he was caught stealing gum at Mr. Pasquale's store, and developed psoriasis from the tension. At age seventeen he got into the BIG TROUBLE that marked all those years of problems for Mamá. Toddy was found with a naked six-year-old boy, Lalo Gómez, a neighbor, whose father owned a shoe-shine stand near the train station. Toddy had given Lalo candy to take off his clothes.

"Was that all, Lalo?" Mr. Gómez said, with restrained hysteria.

"No," Lalo said. "Sometimes he buys me gum."

"No, Lalo, I mean, is that all you do? Take off your clothes?"

At that point in the questioning Mamá Lupita stepped in, yanked Toddy away, and later returned with money, promising Mr. Gómez this would never happen again. It never did. Not with Lalo. Or anyone else Mamá knew about. Mothers think they know everything about their children. Ah, they know a great deal, more than a child imagines, but they don't know everything.

Toddy was sent to Sonora, a small town in Texas, to live with Mamá's sister, a childless widow named Soledad. There wasn't much to do there, except take care of Tía Soledad and her hundreds of plants in old coffee tins and water the rosebushes and feed her chickens and clean and do the chores and go to school. Living there in Sonora with

Tía Soledad, Toddy learned what it was to take care of things. A once spoiled, sheltered boy, he attributed to this exile his ability to adapt to anything life might bring.

Soledad's husband, Tío Umberto, had just died. He'd been hit by a train. The small town of Sonora was built along the railroad and everyone who lived there knew someone who had died in or around a train.

After high school, and the service, and several more years away, Toddy came back to Agua Oscura with a wife and a five-year-old son, Gustavito, and another child on the way. Mamá Lupita thought: Now my Todosio's a man at last. Thank you, Blessed Mother and Saint Joseph, for your many favors. I honor you. I praise you. Sending Todosio to Soledad's was the best thing I ever did.

The next-to-the-youngest child was Josefina. She was fair-haired and blue-eyed, like her Papá Profe. Pina was Papá Profe's favorite, the only one of her children Mamá actively disliked. Why, she couldn't say. Pina was always a sweet child, respectful, even-tempered. And yet there was always something self-serving about her, something egotistical Mamá Lupita didn't like seeing. Her other children weren't like that. Teo was the loner, silent but not selfish. Teeney was dark as an Indita, but she was a wonderful daughter. Toddy was still a mystery; he'd done well since he'd returned to Agua Oscura, and his insurance business was successful. He'd bought a laundromat and was getting a lease on either a roller rink or a Dairy Queen, he hadn't quite decided. Things were looking up for the hardworking Toddy and his plain but energetic wife, Lita Barales, from McAllen, Texas.

Pina was very attractive and yet she married beneath her, Mamá thought. Lorenzo "El Bluey" Varnado was from a poor family, and his hair was always slightly greasy. But he owned the Silver Spur magazine store on the east side, and had worked hard to get it going. It was the only place in Agua Oscura you could buy the *El Paso Times* or the *Houston Post* or the *San Antonio Light* or the *Denver Post* all under the same roof. Pina had put in a small sandwich bar and it became popular for its New York–style hot dogs. They expanded each year, with Pina and her kids helping out. Pina was working hard, and so was El Bluey. So were her kids, Neta and Chepo.

It was Pina's attitude, Mamá thought. Pina felt she was destined for greatness, wealth, fame, a lottery win, something spectacular. She was superstitious and slightly scandalous. She loved a good game of cards, bingo, dominoes, the dog races, horse races, or cock fights, Ed

McMahon's yearly invitation to win $10 million. She loved to answer chain letters and initiated many herself. She collected amulets and good-luck charms, wearing as many as she could around her neck and wrists. On top of all that, Pina saw curanderas, spiritualists, card readers, tea readers, and even Cleto Coño, the son of Don Palemón Coño, a curandero who was referred to irreverently as Dr. Kool-Aid because he gave all his clients a powdered health drink that looked like grape Kool-Aid. Mamá had never gotten used to Pina's many chain letters, offering her happiness, wealth, health, sexual fulfillment, you name it. Upon receiving the letters, which came as many as four or five a month, Mamá would throw them away. She knew from the handwriting that Pina was the sender.

"How can she do this to me? These letters are my cross. Another cross."

Maybe that was what irritated Mamá about Pina, her otherworldly worldliness, her go-get-'em-I-deserve-it attitude, her silly, superstitious, blind, childlike faith in herself and the powers of her mind. That, and the fact that Pina and El Bluey attended the Church of the New Risen Savior, a nondenominational sect that leaned a bit left of hell, where it was reported Pina spoke in tongues at night next to Anglos and then returned to the Silver Spur to sell dirty magazines to all the high-school boys. Something was not right, Mamá thought. She just couldn't pinpoint the problem. Let the Lord take care of Pina. While he was at it: Teo. Teeney. Toddy. And even Profe. "May he rest in peace."

With Luardo, her baby, she had her hands full as well.

"Ya no aguanto esta vida. Ay, I do what I can."

Dolores, too, had to struggle with her background, one full of the ghosts of children who were never born or who had lived, then died, and were forever mourned. She and her older sister, Emanuelina, were the only two living children who survived Trancha's pregnancies. All the dead had been boys, except for one girl, and all of them had been named, even if they had died in the womb.

"It's good," Father Robles said, "to name all the dead children. That way when they get to heaven the Lord can address them by name."

The child that had lived the longest before dying was called Eluid; he had died at age ten from whooping cough. Eluid was Trancha's greatest loss, one she never recovered from. The other children were named for deceased relatives, aunts, uncles, Trancha's brother, Primitivo's father. So every year, on the Day of the Dead, Trancha, Lina, and Dolores—Primitivo no doubt gone, as usual, to a remote mine site—would take flowers to San Pedro Cemetery across from their house. From one end of the cemetery, near Fierro Street, nearly to the other end, at Trujillo Street, Doña Trancha would stop and visit with each of her beloved deceased: first her parents, Elidoro Cádiz and Clotilde Garduño de Cádiz; then her children: Zoraida, Albado, Roque, Biterbo, Nemecio, Matías, Enos, Bríjido, Cesario, and Eluid. The girls, Lina and Dolores, would leave a little tin of flowers at each grave site as Trancha prayed for each member of her family in turn. After she'd finished with Eluid, that last stop taking longer than all the rest combined, the women would return home, empty-handed.

Since they lived so close to San Pedro, it was understood that Dolores and Lina would cross the street daily to do the upkeep on the family's graves. As Lina was always delegated to cook the meals, it fell to Dolores to take care of the public gardens, her family's last resting place.

Dolores used to say she grew up with the dead. As a small child, she was accustomed to and familiar with death. It was an inevitability she understood, given her mother's morbid state of mind, as well as their proximity to their loved ones.

San Pedro's was the poor people's cemetery: slightly wild and over-grown, but very colorful. Behind a high concrete wall you could see the tops of monolithic tombstones, their pensive angels peering out to the world in the torpid heat. Behind this wall was the old part of the cemetery, where nothing was watered anymore. All the graves on this side were surrounded by scrub brush and tumbleweeds, littered paper and dried weeds. This was where Trancha's great-grandparents were buried. Everyone from Elidoro to Eluid was buried in the new part of San Pedro's. While there was little vegetation to speak of, unlike in St. Anselm's, the Anglo cemetery, there were still enough wildflowers to make it bearable.

It was a constant battle. Each plot had its own problem. Zoraida's grave collapsed with every hard rain. Matías's was full of crabgrass. Eluid's had its thorns. Albado's was too close to Mr. Conrado Iturbide's, and the two families kept adjusting the area they believed divided the two graves. Enos's was full of sand and couldn't grow anything but worms. Bríjido's was always full of dog shit. Cesario's was far away from the water font and got watered the least. Nemecio's was next to a hornet's nest on a nearby tree. Tree roots broke ground all over

Roque's grave. Biterbo's was full of ants. But Eluid's grave was always the hardest to keep clean. It was covered in thorns, and was often littered with old funeral wreaths and flowers that blew downwind. Despite these problems, Eluid's grave was the lushest, blooming with early spring flowers and summer ice plant. It was a beautiful grave, the only one Dolores really felt connected to despite its thorns, which appeared every week, undaunted. He had been three years older than she.

Early evenings Dolores would go across to San Pedro with her bucket to water Eluid's grave and to talk to him. She felt she knew him and that as she grew, he grew as well. She was now eleven, he was fourteen; she was thirteen, he was sixteen. Eluid in time became her friend. "How are you, Eluid? How have you been today? Mamá's not well again. I don't have to tell you. It's Papá. He leaves her alone. When was the last time you saw him? He looks so tired, old. But Lina's fine and so am I. More water? You're so thirsty. I better go now. It's getting dark, Eluid. I've done all the boys and Zoraida, so I'll go. Bye for now, Eluid. Sleep well."

With such disparate personalities as Dolores's and Luardo's, how was it ever possible they had gotten together? Had children? And instilled in us a set of rules, a moral code, tastes, dreams, a world view? Luardo gave Hector and me a part of himself, as did Dolores. And they were worlds separate and distinct.

Luardo wasn't concerned about the death penalty, the legal voting or drinking age, the atomic bomb, poverty, the jobless rate, the Equal Rights Amendment, abortion, animal rights, or world hunger. What he did have opinions about was who I could or couldn't date, who I should or should not marry.

"Soveida."

"Yes, sir?"

"I think it would be good to marry an Italian. They're real men, with hair on their chest, maybe a gold chain or two. You should marry above yourself. If not an Italian, an Anglo. Don't date Mexicans, they're low class, probably will never earn much money. Don't date anyone too dark, especially Mexicans, never niggers, never, or chinks. I've known a few. Used to go to a restaurant near my house, One Hung Low, I used to call it. Don't marry someone from another country. You should marry an Italian born in the U.S., not one of those Italian Italians. They're men, all the rest of them pansies. The guy should be able to support you. A real man. Not a wimp. He'll like to go out now and then with the boys, be sociable, have a drink or two. He can hold his liquor. Get married, let him pay the bills, you have kids, stay at home and raise them. I want grandchildren. And learn to type. It's very important for a woman to know how to type. If anything goes wrong, you can always find a job as a secretary."

Dolores, on the other hand, had her ideas and she expressed them quite clearly.

"Soveida, listen to me."

"Yes, ma'am?"

"Find a man who can help you. Someone who doesn't mind working at home, doing his share of the work, who knows how to use a hammer, and a screwdriver, who can go up to the roof to fix the cooler and who doesn't have to be told to mow the lawn or wash the car or take out the garbage. Find a man with no body hair. Men's bodies when they're naked are ugly. It'll shock you what they do to themselves. When I first saw Luardo encuerado it shocked me. It was big, like a bull's. Now it's tiny, limp. Well, it was the last time I saw it. I don't want to see it anymore. Thank God I don't have to see it, why should I want to? We're divorced."

"Whatever you do, don't marry a Mexican. I mean it, Soveida. I don't have anything against our own except that they don't make good husbands. Most of them, now there are exceptions, are too macho. ¡Pendejos! Of course, nowadays, with women's lib . . . oh, they're still macho at heart. Now and then there's a good one, but look to the mother first. See if she brought him up good, respecting women. Most Mexicans want the women to stay at home, thinking that's enough. Let me tell you, that was all I ever had. It was never enough. I should know, I stayed home all those years! It's only after the divorce that I was freed. Don't marry a Mexican, unless you know his mother well. And never marry a drinker! I didn't know Luardo drank until the night of our wedding. Imagine my shock. No one told me. Not even his mother, no one! It was cruel, don't you think? Ask around. Talk to the mother, the sisters, the neighbors. Ask around about how he treated the women he grew up with, and that's how he'll treat you. Marry a man who loves children and animals. And relatives. Marry a man who cries. Don't tolerate someone who won't wash his car or clean his ears or take a bath at least once a day in the summertime. Marry a devout man, a decent man, a Christian, someone who's real, not a hypocrite. Someone who knows how to forgive, who doesn't hold grudges, or remember hurts. Someone who has never hit a woman, much less a child. Someone who loves flowers, is proud of his home. Someone who likes to cook. When a man cooks it's a blessing. See if he loves nature, not the inside of a bar in the middle of the afternoon. Notice if he's honest and reliable and trustworthy. If he lies, or gossips, forget him. Is he career-oriented? Does he love his work more than his family? What was his father like? His mother? Does he accept you the way you are, not wanting to change you? Is he oversexed? Does he pay attention to other women, read dirty magazines, pick his nose? Does he stay out late, rise early? Can you sit with him for a long time saying nothing and not get nervous? Another thing, can he laugh? Don't expect him to support you. Those days are gone. Always have your own money. Don't depend on any man to ration it out to you. Be yourself, do what you have to do, do what you love, and share with him, each of you doing your part. Otherwise, it's hard, Soveida. Soveida? Are you listening to me?"

Archangels

8

Another Year

As a young girl I never wanted to be God. That job was too difficult. What I wanted to be was an angel, one of the First Holy Communion angels, one of two girls who led the First Communicants up to the rail, dressed all in white, in a floor-length satin robe, a braided white cord circling my waist, hands raised high carrying flowers, a silver wreath circling my head.

If I could become an angel, then everything else would be all right, or so I reasoned. Only two young girls were selected each year to preside over the First Communion ceremonies. Most likely a second- or third-grader was chosen, a seasoned veteran, someone who had already made her First Holy Communion. It was important that her soul be uncontaminated and in a state of grace. In our Catechism, examples were used to convey the depth of sin: a half-darkened milk bottle for a venial sin, a completely darkened one for a mortal sin.

"Bless me, Father, for I have sinned. I ate meat on Friday and had impure thoughts three times. I fought with my brother, Hector, four times and hit him twice. I forgot to say my evening prayers six times and I was a bad daughter two times. For these and all my sins I am most heartily sorry."

In 1955, the year of my First Communion, Lucy Robledo, who was in my class and who was very fat and always had tiny pieces of lint in her ears, was selected as an angel along with Mara. Mara was in the fourth grade, and it was highly unusual for a fourth-grader to be chosen for this special job. But for some reason, after years of oversight, Mara was finally seen for what she was: angel material. Of course, I knew this not to be true, but who was I to change the minds of the angel-selection committee; namely, Father Dupey, Sister Emilia Marie, the principal of Holy Angel Elementary, and Miss Trastadero, Prefect of Discipline and girls' volleyball coach.

Mara and I were first cousins, her mother my mother's only sister. To me, Mara was the only sister I ever had. Her mother, Lina, had died when Mara was five years old. Mara was only three years older than I, and yet when I was younger she somehow seemed light-years ahead of me in maturity. After Lina's death, Dolores had taken her in briefly, only to give her away to Mamá Lupita. As the matriarchal head of the family, Mamá demanded that Mara go live with her: an unspoken tenet dictated that one of the grandchildren go and take care of the aging grandparent.

It was a great honor for our family to have an angel selected from its midst. The fact that I was making my First Communion that year was merely incidental, as the preparations for Mara's induction into the host of seraphim proceeded. The order of angels went as follows, from the lowest to the highest: angels, archangels, principalities, powers, virtues, dominations, thrones, cherubim, and, the most esteemed, the seraphim.

Mamá Lupita had Tía Bernardita, Dolores's aunt, make Mara's angel robe. Tía Bernardita lived on Sullivan Street, with her older sister, Tía Adelaida, an extremely large woman who was paralyzed from the waist down. Both single, the two sisters lived together in a house facing the back of Mott's Five-and-Dime downtown, near Saucedo's Bakery, where you could buy just-baked pan de huevo or marranitos de jengibre, gingerbread pigs.

Tía Bernardita and her sister, Adelaida, made biscochos for the neighborhood. For pan de huevo and bolillos you went to Saucedo's, and for biscochos you went to the Santos sisters. Making the Morrell lard-sugar cookies was their basic livelihood and a steady one it was. Both of them were deeply involved in the process: Bernardita measured out the flour, lard, anise, and water, while Adelaida floured the table and got the molds ready: stars, leaves, a spade, a triangle, rabbits, large and small, tiny horses, a crown. Bernardita punched and rolled out the masa, while Adelaida cut the cookies, then carefully put them on the cookie sheets. Bernardita baked them at a steady 350 degrees, then Adelaida gingerly covered the biscochos with cinnamon sugar and placed them in boxes with layers of waxed paper in between. A dozen sold for $1.50. For many years the two spinster sisters made their living this way, supplementing it with Tía Bernardita's sewing.

The satin cloth for Mara's robe came from the widow Davis's store, several yards of it, and the lace came from an old chest Mamá Lupita had in her attic. The crown Mara wore was made of fresh flowers from Oralia's garden, lilies and baby's breath and light purple iris and dark red roses.

The year Mara was an angel was the first year anyone had made a crown of fresh flowers. There was talk of it for some time to come. When Mara appeared from the back of the church, near the choir loft, there were gasps and everyone stared at her. She looked so beautiful, just like a real angel.

All of us first-graders, the girls on the right and the boys on the left, were led by our two angels, dumpy Lucy in her tight-fitting off-white robe which hugged her doughy little breasts, and Mara, bright-cheeked and angelic, with her dark hair framed by a crown of color.

Lucy and Mara slowly walked up from the back, holding flowers and rosaries in their hands. Lucy's crown was made of plastic flowers, all white, with dark green plastic tendrils of vines sticking out to the right, like a tired weather vane pointing east. She looked ridiculous. This made her entrance all the more pathetic. Mara was still petite then, and even though I was in first grade and she was in fourth, we were the same height. She had a very pretty, delicate face, with rosy cheeks that came, Oralia always said, from being pinched by God. I was skinny, rather blotchy-looking, still weak from just having gotten over the chicken pox. Mara, by contrast, looked healthy and holy, not at all like Lucy with her artificial halo and her scraggly hair and her robe that was too long, with a hem undone that had already turned black from being dragged across the floor.

Sister Emilia Marie had been the main proponent in Mara's becoming an angel, and everyone agreed it had been a good choice. Solemnly, with great attention and poise, Mara walked up to the right side, the boys' side, and signaled the first row of communicants to put down their prayer books and rosaries, to step out of the pew and then up to the altar.

Meanwhile, on the girls' side, Lucy nodded matter-of-factly to Susie Atencio and Susie got up, confused. Mary Helen Francis jabbed her and the first row filed and pushed out too fast, so that the boys' and girls' sides were uneven from the beginning. Mara gave Lucy a dirty look and took over from then on, Lucy following her lead. Rows 2, 3, 4, and 5 were better timed. I was in row 2 and smiled at Mara when I went past her to the altar, but she was too busy being an angel to see me. If she noticed me, she never let on. All of us approached the altar scared, and we opened our mouths helplessly, like baby birds waiting to be fed. Father Rudy, the assistant pastor, was there to greet each of us with our first Host.

Father Rudy looked stern. He had to tell more than one person to open and/or close his or her mouth. Sammy Lartone started giggling and Mara looked at him as if she would strangle his brain. He settled down, but then he went the wrong way, to the left instead of the right, ending up on the girls' side, next to Mary Helen and Elaine Portillo. He giggled, but I could see that he was confused, then mad. Mara wouldn't let him out of the girls' side and he had to stay there all the rest of the Mass. He looked at her as if to say: I'll get you later, crumbface.

"Go in peace" came and went and Mara and Lucy escorted us down the aisle. All our parents looked at us as if we'd just climbed Mt. Everest or gone to the moon. Sammy never smiled once after that. He was mad at Mara and mad at himself for being so stupid as to listen to and obey a dumb girl, and he was mad at all the girls for being girls, and mad at God for letting this happen today of all days. He stepped on my white shoes on the way out of the pew and he didn't even apologize. Sister Agnes, the first-grade teacher, bawled him out later in front of everyone.

Once outside, we all scattered on the front steps to take photographs with our families. Luardo had a camera and took my picture and then Mara's and then Dolores's with Hector and then all of us together and then I took theirs and then Mara took ours and then we went home.

The next year I was hoping to be an angel, but I was never asked. After a few years, they discontinued the First Communion angel guides altogether. Oralia always said Mara was the prettiest angel they ever had and and, as result of that, they had to stop.

Every girl at Holy Angel wanted to be a Communion angel and, then later, Queen of the Bazaar. We collected our pennies in old peanut-butter and applesauce jars, a penny a vote. When Mara was in seventh grade, she and I ran for Queen at the same time. It was really hard for me and Mara that year. We'd count our pennies every day together on Mamá's front porch. I'd take mine out of my Hills Brothers coffee can and she'd take hers out of her Skippy's Peanut Butter jar. Casting sideways looks at each other, we'd tally up our votes. Mara had taken her jar to City Drug and was ahead. I had mine at Saucedo's Bakery and we both had one at Tía Bernardita's, for the customers that went there. Mara worked real hard and might have won, should have won, really, if it hadn't been for the Acevedo curse. Neither of us won because Sally Acevedo's mother paid Sister Emilia Marie five hundred dollars every year so one of her daughters could win. It worked out well for them and Holy Angel and became a tradition; all six Acevedo girls were Queen at one time or another.

Sally was in fourth grade with me, and by then she already wore a bra. She went around bragging that she was going to win, and we believed her. She was so fat everyone called her Baby Pig. Her mother was fat, too, so we called her Mama Pig. Mr. Acevedo was really thin, all muscle, like a farmer.

Mara tried so hard, collecting money from everyone she came across. I was too shy really to ask for money. One day, knowing full well Sally Acevedo was going to win, Mara, out of spite, took all her money, a grand total of $24.93, and spent it all on herself. Just like that. She bought a radio at City Drug, and no one ever knew about it except me. She used to hide the radio in her room and would listen to it late at night under the covers when Mamá was asleep.

As expected, Sally came in first, Mara second, and I was fourth. Rosemary Pino, whose dad owned a gas station, came in third because her dad put five cents in her jar for every tank of gas he filled. That wasn't fair, everyone felt, but that's the way it was. All I got out of the race for Queen were a lot of glass containers that said: Vote for Soveida. Mara got a radio, at least, maybe some other things; she never did tell me everything. I always saw her chewing gum in the girls' bathroom, bent over the faucet, curling her eyelashes and putting on her lipstick or eating Valomilks after school with her friends. Sometimes she'd let me listen to the radio with her, under the blankets. Other times she lied about what she was doing or would do.

It was probably good neither of us ever won the title of Queen. Sometimes I wonder if Mara didn't buy that radio with her own money. She had a sock full of dollar bills and she could have. It would have been like her to say she took the Queen money, just for spite, and then used her own money instead. With Mara, you never knew what the real story was.

Mara had already graduated from eighth grade at Holy Angel when I was asked to be in the May Day crowning. My best friend, Lizzie, and I were selected to be attendants to Janie Fernández, who would crown the statue of Our Lady with a wreath of fresh flowers. Lizzie and I were to be escorted by Crunchy Maldonado and Ray Allenport, members as well of Our Lady's Sodality, a religious club dedicated to the Mother of God. All the eighth-graders belonged to the Sodality. This entitled the girls to wear blue capes, which, when tucked back with Immaculate Heart of Mary pins, revealed a silk lining. The only thing the boys had to distinguish themselves were their IHM pins, which they wore on the right side of their blue uniform shirts.

The handsomest boy in school, Stevie Roybal, was Janie's escort. Stevie seemed so much more mature than all the other boys at Angel. He was the only one of normal height as well: the rest of the boys were runty, shrimpy, stumpy—not sophisticated at all. Lizzie and I were thrilled to be standing in front of the church's side altar so close to God, before the statue of our patron saint, Saint Michael the Archangel, and next to Stevie Roybal.

Janie had to step up on a high ladder to reach the top of the Blessed Mother's head. I held Janie's long train and Stevie helped her up. I stood next to Stevie, and Lizzie stood next to Crunchy, who was short and underdeveloped but still the captain of the basketball team at Angel. Stevie played forward.

The crown in place, we all filed down the aisle, as our parents waited, another year for another Virgin.

9

The Boogeyman

When I was young, Dolores never told me stories of La Llorona, the mythical woman who wandered by the river's edge mourning her children she herself had drowned. It was only later that I came to hear about the woman spurned and scorned by her lover. Unable to live without him, she killed their children, whom she loved most in the world.

La Llorona was a sexual phantom, a wailing woman who wandered the riverbanks late at night, a mysterious, haunted spirit of lost love.

La Sebastiana, on the other hand, was a haggard skeleton who sat in her death cart, her fatal arrow pointed toward the living.

El Coco and El Cucui were boogeymen who tormented and stole children away if they were bad.

Although I heard about these spirits, my evil was always formless, never had a name.

As children, we were encouraged to be good, because goodness was desirable as an end in itself, saintly. We knew there was a hell, but goodness precluded hell. To be bad was to be removed from holiness, that ever elusive state of grace. It was to be disassociated from the core of life, to be out of balance with the spirit. It was to be someone like my father, Luardo Dosamantes, a reckless, thoughtless, wastrel alcoholic. "Sin juicio," said Dolores.

Coming from his wife, it was harsh, a ruthless assessment. Juicio was the power of judgment, the balance of faculties, prudence, wisdom. To be without it was to be a troubled, confused multitude of persons within one self, without control of one's higher or lower nature.

"Sin juicio. That would be the name of your father's biography if I were to write it. I'm not interested. I'd rather write about my Tía Adelaida Loera and the night she got paralyzed."

Dolly paused, and then sighed aloud: "He was weak."

She had wanted to say he was a pelado, which was, to Dolly, the ultimate insult to a human being. That vilification was usually followed by vividor/vividora: someone who was a parasite, living off of others at their expense, loyal to no one and nothing in particular. What can be worse than to be a pelado vividor sin juicio, a barefaced, bare-assed nobody without judgment?

Few people received the pelado/pelada insult from Dolores. It was usually reserved for people like the poor, nameless, faceless woman who left her imitation gold-lamé slippers under Luardo's bed and forgot to take them home.

"Whose are these?" Dolores asked Luardo on a visit to his apartment. They were divorced then, had been for years.

"What?" he yelled from another room.

"These slippers, whose are they?" She lifted them up with distaste, squinching her nose as if she had smelled of something intimate, sour. The shoes were old, gold plastic peeling around the toes.

"What are you talking about?"

"These shoes," Dolores hissed, storming into the living room. She held them carefully from the heel, repulsed.

"Will you leave things alone, damn it? They're not mine."

"Oh, they're not? I found them under your bed."

"What the hell . . . what were you doing under there? Leave my things alone, Dolores. You can't come over without snooping around like a bloodhound. We're divorced, damn it! What the hell business do you have under my bed, anyway?"

"Pelada," Dolores whispered under her breath. "Pelada!"

Pelado, pelado was what she really meant. Pelado!

"Okay, okay. They were there when I moved in."

"You told me to come over and get your laundry, Luardo. Anyway, I was looking for socks."

"Just take the clothes, and stop going through my things!"

"Where are your shorts? A week and you just use three pair? Didn't Mamá ever teach you? A pair a day?"

"Damn it, just take the clothes!"

"Hand me that pile of shirts, would you? And bring me your comb. I'm washing all the combs."

"My comb isn't greasy!"

"Just give me the comb. And check your pockets! Last week you left in a roll of Certs. Is this all your laundry?"

"I think so."

"Are you sure you gave me everything?"

"That's everything."

"So whose shoes *are* they, Luardo?"

Unfaithfulness was unholy, unclean, and it was a characteristic of someone who was separated from God. And yet, for all the hurts and sorrows of life with Luardo, his absences and lack of interest, Dolores put up with him and always forgave him. She was his wife in her eyes, in the family's eyes, and in the eyes of God. No divorce could change that.

"He's your father. Someone to be loved, despite his failings. He's weak."

It was always the other woman who was the villain, the faceless, nameless pelada who lurked in the shadows and hid under the bed. The blame was hers, hers alone. It was her fault, hers and that of her gold-lamé shoes.

"You know, Soveida," my cousin Mara said over the phone during one of our many late-night long-distance conversations when we talked about our family, "Papá Profe hit Mamá Lupita."

This terrible news about my grandfather, Papá Profe, came as a shock to me. A word had never been uttered against Papá Profe in the official family record.

"No, Mara, it can't be true."

"Adrino told me that someone told him—some Dosamantes from California who was visiting—he can't remember who, he thinks it was Tío Trebolio, after one of his all-nighters—that Papá Profe used to beat Mamá Lupita and then cry himself to sleep. First chapter of the uncensored Dosamantes history book."

"I can't believe Papá Profe hit Mamá Lupita. No Dosamantes man ever hit his wife. Luardo never hit Dolores, Mara."

"Soveida, he never had to. Pendeja that she was, she would have fallen down in a swoon first, begging him never to leave her, as he cursed and then stormed out of the house, leaving her writhing on the floor. Soveida, are you there?"

"Can't we talk about something else, Mara?"

"What are you thinking, Soveida?" Mara whispered in the darkness.

"Nothing. Nothing," I said.

"You're a Dosamantes. At least you have a history. I'm a Loera. And as far as everyone is concerned, Loeras have never amounted to much, like my mother, Lina."

Years later, Dolores said to me: "It all began when Mara went to live with Mamá Lupita. Mara was my sister's flesh, and still I gave her to your father's mother. Mamá wasn't an old woman then, but she was still hungry for lives to rule. Only God knows what I did to that poor child!"

I wonder if Dolores ever *really* knew what she had done?

I wondered, too, why *I* hadn't gone to live with Mamá Lupita. I was her real grandchild, the favorite. She was the one who pampered me, doted on me. To me, she was never the old woman Mara spoke of late at night over the phone. I never knew that old witch she raged about. Who was that woman? Was she *my* Lupita or Mara's Lupita?

Listening to Mara's late-night monologues about the sad state of our family and her tragic life as a result, I often fell silent after one of the latest devastating revelations about someone I had been taught to love.

"Tío Todosio likes little boys," Mara said with the conspiratorial tone I always disliked.

Poor Mamá! Poor Tía Lita! I thought to myself. And get off the phone, get off the damn phone, Mara. Stop telling me lies! Lies, all of them. Or so I wanted to believe.

It's not surprising that I didn't hear tales of La Llorona, La Sebastiana, El Coco, El Cucui, or any number of names that were used as threats to settle children down, to sober them up, to put them in their children's place of terror and dread. Obedience, parents called it.

We never heard the ghost stories of make-believe people, male or female, who terrified and teased. All our relatives were make-believe, with make-believe lives. But we children really knew the truth. Only we couldn't talk.

Years later, on the phone, long distance and late at night, we corrected the lies: Papá Profe beat Mamá Lupita, Tío Todosio liked the boys, our cousin Adrino liked anyone with breasts. Luardo no tuvo juicio and Dolores was an actress. Mara had a big mouth, and I liked to cry.

Our ghosts were real. There was no need for the wailing Llorona or the demented Coco. Our ghosts haunted us in a way no fantastic demons ever could.

"Dolores and Mamá Lupita were my boogeywomen, Soveida. I had my boogeyman too, hell, and he had me. Luardo would come into my room and touch me. I wanted to scream. I had nightmares that Dolores would find out. That she would tie me to the bed and beat me. She knew. I could never call him Dad anymore. That's when I started calling him Luardo."

"You always talk about the past, Mara."

"You always talk about the past, too, okay?"

"But in a different way. Your past is always cruel."

"It was cruel, don't forget it. It's that way for all women, Soveida, so wake up! I hate to see you play the same damn role that your mother played, Soveida, bowing to all the men who come into your life and then scraping up their crusty filth and saying thank you, sir."

"When are you coming home to see us, Mara? You told us you were coming home for Christmas."

"I don't know if I really want to."

"People don't forgive each other anymore. Have you noticed that, Mara?"

"It's too much trouble and too fucking painful."

"All my life I've been saying I'm sorry."

"That's one thing I've always hated about you, Soveida."

"I don't even know who I'm sorry for anymore. Or why."

"Did Luardo ever come into your room and do those things he did to me?"

"I'm not sure. But I was always afraid of the dark and of something in the dark touching me."

"I'll never understand. Never. And I'll never forget."

"But you can forgive. You can forgive, Mara."

"God, Soveida, you sound like Tía Adelaida talking about the night she got paralyzed. The Old Lady That Forgives Everybody, that's you."

"I've never heard that story."

"Well, someday you will and you'll understand what I'm talking about."

"You're not feeling well, Mara, are you? What is it?"

"The same old things. Shit. Well, I gotta go."

I knew what Mara was talking about. We were a family without a real history. Ours was a history of lies. Someone's invention of what a family should be.

And yet, Mara, I wanted to tell her, we are undoing the lies, you and I. I wanted to make her understand once and for all—there was no boogeyman, no boogeywoman, no imaginary darkened face across the room, peering at us from the window or in the mirror, but *ourselves*, saying yes, why not, go on, suffer.

10

Saints

I have always identified with saints.

Particularly martyrs, young women who choose Christ as their sole spouse, women who would rather have their breasts ripped off them than betray their chastity.

I identify most especially with Maria Goretti, the Italian girl who chose to die rather than succumb to the concupiscence of the flesh. Maria lived on a farm in Italy with her parents, brothers, sisters, and a hired hand, a young man. Drawn to the flesh, he hid magazines of naked women under his bed that he reveled in lasciviously.

One day, while all the family was out working, the young man stayed behind. For some reason, Maria was in the house as well.

The young man cornered Maria with evil intent. She cried out, but no one could hear her. She tried to escape. He chased her, insisting she give in to him, that it would be all right. She resisted, praying to God to save her. Throwing her down, he beat her, raped her, and then killed her.

The young man escaped. He was hunted down, captured, and put on trial. But he repented, calling upon the Holy Father, His Holiness the Pope, to forgive him. Interceding in a way not known before, the Pope took the fellow into his residence, where he was assigned the role of gardener. For many years the man quietly cared for the Pope's roses.

This is the story as I remember it from the little book on Maria Goretti that I used to read in school. There was a series of small books for children, *Lives of the Saints*, which were kept in the window-ledge library of the sixth-grade class of Holy Angel Elementary School. The book on Saint Maria Goretti was one of the most popular. She was a contemporary saint, that's what struck us as unusual, not some bygone Roman virgin thrown into a pit of lions. She was someone who lived in the present.

I myself checked the book out three or four times. It was a mysterious book to me, for it hinted at an unknown world of vice and degradation so evil it could barely be imagined. I could not conceive of it at all. Just as I could not understand the number 69 or the word FUCK seen on the walls on my walks home from school, I had no knowledge of the violent creation sexuality had become, and always was to some.

I knew Maria Goretti was violated, but how?

This book, then, was our introduction to passion. Unbridled, unrestrained, demonic. The book was checked out by everyone that passed through Holy Angel, because it dealt with that secret, unapproachable world of sex, and crimes against the very core of one's self.

Recently, someone tried to correct my version of the Goretti tale. The Pope part was supposedly not true, not to mention all the gardening business. But I do remember reading an article and seeing photographs of the gardener.

To me, it was more just and wonderful that the young man, slave to his baser nature, had found peace and rest in the sweet, cleansing aroma of the roses. To think of him there made me cry. I want to believe that he was the Pope's gardener. It's somehow more tolerable to imagine that he repented in the beauty of the roses, in the sunlight, under the shade of cool trees, than in a prison cell, cut off from all redemption.

Saints come in all shapes and sizes.

I think of Saint Sebastian, showered with arrows and bound by rope to a tree, his magnificent body slumped in death, in perfect stillness, a bloodied male flower.

The Little Flower, Saint Theresa of Lisieux, is the saint of the child in all of us. She is a pure, simple, unaffected child of God. Saints are different to children than they are to adults. When you are a child, saints have more of a sweet reality. Adult saints and the saints adults revere are more desperate, like Saint Jude, patron of impossible cases, or Saint Anthony, who spends all his time looking for lost glasses or shoes. They are gimme-gimme-something saints, help-me saints, incurable last-stand saints, lost-and-found saints.

Saints are also culturally rooted, like San Martín de Porres. He was the first black man I ever knew, very handsome and always, it seems, happy. He is a saint for all displaced people, himself an outcast by color. Somehow he is very dear to mexicanos. He once worked with lepers and the poor. We embrace him like a brother and admire his thick curly hair, not unlike our own. He is a saint for all Latinos, a get-ahead saint, who is loved and accepted by all the viejitas, who would never allow their daughters (¡Ni lo mande Dios!) to marry black. Proudly these old women display large, glass-covered, framed images of San Martín in his brown habit over their antique bureaus in darkened, private bedrooms, bedrooms unvisited by men for over thirty years.

Then there is the Santo Niño de Atocha, who goes out regularly with his worn shoes to help the poor and the defenseless late at night. Returning in the early-morning hours, before anyone is awake, he settles into his tiny niche, his white shoes splattered with mud.

Juan Bosco always draws a crowd of young people to his side, mostly young boys, because all the good women saints are usually ex-whores or breathless virgins, or old women widowed for many years.

Saint Joseph is the surrogate father of Jesus, so all male-related cases fall to him: errant and lazy husbands, sex-starved, shiftless pelados, men with small and/or ineffectual penises, troubled male children who lock themselves too long in the bathroom, incorrigible fathers and bachelors. Mothers who are looking for a husband for their daughters also pray to him, as do young and old women who want either to find or to lose one.

Saint Anne is prayed to by old women and future mothers, those concerned about their wombs in one form or another.

Saint Francis is the saint for everyone, even non-Catholics. What is more universal than birds, and animals, and marauding wolves to be tamed? Saint Francis is also the saint of the once-rich-now-poor or the poor and the spiritually rich and the not-rich-not-poor who would like to give themselves up to nature and the spirit of brotherhood inherent in all men, if only they could. Saint Francis is definitely male and in the upper echelon of male saints. One rarely hears about his counterpart, Saint Claire, or her work. But, then again, most saints are male, except the unfortunate heretofore mentioned limbless, sightless, wombless, or sexless.

For years I wore scapulars, blue, brown, green, white. I carried wood from Jerusalem in my bra, blessed myself with Holy Water, ate sacred bread, and touched wondrous dirt. I carried relics of splintered bone or tiny locks of hair or nails in my wallet and purse, pinned them to my undergarments, and wore sacred wood around my neck and wrists. I said countless ejaculations, short prayers that rolled off the tongue like a litany of breath. My Mother, my Confidence. My Mother, my Confidence. Dulce corazón de María, sálvame. Dulce corazón de María, sálvame.

I always prayed to the Holy Mother, the Virgin Mary. She was Our Lady of Fatima, Our Lady of Guadalupe, the Black Virgin, and Our Lady of Lourdes all rolled into one. She was the spirit mother that held me, small child against her breast.

Later I identified with Saint Mary Magdalene, the supreme woman saint, ultra-whore, no cloying virgin, the top sinner among all the saints, except Saint Augustine. The Magdalene is almost as popular as the Goretti, except she's older, more jaded. She is the saint of hussies, fallen women, and mistresses, something I imagined as a child I would never become. She is the patron saint of Luardo's woman with the gold-lamé shoes.

Mary M. is older, more used up. Saint Anne is the Mother of God's mother, and she, too, is old and shriveled up, despite the fecundity of her womb. It was only through divine intervention that her woman's juices still flowed.

There is Saint Joan of Arc, but she is French, and hears voices. I can't really trust her, somehow. I am more comfortable with the passive lay-down-their-life-and-die-rather-than-screw virgins. Saint Joan is too aggressive for me. I was indoctrinated into believing that having rounded ample breasts and living in constant fear of having them ripped off was the only way.

John the Baptist is a wild man, not your usual saint. It's always a relief to hear about him at the river. God really loves him, so wildness is okay, if you are a man, or look like a man. You can't be wild and a woman. Look what might happen to you. Burned to death on a spit like a witch.

The Good Thief is probably my favorite male saint. On Good Friday I take out my Missalette and read the Passion to myself, beginning with the part about the thieves, the cynical one and the repentant one. Over and over I read how the Good Thief feels the Lord was unjustly punished. He asks to be remembered in God's kingdom. I long to be with him in paradise as well. He is a last-minute dark-horse saint, a God-will-save-your-soul-if-you-really-love-there's-hope-after-all-if-your-heart-is-pure saint. During the Elevation of the Host I am filled with great longing as my nostrils breathe the unforgettably sweet and intoxicating smell of incense. I mouth with the Good Thief the words: Lord, remember me when you come to your Kingdom. Love-filled music instantaneously floats back to me from that holy body wracked in pain: This night thou shalt be with me in Paradise. I am seared, wrenched, and burned further into that ecstatic essence that is my soul.

I like the Good Thief because his story moves and excites me, but to live on that feverish plane is something I could never do for long. Someone like Mother Cabrini is good to cool the blood and settle the heart. Mother Cabrini has a nice face, but I always feel she is a bit stodgy. She looks like a spider in her black dress and dark veil.

Last, there is my Guardian Angel, a saint, no doubt, but faceless, as all angels are. Male or female? Decidedly, gloriously female. Or female with the best of male. For years I depend on her, talk to her, and bless her. Then years go by and I ignore her. When I apologize, off we go again. She never gets mad at me, not like Dolores or Luardo or Hector or even Mara; she is even-tempered, and very kind. No dramatics, no theatrics, just your everyday, dependable variety of saint. Sweet and loving, no fanfare, no trumpets, just old reliable love. A comfortable, spiritual old sock. The best.

And then there is me, for, after all, this is about me. Little Soveida, wanting to *be*, not *become*, a saint. Everybody has their chance at sainthood; what will mine be? What cause will be thrust upon me, what unspoken affliction? And when will it begin?

My grandmother, Mamá Lupita, wants me to become a nun. She often takes me aside and talks to me.

"Priests in the family are a dime a dozen, Soveida. Everybody knows they're jotos and maricones or lusty goats in search of skirts. What this family needs is a nun. Women's prayers, everyone knows, are more powerful. Any man can give up sex for four years, especially if they get him before he knows what to do with that thing between his skirts. Cassocks, that's what they call them. After that, you know what happens. When a woman gives up sex, it's final. Try and sneak sex on a woman, see what happens. Nine months later there's everlasting hell to pay. No, m'ija, you are the one, Soveida. You are going to be a nun, someday, one day, may I live to see it, and if I don't, you'll never rest until it's done or you're done or I'm done. One way or another. One time or another. Every woman wishes she could become a nun. You don't know what I mean yet, m'ija, may the Blessed Mother—

she was a woman, too, don't forget that, so she knows what I'm talking about—may she spare you a drunken man late at night smelling of chicharrones and tequila, worse yet, of frijoles and beer. ¡Dios mío el gas! Worse yet a man in the middle of the afternoon, en agosto, when you're roasting chile, hasta al copete en chile, and he comes in from the farm, smelling of sweat and dirt, and carrying on, as if it wasn't hot enough already! I want to spare you this, m'ija, look at me, listen to me. You need to think about it, now, before it's too late! You like to read. Nuns read all the time and no one bothers them. They can be quiet. They don't have no one belching and scratching and making pedos, you know, farts, on the way to the you-know-what, el escusado. Escusado, bathroom, a word like that, it sounds like an excuse. Well, that's what sex is, but in a different way. But let's not talk about it now. We'll talk about it later. I want to spare you the details, m'ija. And once in the escusado, Dios mío de mi vida, the noises and later the smell. I keep matches in there, but your grandfather, Profesito, he don't use them. Men cannot be trained. They're wild bulls or changos: monkeys, I don't know which. And that's not all. They shed. I could never keep a clean bathtub. Pelitos por donde quiera. Little hairs all over the place. But I want to spare you the details. Think about the Divine Service. I know what Father Escondido thinks marriage is, but remember, m'ija, all priests are men, just men, what do they know? I'd like to see el padrecito take three rounds con mi viejo, let's see what he says. Maybe someday women will become priests, ay, I won't live to see it, may you live to see it, and if you don't, well then, may another woman live to see it. Me, I never wanted to become a nun. A priest, that's what I wanted to be! May the Blessed Mother support me in this, she knows I would have been a good priest. Ay, we do what we can. So think about it, I mean, becoming *at least* a nun. Your mother's childhood friend, Estella Fuentes, became a nun. She's now Sister Mary Margaret Marie of the Holy Magdalenes. She don't have no wrinkles. Her face is as smooth as a baby's nalgas. Look at Dolores's eyes. A road map. Texas. Luardo did it to her, and he's my son. With him, priesthood was out of the question from the very beginning. He was always pulling on his cosita; there was no way he was ever going to be consecrated. ¡Ni lo mande Dios! It's as if some children are born with an invisible sign on their foreheads: Priest. Married Man. Pendejo. Yes, I knew. The man was oversexed from the day he was born, no way he could ever have been ordained. La cosita, *it* would have stuck out between the skirts. *It* should have been, you know, right then and there, for all the shame *it* brought this family, all the trouble *it* caused your mamá, not to mention las otras, putas desgraciadas pintadas chorreadas. En el nombre del Padre, del Hijo, y del Espíritu Santo. He may be your daddy, but he's half man, half goat. Which half the goat, you'll have to guess. But let's not talk about that now. Testudo como un chivo, stubborn as an old goat, that's what I say, he thought with his cosita, not with his head. Look at your mamá. That road map near her eyes. California. All on account of you can imagine. ¡*La cosita*! She didn't have no chance. *It* had a will of its own. Como chile colorado. Think about it, m'ija, think about the Divine Service. Just promise me you'll think about it. IT, the Nunhood, not *it*. We'll talk more later, eh, con más tiempo . . ."

Mamá Lupita and I get up early and walk to 6:30 Mass every morning. We walk because she likes to walk and is too old to drive a car. I am only six years old. We meet on the walkway outside our two adjoining houses. Her Blue House looks so lovely in the morning light. I often see her pass the large blue window that gives the house its name. Once the house was painted white, but now everything is blue, Mamá's favorite color, in honor of the Blessed Mother.

When we go to church I am convinced I am going to become a nun. In the air of sanctity that surrounds me there, it is the only place I feel saved.

At family gatherings, Mamá Lupita prods me and then I will proudly announce that I am consecrated to God. I am going to become a nun. I myself believe this with all my heart. When, I don't know. Perhaps after high school, after a few years of dating. I want to see the world before I leave it. And what harm can there be, really? All the seminarians I've ever known dated during the summer vacations, and a few of them eventually became priests.

Mamá Lupita thinks I should join an order right after high school, the sooner the better. As soon as possible. She knows a few of those same seminarians and has her doubts about waiting too long and having too many distractions. Saint Theresa of the Child Jesus had a Papal dispensation, she went all the way to Rome to beg the Holy Father to admit her to the Holy Life, why can't I?

The only problem is that when I started school I saw Stevie Roybal and fell in love.

But, before, there was my brief year of grace, my one experience of saintliness.

Mamá Lupita was so proud of me that short year. All her friends, the old men and women of the 6:30 Mass, admired me; she told me so. They couldn't imagine a six-year-old child getting up so early every day to go to Mass. "It's unheard of!" Dominga Fierro said. Dominga is Mamá Lupita's best friend. Her only friend other than her maid, Oralia, who has been with her for over sixty years. Dominga is Mamá's comadre. She baptized Teeney, Mamá's oldest girl, when she was small.

"Imagine that! Must have been a long time ago, it's hard to imagine three-hundred-pound Teeney a small baby. Incredible!"

Dominga is fat and wears the waist of her dress over her stomach. She puffs alongside of us, panting and rubbing her belly, talking to it as if she were talking to a child. "Ay, ay, ay 'stá, amorcito . . ."

She looks pregnant, about to give birth to something. The only child she carries, Mamá says, is Death herself. She has cancer. And she knows it. That false fertility she has ignored for so long will finally kill her, giving her life in the only kingdom that to her really matters, Mamá says.

When she dies, part of Mamá Lupita will die as well. Dominga is her best friend, her last friend, besides Oralia. But what lady admits to the fact that her maid is her best friend? Not Mamá Lupita. So when I ask her if she has friends, she replies dryly, "I have one friend, but she's dying."

On our walks to church every day we swing by Dominga's house, a small adobe near the large intersection that leads to Our Lady of Grace Catholic church and the altar where I once again renew my eternal vow to become a nun.

Each day I dip my hand in the Holy-Water font, cross myself, one small fast cross on the forehead, one small fast cross on the chin, one small fast cross on the breast, one big salute to the forehead, breast, left shoulder, right shoulder, and one final tap to the chin, or if you are more pious, which I am, one last prayerful gathering of the fingers to the lips with a small sacred kiss. I then genuflect, full knees to the cold, hard floor, and walk up the aisle, repeating the crossing ritual, crossing myself again, eyes to the altar, where I see the monstrance gleaming gold in the early-morning light.

Later, I kneel at the wooden communion rail, shyly, like a gently submissive bride, lacing my fingers through the dark metal that surrounds the wood, afraid that if I displease my God, the Host will burn out my tongue like acid, or that the unfortunate priest will stop in front of me, refusing to give me the Host, knowing by some innate sense that an evil demon lurks above my head, taunting me in front of the Divine Presence, the Paraclete. I imagine all kinds of last-minute punishments and torments for a sinful mind and a blackened soul. The priest might drop dead in front of me, or worse yet, I might drop dead in front of him, falling downward into the open flames that are always just below the floor of the church, a burning façade for the fires of a never-ending hell.

Nothing like this has ever happened. The most dramatic occurrence is when the Host occasionally gets stuck to my palate; it's not uncommon. If this happens, I have to cluck it down. My eyes downcast, trying to remain calm, I work my tongue feverishly to rid myself of the strange, inhibiting feeling of stuck Host. Hosts are so sticky, and hell seems so close. Just around the corner. Under the floor.

I am always fighting off temptations, worrying myself sick about my eternal soul, not realizing I am too concerned about myself, forgetting all others.

Mamá Lupita looks around to me as she comes back from the communion rail. Her black mantilla falls around her shoulders. Through the spidery delicate lace she winks at me, then nods her chin when she sits down. She strokes several long white chin hairs, her eyes closed, as she rests in deep thanksgiving. She doesn't notice I am still clucking. An unusually difficult Host is causing me to panic. I look around. All her friends are so proud of me. Sister Soveida. Almost a saint.

Whenever I look at her mantilla, with its large black bobby pin holding it in place, it reminds me of a story she told me. A nun friend of hers had told it to her. This was when she still had friends. It concerns a young nun who had just been received into the order. In those days, all the nuns wore black, thick habits, not like today. Today, nuns look like librarians or teachers. But then nuns were nunish, with long, full robes and a headpiece that fell about the shoulders.

On the very first day of the nun's induction, she was being dressed by an older nun with bad eyesight. The old nun accidentally jabbed the long straight pin that held the young nun's habit in place, catching some of the skin on the top of her head. It hurt! But what was the young nun to do? It is God's will! Praise the Lord for his love! If that is what he asks of me each day, I will obey!

The next day the young nun arose, put on her habit, arranged her headcloth, sticking the pin directly in the center of her head, piercing her scalp. The pain grew worse. Blood appeared. This went on some time, until one day another older nun noticed the blood.

"Sister, what is it?" she said. "Let me see."

"Sister," the younger nun replied, "it is nothing but the Cross."

"What are you talking about, Sister? For God's sake!"

"But it is for God's sake, Sister," the young nun answered.

Crying, laughing, the older nun shook her head, and exclaimed, "Sister, Sister! God's will for us is a merciful thing, full of love, not pain. How long have you been doing this?"

"Since the day I became a Bride of Jesus," the young nun replied. "Since the day I joined the order. Since the day I took my vows of obedience and poverty and chastity. Since the day Mother Elizabeth caught my skin. Oh, but, Sister, while I did not question God's will, I didn't know how much it would bleed!"

Mamá Lupita knew many nuns. They told her stories like these. There were other stories as well, about nuns who lost their hair from lack of air underneath those starched habits, of nuns who had skin diseases, stories, too, about other parts of that never-seen body, the body of Christ. I am the vine and you are the branches.

"They are holy women, Soveida. And yet they know what the world is, they know the ways of men. Many of them have been married. And others have brothers. Some of my best friends were nuns. Their prayers, m'ija, are *very* strong. They have dedicated their lives to God, and he is grateful. Little by little the nuns are making God a nicer man."

Mamá Lupita smiles. When she speaks, I listen. When she is silent, I am silent. We have no need to speak to each other. It's she who gave me my first shot at sainthood, and I am grateful.

That year came and went. I'm still trying to recapture the glow of the bright, burning candles. I inhale the incense and Mamá Lupita comes to mind. I see her peering sideways at me through semitransparent black lace. She was a friend to so many nuns. She was never a nun, knew she could never become one. It was only much later I found out she never really wanted to become a nun. She should have become a priest, but when her mother looked at her she'd seen the invisible words written on her forehead: Woman. Wife. Mother. Martyr.

11

Bloody Towels

What did I know of sex? A handbook on the menstrual cycle hurriedly passed to me by Dolores, a book I read and reread in the bathroom; a bloody towel with menstrual blood left there by Mara; and the furtive commingling of Dolores and Luardo when he came home to visit, bringing his dirty laundry with him as a present.

What I later learned about sex was from the previews at the Grand Theater advertising oily, bare-breasted women, their high pointy breasts straining under black leather vests. It was a preview that jolted Holy Angel Elementary School for months to come, a preview not even Sister Emilia Marie the principal knew would be shown between *The Song of Bernadette* and *Animals of the Wild Northern Tundra.*

That fateful, sin-filled day, the lay teachers yelled to us sixth-graders in the flickering, guilt-ridden darkness, as well as to anyone who was within earshot. "Close your eyes! Close your eyes! Close your eyes! Don't look!"

Many of the teachers were unmarried women from the teaching ministry back East who ventured West to evangelize the natives, while not discounting the possibility of finding a husband from the nearby army base. Others were anorexic-looking, demanding young Filipino spinsters who were afraid to laugh and who excelled in typing skills.

Miss Trastadero, the latest arrival from Manila, stood in front of the movie screen hugging the dark thin arm of Miss Bamboa, her Filipino spirit sister, who stood next to her, practically in tears.

"Our Father who art in Heaven, hallowed be Thy name . . ." Trastadero called out in the interminable harsh light of those never-ending previews, "Thy Kingdom come, thy will be done," as the sexy, husky voice emanated from the screen and floated over the tops of our small heads, which could barely see beyond the backs of the seats, but strained, guiltily, to sneak looks.

En masse we continued praying, "On earth as it is in Heaven"— eyes wide open, then closed in terror, then opened, slowly, wantonly, with insatiable curiosity. "Give us this day our daily bread," the boys snickered, while the girls winced in shame. Those were women up there, women like us, women we someday would become, with breasts like that ". . . and forgive us our trespasses," even as we looked, "as we forgive those . . ." Stop! "As we forgive those who trespass against us, now and at the hour of our death." Will this never be over? "Amen!"

No one I knew ever told their parents they'd seen naked women that day at the movies. We were all too afraid. No one ever spoke of it again, except those few boys like Robert Ryan and Willie Melendres who licentiously joined the girls in the women's bathroom and whispered things to us in there, or mumbled under their hot breath to us when we landed on first or second or third base, or murmured in the outfield when no one was paying attention.

Most of the students at Holy Angel were silent, and secretly thrilled, not merely to have seen the naked, conelike breasts of a woman dressed in black leather, brandishing a whip, but to have seen all this on a school outing from Holy Angel—"the Angel," or simply "Angel," as it was called—in the company of the boys! There was talk, quiet, hushed, furtive, from the immodest ones, for weeks. The administration never spoke of the preview incident. We girls were thrilled, yes, to have a secret with the boys, at last.

Later I came across a worn book my cousin Adrino had stolen from his dad. Adrino Sr. had bought it at Manda Pacheco's garage sale. It was a book Manda knew nothing about except that it had once belonged to her nephew, Adolfo, who attended Berkeley for two semesters, dropping out to pursue the T-shirt business. The book was *Psychopathia sexualis* by Krafft-Ebing, and it was far worse than the dirty magazines at Adrino Sr.'s house, stored there on top of the washer that faced the old toilet that bit you when you sat down.

One day I'd gone to my Tío Adrino and Tía Teeney's house with my parents and had found dirty magazines in there, a huge pile of them on top of Tía Teeney's chipped Hotpoint. Why she had the washer in the bathroom was as much a mystery to me as why my Tío Adrino kept his magazines out there in the open for all to see.

As modern and as up-to-date as she was, Tía Teeney, if she could have her way, would have made the bathroom a building apart, away from the main house, so convinced was she by Mamá Lupita's continual harangues about men, their cleanliness and lack thereof, their improprieties, and the uncomfortable matter of attending to one's own body, and that of a household's, and doing it with some modicum of decorum.

I think the washer was in the bathroom because somehow, in her mind, it was all connected. My cousin Adrino, or A.J., as he was called, did his laundry in elementary school, and was surprised to find out Dolores did mine.

"What? You mean, your mom . . . ?"

"Yes, but I wish she wouldn't."

"Yeah, I know what you mean, girls get crusty shorts, too."

"Shut up, grossbag, what do you know, anyway?"

"Let's talk about your shorts, Soveida woveida . . ."

"Talk about your own shorts, peaface!"

This taunt upset A.J., so he'd go on at length about the state of women's drawers, especially what he imagined mine would be like. He'd had the misfortune, as he told it, to have one day accidentally seen his sister M.J.'s panties in the bathroom where she'd left them after a bath. So he knew all about the crusties.

"Don't call me peaface, toilet breath."

"Let's talk about how *you* got a pea up your nose. Nobody gets a pea stuck in their nose. I mean, it's pretty hard to do."

"It was an accident, Tampax butt!"

"Yeah, sure, peaface!"

Tía Teeney's bathroom was small, painted a bright pink, with chunks of cement missing from the walls, which always seemed moist. Rivulets of water fanned out over the ceiling above the shower; the little window that faced out into their large back yard was stained with rust.

The washbasin was full of hairs: short hairs from Tío Adrino's beard, other bristly ones that looked suspicious, and still others—longer, half-dyed ones that could only be my Tía Teeney's. I hated to use their bathroom, but it was inevitable I would have to go in there at least once each visit. Tía Teeney, while not a bad housewife, purposefully neglected this room. A seldom-used can of Ajax sat forlornly beside the toilet, a hard gray rag draped on top.

The washer was old, feisty, hairy as well, with an accumulation of impacted navy-blue lint inside that Tía Teeney saw fit to leave unattended. Often the machine would stop mid-cycle, as if for a much needed rest. Then someone would have to come in and kick it to start it up again.

I remember the first time I discovered Uncle Adrino's magazines.

They had names like *Cavalier, Gent, Stud.* I had never seen such magazines before. Sitting down, forgetting the biting toilet seat, I looked through his pile, amazed and aghast at the same time. I was locked in there at least half an hour when A.J. called out to me: "Hey, Sove, what you doing in there? Cut it short, I gotta go!"

Caught in the act, I picked up the stack of magazines that I had spread all over the floor near my feet and decided to hide them behind Tía Teeney's washer, in one of the cement holes in the wall.

At that moment the washer started up and feverishly chugged through a delayed rinse cycle. I could hear Tía Teeney behind the door now, yelling at me to kick it good, the thing, kick it good, so that it'll remember this time. Kick it I did, and the washer stopped its gyrations. Red-faced, I came out of the bathroom. Tía Teeney raced in with a handful of flaming matches and kicked the washer a few times with relish and went out, holding her nose with two red-lacquered nails.

I was finally free from the evil hold of those magazines, and awkwardly tried to resume my usual, nondescript place at my Tía Teeney's court, where she played queen, regaling her sputtering brother Luardo and his silent wife, Dolores, with tales from her vast repertoire of adventures. She loved talking about the neighborhood now, the same one she and Luardo had grown up in, how it had become run-down, full of Mexicans, hell, it was always full of Mexicans, but now they were from México. She mentioned Esau Portales, the viejito borracho, the little old drunk down the street.

"Pobrecito," Dolores said.

"Well, I don't feel sorry for him," Teeney said. "He's been wandering drunk through the neighborhood near the Güero Solo's all week in stained shorts, those ragged calzoncillos he wears summer-winter-spring-and-fall."

"I didn't know the Güero Solo was still alive!" Luardo exclaimed.

"Well, he isn't. Where have you been all these years, brother?" Teeney said. "He died years ago when we were still kids."

"Oh yeah, I remember now."

"Who was he?" I asked.

"Some crazy, blond Anglo who lived all alone here in the barrio con los mexicanos. Hell, we didn't call it a barrio then, it was home. He came from other parts, and lived here in Chiva Town, of all places. And just imagine that I'm still living here!" Teeney said.

"How old was he? Was he old?" I wondered.

"No, he was in his thirties," Luardo said.

"Not bad-looking, either. I myself would have gotten closer to have a better look. All the eligible girls had their fancy. Everyone wondered what the heck he was doing here with all the plebe, us common folk. In his tin-roofed house, all alone like that."

"Yeah, I remember him."

"And so Esau the drunk comes by the house, in the direction of the Güero Solo's, estoy tendiendo la ropa afuera, I'm hanging the clothes outside, and he wants to *borrow*, that's how he says it, *borrow* a pair of Addie's shorts, or shortes, como dice la mamá. Don't you have no home, I say, and water to clean yourself? You're a disgrace to everything decent I've grown up to know and love. Get out of here, you shiftless pelado. You think I'm going to give you a pair of my husband Addie's shorts? You're crazy! I'll call the police!"

"Why didn't you give him the shorts, Teeney?" Luardo said, through tears of laughter.

"Me, no way. He'd want to come and start borrowing things—sugar, a mop, tools. And, besides, Addie don't have so many pairs."

"So who says you never concern yourself with other people's laundry, sister?"

"Shut up, Luardo!"

"You didn't give him the shorts?" Dolores asked sadly.

"No! What kind of woman do you think I am!"

"Was he married?" I asked.

"Esau? Esau Portales married? No way in the world, Soveida, are you crazy, girl?" Tía Teeney scoffed. "What's wrong with you? He's a crazy man ever since they shot off his como se llama during the war. Dolores, you should give her some Milk of Magnesia, or Lax-ol, the girl has problems! How long were you in there anyway, m'ija? When did the problem begin?"

"I mean the Güero Solo, did he ever get married, Tía?"

"Him? What do you want to know about him for? He's dead and buried for over fifty years."

"I remember him," Luardo said reflectively. "El Güero Solo."

"I shooed Esau away like an old dirty dog. Ssst! Ssssst! ¡Imagínense! The nerve of that old man, he wants to *borrow* Addie's shorts, and he don't have nothing to put in them shorts once he gets them! What is this neighborhood these days, anyway, but dogs and old men with loads in their pants?"

"But you just said, sister . . ."

"I said he don't have nothing to put in the shorts, front, not back! Will you leave me alone, Luardo? This neighborhood going to the dogs just makes me want to run away and move to California!"

California was one of Teeney's dreams. The Dosamantes family had lived there briefly when Teeney was in grade school and she still had the California fever in her blood. Luardo, too.

"I know what you mean, Teeney," Luardo joined in. "Agua Oscura isn't worth a damn anymore."

"Don't cuss, Luardo, please, not in front of Soveida and Hector," Dolores said.

"Hell, it isn't, brother. Let's move to California."

The consequences of my unchaste actions caught up with me full force, as A.J. found out about the hidden magazines and told his best friends, Bobby González and Willie Melendres and Robert Ryan, and some of the other boys at Angel. Bobby was in my class, and naturally, the story spread to the whole sixth grade. Not a day went by when Bobby, A.J., and one Sammy Lartone, also from sixth, didn't present me with the facts of my indiscretion.

The only good that came out of all this was that for a while Tía Teeney's washer was momentarily fixed. But even that was short-lived.

If it hadn't been for Tía Teeney getting a new used washer and Tío Adrino looking for his magazines and the noise everyone heard testifying to my guilt—the stopping and then the starting and then the stopping of the old washer—I think I might have gone unnoticed. But what really got me was my own stupidity. What possessed me to hide the magazines? How was I to know Tía Teeney kept her mad money back there?

Sex, to me, was never love.

Sex was for those other women, desnudas, encueradas, peladas, with their gold-lamé shoes, "bitchy" shoes, as Dolores called them. She saw these "bitchy shoes" on the naked women in the nightclubs and seamy dance halls Luardo took her to, an unwilling but obedient spectator. I joined them after a while, as did Hector. We saw countless strippers and exotic dancers in Juárez and other back-street towns Luardo frequented. Morals were a bit more lax; everyone wanted to sell you his sister or brother or cousin. Donkey shows were popular.

One of Luardo's favorite clubs was called the Golden Dragon. Its façade was covered by a huge neon dragon emitting long curly flames out of its leering mouth. Luardo had coerced Dolores into going with him, and unable or unwilling to fight or to find a babysitter on such short notice, she had taken us as well. I liked going out at night, but

Hector hated it. I liked the lights and the music and the Shirley Temples that I used to order, with a bright red cherry or two or three in my glass alongside a split circle of orange.

Dolores went along, she said in justification, to take care of Luardo, since he had problems with liquor and women. She thought she could control him, encourage him to return home soon, help him out. And so we went—the four of us, Hector in diapers—to these late-night clubs where women paraded across large wooden dance floors in bitchy shoes and nothing else.

On our way, we might stop at one of the many arcades near the old bridge crossing into México, where Luardo would give me a quarter to see naked girls washing cars. He would hold me up to the peephole so I could place my little eye there, peering inside the moving-picture machine to see several young naked soapy women washing and then rinsing down an old Studebaker or Rambler, the foam dripping from their large breasts.

I was fascinated by the moving pictures and the strange incongruity of naked women washing a car in daylight. I was fascinated, too, by the close proximity to my father.

Luardo wanted me to see, and so did I. He would hold me up that way, until the peep show was over, and I cried for more. I never knew what the naked women really meant to be doing other than washing a car. It seemed relatively natural, despite its oddness. I was enthralled by the picture moving fast like that in such a small space.

When we finished with the peep shows we either went to the Golden Dragon for the early show or to the Tenampa Bar to hear the marimba band. Luardo would drink his beers, Dolores her Cokes, me my Shirley Temples, and Hector would nurse from his plastic bottle. Later we would go get a bite to eat at Mundo's sandwich place on the side street near the Old Basilica.

Dolores would finally have to drag Luardo home. Even though he was tired, he was still eager to go on. He held his liquor well then and he would argue with her as she finally convinced him that she should drive home. He sat in the back seat with Hector, the two of them sleeping side by side.

At times Luardo went off by himself. Days later he returned, totally exhausted, needing three or four days of sleep to recover. Dolores would call in sick for him at the city office where he was a jobs counselor. Then she would tiptoe to his workroom, off the kitchen, and quietly place a quart of milk by his bedside. He would rise at various times of the day and night to drink milk and then go to the bathroom.

The 25-cent movies were part of my sex education at the hands of Luardo. He loved to show off to us, his children, and to make Dolores wince at her prudishness. He'd laugh and laugh and then smile and leer at her. Always, there was talk between them, in strained whispers, of "other women." Many of them. Luardo never had any regard for women. None at all. They were things to be used, played with, ruined. Luardo's sick, sordid life drew us along with it, and for Dolores, Hector, and me, there was no escape as long as he lived with us.

Sex was dirty women and dirtier men and smoky nightclubs with my mismatched parents.

Sex was an ugly thing, a hidden bruise.

Once Mara stayed with us when Mamá Lupita went to visit her cousin Fidela in Riverside, California. During that time I found some bloody towels in the bathroom, on Luardo's towel rack.

It wasn't until years later I found out that it was Mara's menstrual blood, there for all of us to see, a crimson banner of pain.

I somehow knew then what I now know is undeniably true.

One night I found myself sleepwalking, a thing I did occasionally. My sleepwalking was usually a result of trying to escape something powerful, dark, and frightening. This time I moved from my bedroom to Mara's room. Usually I awakened with my hands on the tarnished doorknobs in either the bathroom or the front room. Not this time.

When Mara stayed at our house, she usually slept on the pull-out bed in Luardo's workroom. It was a small, dark room next to the kitchen, at the back of the house. Only Luardo had a key to this room, and he always kept it locked. The only time the door was left unlocked was when Mara stayed with us. The room was always warm, since it was next to the hot-water heater and had a radiator. A hot room, even in winter, it was reserved for Mara.

Somehow I wandered into Mara's room, and into her bed. Mara woke up and folded me in her arms, an older sister, without questions. We fell asleep, two halves of a troubled whole.

The next day, Mara went back to the Blue House. Mamá Lupita had returned and I found myself in Mara's bed, alone. Luardo came in and told me to get out, that he had things to do in his room.

The bloody towels never appeared again.

Sex was a promise to myself: never to get hurt, or caught, to be a good lover, to search for that Face, to remember the others, to love them all as completely as I could, and never to forget.

12

J.M.J.

Mara. Just thinking about her makes me tired. Goddess. Troublemaker. Distractor. Destroyer. The woman all women know and fear. The other half of solid self. Dream sister. Cousin.

Whenever I think of Mara, I think of her missal. She had written J.M.J. at the top of page one in her new missal, for Jesus, Mary, and Joseph. Mamá Lupita had given us identical missals for Christmas, but Mara quickly lost hers.

J.M.J. is what the kids at Holy Angel Elementary wrote at the top of each page of homework, and also in our notebooks. One year Mara had J.M.J.'ed all her new notebooks, including several Big Chiefs in the late summer, before school had even started. She said she'd never do that again. The problem was that she lost her faith the first week of school and now her pages were ruined. Mara said she never wanted to see another J.M.J. as long as she lived, and it was going to be a long life.

The real loss, though, was her holy-card collection. Mara had one card dating from her First Communion. The most valuable holy card, by far, was one that was a memorial to her mother, Emanuelina "Lina" Loera, who had died on August 3, 1950, in Agua Oscura, New Mexico. The picture on the card was of Junior in his costume as the Good Shepherd. Mara always referred to Jesus the Son as Junior. Underneath the picture of Junior wearing a long white robe and holding a wooden staff in his hands were the chilling words: The Lord is My Shepherd. I shall not want.

Whenever Mamá Lupita spoke to Mara of her poor unfortunate mother, she sighed and then began her familiar litany. "May poor Lina rest in peace. She wanted too much. She fell in love with your father, and followed him at a time when women didn't follow men and men did not want to be followed. She followed him when she was already four months pregnant with you in her stomach. Well, she caught him and she brought him back here. He stayed in Agua Oscura until you were born and then one day he vanished. Just like that. Forever. And that was when your mother's sex rebelled and she got the cancer that killed her and Father Cantucci buried her in the cemetery across from your grandmother Trancha's house, next to all her other brothers and sisters. Just remember what it is to want too much. It can only bring you sorrow and death."

Mara thought the Good Shepherd card inappropriate for her mother, Lina. It was just the way it was printed, with the "I shall not want" in large black letters near Jesus' sandaled feet.

Later, Sister Loretta explained to the sixth-grade religion class that this Psalm had to do with God completely and fully taking care of you with cool water, green grass, and hope, even if you were dying. If you thought about it that way, then the "I shall not want" made sense, after all. What didn't make sense to Mara was the wanting in her mother's life. The eternally unfulfilled wanting. The wanting of love from that one man, and that one idea of happiness. It was enough to make you crazy if you thought about it.

A throbbing Sacred Heart card would have been more suitable for Lina, the embossed kind with an exposed chest cavity, a heart swollen with love, pierced by arrows, with a circle of barbed wire surrounding the still pumping organ.

Mara thought Lina should be remembered in her glory, assumed into heaven bodily like the Blessed Mother, without passing through the cycle called death. Try as she had, Lina could never call her existence living. Why now in death couldn't Lina lay claim to the greatest of God's mercies?

In the 1950s, God was still a man. And only one woman ever ascended into heaven to be with her child. The Assumption card was out, and so was the Good Shepherd card, and so were any other number of cavorting-angel cards or rose-diadem cards with scrolly words like God is my Consolation and Blessed be the Meek.

If Lina could have a card that was truly hers, then Mara would have to make it. And so for days Mara, who had little artistic skill, designed a holy card for her mother that seemed appropriate. I offered to help her, but she was determined to do it on her own. In the card Lina hovers in midair, in transit to heaven, holding Mara up, as Miguel

Angel Fortuna looks down from on high and, with his hands extended, takes both mother and child into his waiting arms.

It was a crude drawing but it gave Mara great peace. She loved and treasured it and kept it in her old and then her new missal, along with all the other images of hell and salvation that reminded her that although her parents had never had an occasion to tell her so in this earthly life, she was still loved.

The missal disappeared on a Tuesday. On Wednesday, Mara still hadn't found it. On Thursday, after Father Pendergrast's usual sermon about the concupiscence of the flesh, I came up to Mara at recess where she sat glumly near the teeter-totter watching Anna Lou Mirabal's lardy rump go up and down. Anna Lou was seated opposite the Becker twins, each of whom weighed probably about fifty pounds to Anna Lou's hefty 133, which for a fourth-grader was quite a lot. The Becker twins, Tania and Toni, were stuck at the top of the teeter-totter once again as Anna Lou unceremoniously lifted one glutinous buttock from the wood and in the process released a small whine of gas as she pushed herself up in the air. The teeter-totter came down hard on the Becker side as I ran up to Mara.

"I saw it!"

"What?"

"I saw the missal! I mean, I think it's your missal. There were lots of holy cards in it. I was in line for confession behind Lorraine Martínez. She had glued a white piece of paper on the front page of this new-looking missal."

The next day at Mass, when Lorraine went to Communion, Mara picked up the missal that she'd left behind on the pew and lifted up the white sheet of paper. Inside she saw her name and address:

> *Mara Fortuna*
> *758 Esperanza Street*
> *Agua Oscura, New Mexico*
> *Please return if lost. Reward!!!!!!*

Mara saw her unmistakable J.M.J. at the top. Lorraine had stolen her new missal! During the afternoon recess Mara finally went up to Lorraine and confronted her. Lorraine at first denied everything, but eventually admitted she had stolen it.

The missal was never the same. Jesus, Mary, and Joseph! The special holy card was missing, too. Lorraine had probably thrown it away, thinking it was a joke or a mistake. Some foolish dream, what Mamá called "some poor fool's wanting." Mara put the tainted missal away in her room, behind a row of books. She decided she would find new ways to pray.

Mara knew I loved her as a sister and I knew she loved me as well. We'd grown up together, one of us in the Blue House, the other in the Brown. Not only were we neighbors, we were the best of friends. We would often spend the night at each other's house, sharing the two houses and their worlds as one. If one ever needed to find Mara, I was always nearby, and if ever I was lost, Mara would be lost with me as well.

We spent nights together in each other's rooms, going through each other's possessions. If I got a new dress, or a new pair of shoes, Mara was the first to see me wear it. And if Mara had found some new game to play or had picked up another of her "treasures" in one of her neighborhood forays, I would have been there with her or would have known about it shortly afterwards. Mara had a collection of small animals and natural artifacts. Against her will, Mamá had allowed first the captive tadpoles into the house and then the frogs and then the collection of birds' nests and the rocks, after which came the pressed-leaf collection, the plastic doll's heads, old buttons and smashed metal parts that would someday "go into something."

While my room was full of the usual teenage posters and paraphernalia—matching pen-and-pencil holders, upholstered wastebaskets, lipstick holders, and Kleenex holders—Mara's decor leaned toward the jungly and Oriental. The walls were draped with printed Indian bedspreads and a few select posters of Dion and Frankie Avalon tacked to them. On the ceiling directly above the bed was a photograph of Fabian Forte. A large table full of plants was placed underneath the grated window that couldn't open anymore because Mamá had removed the knobs for security purposes.

Each of us found a missing part of ourselves in each other's room, and within each other's presence.

Sometimes we'd lock our bedroom doors, move all the furniture, and work on each other chiropractically. Mara had mastered the head snap and would crack my neck at least twice a day. I, on the other hand, had a good back-popping technique and would proceed to realign and loosen up Mara's spinal column on demand. Both of us were limber and athletic, and we kept ourselves fit by exercising our joints and by

self-taught chiropractic adjustments. When Mara learned yoga, I studied ballet. The two of us would meet in my room to swivel our hips
and gyrate to music forbidden in Mamá's house, music that made us
feel sexy and a little drunk.

Once, when Mara spent the night, she found some old papers of
mine in one of my drawers. It was an autobiography I'd written when
I was twelve years old. *Saint or Sinner*, it was called.

"What is this, Soveida?"

"Nothing, Mara."

"Saint or Sinner?"

"Come on, Mara, leave it alone!"

"Let me read it."

"No, it's mine."

"So what is it? Come on. If you won't let me read it, then you read
it to me."

"It's my autobiography. Don't laugh."

"I'm not laughing. So read it to me."

We sat down on my bed and I did read it to Mara.

SAINT OR SINNER
(Preface)

*This is my very own story. It tells about me, my life, and my future
in this world. In this book I try to make others understand me. And
yet, no matter how hard I try, I am still a mystery to myself.*

Sincerely,

Soveida Dosamantes, age 12

CHAPTER ONE
MY CHILDHOOD—AGES ONE TO THREE

*One cold night in February I was born María Soveida Dosamantes.
Everyone thought I was dead because my face was blue and I wasn't
breathing. They took my mother into another room and left me alone
in the dark. People say you're not supposed to remember anything
when you're born. You're a baby, how could you? My Tía Teeney says
if it weren't for her forgetfulness and her purse that she left in the
room, I'd be dead. From that day on I've been afraid of the dark. I
sleep with my arms on top of my head, one crossed over the other,
like a shield.*

*I was baptized on April 26, 1948, by my Tía Teeney and my Tío
Adrino. I cried a lot when the priest poured Holy Water on my head*

but later I got the feeling of secureness that babies get wherever they go. A secureness that only God can give.

CHAPTER TWO
NO LONGER A BABY — AGES THREE TO SIX

Soon I was no longer a baby. I began to take notice of the world and the things about me.

My grandmother, Mamá Lupita, started taking me to church. I would only be happy if I went to church at least once a day.

I often wonder what went on in my mind? If I could only remember I am sure I would understand the mystery of my childhood.

CHAPTER THREE
SCHOOL DAYS — AGES SIX TO NINE

When I was seven my brother, Hector, was born! I really wanted a sister, but it was okay, at least in the beginning.

That year I finally got to go to school and it made me feel so good, and very grown up.

But the greatest day of my life was the day I made my First Communion. I felt my heart would break of happiness. Father Dupey said to us kids that every second on earth without God is about a thousand years in Purgatory. And every second in Purgatory is like a grain of sand in Hell. Patience, he said, that's what living is.

CHAPTER FOUR
GROWING UP — AGES NINE TO ELEVEN

Yes, I was growing up.

I tried so hard to be good, and I still try. And yet I knew something was missing.

One of my greatest dreams is to be accepted because of MYSELF.

CHAPTER FIVE
THE PRESENT — AGE TWELVE

Now I am twelve years old.

Every week I have a crush on a different boy.

And yet my life is worth so much more. I am torn between Heaven and Hell. Somedays I want to be a saint or an angel or even the Blessed Virgin. Other days I just want to be Me.

So what am I? Saint or sinner?

"So who wrote this stuff here at the bottom, Soveida? 'We are all saints insofar as we love God and our neighbor and make our wills be the will of God. Just love and everything will take care of itself.' "

"Oh, that? Sister Emilia Marie."

"She wrote that to you?"

Mara put my autobiography back in the dresser drawer and turned to me. "How come you don't talk about me, Soveida? Aren't I like your sister?"

"Yes, you are, Mara," I said and hugged her.

We looked at each other and somehow knew even then how far apart from each other we really were.

A year later Luardo and Dolores took a trip to Colorado to visit Nora, one of Tía Ismindalia's daughters, and invited Mara to come along. I had been there before, but it was Mara's first trip. Together we toured Seven Falls and Pikes Peak and Santa Claus land. We got to share a room and spent several happy days together, giggling and telling stories to each other until late at night. We were sad when we had to return to our separate households. Mara asked me to ask Dolores why we couldn't live in the same house.

I did ask, in the car just outside the Walsenburg city limits.

"Dolores, why can't Mara and I live together?"

"You want your own house now?"

"No, I mean, why can't we live in the same house? We're so happy together, aren't we, Mara?"

"Yes, we are."

"You know why, Soveida."

"No, I don't."

"It's Mamá."

"Mamá? What does she have to do with this?"

"Mara lives with Mamá. She helps her. And you live with us."

"But Mamá has Oralia."

"They're both getting old."

"They're not *that* old."

"You girls are together all the time."

"Not all the time and it's not the same."

"Isn't it enough? You're right next door to each other."

"We want to live together. Like sisters. Please."

"Mara has Mamá, Soveida, and you have us. Think of Mamá."

Dammit. Oralia could crack Mamá's back and pop her neck and

bring her hot teas and rub her tired feet and tuck her in bed. Why did Mara have to be there, just in case? Mamá never let Mara touch her anyway. It wasn't fair. Mamá didn't even really like her. She just tolerated her as poor Lina's girl.

"You tried, Soveida."

"I don't understand, Mara."

"It doesn't matter. It's okay. I'm going to leave someday soon anyway."

"It does matter! And it's not okay!"

"We spend a lot of time with each other."

"Promise me, Mara, that you'll always be my sister. That you'll never be so mad at me you'll tell me that you hate me and that you never want to see me again or that you're dead to me or that I'm dead to you. Promise me! Even when I'm dead and gone and nobody remembers my name, promise me that we'll still be friends and love each other. Promise!"

"I promise, Soveida. Now you promise."

That shame of the lost holy card is what I always felt when I was with Mara. Some kind of grace gone wrong. It's true we were related by blood, and yet how could two cousins grow so far apart? How could two families, the Dosamantes and the Loeras, ever be so in conflict? Dolores had ceased being a Loera when she married Luardo. I was always a Dosamantes. Mara was a Loera first and foremost. And once we were sisters.

But there was always shame between us, shame that had been inflicted on us. All of it was nothing more than Mara's imagined shame, but it was nonetheless real. Miguel Angel, Luardo, Dolores, and Mamá—they were the ones who should have been ashamed.

Later there was the shame of Mara running off and getting pregnant and getting married and divorced and married and divorced and married and then . . . Things I didn't know about until I was much older. Things she didn't tell me until later because she couldn't. Things consigned to late-night conversations across the miles.

Even Mamá Lupita's prayers weren't strong enough to stop all the suffering:

En el nombre del Padre
del Hijo
del Espíritu Santo
What are prayers in hell?

13

T.D.T.M.T.T.F.I.T.W.

In high school I once went on a retreat with a group of Catholic girls from the area. We all converged on a conference center in an idyllic country setting. We were to obey vows of silence, yet it was in the darkness of the individual rooms that one heard and felt the buzz of sexuality, that impassioned religion of the very young.

My girlfriend Lizzie and I stretched out on our bed, legs dangling, across from two other girlfriends, relating stories of sexual adventures to one another, while our chaperons were just rooms away. We huddled that way, in the agitated darkness, whispering litanies of unbounded, tumultuous yearning.

"Oh, I wish I was eighteen and had my own car and my own apartment and my boyfriend was handsome and in college . . ."

"He has dark hair . . ."

"He's a blond . . ."

"He's very nice . . ."

"Not only rich, but very nice. Good to me."

"Not too good. Men shouldn't be too good. Then they get boring, that's what my cousin Mara says."

"Okay, so his name is George . . ."

"How about Paul?"

"Whatever, the name doesn't matter . . ."

"It does to me."

"He's tall."

"Not too tall."

"Sexy, like George!"

"Yeah, sexy! Like Ringo!"

"Give me a break! And he wants to marry me, Lizzie."

"Who said anything about marriage, Soveida, I'm talking about sex."

In those narrow, prayer-filled rooms we accounted for ourselves, comparing notes, murmuring fantasies, inchoate dreams.

"My boyfriend and I French-kiss."

"No!"

"Yes, we do. All the time. And sometimes I let him touch my breasts."

"No!"

"Sometimes I'll let him unbutton my blouse and put his hands in there. But I don't pet. No way."

"What do you think that is, anyway? That's petting!"

"It is not!"

"It is!"

"So what *is* petting?"

"Oh, come on, Soveida. It's anything below the neck."

"I thought it was below the waist."

"Above the neck. That's necking. And below the neck, that's petting."

"It is?"

"Sometimes I wish I could just do IT and get it over with."

"My boyfriend says he loves me and that it's okay to do IT if you love someone."

"Did you hear about Gloria Gabaldon? Her dad has the mortuary. My friend Delilah is in P.E. with her at the high school and she saw her legs in shorts and she said Gloria had hickeys on her thighs!"

"Noooo!"

"That's what I heard."

"No way, it takes a long time to give yourself a hickey. I've tried."

"Oh, Soveida."

"I mean it, Lizzie! I've tried to give myself a hickey on the arm and it didn't really work."

"You're so stupid. Remember you were the one who thought Frances Leyva had bruised her neck in a fall? Didn't you ever see a hickey before that, Soveida?"

"Gloria probably goes all the way."

"I bet she does."

"Probably."

"Were the hickeys all up and down her thighs or where?"

"She was wearing her gym shorts, okay, and you know how low cut they are and how Gloria is . . .

"Nooo! That high?"

"That high!"

"Wow!"

The other girls had been kissed. I had not. Some of them had been touched. I had not. One of them had—I had not.

The chaperons, in pastel flannel nightgowns, knocked at the door, admonishing us to be still, to go to bed. Our two visitors scurried to their room, leaving Lizzie and me to our ruminations.

There was silence. Each of us saw herself, her face, in a car, on a long deserted stretch of highway. Longing was that flashing face in the window, passion the speeding car.

It was only later, Lizzie and I in our separate twin beds, that there was noise again. The sighs of imagined lovers, their hushed, often violent words, our unspeakable yearning that sizzled, smoldered, and eventually burst into flame.

"Ahhh . . ."

"Was that you, Soveida?"

"Lizzie, I can't sleep . . ."

"Me neither. I'm horny."

"Lizzie!"

"I can't help it. I was thinking about French-kissing and my panties got wet!"

"Lizzie! Go to sleep. It's late."

"I can't, Soveida. When I get this way I just can't sleep. I'm going to get a wet washrag to put between my legs."

"Go to sleep. We have to get up early for Mass."

"If I can, I will. If I can't, then just leave me here."

It was on this retreat that I saw him. He was the first person I was destined to desire. He wasn't particularly handsome. He was a brother who worked at the retreat, one of the waiters who served us lunch in the large dining room, one of several who deftly, quietly, and un-equivocally proclaimed their manhood among the legion of anxious-eyed, self-effacing young women who sought the silence of the spirit inside.

Tall, with curly, brownish-red hair, he had a wayward, twisted smile.

Once, while removing a plate that lay on a table across from us, he smiled at me. Did I imagine it? Surely he smiled at everyone. Or did he smile only for me? It was hard to know, for that year was one of so many dark imaginings. The year of Miracles. The year of the Bloody Towels. The year of the Bloody Tears.

He came up alongside us to remove our empty plates, leaning in to take our dirty forks, and he returned with dessert.

It's hard to say how I singled him out. There were other men there, blond brothers, dark priests. Perhaps it was because of his height. The majority of men I knew were short. I found myself thinking about him. Who else was there to think about? The faceless, bodiless men in the car windows late at night?

His lopsided grin was dark and deep, as mysterious as the questions asked in the question-and-answer session.

"What is necking?"

"Is petting a mortal or a venial sin?"

"Who is God?"

"Where is He?"

"Where is heaven? Is it above the sky?"

The elderly, thin-haired priest had laughed at me, snorting with incredulity at my juvenile question. "God isn't *anywhere*. He isn't *up there*," he brayed, "for Pete's sake. God isn't a fairy-tale giant, as in *Jack and the Beanstalk!*"

He had laughed at me, my only question. "*Where* is God?"

No one knew it was my question. Even now I deny it to myself. Where is God? Is He in the sky? Only a fool would ask a question like that.

I found myself alone, meditating by the pond, near the willow trees in front of the chapel, trying to be silent, with a borrowed book from the retreat's library, *Ten Tips for Teens: Seeking God Through Everyday Holiness* by Father Wynton Spindler, OFM.

I heard a noise, felt movement behind me. Then, from the corner of my eye, I saw the redheaded brother. He stood across from me. The shock of being alone with him was unsettling. I couldn't see clearly. He was holding a frog in his hands. It *was* a frog, if I wasn't mistaken, a large, grayish-green frog. With what I thought was a lusty grin, the brother threw the frog into the water. He watched it move away without a word. I sat there with that lingering, salacious smile of his locked in my heart.

Later I wrote the initials T.D.T.M.T.T.F.I.T.W. across one entire page in my diary. I figured that whoever read the diary would never really guess what was written there. Never. It was too sacred.

I had wanted to kiss the brother hard because he was the first of many who touched my great, unfulfilled, burning dreams. And because I knew that I would never get close to him. Ever.

I knew the kind of commitment it took to give oneself a hickey. That hickey was the symbol of a secret life, a life of intimacy unrelated to family, full of reckless passion and excitement. I knew as well that I had fallen unwittingly, almost against my will, out of a state of grace. And what tormented me most was the unattainability of that dream lover. My private, undeclared, woman's itch.

I felt it that first time in the red-haired brother. When I closed my eyes I tried to imagine the vague outline of his face. It was a face hidden to me, a face I longed to know. Was his the face? The eternal lover's face?

I am the woman with the issue of blood. Waiting for years like that biblical figure for my Christ to appear. Bleeding endlessly my woman's woes. What Christ has touched me with his hands? Or even really come near? As suddenly as he appears, he is gone. A mirage.

When will I be done? Free at last? Free of blood. Unnatural blood. And of certain men.

14

The Exorcism

Dolores and Mamá Lupita were forced to tie Mara to the bed. Now that she looked like a woman and her body had changed to a woman's and she had the desires of a woman and men looked at her like she was a woman, it was certain as well that the devil had entered her flesh. This is the same bed Mara had been tied to before by Tía Lita and Oralia when she had screamed and cried out and had those other fits that were surely a sign of possession.

In Mamá Lupita's mind there was no recourse but to call in Father Dupey, the pastor of Our Lady of Grace Church.

"Ay, Padrecito Dupey, come and pray over Mara. She's not well. Troubled. A sick child. Always has been. Her mother Lina's dead, her father is who knows where. She never knew him. He left her mother when Mara was born. Ran away. They never got married. Her aunt, Dolores, is my son's wife. I took Mara in, an orphan without a home, I took her in when no one would. I brought her up, fearing God. In this house there are no secrets, no darkness. Everything changed when she came into this house. Pray for her. She's sick. From the time she was a little girl she never had anyone. Except herself. All she's given me is trouble and now I know why. Pray over her, she needs to be healed. I've given her everything. I loved her as my own grandchild, fed her, clothed her. I don't know her anymore, she's changed. There's a presence here. My heart shudders to think *what*? *Or why*?"

On Father Dupey's advice, Reverend Pendergrast was called to 758 Esperanza Street. Home of Lupe Dosamantes, and her ward, Mara Loera. Or Mara Fortuna, which was what she called herself.

Mara had been having nightmares, screaming and crying out in the middle of the night. Mamá was worried. There was a demon, perhaps more than one, in the house. Late one night, Mara had screamed out from her room at the back of the house; it was a horrible cry, strangled in terror. When Mamá got to her, Oralia was comforting her, as Mara told them in horror whom she'd seen: Evil Incarnate. Mamá's heart stopped, then started again, but not in the same way. After that night, her heart was always cold.

The gray evil had come into her house, a blinding flash of powerful and indescribable light, and Mara had looked into it. It was so horrible, so ghastly in its spurious grayness, hovering there to her left, with its intelligence and its intensity, that all she could do was scream, a swimmer struggling to find her way to the surface where the air was, a dreamer in that underwater sleep, attempting to slough off dread.

This wasn't the first time Mara had seen the Evil. She had seen it as a child, but it was only now in the telling that she had remembered seeing it before, back then. Hovering.

When Reverend Pendergrast arrived, Mamá Lupita stood outside the room until the exorcism was completed. She was afraid to enter. Her prayers could be heard behind the dark wooden door. Mara's room. Mara's demons. Lupita's God.

The exorcism had been brutal.

And yet no one ever spoke of it. Not Mamá Lupita or Mara. Not then or afterwards. It was only years later that Oralia one day alluded to it. Only after much prompting on my part did she speak to me about "Mara's limpia, and yours, Soveida, which was part of the same healing."

Mara's room was the same room in which I, too, would be prayed over, this time not by Reverend Pendergrast but by the Traveling Prayer Team, a phenomenon of the late sixties and seventies, when speaking in tongues became the norm.

It was common for the women in our family to be prayed over at various stages of their lives, without giving thought to why. Perhaps the mere fact of being a woman necessitated prayers of a certain sort and at specific times. Adolescence and old age with their uncertainties require much grace. It seemed logical that I, as well, would need this cleansing, having exhibited signs of "unrest" that Mamá said stemmed from "contacto con esa Mara. Ay, Soveida, if I had only known. I would have never brought her into my home."

My "unrest," as Mamá called it, began around the same time as Mara's illness. I would lock myself in my room for hours, only coming out to go to school, and to eat. I had few friends. Lizzie was the only one I could talk to about so many things. And yet I could never tell her about Mara. About Luardo. How he was becoming uglier to everyone. How he rarely spoke to me, and how I avoided him.

Outwardly I wore my fishnet pantyhose and wiglets and false eyelashes and imagined myself with all sorts of lovers, men who desired me and then promised their undying love. But alone, in my room, I wondered if I weren't possessed. I wondered if unknowingly, during some moment of weakness and desperate humanity, I'd called out to the devil instead of God, and sealed my eternal fate in that timely instant.

Mamá noticed my moods, and decided that what I needed was prayer. Someone to lay hands on me, to uplift my spirit and cleanse my soul. Brother Michael and Sister Rosario were called in. Rosario, in turn, invited her husband, Brother Raúl, who, it was reported, not only spoke but sang beautifully in tongues. Arabic, some believed. Greek, others thought. No, it was our Lord's tongue, whatever it is they speak over there.

Sister Rosario chimed in, "It's God's own language. How else could he, Raúl Rojas, head janitor at Almira Elementary School, know God's language, unless God himself was speaking through his mouth? It's impossible through earthly means. I've known my husband for thirty years, and he's still trying to learn all the words of the Pledge of Allegiance in English."

Raúl, despite his apparently lowly job, was the diocese's reigning religious superstar, having won many converts in the last few years since he was slain in the spirit. Brother Michael had been there himself to witness that great coming to God. It was the winter, a chill, gray night, even colder in Our Lady of Grace Church. Everyone was listening to María Estefanita Galindo give her testimony for the third time that year, and at the moment she gave her life to God, Raúl got up, stripped off his coat—which was a divinely motivated action in view of the cold—and cried out: "Alleluia Lord of Power and Might. My Lord and Saviour, Jesucristo Redentor," and fell over backward in a swoon, slain in the spirit, his baser nature overwhelmed, extinguished, and then reborn in a quiet, all-embracing grace. Raúl barely missed hitting the pew behind him. María Estefanita carried on with her testimony, crying out: "Take my life, Lord, it's yours. I'm a poor woman, it's all I've got. I don't have no money, I don't have no property, I don't have no t.b. set, all I have is my soul. Take it!"

Raúl had fallen back and accidentally kicked the edge of the wooden pew where Pablo Papiro, the town drunk, was sitting to get out of the cold and away from his nagging wife, Merced. It was Rosario who ran up to Raúl as he lay there, legs splayed in the aisle. Pablo eyed Raúl suspiciously and stared as Rosario attempted to cover Raúl with his overcoat. Raúl immediately threw off the dark garment. Twice more Rosario tried to cover him, and twice more Raúl pulled off the coat and lay there on the cold black-and-white linoleum, eyes rolled backwards, hands upraised toward the heavens. Suddenly a cry leaped from his body. It was the cry of a once-muffled heart which now began to sing long-withheld songs of praise. Yahweh Alleluia and other words and phrases in the ancient language that came from that holy place, that sacred world; it was Jerusalem's own echo, God's own tongue.

Raúl lay there as Pablo quickly sobered and María Estefanita resumed her dedication to the one Christ: "I don't have no diamonds. I don't have no swimming pool. All I have is my heart, take it . . ."

The devout group of fifteen or so sang *De Colores* and *O María, Madre Mía* and *Amazing Grace*, ending with the usual cries of: "¡Qué viva la Virgen de Guadalupe! ¡Qué viva!"

All told, Raúl lay there on the very cold, newly waxed linoleum for probably thirty-five minutes, his hands now to his sides, his eyes closed, his dark purple lips mumbling mysteries in that rarely heard tongue few could unravel.

From that day on, Raúl Rojas, the short, squat, swarthy-skinned janitor with the large head, small eyes, big hands, and the bad breath, became Agua Oscura's spiritual wonder.

Rosario Rojas followed her husband in the Traveling Prayer Team, but she was never to overshadow him, ever, despite her constancy, reliability, and goodwill. Taller than Raúl, and twice as wide, with a large, discolored, spotted face that cried out yeast, she had the bulging brown eyes and the stomach of a pregnant frog. She was not a lovely woman by any means. Seeing the two Rojases side by side, both of them hunched over in prayer, calling out: "Praise you Jesus, heal him, Lord, Lord, have mercy, we love you Jesus," it was hard not to wonder what exactly they had going for themselves matrimonially. They had two children, that was a fact. But there appeared to be some higher linkage between these two, with their grossly unequal bodies.

Brother Raúl was the last person to join the Our Lady of Grace Traveling Prayer Team. Together, Brothers Raúl and Michael and Sister Rosario visited the bedsides of the dying, comforted the bereaved, laid prayerful hands over the living—young and old—anointing them with Holy Water. They liberated the newborn from Original Sin with holy salt and water, and buried the dead, consigning their spirits to the eternal spirit of God's merciful grace.

Together, these three mismatched individuals traveled around Agua Oscura, casting off the chains of the oppressed, shining God's blessed light on the darkest of sorrows, and, in general, easing and consoling the troubled. At times, they were joined by Sister Winona, Brother Michael's wife, who tried her best to keep up with the other three vagabond evangelists. Everyone called them the Holy Ones because of their reputed sanctity.

Brother Michael Trainor was a tall, thin man of fifty-six, soft-spoken, with a limp handshake, round shoulders, and steely blue eyes. He knew right away if a person was in need of healing when he saw them. He knew if they needed prayer or confession, a laying on of hands, a verbal casting out of demons, or a blow to the back, a loosening up of the Evil One's hold. There was a goodly cast to Brother Michael's eyes, a thin, ever-present smile to his lips, a self-contained, unruffled happiness that he carried about him that could only assure irritation and unholy vexation, even dislike in the unsaved soul, and which, on the other hand, won love and admiration and respect from the saved. Sallow with grace, stooped by understanding, and thin-haired by heredity, Brother Michael was the saved man's saved saint, the broken man's instrument of redemption, and the skeptic's unlikely thorn.

Sister Winona Trainor was tall like her husband, a lanky six feet two, all of it leg and sinew and bone. She was so restrained she was always constipated. To be quiet, to be efficient, to be thorough, that was Sister Winona's life goal. But just let her lay her hands on you, and up went a whooping cry from that enormous heart of hers. It would swallow anyone whole if it could, it had so much desperate yearning for magic, call it the spirit. Her shrill voice ascended a scale of emotion, and as it grew in intensity, the stronger her resolve became. Pushing, pulling, and pounding the one being healed, she called out with a mighty, piercing, orgasmic fervor: "Alamalalarante melola. Save him Lord shante molina rante meloa alamala, thank you, praise you, bless you, yes, out, out, ahh, Jesus! Amen! Amen! Bless him, praise him, out! Praise you! Lord God of the universe Alamalalarante ala rante alamala!"

Sister Winona went out healing whenever she could, and it so happened that the Friday night of this particular healing she was free. She didn't have to take a shift at the Border Cowboy Truck Stop, where she worked as an accountant, until the next Monday.

The last home healing session she'd participated in had so exhausted and depleted her that Brother Michael had forbidden her to go out until she felt strong enough again. It had been two weeks and Sister Winona felt herself in rare form. When Brother Michael got the call from Mrs. Dosamantes the elder, Sister Winona knew that she was ready. She and Brother Michael went to meet the Rojases at the big old blue house on Esperanza Street. She'd always wanted to go inside the house and had never been invited. Now she would finally get to see it.

"We'll be there, Mrs. Dosamantes. Friday night. Around 7 p.m. We'll pray for your granddaughter then. What did you say her name was? Be peaceful, the Lord wants this healing."

When Friday arrived I was sequestered in Mara's room in Mamá's house. The Traveling Prayer Team circled me and called out: "In the name of Jesus we command you, out, evil spirit! Shananana leave this young woman, what's her name, yes, Soveida, leave her, I say! Rantelanmalala, heal her, Lord, praise you, out, evil one, begone!"

I stood in the middle of Mara's room, near the place where Mara's Evil had once stood, underneath one of Mara's posters of Frankie Avalon. No stranger could have walked in on us or ever heard all the noise that went on from that part of the house, so tucked away it was. It was a place familiar only to the house's inhabitants. In this room, the rite of passage from the state of evil to one of healing was once again enacted. In this room both Mara and I were expected to move from darkness to light, from depravity to grace, from sinfulness to holiness.

A person on each side, front, back, to my right and left the Brothers and Sisters stood, their hands on my shoulders, my head, my back, my arms, praying together, all of them breathing new life into me.

Raúl Rojas faced me and exhorted God to free me. I noticed his sour breath and closed my eyes, putting my left hand to my nose to block the smell. Sister Winona grabbed that hand, shook it, released it, and then let out a stifled cry, begging me: "Say your Father's name, say it, go on, say it, go on, go on, say it. Jesus Lord God, heal uhh . . . Soveida, heal Soveida. Go on, say his name. Father. Master. Lord God."

No, I thought. I can't pray to your father, to anyone's father. I don't have a father.

"You can say Father! Say Father! Oh Lord, praise you Father, Alamalalalala." Sister Winona nudged me lightly and then punched me roughly in my side: "Say it, say it!"

"I can't." I whimpered. "I can't!"

"Father! Say it!"

"No!"

"Father, heal her. Say it, Soveida. Say Father heal me!"

"No. No!"

Raúl Rojas blew his stale acrid breath at me again. I stared into his bloodshot eyes and then followed the sweat from his forehead to his dark, pitted cheeks. Sister Rosario had her eyes closed. Her large bosom heaved mightily and she broke into sobs.

Brother Michael never once released his cold, determined look, admonishing the Evil which had once manifested itself in this room. The Evil once Mara's, which was now mine. "Out, demon, out!"

"Go on, say it! Lord Jesus." cried Sister Winona.

Go away, go away, all of you, I thought. God's not a man but a woman. A woman!

"Aleluia mi Dios, Lord God of Power and Might. ¡Qué viva! Alamalalala rante rante."

"My tears are tears of joy, of healing!"

"God the Father comfort you, Sister Winona! Shanbanana!"

"Praise him, Brother Raúl!"

"Shanbananaanana . . ."

"Sing it, Brother Raúl! Rante alalalalmala . . ."

"Praise you, Father."

"Rante alalalalalala rante molina . . ."

"¡Que viva Jesucristo Salvador!"

"Go on, go on, say it, say it!"

"God the Father. Praise him."

"Yes, amen, amen, amen!"

Not Father, not Father. Mother. Mother. *God the Mother*. Praise Her.

15

The Bride of Christ

"Damn the old woman to everlasting hell!" Mara said to me when I went over to the Blue House to see what had become of her plans for the Spring Dance. She was a finalist for Queen, but she hadn't told anyone else in the family yet. We'd both been excited for weeks. Mara had put a dress on layaway at Margie's Mode and planned to make her final payment today.

The week before, she had told me to meet her in front of school after classes and we would walk to Margie's together to see her dress.

I was elated, because Mara had deigned to meet *me*, her little cousin, a freshman, in front of Agua Oscura High, where it was possible for everyone to see us. I was as thrilled about the dance as she was. Her date was Mannie Morales. Never mind that his family owned the most successful bar in Natividad County; Mannie was handsome, wealthy, and had his own Thunderbird.

Mara greeted me impatiently at the designated hour, and we walked the seven blocks from Main Street to Margie's. She had laid away her dress with a twenty-dollar down payment and had only eighty-seven dollars to go.

"Mara!" I said, amazed, "your dress is over a hundred dollars!"

"So?" she said with irritation. "I'm worth it."

And she was, no doubt about that.

The saleslady, Mrs. Armijo, was a friend of Dolores's, and when she brought the dress out, I felt my face flush. I had never seen a more beautiful dress. White tulle, strapless. Oh, Mara! When she tried it on, she looked like an exotic angel, just sexy enough to take your breath away. Mara would be the most radiant Spring Dance Queen in the history of Agua Oscura High, just as she had been the most lovely

First Communion angel on record at Holy Angel Elementary School.

"You really like it?" Mara said, twirling in front of the three-way mirror, piling her long, dark brown hair on top of her head to see how she looked.

"Your hair is so pretty, Mara, just wear it like you do."

"You don't think I look more sophisticated with it up, Soveida?" Mara said, pursing her lips and pulling in her cheeks to make her face more angular.

"I like your hair down, Mara, and besides, you might need it if you get cold."

"Oh, Soveida. You're such a baby! Everybody's wearing strapless these days. Well, I'll think about my hair. When we get home, we'll try different hairdos. How about a French roll in the back, with the sides kinda draping, like this?"

"It sure is a pretty dress, Mara," Mrs. Armijo said. "Do you want to take it home today?"

"No, I'll make a payment and pick it up next week. Thank you."

"Say hello to your mother for me, Soveida, and you, Mara, you say hello to your grandma. How's she doing?"

"She's okay," Mara said without enthusiasm. I knew she was worried because she hadn't told Mamá about the dance yet, and she'd already told Mannie yes. Yes to him and nothing to Mamá.

Mamá hadn't allowed Mara to date anyone. The only time she went out was in the company of her girlfriends. When they arrived at their destination, they would break up and set off on their own. On one such occasion, when they went to see *Imitation of Life* at the Grand Theater, about a back-street affair, which Mamá had allowed Mara to see because she thought it was about the life of Christ, they met some soldiers from Fort Bliss on weekend leave. Danny Philprin was among them.

"He's tall and cute and he kisses real good," Mara confided in me.

"Mara, God, you mean you've kissed him? When? Where?"

"He likes me and I like him. So what if we sit in the balcony at the Grand in the back where Mr. Gurulé the projectionist can't see us kiss each other?"

"What about Mannie, Mara? Does he know? I mean, he's your date for the dance."

"*Date*. He's a *date*. He doesn't own me."

"Who's this guy, Danny?"

"He's a tall white guy. And shut up already, Mrs. Armijo's giving me the big buggy bird eyes, and you know I haven't told the Eagle about the dance yet, much less Mannie, much less about you-know-who."

Mara had started referring to Mamá Lupita as the Eagle when we were alone.

"Although maybe I should call her the Hawk, she's always spying on me. She gets upset if I close my bedroom door. I'm telling you now, someday I'll move away and never come back."

"Don't say that, Mara."

"I mean it, I've just about had it, Soveida."

"So who am I going to rent an apartment with in college if you're gone, Mara? Who's going to be my roommate?"

"You can move over to the Eagle's. Ha, I'd like to see you try that out. Come on, let's get out of here. I want to play with hairdos."

The Monday of Dance Week, Mara finally girded herself for battle and approached Mamá.

"Mamá, I'm a finalist for Spring Dance Queen."

"Oh."

"And I have a date."

"You have a date? Who's the boy?"

"Mannie Morales."

"Who's his father?"

"Mo Morales."

"Who's his mother?"

"Mary Morales."

"Who's his grandfather?"

"Meliquior Morales from Mesquite."

"Meliquior Morales who owns the Mil Recuerdos bar in Mesquite? You can't go!"

"Mamá! I'm a finalist!"

"I don't care if you're Queen of Heaven. I said no, Mara, and I only say no once. Ya."

"Mamá, please. I've been saving up my money from my job at the library to buy a dress I saw at Margie's Mode. Please, Mamá."

"No!"

"I'm almost Queen this time!"

"Ay, Mara, why must you fight me? You want to go, is that it, then I'll go with you."

"No, Mamá. I have a date."

"Since when are you dating?"

"I'm not dating, it's just that Mannie asked me and I thought, I'm a senior in high school, I have good grades, and I can buy the dress."

"I'll go with you!"

"Mamá! I don't want you to go with me. I'm the one running for Queen, not you. You won't have to buy anything."

"Mara, that's enough."

"No, it's not enough. I'm going to the dance and you're not going to stop me. I can't go anywhere because you're always following me to see if I'm going to do something wrong. Just let me be me. I'm seventeen years old!"

"None of my children ever spoke to me the way you are speaking to me now, Mara Loera."

"I'm not your child, Mamá. Let me go, please. Please, Mamá."

"I never imagined the day I would be defied by you, Mara, after all I've done for you, an orphan, your poor mamá . . ."

"I know to you she was just a whore, but she's dead, Mamá. And I'm alive! Let her rest in peace."

"Mara!"

"Why can't you forgive her? And why can't you forgive me, Mamá? I've been here all these years. I've helped you and loved you. What do I have to do to prove to you I'm not Lina or Dolores but just me, me?"

"We'll talk about this later. Stop your crying and carrying on, Mara. I'm going to my room to pray."

"It's because I'm not a Dosamantes, is that the problem, Mamá? Is it because of that, or because Luardo has made me do things, Mamá? He hurts me . . ."

"I don't want to talk now, Mara."

"It's not the dance, it's—"

"Get a hold of yourself, Mara Loera."

"Why should I, Mamá? Why can't you hear what I'm trying to say? Luardo hurt me. He hurts me still."

"Mara! We are not going to talk now. I said no. No. And you leave Luardo out of this, he's been nothing but kind to you. For once think about someone other than yourself. Why can't you give thanks for what you have, instead of throwing your Loera ugliness in our faces? You're just like your mother. Now go to your room!"

———

Mara didn't go to the dance. She won as Queen, but because she wasn't there, Mr. Catchman, the principal, gave the crown to Debbie Le-Lorstier, who had come in second. No one knew, anyway, except Punky Piñeda, who counted the votes, and, of course, Mr. Catchman.

Leave it to Punky to tell Mara.

"Damn the old woman to everlasting hell," Mara said again.

We sat glumly on her bed, Mara staring out the window and crying a little from time to time.

"It wasn't only the dance, Soveida, it was more than that. Mamá hates me and I hate her."

"Come on, Mara, you don't mean that."

"Why doesn't anyone ever believe what I say? I hate *everything*: this house, this room, Lina for dying, me for being born, your mother for giving me to Mamá. And you for sitting there like a dumb cluck while I'm crying. Go away and leave me alone, Soveida. If you stay here any longer, I'll hate even you."

I slipped out of Mara's room and wandered back home. Oralia was outside, tending to her garden. Her young plants were already breaking through the hard earth. I didn't know where Mamá was, but I was glad not to see her. I felt she'd been so unjust to Mara, but I felt incapable of saying anything to her. After all, she was my grandmother. The Eagle.

After several weeks of Mara's unpleasant silence to everyone, including me, Oralia came over to Dolores's, yelling to Mamá, who was making sopaipillas for Luardo.

"She's gone, Señora Lupe," Oralia said, out of breath.

"Who's gone?" Dolores asked.

"Mara. Mara's gone. Se nos fue."

"What?" said Mamá. "¿Pero comó?"

"What are you talking about, Oralia? Soveida. Soveida! Are you there?" Dolores called out to me.

I came running out of my room to see what had happened. I could barely hear Dolores's shout above Donovan's song "Mellow Yellow." It was Mara's record, but Mamá never allowed her to play anything stronger than Johnny Mathis, whom Mamá didn't know was black. Now that Mara was mad at me, I listened to all her forbidden records alone.

"Mara's gone, Soveida," Dolores said, her face flushed and angry. "She just took off without a word."

"Mara's gone?" I said, without comprehension.

"She's run away," Mamá said with a heavy heart, putting her flour-covered hands to her heart. "No child of mine ever ran away from home. I would have beat them first. And she had everything, everything!"

Everything except freedom, I thought.

"She left a note, Soveida," Dolores said. "See for yourself."

"Mamá," I read. "I'm leaving. I know you'll be alright without me. Don't worry. I can type. I have to go, Mamá. It's time. Say goodbye to Soveida for me and tell her to check the radio in the dark corners where the Eagle doesn't fly. Mara"

"What's this about checking the radio, Soveida?" Dolores questioned suspiciously. "What does she mean?"

"Call the radio stations and put out an alert, that's what it means, Dolores," Mamá said excitedly. "Call the police and then Luardo at work and then Father Piedoso. Oralia, go get some yerbabuena to make us some tea, we've had a terrible shock."

"Sí, Mamá," Oralia said and then bowed before she made her way to her garden in search of her healing herbs.

Everyone was in a battle mode, and somehow it suited them. The women seemed more real, more substantial, as if they welcomed adversity.

"Read the Eagle part of the letter again," Mamá said. "I think it means Mara's gone to Eagle's Nest, New Mexico," Mamá offered. "We'll find her there."

It took all my strength to keep from laughing, as sad and miserable as I was at Mara's running away. Her secret code told me where to find her new radio, hidden in the hole in the back of her closet, close to the bathroom water pipes.

"Eagle's Nest," Mamá ruminated. "We don't have any relatives in Eagle's Nest that I can recall."

"Is that what Mara meant, Soveida?" Dolores asked, looking at me.

"I don't know," I muttered, then broke into tears. Mara was gone. Mara, my best friend. My almost sister. And I knew then that she was never coming home. Because to her this never *was* home.

Mamá cried to herself softly, beading tiny balls of masa from the base of her fingers to the tips, easing her hands of the gummy dough.

I almost felt at that moment that Mamá loved Mara, but because of who Mamá was and what she imagined herself to be, she could never publicly show her love to anyone.

Dolores ranged around the room, her voice shrill and unpleasant. "Run off! A fine thing to do. What will people think? ¡Ay, que vergüenza! The shame!" she said with disgust.

Through tears I looked at her and realized sadly who Mara's real enemy had always been.

"We'll find her," Dolores said firmly. "She'll be back, Mamá. No te apures."

"No, I don't think so, Dolores," Mamá said, rinsing her hands with water. "Not this time. I should have let her be Queen."

As soon as Dolores and Mamá were off, one calling the state police, the other a priest, I snuck into Mara's room and found the radio she'd hidden in the back of her closet. Mamá told us many times that all the radio played was ese cochino rock 'n' roll. She never even allowed us to have a radio on in her presence.

That night I lay in bed crying to myself, missing Mara like I'd never missed her before. The radio was pressed up against my ear as I listened to KOMA from Oklahoma City. In between sobs, I sent Mara my love across who knows how many miles to who knows where. I finally fell asleep that way, only to find the batteries dead the next morning.

When we eventually heard from Mara she was married, pregnant, and working in a dry cleaners in Fort Huachuca.

"¿Dónde, Dolores?"

"Fort Huachuca, Mamá."

"¿Cómo qué Pachuco?"

"Fort Huachuca!"

"No me grites. I can hear you all right. No te entiendo. I just don't understand you."

Mara wrote me to say she'd be coming back to Agua Oscura for a few days to gather up her things. She wanted to know if I'd pick her up at the Greyhound bus depot and take her to a motel. A few days later Danny would meet her with the car and they'd drive back home together.

"How can she be staying at a motel? She has a home, or had one," Mamá said.

Dolores had seen the Fort Huachuca postmark and had opened my letter from Mara. From then on, Mara's visit became a family affair.

Luardo, Dolores, Mamá, Hector, and I would pick up Mara and take her out to eat, but not at El Farol.

"She needs meat for the baby," Mamá said. "We'll take her to the Branding Iron, my treat, I mean for Mara, and after that, we'll come home for sopaipillas."

"She ran away from home, Mamá," Dolores reminded her. "She doesn't want your sopaipillas for dessert. I doubt very much if she wants to see any of us. Why can't Soveida just pick her up and take her to a motel?"

"She's staying at her friend Margaret's house," I interjected. "For a few days until her husband comes."

"Mara married!" Mamá shook her head. "¡No es posible! No, we'll all be there to greet her. Baby or not, we're her family. The child is innocent."

The 8:15 bus from Oklahoma City was late. The October night was unseasonably cold. The bus depot, a small tin shack barely large enough for the ticket agent, was closed. We sat in Luardo's car with the heater on, waiting for Mara to arrive.

Mara was the last person to get off the bus. The bus driver helped her down the steps. She looked pale, and when she came in our direction we saw she was very pregnant. She wore an ugly gray coat I'd never seen before.

The first few moments were awkward. I knew Mara was surprised to see everyone, including Hector, there. I hugged her warmly. Then Mara let Mamá hug her without responding, Dolores said hello, and Luardo hung back.

Mara agreed to stay at Mamá's provided that I would stay there with her. We spent two nights together and tried to catch up on everything. Everything that she cared to tell me.

"Danny's an angel," Mara kept repeating, but I knew she wasn't really happy. "Pretty neat on the code, huh, Soveida?"

"Yeah, I knew you meant the radio."

"Can I have it back?"

"Sure, it's yours, Mara."

"We don't have a TV, and it'll help pass the time, I mean, until the baby comes."

"Yeah, I'll bring it over before you leave."

"So no one ever knew what I meant, huh?"

"Never. No way. Not even the Eagle."

Just before Mara left the house she took me aside and hugged me hard. "Soveida, look, if anything ever happens to you, I mean it, Soveida, you can always become a nun!"

"Mara!"

"I mean it! Marriage isn't what it's cut out to be."

"You sound like Mamá."

"Don't tell me that."

"I mean it."

"I mean it, too. All I wanted was to be rich or famous and here I am a pregnant mama pig with a little tiny baby pig inside me and all I ever do for fun is cut out Spam and potted-meat coupons. Okay, so maybe later I'll be a sexy broad. Desirable. And single."

"Don't you love Randy?"

"Danny, his name is Danny. Yeah, I do, that's not it. It's just, oh, what the hell, your body betrays you."

"How's that?"

"I mean, we're taught one thing, one solitary goddamn thing. I always thought it would be different for me."

"Mara! Do you mean that?"

"No. Oh hell, all I ever wanted to do was to get away."

"I know."

"You don't understand, Soveida, not yet, anyway."

"What are you talking about?"

"The training for service."

"What?"

"Hey, I've missed you."

"I've missed you, too. What training, Mrs. Philprin?"

"Shut your stupid mouth. This, Miss-Bride-of-Christ-Suffering-assed-little-Virgin," Mara said, patting her large belly. "*This.*"

Principalities

16

The Memory of Waits

"¿Como le ha ido, compadre?"
"Puro dale dale."

"How's it going, compadre?
"Just going at it, just going at it."

—*Conversation overheard*

EL FAROL MEXICAN RESTAURANT
For over forty years El Farol Mexican Restaurant has been doing business in the heart of Agua Oscura, New Mexico. Founded by Consuelo Carrasco Larragoite LaPoint Bexler, this well-known and famous restaurant lives on under the management of Consuelo's son, Larry. Known for its outstanding Mexican fare, El Farol invites you to taste its unique blend of culinary excellence.
¡Bienvenidos! Welcome to El Farol!

I first began working at El Farol Restaurant when I was fifteen. That unbearably hot and memorable summer, I was an eager but unsure public servant. My younger cousin, A.J., had dragged me along to his job interview for moral support. The owner, Mrs. Consuelo Larragoite, questioned A.J. about his schedule, but he was too busy with sports to work the hours she wanted. Mrs. Larragoite turned to me and asked me if I was available. I said yes, and got the job as bus person instead.

"*You* got the job! You didn't even *want* a job!" A.J. yelled at me outside the restaurant.

"I know."

"Why did *you* get the job?"

"I was free. You weren't."

"It's more than that."

"Oh, you!"

But it probably was true. I didn't say that to him. I just kept my thoughts to myself.

Mrs. Larragoite was divorced and had been for a long time. Her son, Larry, older than me by five years, was working that summer as a cashier. The summer before that, he'd been a waiter, and before that, a busboy. Mrs. Larragoite wanted her son to know everything there was to know about a restaurant and its management, but I didn't know all this until years later when Larry was owner and manager of the new old El Farol and I was his headwaitress. Larry and I weren't really friends then, but now that we are, we say we became friends that summer.

I got the job because I was ready, willing, and sure about how very unable I was. As Oralia, who always had a dicho for every event in life, explained to me later, "Cuando andes en la silla, maneja bien," which means "If you're in the saddle, ride it."

I got the job on a Friday. On Monday I began my official service. I haven't left it since, except for two occasions, but that's another story.

I began as a bus girl to Milia Ocana, who later became Mrs. Tosty Krungler. Everyone knew her then as Milia. Milia was forty-two years old at the time of my internship with her. Her name still conjures up strong memories: Milia in the little hallway off the Turquoise Room leading to the patio, totaling up her bills, a stubby #2 lead lifted to her mouth, causing the lead to soften and darken. As if crossing herself with Holy Water, Milia lifted that pencil to her mouth to be blessed. Long before pocket calculators were popular, Milia accurately tallied a multitude of meals, most ending in 95 cents. El Farol Special. New Mexican red pork chile stew with vegetables. $6.95. Enchilada plate with blue corn tortillas. Red or green. Or Christmas style with a combination of both red and green chile. Sour cream or an egg. $5.95. Burritos. Meat, bean, guacamole, chile relleno, chorizo, eggs, or any combination of your choosing. $3.95.

In Connie's mind, her prices were always bargains, and could be rounded off easily. No one bothered to be exact, except Milia, who had been with El Farol since its inception in 1943, and could, on demand, give out the total of any number of dinner permutations: 3 tacos, 1 guacamole salad, 2 enchiladas, 1 fideo, 1 tampico, 3 nachos, 1 sopaipilla, 4 con queso.

Milia never got past the third grade. She learned to add by counting bags of grain at her father's feed lot in Waterwell, New Mexico. When her father died, Milia sold the feed lot and moved to Agua Oscura, a distance of forty miles. An only child, she had lost her mother when she was four. Milia's inheritance bought her a small house on the edge of Chiva Town, as close to the Anglos as you could get without being kin. At twenty years old, Milia was not the kind of woman to sit home, so when Connie opened El Farol, she enlisted the aid of her neighbor, Milia Ocana.

Milia was El Farol's first and only waitress when the restaurant was on the east side of Gonzales Street. Located in a former billiard parlor, El Farol opened the year Larry Larragoite, Consuelo's only son, was born. It opened amid much doubt that it would survive, but flourished due to Milia's hard work, Consuelo's determination, and a dedicated kitchen staff consisting of Chilo Díaz, the cook, his wife, Pinga, the assistant cook, and Chuy Barales, dishwasher and custodian. At the end of the year Consuelo was able to hire another waitress and move into a building down the street. The following year El Farol moved to its current location, a large adobe building that had once been the town's Opera House and Community Center.

El Farol's dining rooms—the Kachina Room, the Stalactite Room, the Roadrunner Room, the Tepee Room, and the Turquoise Room—radiated out from a plant-filled central patio, the former site of the Opera House stage. The long wooden bar stood at the back of the patio, facing the lobby. An enormous glass-covered ceiling screened the patio, and was always leaking.

Milia was at El Farol from day one. She was reputed to be a business partner, but that was never proven. What was evident was that the woman had found her calling.

She was still a good-looking woman, after years of lifting feed and then large round brown plastic trays full of plates. Milia showed no signs of stopping. She had a head full of dark hair which she pulled into a rat and then fanned out like a sausage roll across the back of her head.

There was much speculation about the fact that she hadn't yet married. When pressed or teased, Milia replied that she "didn't need no sex to feel like a woman." It came as a great surprise when Milia got married at the end of the summer.

I arrived at El Farol to begin what I thought was a short-term job, and I hoped that no one would notice I'd come ten minutes late. I found Connie, who told me I was to report to Milia in the Kachina Room. Milia hugged me warmly and welcomed me to El Farol. She then took me aside and scolded me briefly. We stood under a large mother storyteller holding a multitude of her sleeping children.

"I was here at eight-thirty. I expect you to be here at nine. Now let's get to work. Take that towel and help me dry the silverware." A large plastic dish rack between us, we dried first the knives, then the forks, and last the spoons. This ritual never varied while I was under Milia's tutelage.

"People notice forks first. Then knives. Spoons come last. Check to see there aren't any spots or dried food on them. I won't have my customers insulted. We can sit down when we do this, but never let me see you sitting or eating or chewing on anything, not even the fat with anyone else who works here. Now put the tray back on that stand and get me that pile of white tablecloths. Start from the front of the room and move back. It'll save you some time. You see that little room off the side? That's where we keep everything you'll need. Now, Soveida, I want you to listen. A person who listens is a good waitress, remember that. Do you hear a cough? It could mean someone is ready to order, or they need water. Tapping on the glass or tables means impatience. Shuffling means there's a bill to be totaled and placed quickly on the table. Silence means the customer is either happy or mad. Things could go either way. Learn to know the difference. There are so many degrees of sound. Like a musician, you'll come to know them all."

"I'm done with the tablecloths, Milia."

"Good girl! Now bring me that tray with the salt and peppers. Take the silverware rag and clean each one. You might have to wet the rag. Make sure the rag is still clean. If it isn't, get one from the back. Ask Chuy where they are. Fill up those salts with salt from the container there. Careful. Soveida, you're more than a bus girl. You're more than my assistant. You're the left hand of God extended. I say the left hand because I don't want to be so presumptuous to say the right hand. Only God can act with the right hand. I am God's left hand and you, Soveida, are God's left hand extended."

"I'm done with the salts and peppers, Milia."

"Put a set on each table. Now get the sugar containers and make sure there's enough of each. Sugar. Sweet'n Low."

"Okay, and after that?"

"After that, you slow down. You're moving too fast already. Start pacing yourself. You put too many sugars in here and not enough Sweet'n Lows there. It's all about balance. We are responsible for each other. What I do, you do. What you do, I do. Now get the sauces in the back. They're in a tray. Catsup, Lea and Perrin, Tabasco. Make sure all the bottles are clean. I won't have me no sticky fingerprinty bottles. Consuelo said your name was Dosamantes. From Agua Oscura? Any relation to Lupe Dosamantes?"

"She's my grandma."

"I thought so. I know your grandmother from the altar society. Now, that's a good girl. I like the way you work. Steady and careful. That's the way. Just like me. I get paid very well. I have my regular customers. They're used to me."

"How long have you been here, Milia? I mean, you don't mind if I ask, do you?"

"Not if you keep working. I've heard people say: 'Why does she work at that old job? It pays little to nothing.' They don't know how stable this work can be, if you're good at it. Bring me the candle holders. They go on the table last."

"Should I clean them, too?"

"Does a waitress have legs? Look at me, Soveida. You are not here to be served. You are here to be of service. Remember that. You're not going to be a bus girl forever. After you move up, and you will, you'll become a hostess, and yes, that will be good for you, to seat people, to deal with them when they are impatient and hungry, and to work with us out here in this ocean of tables, all the waitresses and waiters waiting for a good catch: a tip. Know how to rotate and who to sit where and why and know how to share. We'll be grateful. But that's just the first step. Learn to be strong and fast. And don't talk too little or too much."

"What if someone asks me to get them something?"

"Well, you get it and then you let me know. Or you let me know and then you get it. It depends. Now, I demand a lot. I expect the best from you. My money is yours, because what little you make an hour goes to pay the Big Buitre, the President, that vulture and his taxes. I've been waitressing since before you were born and I know what waitressing is. Work with me and around me, mi bailarina."

"I'm done with the candles, Milia."

"Now stand back, admire your work, and get ready to dance."

That summer I followed Milia around like an eager partner. I learned quickly.

"Too quickly," Milia said. "Now Consuelo wants to take you away from me. She wants you to be a hostess three week nights. Soon you'll be working weekends. I've trained you too well!"

"It's only three nights a week, Milia."

"Then it'll be four."

"I can still help you."

"And soon you'll be working tables. They'll give me some overfed mama's boy who'll faint the first time he sees the dish pile, or else some toothpick who can't lift a tray full of food higher than his ombligo. I knew when I saw you, Soveida, that you were like me. A waitress de deveras. A true waitress. Someone who loves people and enjoys the craziness of this work. Someday you'll replace me."

"Replace you? Never! I'm just a bus girl!"

"You're a hostess. Let me give you some advice: Stay away from the tostadas. They'll make you fat. All the other hostesses keep a bowl of chips and salsa behind the podium where they keep their charts. Don't do it. My last bus girl gained fifteen pounds one summer. Never let people see you with anything in your mouth or in your hair. No pencils, no pens. Keep your uniform clean, no manchas, never a spot. Clean nails. No low-cut blouses. No chichis caidas. Get a good lift on the bra. Make sure you are wearing the right cup size. Many women have been wearing the wrong cup for years. You don't want to fan out on the sides. Yes, soon you'll be leaving me!"

"I'm just a bus girl, Milia!"

"But at least I can retire now that I've found someone to take my place."

"What are you talking about, I'm just going to hostess three nights a week."

"Someday you'll be a good waitress and then a wonderful waitress and then very soon you'll be the headwaitress, training other waitresses, and then the best of all waitresses in Agua Oscura."

"But it's just a summer job!"

"That's what you say, mi bailarina. Listen to my words. The food gets to you."

"Are you really going away, Milia?"

"I could never go too far, but yes, someday I'll go away."

Milia had recently acknowledged her romance with Tosty Krungler, one of her regulars, a man who had courted her, unknown to anyone, for over twenty years. Their dates consisted of going to church and eating ice cream afterwards. No date had been set.

"You're lucky, bailarina, that you have *me* to show you how to do this work."

"Why is that, Milia? I mean, I know why, but why?"

"I didn't have a mama, she died when I was little. My father was just a poor man who didn't know much except oats and sheep. What I did have was silence and the power of my hands. Anyone would walk in here and just see tables, with people sitting around them eating. I look around and I see a world. A complete world."

"I never thought of things that way."

"How could you, solita? Without me, you can't see this world. Only yourself in all the noise. Learn to separate the noise from the silence. And to love both. It's here I fell in love with mi Tostadito. Like you'll fall in love with quién sabe, and the one after you falls in love with fulano, and so on. I knew I wanted to marry mi viejito ten years ago."

"Why didn't you?"

"He didn't ask. But, anyway, I was busy, and as I say, I didn't need no sex to feel like a woman. When you get older, you see things differently. I see ese pobrecito, Lenchito, Consuelo's son . . ."

"You mean Larry Larragoite?"

I looked in Larry's direction. He was directing someone our way, and doing it with an air of superiority. A tall, thin young man, he was unappealing to me in so many ways: big-lipped, unattractive, stuck-up as well, he still had his delusions of importance.

"El mismo. Someday he'll become the manager and then he'll retire. Probably early on, it looks to me. And then, who knows, *you* might take over."

"Me? Ay, Milia!"

"Don't you *ay* me, bailarina, it's possible."

"But I want to go to school, Milia. Get a degree."

"You will someday."

"Someday better be soon!"

"Someday, bailarina, is never soon enough! Just remember what I said. Watch that boy. Mira, here he comes. How you doing, Mr. Lenchito?"

"Hello, Milia. So, you're the new girl, huh? Are you going to seat Dr. and Mrs. Pincely or what?"

"Are you talking to me?" I said with irritation.

"Yeah, I'm talking to you. You're the hostess, aren't you?"

"Esos viejitos, Soveida. They're my regulars. She doesn't see too good and he's medio sordo. D2, the table in the corner. Water. No chips. Yew-hew! How are you, Dr. and Mrs. Pincely? Miss Dosamantes will be right with you."

"Right this way, Dr. and Mrs. Pincely. If you'll follow me," I said, turning my back on Larry, thankful that I would have to tolerate him only for the next few months.

Days and then weeks went by. I became a hostess and by the end of the summer was waitressing full time. Larry was cashiering and, against his will, pinch-hitting now and then as a waiter, a job he abhorred.

"Devil or Angel," sang Larry off key. "I hate waiting on tables, Soveida."

"You do? I love it!"

"I hate to see how people eat."

"I never think about it. You see things as good or bad, you start making judgments, you won't be able to do the work."

"You sound like Milia."

"I guess I do. I really miss working with her. I can't believe I'm staying on. The food's gotten to me!"

"Call it by its real name: slime. Have you ever really looked at a dirty plate after someone has finished a meal? It's disgusting! It's full of discarded chile skins, fat globules, wilted lettuce, old beans like dry turds, soggy tortillas. Yech!"

"I never think of it that way."

"Pork entrails, half-chewed steak, greasy rice, tough gristle, watery vermicelli! Go on, think about it! It's nauseating! I hate food! Especially Mexican food!"

"Don't let your mother hear you say that!"

"Sticky honey, gummy con queso, red chile diluted with Coke. Shall I go on?"

"Okay, okay! I got the picture."

Everyone who now worked at El Farol had trained with Milia at one time or another. It was Milia who discovered Eloisa Ortiz, the night cook, who immortalized the El Farol menu. Initially Eloisa was hired as a waitress. Milia had given her a talk as well.

"You don't seem to have what it takes to be a waitress, but you do have the serving in you, and you love food, I can see that. Let me give you some advice. Watch the tostadas. Do you cook?"

"Sí, señora . . ."

"Señorita . . ."

"Sí, Señorita Milia. I love to cook. I grew up in a family of thirteen, and I was the cook. It's my favorite thing in the world, well, except for one other thing. I'm married."

"Remember what I said about the tostadas. And when you get a free moment—not that I know when that will be—but go talk to Chilo the cook. He needs some help in the kitchen."

So Eloisa moved into the kitchen, which lasted until Chilo's retirement, when Eloisa took over as head cook. Everything happened as Milia predicted: I became headwaitress, Larry Larragoite the manager, Eloisa the head cook. She left everything else in order, that was her way.

Milia was right about so many things. There were only two things she hadn't prepared me for. The first was error. Error caused by timidity, insecurity, carelessness, and haste. Only practice made perfect. Milia no longer had such problems. She was way past adding a bill incorrectly, or losing a ticket, or being stiffed by various sets of customers, whether a group of rowdy Chicanos on their way to the rodeo, or an old Anglo lady who looked like she wouldn't harm anyone and then, when confronted in the lobby for not paying her bill, threw me the finger and stormed out. There was the table of Native Americans, quite drunk, who'd driven across the state to sell jewelry in Agua Oscura at the Annual Roadrunner Festival, rang up a bill of $162.93, and then walked out of the bar while I was in the bathroom. Romilio, the kind, usually silent bartender, rang up the bill, allowing El Farol to absorb the loss. I can honestly say that I've been stiffed by every ethnic group you could name. Meanness has nothing to do with race. I've seen them all.

There were other mistakes early on as well: the splattering of hot Tampico steak grease on a light brown suede jacket, the serving of soup with the meal and a consequent complaint from an irate customer who chastised me: "Soup comes first, don't you know that?" There were late waters, and forgotten Cokes, encounters with the grouchy, the impatient, the unfriendly.

I knew I was finally getting it right when a businesswoman who had been so unpleasant in the beginning apologized to me later. "I'm sorry. I was rude and you were so nice. It wasn't right." I started having my regular customers after that summer and I've kept them ever since.

The other thing Milia had told me about, but hadn't prepared me for, was falling in love with a customer. The object of my desire, whose name was unknown, was dark, handsome, watchful, and he never smiled. His mother was large-busted, imposing, with a mole the size of a small cucaracha on her upper lip. The father was small, sunken-chested, with a swirl of dyed black hair.

"Good evening, I'm Soveida Dosamantes. I'll be your waitress tonight. Can I help you?"

"Where's Irma?" the mole asked. "This is her room. We want Irma."

"I'm sorry, Irma's off tonight."

"We always come on Thursdays. Irma's always here then."

"I'm sorry, but she's off. Her sister got married."

"On a Thursday?"

"Just order, Lourdes."

"I've never seen her before, Cuti."

"She's a new girl, Lourdes."

"What do you want, m'ijo?"

"I'll have enchiladas, Christmas. And a large Coke, miss."

"Ivan Eloy Torres! ¡Por Dios! He always orders the same thing! And you, Cuti?"

"Tampico steak. Rare."

"Make that two. The other well done. Mr. Torres will have his coffee now. I'll have iced tea. No lemon. Diet sweetener."

"And two orders of sopaipillas."

"Will that be all for you?" I stammered, staring at the beautiful young man at table 5.

After I met Ivan Torres I remembered Milia's words: "You'll fall in love with quién sabe, and the one after will fall in love with fulano, and so on . . ."

The next Thursday night Irma returned, so the Torreses asked for her. But it was too late. I'd already fallen in love.

At the end of the summer Milia retired her apron amid much teasing about her "not needing sex to make her feel like a woman," and married Tosty. She sold her house and moved, "at her ripe old age," to LaDonna Street, where all the rich Anglos lived. Milia cooked, cleaned, and ran the house, "Pa' mi viejito, mi Tostadito."

Connie threw a huge wedding party at El Farol. Chololo Chiwiwi y los Chingazos were hired to play a mixture of pop, rock, ranchera, salsa, with a little cumbia thrown in. The patio was cleared, so people could dance.

Milia winked at me when we had a moment away from the madness. It happened too fast for anyone else to see it, and it was simply a quick movement and expression of the eyes that said: "We did it, bailarina!!"

17

El Jester

"Y our breasts are so small."

That's what Jester told me. He was the first man I had ever lain with, full body on a bed, in a darkened room. We hadn't made love, just moved around in some kind of simulated ecstasy. Jester was twenty, I was seventeen. I met him after I had been working at El Farol Restaurant for a couple of years.

Jester was a cousin of Belisa, who was one of the waitresses. I was setting out the silverware when he ran in to give her a message. Belisa was in the bathroom. She had just gotten positive test results from Dr. Wenchy. She was carrying her boyfriend Jerry's baby.

"Tell Belisa to call Tía Pepa. Tío Nati got some fingers cut off on the farm. Chipi can't pick him up at the hospital because Fernie took off with the car. Maybe Tin or Pollo could do it."

"Could you repeat that?"

"This is an emergency! My Uncle Nati got his fingers cut off!"

"I got that."

"Chipi can't pick him up."

"Okay, I got that, too."

"Maybe Tin can. If not Pollo. You got anything to drink back there? Man, am I thirsty!"

"Nati, Chipi, Tin, and Fernie . . ."

"Fernie, then Tin. Just tell her El Jester said to call Tía Pepa. Hey, you got some iced tea you can give me?"

"Who's El Jester?"

"Me, sonsa! Shit, I'm full of blood. You got some orange juice? I got a thirst you won't believe. Had to go to the farm, way the hell over to Four Points and then back, pick up two dedos—all I could find was the two—the thrasher probably got the other one, and race back to the car. Y me pegó un asco, babes, like you can't imagine, no te imaginas, I got these two bloody dedos on the passenger seat of my TransAm, on my simulated sheepskin, wrapped up in my chamois I had in the back seat. Had it ten years, esa. Peeled out a todo dar straight for the hospital, barely holding it in, me pegó un odio, eeh, I was like repulsed, mana, to the max! I can tell you, babes, it was the longest twenty-five minutes of my whole damn life. When I got to the hospital, there was three, count 'em, three doctors waiting for me by the emergency entrance with an ice chest. I'd radioed them on my CB. When I saw that ice chest, all I could think of was cold beer, but no way. The chamois was ruined."

"Did you want a Pepsi or a Coke, Joker?"

"Joker, Jester, what the hell. As long as you call me something. It don't matter. I'll take a Coke. So, what's your name, babes?"

This was my first meeting with El Jester, as he called himself. His name was really Juan Alfredo Ramos, or Yonny, as his grandma called him, not being able to pronounce the J.

Jester would come in from time to time to get a free Coke from Belisa. Then one day he asked me out.

At first, Jester wasn't boyfriend material in my mind. He was handsome, though, with long black hair that he wore tied back with coiled red yarn in a thick chongo. Always slightly unkempt, he was taller than most men I knew, thin, but strong, with defined muscles you could clearly see in his sleeveless tank tops. He always smelled a little sweet, of fresh sweat, and excitement. I liked his casual indifference toward most things in life, the long look of his almond-shaped eyes, quick as fish to register emotion, his rich hair and his soft lazy lips that taught me how to kiss.

So that summer Jester was my unofficial boyfriend. I always liked him much more than he liked me. That was the unofficial part of our romance. The official part was that he never acknowledged that he cared for me, never told me he loved me, and yet he did introduce me to his mother and his grandma, who lived together in a project house near my Tía Adelaida's.

Jester's black TransAm was his greatest joy, and it was in the bucket seat of that car, on the side that held his Uncle Nati's bloody amputated fingers, that I first discovered what it was to have desire reciprocated.

Jester's luminous black hair flowed freely, opening up in the wind as we sped along Highway 70 in his car, all the windows lowered, my arm around him like a living bandage. We would drive out to the river after my shift at work, and sit by the low muddy water underneath an ancient cottonwood, on a soft faded serape the color of old blood. This was the blanket Jester said his grandfather Nicanor sat on every morning at daybreak, atop his favorite cerrito, no matter the weather, praying to the sun god. Each afternoon we lay on his grandfather's serape, sheltered in the shade of that ancestral tree, far away from the noise, from all human preoccupations, drawing sacred life with our tongues in each other's mouth.

Jester taught me the game of kissing, the push, the pull, the ever widening net: the prize. We made a delicious dark love with our tongues. He left me wet, full of juice, confident in my ability to love. But we never spoke much. He was the pachuco from the other side of town, the low-rider from the barrio, my Chiva Town boy, and I was la princesa, admired, inaccessible, and inexperienced, a member of that once wealthy, still regal, family, the Dosamantes. Jester's father came from México, from Nuevo León. Mr. Ramos spoke English with a broken accent, while Luardo spoke Spanish only when he had to, or because he needed something from someone lesser than himself. Jester was El Indio to Dolores, el prieto greñudo, to Mamá, the dark one, full of hair. Once Mamá took me aside and said to me, "Soveida, when you go with him, m'ija, and then come home, you smell. You smell of man."

One morning when I got to work, Belisa told me Jester had been in a car accident. He was driving too fast on a dirt road. He flipped over, knocking himself and his front teeth out. Those same beautiful white teeth that had once played a long and lovely tag with my tongue and lips and ears and neck.

Later that day I saw Jester in the hospital emergency room.

"Are you all right, Jester?"

"Yeah, I'm all right. Hey, can you believe this? This is where I brought my Tío Nati's dedos. It's like what do you call it when you think you've played this scene before in your mind only you haven't. Or maybe you have. It's like that. What do you call it?"

"I don't know."

"It's called something. So, you want to go to a party next Saturday afternoon, Soveida?"

"Are you sure you'll be okay by then?"

"Hell, they're letting me go home today. Only I got to lay low, the doctor says. My compa Cheno's having the party. So, you want to go or not?"

Cheno lived out of town, off Frenly Road, near the orchards that led south into Texas, in a big adobe, with two male roommates, both of them best friends since the second grade. The next Saturday we drove up in Jester's dented TransAm. Cheno was in the living room drinking beer and watching a game show on television. The two roommates were gone. Jester brought himself a beer, which he drank quickly. We watched TV with Cheno for a while and then one of the roommates came back with a girlfriend. The couple went into the kitchen to whip up a meal. Jester and I walked to the back of the house, the smell of frying carne adovada floating to us from the stove. I could hear the sharp metal clip of Cheno trimming his fingernails as he sat laughing to himself in front of the television.

Jester had been staying with his compas since the accident. He wanted to move to California, but when he told his mom, she had said no way; he needed to stay home and help out his grandma and her. In a fury, Jester moved out.

Jester guided me down a hallway. His toothless smile was crooked and sexy as he took my hand. We slid through a train of rooms to his small bedroom and his single bed shoved into a corner. He pulled me down to him, drew up my summer top, and then thumbed my breasts.

I turned over with my back to him, my breasts pushed together. I felt more attractive this way, less shy, and he held me that way awhile.

"Your breasts are so small," he said.

I froze inside, and then went for his mouth, the mouth without teeth, the lips now without words, the hair that I loved to touch covering my hidden face. He was a warm, hungry animal, and he was dear.

Jester rubbed up against me and sighed.

Then his roommate called everyone to come and eat, and we left.

My romance with Jester was short-lived. It lasted only a few months. Jester kept telling me that he was moving soon to California to get a job and I had no reason to doubt him. I can't say that I wanted him to stay, and yet I did find myself drawn to him, his wildness. Our times together were mostly limited to afternoon trysts, beginning after my work shift, ending just before dark when he would drive me close to home. I would walk the half block remaining, because I didn't want to have to face Mamá or Dolores. For all they knew, I had just gotten a ride home from work with "that nice boy, Larry." To me, there was nothing nice about Larry. He was obnoxious and ill-mannered, ugly as well, not like Jester, with his handsome face and crazy, hungry eyes.

One afternoon at the river, shortly after Jester got his new front teeth, he asked me if I would like to go to the drive-in with him that night. He'd given me such short notice I wasn't sure Dolores would let me go. I lied to her, saying that Connie wanted me to help with a banquet. I told her that I would be back around midnight, and that Larry would drive me home. Never doubting my word, Dolores gave me her permission. I wasn't dating at the time, although I was almost eighteen. The secret thrill of being with Jester after dark—at a drive-in, no less—was something new and forbidden to me. I was sure no one would find out. Twenty years old, with his own car, he was all the man I ever wanted.

The Río Grande Drive-In was situated at the north end of Agua Oscura, and was a place I had been many times with Dolores and Hector. We would always park in the middle row and during the film Dolores would inevitably ask me to take Hector to play on the swing set that was just in front of the giant screen. Sidestepping our way between the parked cars, I would hold Hector's hand as he blatantly peered in parked cars where couples were making out or sleeping. Cautiously avoiding the speaker wires, Hector and I walked toward the changing lights of the enormous screen and through the gate that led to the children's playground. When I was younger, I, too, had yelled and cavorted like all these children, happier to be out here in the grass than sitting in a stuffy car with my parents.

Hector ran around the grassy recreation area beneath a huge image of Cornel Wilde scrambling through the African desert in *The Naked Prey*, restless natives in hot pursuit. The children's squeals and cries always drowned out the movie's words. While Dolores sat in the car peacefully eating popcorn, I watched Hector go up and down the slide, in those endless, tireless games of his, as I swung back and forth on a swing, straining to get ever higher, ever closer to the screen. I wanted to go over the top of the movie screen and fly far away. Or at least get close to those passionate lovers, their lips fixed on each other as if they would never part, their lives always connected. Their joys and sorrows seemed more interesting than mine; I wanted to melt into them.

Jester snuck in the theater the back way. While he drove his car, I got out and undid the metal chain so that his TransAm could get through. It was either this or pay the three dollars. I offered to lend him the money, but he refused, saying this was what he always did. How many times had he been here, I wondered, and with whom. I'd never been to the drive-in without my mother or my younger brother or without a car full of girls, Dolores as chaperon.

Jester looked so handsome in the growing darkness. We parked at the back of the drive-in, near the high wooden fence that was supposed to keep people from seeing the movie without getting in. I thought we might get something to eat and drink, but we never did. I'd looked forward to going to the snack bar with Jester, showing him off to whoever might be in there. I wanted us to be a couple, to stroll in with our arms around each other, as if we belonged together, or to sit in the darkness of the car in silence, holding hands, the way old married people did, with a quiet reverence.

The movie was halfway over, and I was disappointed, since I hadn't yet seen *Doctor Zhivago*. There was a lot of noise and I couldn't quite gather what had happened up to that point.

Suddenly Jester unzipped his pants. He took my hand and put it around his penis. For a minute I didn't understand what I was supposed to do. Without any words, Jester put his hand over mine and began to move it up and down. I had never seen a man's penis before like that, unfurled so suddenly and with such deliberation. It seemed enormous, a rubbery mass I couldn't quite grasp. It was warm, and very hard. I was overwhelmed—embarrassed and aghast and quite nearly sick. What had I done to encourage this behavior? There was nothing exciting or sexy about the way Jester treated me, nothing personal or even real. I watched myself disassociate from my feelings, as the poor unwitting Lara had. Trapped by an older, selfish lover, she hardly recognized her own haunted face in a shadowy mirror. Why had this night gone so wrong? I liked Jester and he had once liked me. But now I no longer existed. I was Jester's plaything, without a voice. I was too shy to say or do anything, except follow the motion of Jester's hand, as he guided me. It was obvious I'd never touched a penis before, and could feel Jester's irritation in the flickering silence. I wanted to get away, but I knew I couldn't. I realized I was someplace I shouldn't be, with someone I shouldn't be with, and that no one knew where I was, nor would I ever tell anyone where I'd been. The grandiose spectacle of *Dr. Zhivago* took place before my eyes as I sat close to Jester and pulled his long thick penis. He was frustrated, I knew, and I wasn't helping much. My resolve to get away was buried in the snow of that endless Russian winter. I was trapped in my own silent, suffering inner revolution.

My life flashed before me and I knew the absolute interminable stillness of eternity waiting for my first penis to explode. I wanted to jump out of the car, run to the snack bar, hide in the bathroom until everyone was gone, and then escape. Instead, I sat there as Jester moaned to himself and put his hand over mine every once in a while, teaching me what to do, his legs splayed, pants around his knees. My hand grew limp and tired, as I slid Jester's penis back and forth without enthusiasm. Frankly, I was grateful he hadn't pushed my face down and asked me to kiss him. I wondered if anyone I knew was in the drive-in, or walking by with a little brother in tow. I could hear the screams of the little kids in the playground, one little girl in particular, as her swing went higher and higher, and floated out into the starry sky over Agua Oscura.

I thought of a story Lizzie had told me about a date she'd had with Gerónimo Flores, one of two horny cousins from T. or C., renowned for their sexual conquests, Agua Oscura's reigning hickey masters. It was reported that Herman, the older cousin, had a mistress. Lizzie knew who she was: an Anglo college girl with big breasts. The younger cousin, Gerónimo, was a college freshman, and on their first date to the drive-in, he'd tried to rape Lizzie. He had come on so strong that Lizzie had gotten sick and had to lean out the passenger seat to throw up. I wished I could do that with Jester.

I peered up at the screen, which seemed so tiny and far away, and wondered what Julie Christie would have done in my shoes. Hell, she was a woman who must have been used to such things. But would I get used to men, and to things like this?

In disgust, no doubt, Jester took over from my uninspired pumping and finished the job for himself. With a number of forceful thrusts he completed what he had begun. I was drained, and oddly grateful. Cleaning himself up with a handkerchief, he zipped up his pants and started the car engine. I knew that he would take me home now, that our date was over, and that I would never see him again. I would never be his lover, the way I'd once wished. Jester was a man of the world, ruthless and unconcerned about little girls like myself. I was relieved that the night was nearly over. I consigned his memory to that dark place that no one visits, full of the corpses of dead dreams, lovers who never loved, where twisted fantasies become nightmares. We had never spoken much, much less now. Words filled my throat and were pushed down, and yet they filled the distance between us, as I pressed my body against the car door. Silently Jester drove me home.

"Leave me here," I finally said, my voice strained. "I'll walk home the rest of the way." "Are you sure?" he replied indifferently. "Yes, leave me here." "See you," he muttered. The car stopped and I got out, not looking back, as Jester spun around, making a loud U-turn in the middle of the quiet street. He had left me a full block away. I walked home feeling sullied, sad. I promised myself I would not cry, not now, not until I was alone in my room. Dolores wondered why I was home so early and I told her that Connie had more help than she needed. "Be sure and thank that nice boy, will you, Soveida?" Dolores called out to me as I went down the hallway to my room. "Which one?" "You know, Larry, he did give you a ride home, didn't he?" "Oh yes, him. I will," I answered in a strange voice, a voice that only I could hear inside of me, wondering to myself why Jester had done what he had to me, to someone who had thought so much of him.

Later I found out Jester had moved to California to work on car engines. He had a new girlfriend. Someone half white. Someone who was older than me, someone who had real breasts and let him make love to her the way he wanted. She was short, blond, spoke with a lisp, had legs thick from gymnastics, and was no prettier than me.

I now realize that Jester had taught me well. He prepared me for rude men, crude men, the ones without shame, who use women like me and then discard us when they're done. In the silence of my room I had many questions for Jester, all of which went unanswered. Eyes open, I stared at a ceiling of stars as my mind soared high over the rooftops of Agua Oscura, and higher still, into the dark navy-blue sky where there was nothing but silence, and everything below looked helpless, insignificant, and small.

18

Whispers

I never learned to whisper. My mother, Dolores, could have taught me how. She herself had learned to whisper from her mother, Doña Trancha.

Doña Trancha would whisper even in the quietest of places. Not one of the ten solemn old women who were in attendance at the 6:30 Mass could hear her, nor could that solitary old man, Don Juan Hidalgo. Nor could el Padre Cantucci, with his very acute hearing, understand what she said. He stood with his back to the congregation, facing the altar, his hands upraised in prayer.

Doña Trancha whispered to Dolores, who knelt next to her: "Straighten up and now, young lady, or the demons will come and take you away. Don't think it's impossible. They're right under these floorboards. Why, if it weren't for that crucifix . . ."

Doña Trancha was a whisperer, one of desperate, unpleasant, and unspeakable things—things a daughter never wanted to hear. Dolores often wondered if Trancha was really her mother. She couldn't be! "Malcriada, disobedient, misbehaving, naughty child, I don't know you, I never have. I'm not your mother. You're the child of the devil, no child of mine would ever behave the way you do."

Everything about Trancha went on and on. Hers was one long tirade of uncompleted, unresolved, and certainly never happy realities. Whisper whisper whisper, when Dolores was trying to smile at someone across the room. Whisper whisper whisper, when Dolores didn't look the way she was supposed to look. Whisper whisper whisper: Be quiet, be still, don't touch, awful girl, not like your sister, Lina, who always behaves.

"God help you, you're like your father. Cara de beato, uñas de gato.

What good will it do you to have a devout face and bad habits? You're still a kitten who thinks you're a coyote howling under the full moon. Always dreaming!"

Trancha never hit Dolores. She didn't punish or hurt her, except with her words. Worse than physical blows, they would pull her up, make her step aside and pause wherever she was standing. The high, sharp Psst! of Trancha's voice snapped the desert air, stung and burned like sand in a dust storm. Only Dolores could hear the piercing decibels that brought her pain, the pain of a dog unused to certain soundless whistles. These were words from one woman to another, a mother to a daughter, unacknowledged words that neither could deny. They were damaging and remembered words. Scaring words. Welts underneath clothing. Cold disturbing words from one woman to another, one who knows your most intimate smell. Words from a woman who sees you as the man who makes love to you would. A mother.

Some people can whisper and others will never learn. Now, Mamá Lupita could whisper and so could Luardo. All the Dosamanteses were good whisperers, and that extended to Mamá's grandchildren, M.J., A.J., R.J., Butch, Baby, and even Hector. I am the only one of Mamá's grandchildren who can't whisper. I consider it a blessing when I think of my cousins, especially M.J. and Butch.

M.J. is my closest female cousin in age, after Mara. She got the worst of her parents' qualities. Just like her mother, Teeney, M.J. is finicky to the extreme when it comes to bodily functions and physical tics or deformities, or any personal oddities of habit. Just like her father, Adrino Talamantes, she has always secretly delighted in other people's misfortunes and disappointments. The end result is a person who doesn't like anyone or anything.

You wouldn't know it, talking to Tía Teeney. According to her, M.J. and A.J. were always the brightest of the Dosamantes grandchildren.

"They've gone to college, unlike all the rest of their cousins. A.J. even has a master's degree in counseling. It doesn't matter that he hasn't used it the way he was supposed to. My A.J. has the largest and most successful hamburger franchise in southern New Mexico. M.J., on the other hand, is the brain of the family. If a person can be too smart, then m'jita is. Every week she finishes at least seven paperbacks. She even has several bookcases full of hardcover books. Big ones. With lots of words. My M.J. is now chief accountant for her brothers' hamburger business. How do you like that? One burger led to another and now they're both doing very well, thanks be to the saints. And it's because my kids were the only ones to go to college. I'm not bragging. Yes, I am bragging. Not one of the other cousins went very far. Not even you, Soveida, and you showed such promise."

A.J. was the cousin who got a pea stuck up his nose. And M.J. made some disparaging remark that caused A.J. to snort with such juvenile gusto and ferocity that the pea finally popped out: Some successes!

"Don't let what your Tía Teeney says bother you, Soveida. Her children may be doing well, but so are you, m'ija," Mamá Lupita consoled me when Teeney stepped out of the room. I had decided to keep working at El Farol, and yet someday I knew I would go to college.

"Besides, a la Mary Jane le sobró algo. Her cesos moved out of her head and down her face and onto her nose, and got stuck there. Yes, her brains came out and landed on the very end of her nose! That's the reason why my granddaughter has a nose with a mole like a shriveled pasa, a yellow raisin on the tip. If only the mole were dark, it could pass for a beauty mark! If only la pasa didn't hang down like a moco!"

All the kids at Holy Angel had called M.J. Moco Head or Snot Brain or Raisin Nose. M.J. went to school there until she couldn't stand it anymore and begged her mom to send her to Loretto Academy in El Paso. Tía Teeney was against it at first, but finally relented. M.J. went on to graduate with honors, far away from the voices of those nasty children from Holy-fucking-Angel that she privately referred to as a bunch of aggie-dork-brained-jerkheads from the sticks.

As much as M.J. tried to get upstream from Agua Oscura, she still had her nose to contend with. Her large mole made all the stereotypes of mad witches seem so real.

"Ay!" Mamá whispered to me. "If only la Mary Jane didn't have that mole. Then she could think about conceiving a child. She might even possibly have a chance at redemption. As it stands, or hangs now, she'll take that mole to hell with her and her money bags. How can a man love a woman like that? She's too macha. Too ready to trip you and then help you up like it was your fault. How can a man look at a woman like that and not see bitterness in front of him like sour fruit for the rest of his life? You can't hug a brain. It won't warm your feet. No, she's not beautiful. She's not even pretty. Nor is she attractive. But she has all the essential parts. She's not bad-looking from the nose down. Big flat feet like her mother, Teeney. The only one of my children with flat feet like their father. Maybe that's why Mary Jane is so good in business. Her feet are planted firmly on the ground. She's a bit on the chubby side, like an overripe melon. Now some people like melons a little over, like that. To get on with it and to get down to it, Soveida, no one wants to reproduce a nose like that, or reproduce with someone with a nose like that. Do you understand me? It's good she likes to read. Pero pobrecita, she's too mean to be a nun. Not that there aren't any mean nuns or ones with big noses. It's not that. It's the mole. With the mole she's the incarnation of Judas, only female. Ay, Diosito, I've said too much," Mamá whispered sadly.

That is what I hate the most about the Dosamantes family: their whispers that pull the rug out from under you, leaving you forever off-balance, like Mamá's whispers about Mara.

"Mara wasn't a Dosamantes. Never could be. She came to me like a stray cat with the meanness and madness of her own family, the Loeras. The girl always gave me a hard time. She couldn't help it. Just think about her poor mother."

When I was eighteen years old my cousin Butch, otherwise known on his baptismal certificate as Gustavo Fernando Dosamantes, came up to me at a family gathering at my Tío Toddy and Tía Lita's house. Everyone had gone into the dining room to get their plates. I had forgotten something in my purse. Butch came in from outside, where he'd been smoking a cigarette.

"Come on, Butch," Tía Lita called. "The food's ready!"

"I'm coming, Mom. Hey, wait up for me, cuz."

I waited for him by the door. He smelled of the hot sun. His skin was pale, gleaming like his mother's, with freckles no Dosamantes had, a smell no cousin had, just a hot man whispering up close: "When I was at your house last week helping your dad I looked in your room. I saw you in bed with your nightgown pulled up."

I got away as fast as I could and went to get Tía Lita's greasy fried chicken as if nothing had happened. After that, my cousin Butch always stared at my breasts and made comments to me about them or the way I looked in bed.

Butch was married at the time. His wife, Cheryl, was so nice, and they had two cute kids, Terry and Tommy. I never liked being alone with him.

And yet, as much as I didn't like to think about it, Butch was a handsome guy, with his pale skin and all those freckles. He had soft light brown hair with curls near the hairline, like a small sweaty boy. And he wanted to hurt you like the Sánchez brothers, the neighborhood terrors, who lived the next street over. They chased you, grabbed you roughly, and then pushed you to the ground, pulling down your panties and then running away, jeering to themselves. The only girl whose panties they never touched were M.J.'s.

Butch was much older than the Sánchez brothers. His wife, Cheryl Halbrecht, was a blond, blue-eyed Anglo from California. They met in San Francisco when Butch was stationed out there. Cheryl's brothers and sisters were all blond and blue-eyed, and brought a new and interesting dimension to our dark-eyed, solely Mexican family. Now that she and Butch were married, the Halbrecht cousins came to visit regularly and stayed with them during the summer.

During the summer, I met Stewart, Cheryl's nephew, at some family gathering at Butch's. It was love at first sight for me. Stewart was very quiet, and very fair, unlike all the brash, impetuous, horny Agua Oscura boys. He wasn't mean or hard and he didn't drink. Cheryl invited me to dinner, "so Stewart and I could get to know each other better." When I got over to Butch's, I found out that Cheryl had been called in to work at the hospital where she was an R.N. I decided to stay and at least eat, since Cheryl had left everything prepared. We had wine and then mixed drinks, and while Butch remained perfectly sober, both Stewart and I gradually became quite drunk, especially Stewart. Suddenly he got sick and finally ended up asleep, curled up on the couch. He tried to rouse himself, but he was unsteady and once again fell back on the couch.

Then Butch moved closer to me. "Turn around."

"What?"

"I'm going to rub your back. You look tense."

"I'm not tense. I'm *too* relaxed."

"Just turn around."

"Butch!"

"Turn around!"

Butch massaged my shoulders and back. I remembered I was wearing my old white bra with the safety pin holding the hook together to the main part. I wished I could die and disappear, because it felt so good. Butch rubbed my shoulders and then he ran his fingers lightly over my neck. He moved my hair out of the way. I pulled my hair on top of my head and then he bent down and kissed my neck. The door opened. It was Cheryl. They'd let her off early. I got up quickly and said goodbye and thank you and drove home slowly. Later Mamá heard about it and she bawled Butch out. "Shame on you, Gustavo, giving liquor to minors, especially your cousin Soveida. Who is this Stewart fulano? ¿Quién lo parió? Who are his parents?"

Later I thanked God and Cheryl and even Mamá, who had saved me from Butch and from that desire I'd felt for him. Nobody ever talked to me about anything like that but Mara, saying she was in love with at least two of my relatives at one time or another.

"Thank God they're not my relatives. So I don't have to think about it twice."

I saw how easy it could be to get lost in Butch's whispers. I had wanted Butch in as pure a way as I could, the purity of drunkenness. What would I have done if Cheryl hadn't come in to save me from Butch's massage while Stewart was passed out on the couch?

When I think of that night with Butch I cringe. But I'm glad I never fell for those whispers of his—lies, all of them lies.

Now that I am older I remember the whispers.

Wear your hair up. It looks ugly down.

You have the nipples of a married woman.

I saw you. I saw you with your nightgown pulled up.

Many have whispered to me, wanting things, desiring them, professing belief. Murmured secrets dark and unrepeatable. I even heard Mamá Lupita whisper to Dolores, "Luardo's always been a good boy. A blessing to the women of his family."

And then she coughed to resume the lie.

I looked at Mamá, a gentle, tender, and honest woman, and I thought to myself: How long can we carry these burdens?

At once I knew the answer.

If we want, forever.

19

The One

The Torres family continued coming to El Farol to eat, and of course they always requested Irma as a waitress. One quiet off-night, Ivan showed up by himself, requesting a table in my section. I was surprised to see him when I came out of the kitchen, where Larry had been telling jokes. Still laughing to myself, and caught off-guard by the sudden appearance of Ivan, I approached his table, flustered.

Ivan looked up at me and smiled. I smiled back, forgetting to ask him about his order. "Your name is Soveida Dosamantes and you're my waitress tonight, right? I'm Ivan Torres."

I know, I thought to myself: You're the Ivan Torres who lived in California, the only man in Agua Oscura who doesn't wear socks with shoes, the person who's caused every woman's heart to race and then stop and never want to start again. "What can I get for you?"

"Enchiladas Christmas with an egg."

"Is that all?"

"Can I meet you after work, I mean, would you like to go dancing?"

"Dancing?"

I mumbled something to Ivan and made a hasty retreat to the small workroom where we tallied our checks, and where I poured myself a glass of water. I didn't know Larry was standing there in the darkness, and I yelped. "God, Larry, you scared me. How long have you been hovering?" "So, who's the guy?" he asked. "It's like you saw a ghost or something." I muttered something and finished writing the order. Side egg. What to drink? Larry looked at me suspiciously and then a little sadly. He left me alone to ponder the unthinkable: Ivan Torres.

I didn't go dancing that night. I wasn't quite ready to repeat any past mistakes by jumping at anything on such short notice. But I did go out with Ivan the following weekend, and we did go dancing.

Have you ever loved anyone immediately? It had something to do with the way he looked, that was a great part of it, but then again, it had something to do with how he did things. Ivan was incredibly handsome to me, like a movie star, with a full head of dark hair, beautiful teeth, and a great, all-embracing smile. He looked so clean, so healthy. He moved like a dancer, too, sure of his actions, without wasted motion or effort. To a small-town girl like me, he was the city personified: glamour, and effortless elegance. As a matter of fact, he looked nothing like anyone I'd seen around Agua Oscura. I hadn't seen penny loafers in years, and somehow on Ivan they looked worldly, debonair. There was a glowing naturalness about the way he did things, he seemed so self-assured and able to cope. All the men I ever knew seemed helpless brats, incompetent in the matters of the world, and selfish by comparison.

Ivan picked me up at Dolores's promptly at seven. Dolores was taken aback by him, I know. I don't think she knew he'd be so good-looking and it shocked her, I could tell. Mamá came over when she saw him drive up in his Ford truck and wondered what all the commotion was about. She didn't recognize the vehicle, much less the young man who emerged from the truck carrying a bouquet of carnations. He gave several to Dolores and, when Mamá came in, a handful to her. She shooed him off with a look, but he was gracious and courteous to her. Before I knew it, we were out of the house, Dolores waving happily to me from the front door, Mamá behind her, with a curious look at his sockless feet.

We went to Evangelina's, a lounge near downtown, where on Saturdays the Desperados played. I wasn't yet twenty-one and didn't have an I.D., but Ivan got us in with the motion of his hand. He knew the bouncer, the cocktail waitresses, the bartender, and everyone sitting at the tables.

We danced nearly every dance, and I was so happy to see that he knew how to hold me right, the way Mara did when we practiced dancing together in my room and she played the man and I the woman. Ivan held me securely, without fear, his right hand high, without any sign of strain. I was a good dancer, but he was better than me. "If a man can dance," Dolores always said when watching the Lawrence Welk show, "they're really better dancers than women. The same holds true if a man can cook. *If* he can cook, a man is always a better cook than a woman. Now, your father, Soveida, he could never cook. One time I went over to his apartment, and you should have seen what he did to a cow's tongue. You know how much your dad likes tongue? It's a Dosamantes thing, I can tell you that, I was never one for tongue. Well, he'd put a tongue, and I imagine it was a good-sized one, in a pot to cook, but he'd forgotten it. All that was left was something like a miniature chicken's liver when you forget to put enough water in the pan. About the size of a small black you-know-what. And don't make me tell you what."

Ivan could dance his way around any dance floor, with any woman, and I knew that every woman in Evangelina's would have given her tongue or even part of her liver to dance with him the way he danced with me that night.

I never knew a man could be so self-possessed. All the men I'd known had been reckless, without any discipline. Ivan may not have worn socks, but his taste was otherwise impeccable.

Okay, so the outside package was divinely inspired, what about the rest of him? I had never met anyone before who called himself Chicano. I didn't know what the word Chicano meant then. I knew I was a Mexican-American and that was it. I knew vaguely that my family's roots were in México, but what did Chicano mean? To Ivan, it was a political connection with the workingman's struggle. "You just look at me and see this California guy who comes back to Agua Oscura and thinks he's the greatest thing in the world." Yes, I thought, that about covers it. "But what you don't see is what is really going on in the world. I've seen how the campesinos are breaking their backs in our lettuce fields. I've seen families torn apart by the great farm machine, and children hurt and damaged by pesticides. I know César Chávez's struggle and I've even met him. What I want to do, Soveida, is bring some of that struggle back here to New Mexico. I want to do something for my people, I mean, *really do something*. Not just talk about equality, but make some kind of impact on our life here. I mean, isn't that what we all want to do? What do you think about the farm workers' struggle?"

I honestly couldn't answer Ivan. I had never thought about the farm workers. To Luardo they were always mojados from el otro lado, and to Dolores they were people who needed jobs, jobs she let them do for her, at little pay, because she never had a man around to do the things she needed done. Mamá, too, thought little of her workers; you could see that in the thoughtless way she sometimes treated Chata, the cleaning woman, or even Oralia.

What did I think of Chicanos? The United Farm Workers? César Chávez? First of all, who were they, what did they do? I just didn't know. But in the course of that first evening with Ivan I became a Chicana. In between frenzied, passionate dances, I learned about the people I was supposed to be connected to and yet barely knew. I hardly understood what Ivan was talking about. No one cared about the Vietnam War in Agua Oscura, and when a few brave souls marched opposing the draft, I'd wondered why. I was always too busy doing something else, and when I suddenly woke up, the injured soldiers were coming home. Some of them, like Lizzie's cousin, Felipe, were shipped back in plastic bags. I don't think the Vietnam War affected me until then.

I believed in Ivan, and as a result of that, I wanted to align myself with his causes. He opened a door for me that I had seen before but never walked through, a door that led to knowledge of the outside world far beyond conservative, backward Agua Oscura. He also aroused longing and desire to be held in the warm arms of someone who had confidence in himself, in the power of his beliefs. And, God, did he know how to dance! I had never been held by someone so mature, so proud, so hopeful. All the men I knew until then were creatures injured and bruised by sunlight, men who loved the night. They operated in darkness and let it conceal their many sins. Ivan was so full of light, an archangel like Saint Michael, with his drawn sword. Not the meek and mild-mannered angel who led the small children gently over the bridge that crossed a placid stream, he was the powerful avenging angel who came to save and protect and defend. That is what I wanted then, a man to save me from myself, my shadow-filled world. Ivan was that to me, and more.

"There are two kinds of men," Dolores said to me once. "The nice ones and the ones who dance." Ivan was definitely the latter. And yet he was the first man who'd ever been a gentleman to me, bringing me flowers, opening the car door, always picking up the tab. What more could any woman want?

We left Evangelina's and drove to the scenic point above Agua Oscura where all the tourists stopped to see the Lagrimas Mountains, and parked in the nearly empty lot. It was a popular hangout on the weekends for young people. They came to make out, far above the valley floor, as close to the moon as you could get.

Ivan leaned over to kiss me and in my nervousness I averted my face and he kissed my ear. Laughing softly, he took me in his arms and kissed me with great tenderness. I felt my heart full of lights and swirling music and moved into him. Ivan Eloy Torres had touched me and no one could undo the tie. Our lips together, we molded ourselves into one another.

We first made love in my room, when Dolores and Luardo and Mamá went out of town, leaving me at home, Oralia in the Blue House looking in on me from time to time. When it was dark, Ivan tiptoed in, his truck parked down the street, a block away, so no one would know.

I was a virgin and yet I wasn't afraid. Ivan took out a condom and put it on, and I watched him as he did so. Then he took out a small bottle of tequila, "the sacred plant, to drink it makes you holy," he said, and we toasted each other.

I opened myself to Ivan, and he made me feel more beautiful than anyone had ever done. The next morning he rose early, and left the same quiet, secretive way he had come in. After that night I knew I loved him, would always love him.

My insides ached as I sang to myself: Ivan! Ivan! My thighs were weary. I walked with a proud discomfort, a woman fatigued, exultant. Could anyone see the change in me, I wondered. From the porch window I saw Oralia look out of her window, across the way, at the Blue House. No matter. My insides were pulled in tight, complete with loving.

I would call Lizzie and tell her. Tell her what had happened. That I was in love with Ivan. That he was the one. Which one? The one.

20

A Heart Full of Holes

"Soveida, ¡ven! Come and eat some watermelon with me."

Oralia yelled to me across the yard. She stood next to her wild, lush garden, triumphantly holding a large sandía.

"The watermelon will spoil," she said.

Hot, eager to be alone, I tried to make excuses. "I'm waiting for Ivan to call me." It was true. We wanted to meet one last time before Luardo and Dolores and Mamá returned home.

"How are you, m'ija? You look pale. Are you eating well? Let's go inside and have some sandía. I haven't seen you at all since everyone left us alone. Let me cut you a piece."

"I don't want much."

"Since when is the sandía I give you too much? Take this. Now hand me the flyswatter from the washroom."

"I can't stay long, Oralia. I'm waiting for a call."

"You're always in a hurry, Soveida. It's not good to be so much in a hurry that you forget to eat. ¡Diosito! The flies come in uninvited and just make themselves at home. They must have come in with me when I went out to the garden to get my herbs for Doña María. Probrecita, she's dying. There's a fly next to you. Sit still, that's it. Sssaaass! Got him!"

I sat at the old-fashioned wooden table in the kitchen that was Oralia's domain. The kitchen was large, fairly organized, and yet everything in it was slightly oily, having sat unattended and neglected for too long a time. It was evident that the two old women used the same pots and pans, the same plates, the same silverware every day. As a matter of fact, when I sat down, Oralia apologetically ran to get a long unused plate from the cabinet, rinsing it with hot water from the tap. Mamá was not the housekeeper, Oralia was, and she did the best she could, but she was already in her eighties and her eyesight was beginning to fail. I didn't think she had seen me chip off a bit of dried egg from the dish she handed me, but she had.

"Here, Soveida. Use Mamá's plate. She's not here and she'll never know. You know how your granma is about her things."

The watermelon she gave me was sweet, and full of juice. As I ate, Oralia moved around the room, killing flies with a greasy flyswatter from the Natividad Credit Union, leaving them where they fell until she could bring out her dustpan and her ancient broom, one she'd cut and wrapped herself.

Swat went the flyswatter, and another fly would drop.

"There's no hope for Doña María, Soveida. She's dying from cancer of the blood. Too many pan dulces and sugar candies. Sweets to make up for the bitterness in her life. I've tried to help her live, now all I can do is help her to die. She's a good woman, although many wouldn't say so."

"Who is she, Oralia?"

"Your grandfather Profe's other wife."

"Other wife? He had another wife? Mamá never told me."

"She was the daughter of Papá Grande's ranch hand, Don Augustín Mejía. She worked in the kitchen. She and your grandfather Profe fell in love when he was forty years old, and they had a child they named Manuelito, after your great-grandfather.

"Your grandparents had been living on Papá Grande's farm, De los Campos, which was about ten miles south of Agua Oscura. Once that farm was over five hundred acres. Now where is it? All sold. Nothing left. It's very sad. Papá Grande's oldest son, Teodelfiño, wanted to be a judge. How could a Mexicano from Agua Oscura become a judge? Impossible! Teo enlisted in the army to get away. Then the news came that he had been killed at Castigny. Papá Grande never recovered from that stab wound. He had wanted Teo to take over the farm. You should have seen the way he carried on with the corpse! He slept in the sala with the body for three days, until it was time to bury it. When Teo died, the responsibility of the farm fell to your granpa Profe. He thought he would eventually inherit the farm, but when Manuelito was born, Papá Grande divided it equally between Profe and the girls, Amparinata and Ismindalia.

"Your granpa Profe was so angry that he moved with your granma

Lupita into town. Then he built his grocery store, La Esquina Market. That was the beginning of your grandfather's food stores, the end of the Dosamantes' farms, the beginning of Papá Grande's bad health, and the end of whatever peace there ever was in the Dosamantes family. Do you want more sandía? It's good, isn't it?"

"So what happened next, Oralia?"

"If there's sandía, there's flies. You can't have one without the other. It's like love. I never married. It's not that I didn't want to. But the man I loved didn't love me. María never married, either. She was a beautiful woman, but she wasn't refined, like your granma. She wasn't a lady. Well, that's what everyone thought. And I admit, I used to think that, too. Profe set her and Manuelito up in a small house and everyone lived without talking about certain things.

"When your granpa Profe died, the base that supported María's spine gave way as if a willow's trunk had snapped inside her chest. Her posture twisted overnight, and her shoulders caved in. The children called her La Jorobada, the Hunchbacked Hag. A witch. Some believed, like Señora Rascana, her neighbor, that she was a demon worshipper. No one could explain the strange odors that came from that crumbling house: cinnamon mixed with coal, comino, and decaying flesh. There were screeches and whimpering, sounds that would make you crazy just to hear them. Soveida, it's a long story."

"Go on, Oralia, tell me. You can't stop now!"

"What about your telephone call?"

"Go on, tell me the rest."

"Most stories are sad when you get to telling them, but anyway, what is life but stories? Some just a little sadder than others. I was there, Soveida, working first for Papá Grande and then later for your grandfather Profe. But I never knew the real story. Not until María shared it with me. She's needed someone to talk to, and I've listened. It breaks my heart to see her die this way. Yet she says she would do it all over again. She served food to the Dosamantes family. When Profe would ask her to bring him something, she would always forget.

" 'María, my drink,' or 'Where's my bread?' he'd say, and she would giggle and then forget to bring his bread. She was not a good server, like her mother, Doña Luz. She was too full of pride to ever bow to anyone, master or not.

"It was a summer night. A party to celebrate new land. There was music and drinking and all the rest that goes with celebrations: overeating, sleepiness for some, melancholy for others. Everyone had gone to bed: all the children, all the adults, anyone who was old or tired or still nursing or sleepy. Only Profe was awake.

"Doña Luz worked in the kitchen while María gathered the dinner dishes, humming to herself: 'Cuando me encuentres, amorcito, no me dejes, nunca.'

"Profe stopped her as she made her way past the darkened living room.

" 'María, come here,' he said.

" 'Good night, Don Profetario.'

" 'Do you want a glass of wine? Here, I'll turn on the lamp.'

" 'No, thank you, I don't drink. Can I get you something, Don Profetario?'

" 'Everyone is asleep. How quiet it is!'

" 'Good night, then.'

" 'Wait, María. Please. Sit here, for just a moment. Now listen to me, don't say anything.'

" 'Don Profetario . . .'

" 'Nothing, don't say a thing, María . . . Just listen to me.'

"Soveida, a person gets so tired of her past trailing her like a hungry animal, one that whimpers until it is fed. Unless you heal yourself of memories when you are alive, there is no telling what death will bring. That poor woman never had anyone to talk to, it's no wonder her blood is hot and full of worms. Or that she has that hunchback full of worries that she's carried alone through her sad life.

"When she talks to me, I feel as if I were there with her as well. She remembered how Profe's words were music from another world, and all she could do was listen.

" 'My heart is full of holes,' he said to her, and she knew exactly what he meant.

"There was no turning back.

"He loved her and she loved him. And no one could ever change that: no wife, no children, not the Dosamantes earth, not even Papá Grande, nor Agua Oscura, nor the people who lived there and would later call her a whore.

"Do you ever wonder what la Santísima Virgen felt when the angel called out to her and said: Your womb is full and what you carry inside of you is God?

"That is what she clings to. Imagine it, Soveida, when the pain becomes too much, and she spits out her own poisoned blood that comes from the soles of her feet and rises to her heart and then her head. I hold her hand, give her my teas, and try to get her to rest, at least a little while, until she can breathe again.

"Pobrecita, she still lives inside that summer night, when all life closed in on her, then became a spiraling tunnel at the end of which stood Profe Dosamantes, an unlikely, desperate lover. I know that when she dies she will see him. She and I never married. Both of us knowing love like that, born out of hopelessness, and rage against fate."

"Oralia! You're crying!"

"Excuse me, Soveida, but I told you, it's a sad story. There"—she turned back to the work at hand—"I got the last mosca. He couldn't escape. Bring me the dustpan and my broom. How was your sandía? Full of seeds, or sweet?"

"Let me clean up, Oralia. Por favor."

"You love him, Soveida, don't you?"

"What?"

"You love that boy? The one who comes to see you?"

"Oralia . . ."

"Do you?"

"Yes."

"That's all I need to know. Now let me take Mamá's plate and wash it. She'll want everything in place. Promise me, Soveida, that you'll listen to the stories women tell you. They are the ones you should remember. Otherwise, how will you ever expect to understand the human heart?"

21

The Mouse Woman

I left Oralia at the Blue House and walked home, lost in thought. I went straight to my room, lay on my bed, and reviewed everything she had said. I'd realized that day that I was falling deeply in love with Ivan, and somehow I'd sensed Oralia's concern. But would I be like the little gray mouse Oralia used to tell Mara and me about when we were children?

"There was a little gray mouse who saw a pot boiling on the stove," Oralia had said as we sat in her kitchen. "Twice its mother told her not to look into the pot, to be careful. The third time the curious mouse peered into the pot, fell in, and became mouse stew. The moral of the story is: Little girls or little mice can sometimes be too curious for their own good."

"It's such a sad story, Oralia! Don't you feel sorry for the little mouse?" I asked.

"No, and you know why, Soveida?" Oralia said. "The mouse was muy traviesa, so naughty she didn't listen to consejos. You and Mara, on the other hand, you listen to me and I'll help you when I can. When you begin to get into things that you shouldn't, most often they will hurt you. But enough about mice, bring me the calabaza from the countertop, and you and Mara can help me roll out the dough for the empanaditas."

Oralia cleaned the table with a washrag, dried it, and then spread flour all over the table surface. She then brought over a large ball of masa and with easy, rhythmic motions folded the dough into itself and then plucked off little clumps, ending up with ten perfectly shaped balls. Oralia's dough was unlike anyone else's; it had such elasticity, and could meld into any shape. The rest of the dough she put aside, covering it with a clean dishrag.

Handing Mara and me two small rolling pins, "children's size," that she had carved out of wood, Oralia gave us each five dough balls to roll out. Mine held such promise, but after a few moves of the rolling pin they were already distorted and misshapen and looked more like elongated islands than like circular worlds.

"The trick is in the turn," Oralia said, showing us. "You have to keep turning the tortilla as you work it."

"I can't do it, Oralia," I protested, gathering up two ugly islands and plopping them down next to the three remaining balls in my pile.

"Like this? Is this what you mean?" Mara said, rolling out her first masa ball slowly and carefully. It didn't look too bad.

"That's the way. Now you try it again, Soveida."

As much as Oralia tried to teach me, I never did learn to make a decently shaped tortilla. They always ended up looking like a map of Cuba or Puerto Rico. They were stiff, too, and never folded well, the way they were supposed to. On top of that, they were ugly.

"Don't give up, Soveida!" Oralia encouraged me. "Someday you'll get it right."

It was just like Oralia, coaxing me to learn something right, something I always thought I could never master. It was she who taught me to make tamales, showing me how much masa to put on the corn husks and how long to cook the red chile with pork that went inside.

"Who cares about making tamales?" I had said to her. "We're Americans."

Oralia stopped stirring the pork at her wood-burning stove, which was right next to the new gas stove Luardo had bought Mamá for Christmas, and faced me sternly.

"Soveida, let me look at your hands. There. Now turn them over. Now hold them out a ways. You may be an American in your little finger, but the rest of your hand is brown, like mine. And that means you're an India like me, although Mamá Lupita might not agree with me. She's got her Indian blood as well, and she knows it, only she won't admit it. Now bring me the hojas and call Mara and Dolores. We're ready to spread the masa. This job calls for every woman on hand. Call Hector, too, he can help as well. No reason why he can't learn to make tamales, just because he's a boy."

Standing in a circle around Mamá's old green Formica-top table, Dolores, Mamá, Mara, and I spread the masa on the hojas, placing a little bit of chile pork in the middle. Oralia folded the tamales in her special way and put them in a large steamer. Hector punched a lump of dough with a spoon, sticking his thumb into the center of his ball, and then rolled it out again.

I remember those many times in Oralia's kitchen, making empanadas, sealing the edges with fork grooves, or boiling oil to just the right heat so that the sopaipillas puffed up high once they touched the hot grease. Oralia's only attempts at cooking American were her donas, special doughnuts she made from canned biscuits, with the center punched out with a thimble. She fried them in hot grease and then turned them over in brown sugar.

I always associated Oralia with food, and with the smells in her kitchen: hot grease, comino, oregano, canela. You couldn't call it Mamá's kitchen, for, although it was Mamá's house, the kitchen belonged to Oralia. It wasn't a large kitchen, but it was large enough for the two stoves, which sat side by side. The first year Oralia refused to use the gas oven, preferring instead to use her faithful cast-iron, wood-burning stove. She said it cooked mexicano and that was what concerned her. "If you want to make gringo macarrón, and white bread, well then the new stove is what you want, but for my tortillas and my frijolitos, there's nothing better than wood."

Little by little, though, she began to use the gas oven for certain things, "because it's easier and I don't have to cut so much wood." One thing Oralia did still cook on her old stove was her morning atole, the blue corn mush she ate every day. Gradually she began to cook other meals on the new stove, but always in her old cast-iron pan, her one and only and favorite, the one she called Jesusita. "No gray plastic pans that say they don't stick. Just let me look at the stomach of a person who uses them."

When Oralia cooked her meals in her little yellow kitchen, she always made an extra olla for us. Oftentimes, when Mara and I got home from school, we'd go straight there. She would wrap her tortillas in a clean dishrag she had embroidered herself, and place them in a round straw basket. We'd warm the tortillas directly on the gas flame, and when they were hot, we'd melt butter on them.

I rarely saw Oralia eat; she usually ate alone, when everyone else finished. Sometimes she ate in the little alcove off the kitchen, a small bowl in her hands, as she sat on a kitchen step chair, waiting nearby in case someone needed her. When Mamá called her, she'd put down her little bowl still full of uneaten food and attend to us.

Only once do I remember sitting down to eat with Oralia, the two of us facing each other at the little kitchen table. Oralia ate very slowly, she didn't have a full set of teeth, and yet she ate in a delicate and ladylike way. With her, there was never any excess. She served herself small portions, never quite a full plate, and yet she said it was enough for her. "I eat a little less than I always want, or could eat, and somehow it fills me up," she told me.

Oralia was always wonderful company, whether on a cold winter day, shelling peas quietly in the yellow kitchen, telling her wonderful stories, or, on a hot summer afternoon, making tortillas, which she served with her homemade lemonade. When you were sick, she would appear with her ponches, her special punches made with egg whites. To her, the white of an egg had special healing powers. Once, when I burned the back of my calf on a heating grate, she came over to give me a treatment with an egg white, spreading it over my burned flesh, and telling me it wouldn't scar. And it didn't.

Oralia was famous for her medicinal teas, especially a blend she called té del caballo negro. A concoction all her own, it was made from herbs she grew in her little garden, which thrived between our two houses.

She was also an excellent masseuse. No one gave a sobada, a deep rub, like Oralia, with her warm, strong fingers, which she used as prongs to gouge, press, and pull away pain. She was a firm believer in Absorbine, Jr., and used that liniment on all sorts of muscular aches, one of her few concessions to the twentieth century.

When she wasn't cooking, she was busy cleaning the pebbles out of a pot of beans, weeding her garden patiently every day, or sweeping the ground in front of Mamá's house until the earth shone like skin, work she found joyful and never monotonous. She performed her tasks with a sense of novelty, even if it was for the thousandth time and she knew every nuance and permutation of the job at hand.

But, for all her compassion and understanding, Oralia was a disciplinarian, and she could be hard on us. In the summertime, she was the designated nap enforcer and would round Hector, Mara, and me up to take us to our respective rooms. She made us lie down as she said her dark rosary for the world, moving occasionally from room to room, as we fought sleep in that long, interminable afternoon.

It was then I resented Oralia's presence like a dusty old watch ticking away the time. And yet there was something reassuring about her hovering in a nearby corner as we fell into a deep, damp sleep. To wake up to Oralia was good, too, for she was always cheerful and prayed over anything you did or said, bestowing a blessing on every act. Every utterance of hers was prefaced with a "Si Dios quiere," or "Con el favor de Dios," or "Dios primero." If God wants, with God's favor, God first. That was her way.

She herself slept near Mamá, in a former utility room that had been made into a bedroom. Spartan, austere, it looked like something you'd see in a religious order: a large crucifix over the bed, a dark wooden bureau with a statue of Jesus, his Sacred Heart exposed and bleeding, a supply of the previous year's dried palms from Palm Sunday laced through Christ's arms. In the center of a table next to her bed was a small loaf of holy bread in a small glass bowl. The bed was covered by a thin brown blanket and the pillow was an old cushion Mamá had thrown out years before. The door to Oralia's room was always slightly ajar; she never kept it closed. We knew it was off-limits, and yet Mara and I couldn't resist peering in. There was an unassailable smell, pungent as raw vinegar and roots.

No taller than four feet six inches in her black, old-lady shoes from another era, an apron covering her simple, dark, long-sleeved dress, her back as small as a child's in front of her magical stove, Oralia was a world to me. Her soft high voice like rustling leaves, her hands like gloves, kind and loving when they should be, comforting when you needed warmth. I really believed that when you ate her food you became a better person. Her little kitchen hummed in the heart of Mamá's house, *was* the heart of Mamá's house.

As I lay in bed, I thought of Oralia's fairy tales, always full of mystery and darkness—things one never talked about in daylight. Was I the little gray mouse peering at the edge of the boiling water? Was I getting into something I shouldn't, something that would hurt me?

22

Larry Larragoite

"I hear you're getting married on us, Soveida. Does that mean you'll still be working here, or are you going to stay home now and knit baby booties?"

"Connie! Of course I'm staying here. I mean, for a while. Ivan wants me to quit, but I don't want to. Anyway, the wedding's in three months."

"Just elope. That's what me and Larry's dad did. We had a hell of a great wedding. Too bad the marriage went downhill from there. I always have a great wedding, come to think of it. The one to Willie was fantastic, and my last one, and I mean *last one*, to Herman Bexler was one of the best parties I've ever been to. But day-to-day marriage, forget it. I was never meant to marry."

"I'm very happy, Connie."

"That's what I said, until I found out Eddie was two-timing me with half the day and one-third of the night waitresses. Not to mention the hostess he got pregnant. Ivan's a pretty man and pretty men are dangerous. You have to think about these things long and hard before you tie the knot, Soveida. I mean it. Thank God my Larry's un poco feo, not that he's *that* ugly, but you know, a pretty man goes far, too far. Come on, is there anything that would make you change your mind about marrying Ivan? You can tell me. Door's closed, no one is listening. He can't be *that* perfect."

I didn't tell Connie, but if there was someone who wasn't perfect, it was me, not Ivan. I always felt he was watching me from afar, like he was hidden behind a tree, watching the way I did things. If I thought about it too long I became afraid, knowing that I could never meet his expectations.

Ivan didn't like the way I ate my eggs. Fried medium, with the yolk still soft, but the white a little crispy. Once the egg was on my plate, I'd mash it up into a pile, salting it heavily. He thought my method uncultured.

Another thing he disliked was my posture. He worried I would end up hunchbacked and suggested I buy a back brace.

"You have a bust." And by then I did. "Show it off, Soveida!"

"That's not it, Ivan," I said. But it probably was. Low-cut blouses were never for me.

Ivan began to take more notice of what I wore. Sometimes he disliked my clothes and let me know it in no uncertain terms. The wonderful pink-and-orange crushed-velour pantsuit Dolores gave me for Christmas was out. "Too cheap." The black one-piece bathing suit was "too matronly." The skirts were "too long," the boots "not the right color." The white peasant blouses and multicolored skirts I wore were "too Mexican." My hair needed to be cut one day and the next day I should let it grow long. I should wear more makeup or less, depending on how he felt.

As far as being pretty, he was. And he was faithful. He told me so and I believed him. I doubted at that time that he had energy left for any other woman. Our sex life was so good.

Ivan said he wanted me to be myself, and that he was giving me the greatest gift any man could give to a woman. Freedom. He said our love would never be tinged with jealousy or spite or any sort of disharmony. I was free. He was free. We both were free, singly and together.

Ivan never realized that I would go anywhere with him, do anything to be with him, leave any place, any person, anytime, to be with him. And that this fact would never change. His greatest gift to me was what terrified me the most.

So I never wore the pink-and-orange pantsuit, and finally gave it away. I ate my eggs scrambled, tried to walk straight, bought a two-piece bathing suit we both picked out, raised my hems, and had a Mary Kay makeover, with makeup styled for both day and night. I gave my comfortable white panties and my long flannel nightgowns to Goodwill and purchased my first pair of bikini underwear. Some unidentified animal print.

There were just some things I could never tell Connie. Anyone. The wedding date was set, the invitations were at the printer's, and by God, I was getting married.

"I was just wondering, Soveida. I always wished someone had taken me aside those three times and asked me some good hard questions. They would have saved me some heartache. The only good thing that came out of it all was Larry. Now he's the boss of El Farol and I just come in to get my paycheck. I'm glad you're staying, dear. Larry needs you more than he knows. Watch him, will you? The older I get, the more I think he reminds me of Eddie."

"I'm not leaving, Connie, don't worry."

"Just remember, when the mierda starts accumulating in between the grooves of your wedding ring that the only thing that matters is the work. Keep working. It saw me through the pain, the divorces, through the good nights and the bad. I gotta go. I'm going to the travel agent to pick up my reservations. Me and Herman are going on a cruise to the Bahamas. Yeah, I know what you're thinking. And the answer is no. We are *not* remarrying. It's just our divorce anniversary. We both get sentimental. Like I tell him, honey, let's get together about once a year. Maybe every three months. Keep the romance alive. Bueno. I gotta go. The best of luck to you, Soveida. I mean it, girl, you'll need it."

Connie was right about many things.

Milia had been right, too. I was now the headwaitress and Larry was now the owner and sole proprietor of El Farol.

Still referring to all women as "girls," Larry, for all practical reasons, was still a "boy." Some men hardly seem to age, and Larry was one of them. Oh, there was a slight, almost indiscernible stooping, a bowing in the back, but that was all. His face was soft, unlined, the eyes clear, the teeth sound. Larry was thin, too thin perhaps, but he seemed fit, although he did no exercise that anyone knew about, none at all. He was a walker, a pacer, a mover, restless, and relentless. Activity was his wife, anxiety his mistress. He was twenty-seven. He felt seventy. Inside, his heart ticked, ever tired, now and then skipping a beat. He had a cot installed in his office. The heart thing would come on, he'd hurry back, close the door, lie down, and try to breathe normally. Arrhythmia, irregular heartbeat, was the medical term, but he always had excuses. Must have been the red enchiladas he ate for lunch. Hell, he worked too hard. And it didn't happen often, he'd tell me.

"I'm a young man, a boy, full of life. It's harder for guys. Girls, all they have to do—you know. Turn on the charm. Bat the eyes. Lower the lids. Pucker those lips. Straighten their backs. Smile."

Connie had handed El Farol Restaurant over to Larry, lock, stock, and barrel, when Larry was just a few days short of receiving his M.B.A. He'd gone back East to Vermont because his uncle, Milo Larragoite —or, as he chose to be known there, Mr. Laragotte (pronounced the French way)—lived there, and because Connie secretly didn't want him to marry a Mexican. Connie's first marriage had been to a Mexican, Eddie Larragoite, Larry's dad, but he had left her for countless other women, and she couldn't take it anymore. One day Connie just walked out with Larry and never went back.

Larry told me that his mom thought that if he got far enough away from the state he'd meet someone nice. And that meant someone *Anglo*. To Connie there were two main races: Anglo and Mexican. She was a *Mexican Mexican*, a once-middle, now-upper-class American who was proud of her Mexican roots, just make sure they're clean and don't shove them in my face. And please, don't start playing no honky-tonk-whiney-cowstomping-lovelorn Mexican polkas on me and expect me to start wearing a brown beret. Eddie had been a Mexican Mexican. He spoke with a broken accent. He and Connie had both grown up in Chiva Town, they were neighbors, and he always loved his corrido two-steps and his all-night drunks in Juárez, where after the second beer he would sing along with the mariachis. Not only that, but he was a card-carrying member of La Raza Unida. The combination could never work.

Larry said she'd taken him aside and laid down the facts.

"Larry, I know from experience the hell from which I am saving you. I'm saving my grandchildren, hopefully all girls, from the badness in the blood and genes. I want them to find men who will appreciate them, the way Willie LaPoint and Herman Bexler appreciated me. Not that I didn't love Eddie, goddamn I loved that man, even though he had athlete's feet from the war. I know what it is to love a man with stenchy, moldy feet. The man was the best lover I've ever had. I could have lived with his gold teeth and musky, putrid feet, but he just wasn't dependable. If Eddie wasn't dipping his fingers into the cash box, he was monkeying around with the hostesses and waitresses. It was either Eddie and my sex life or your future, son. I really tried to work it out. Eddie had his past and present, and what future was there for an out-and-out in-and-out? You, on the other hand, were my firstborn, my only born. To this day, I can't eat red chile. The night you were born, I ate a plate of red enchiladas which Chilo the cook had prepared for me. I was up and about until the very last moment, and firmly believe Chilo's chile brought the labor on. And what a labor it was! Later the next day, the hospital staff was still cleaning up chile from the floor. I can't look at red chile now without thinking of you, and of my decision, then and there, to tie my tubes. No man nowhere is ever going to cause me that pain again, red chile or not! I love you, son, but I swear to you, Blessed Mother Queen of Angels, on my mother's grave, it hurt like hell. Don't you ever tell me that the pain was worth it. I love you, but, goddammit, no way in hell, forgive me, little Mother, any man, especially one I love, gonna do that to me ever again, may I burn in an everlasting hell full of unfaithful, lying-through-their-teeth men, no man ever gonna do that to me.

"Eddie Larragoite just wasn't husband material. Lover material, maybe, but not husband and father material. No sooner had we gotten divorced than I heard that he'd moved to California and gotten married. Now he has three daughters that look like him. Bastard. I fared better with husbands number 2 and 3, Willie LaPoint and Herman Bexler, each of them rich Anglos who knew how to treat a woman. And yet there was that nagging worm in my soul whose name was Eddie Larragoite. Even now, when I close my eyes, I can still smell that sweet-sour wave of crusty yellow putrefaction that the man I still love—wherever and whoever he was—calls his feet. The feet of an old miner, a gone-to-seed sportsman, a prisoner-of-war, they were the feet of Eddie Larragoite. The only man I ever loved. The only man I swore I ever wanted to grow old with. The only man who gave me his seed, a seed I allowed to remain in my flesh."

Larry eventually moved to Vermont and his Uncle Milo Larragoite did help him out. Milo had married blond and was part of the Eastern establishment, a success with his swimming-pool-equipment business.

"In Vermont?"

"You know New Mexico, I know Vermont, Con. You leave me mine and you keep yours."

"If you want to go and sell swimming pools in Vermont, go for it. You make a great living, and that's all that matters," Connie told him.

Sure enough, Larry met someone in Vermont. Someone female, someone blond. Her name was Bonnie McNuff, a classmate of Milo's half-blond daughter, Yvette, who went to Bennington. All of Milo's children, Monique, Jean Yves, and Yvette, loved the French language and had studied it at school.

Bonnie thought Larry was an Arab. It was only logical. She knew that the French had been in Morocco. Lar was dark-haired, dark-skinned, and he had a mustache.

"I'm Spanish, Bonnie."

"Funny, Yvette never told me."

"I don't think she knows, Bonnie."

"Your parents were born in Spain?"

"Well, no, they originally came up from Mexico, but I was born in New Mexico and Larragoite is a name common in—"

"You're Mexican."

"No, Spanish."

"But you said—"

"I'm Spanish. A Spanish white man."

"You're the first Spanish Mexican—I mean Spanish white man I have ever met and known, Lar." She called him Lar, pronounced lair and rhyming with bear.

"No kidding!"

"Yeah!"

"Golly, Lar!"

"Yeah. Golly."

There weren't too many Mexicans in Vermont. Bonnie was intrigued. She'd never met a real honest-to-goodness Mexican, I mean, Spanish Mexican or Spanish white man, in all her life. Lar was so different, though, she wasn't even sure what a Spanish Mexican should be like, but Lar was so cute. She was definitely interested. Larry had many adorable little ways, ways that others might find actually annoying. To Bonnie, they were part and parcel of the man she now loved. For example, his chronic gum chewing, bubble popping, toothpick sucking, ear cleaning, eye wiping, nail chewing, surreptitious nose picking— the list went on and on. He was like an adorable little monkey. *Her* monkey.

Bonnie was a tall, muscular woman with strong blond-haired legs, ample thighs, and large, swollen breasts. She was always in a semi-excited menstrual state of engorged sexuality. She was attracted to Lar, there were no two ways about it.

Lar, by contrast, was thin, chicken-legged, brooding, and hairy. He wore glasses, and he had always been attracted to large, swollen-breasted blondes. In fact, his heart, soul, and lips were made for swollen-breasted blondes. It was a perfect match.

Bonnie had been majoring in architecture, but after she met Lar, she switched her major to Spanish, with a minor in Home Ec.

"Why not?"

"It's not necessary, for chrissakes, Bonnie! New Mexico *is* part of the U.S."

"I know, Lar, but I need to be able to talk to your family."

"Herman is Anglo and Mother talks English!"

"What about the others? Your tíos and tías, the abuelitas and the sobrinos?"

"There are no others, Bonnie! I'm an only child. My father, well, let's forget him. And Mother only has her brother-in-law, Milo. His Spanish, well, let's face it, his French is better than his Spanish. Everyone speaks English, this is the U.S., for pete's sakes. Hell, I don't speak Spanish, Bonnie, why should you?"

"That's not the point, Lar. The point is, honey, you're Mexican, I mean Spanish Mexican, and I won't be a token Larragoite! And I mean, I mean, I mean really, how can a Mexican not talk Spanish?"

"Hell, I can't speak well. Hell, I can barely speak at all! Just drop it, would you?"

Larry wasn't kidding. This was the same Larry Larragoite who had ordered chocolata caca for dessert at Maxim's in Mexico City on his seventeenth birthday, where he'd gone with Connie, and her then husband, Willie LaPoint. The waiter was disgusted, but Willie, who spoke impeccable Spanish, had gotten a hoot out of it. Larry never forgave Willie for laughing at him, and he persuaded Connie that Willie was nothing short of loud-mouthed, crude, and thoughtless. In reality, that wasn't true. Connie later realized what a gem Willie had been, how delightful, charming, and vivacious. At the time of the chocolata-caca episode Connie had sided with Larry. What marriage can survive the hatred of a maligned and revengeful son?

From there on in, until he returned finally to New Mexico with Bonnie at his side, Lar had refused to speak Spanish. Now Bonnie was teaching him, correcting him, and he was learning. If you call "Pablo tiene un lápiz azul" Spanish.

After they married and moved back to New Mexico, it was Bonnie who really ran the restaurant, who hired and fired and reprimanded the staff—in Spanish—who could be heard swapping jokes with Chuy, the custodian—in Spanish—and who praised the staff—all in Spanish. Lar still couldn't speak much, only what he'd picked up from Bonnie. He avoided the food, because it gave him gas. He loved red enchiladas but they always made him sick. He wondered if it might be a family curse. Besides, he thought of himself as a steak man all the way. He could pronounce what was on the menu and describe it at length, though even then he spoke with an accent.

"En-chill-ya-dah. A rolled tor-till-ya with a green sal-sah sauce," he explained to a customer.

"Empinada. It's a greasy Mexican egg roll," he counseled another, until the day I corrected him.

"Larry, it's not empinada. In New Mexico empinarse means to squat. It's an empanada, an empanada!"

"Dammit, Soveida! Here Preddie Pacheco the dishwasher, that little prick, had me calling them empinadas for so long! Some Spanish tutor! Never trust a dishwasher, that's what I say. No wonder all the old ladies looked the other way. What do you expect from a Mexican who washes dishes for a living? Mom is right about that. Preddie Pacheco. Shit! The food slush is part of his brain already. But it isn't only the food slush, it's more than that. It's the years of food slush, years of soapy, watery congested dreams. In fact, whatever dreams the guy must have had, probably still has, are floating in front of him, suspended in that filmy, greasy, reddish-colored water that clogs and traps him. The problem is that Preddie Pacheco is definitely what my mother would call a Mexican Mexican."

"Jesus, Larry!" I said to him. "What's *your* problem."

What was Larry's problem? He was a Spanish white man.

23

The Man with Chicken Feet

"Tuna fish? I don't want any, Mamá. I'm not eating tuna fish on my wedding day."

"What's wrong with you, Soveida? You haven't eaten tuna fish ever since you took up con ese fulano. I've been keeping track. Look, your mother has the sandwiches already made. See how pretty they look, cut in four, with parsley stems on the side. Ay, que cute, a toothpick with an olive going through the middle."

"I don't want tuna, Mamá."

"She fixed it the way you like it with mayonesa and the onion finito finito, so finely chopped, the way only your mother can make it. You've been eating it for twenty-two years, since you were a baby. Do you think you're too old to eat it now? Gracias, Dolores. Just put the plate down, she'll eat it. Oh, Dolores, bring me some chilito, will you, for my sandwich?"

"Take it away, please, Dolores. I can't eat tuna. It smells, and with the onion it smells more. I can't eat it!"

"Egg then, Soveida. I'll fix you an egg sandwich."

"Dolores, she has the tuna, bring it back, let her eat the tuna."

"Egg smells. I can't eat egg!"

"Since when do eggs smell, Soveida? This is the child who always wanted a fried egg for breakfast, lunch, and dinner. Bring me an egg, Dolores, let me smell it. It doesn't smell!"

"I can't eat eggs, they're too feathery, please!"

"You're not going to eat anything, Soveida?"

"I can't. Not what there is, anyway. Not now. No fish, no eggs, no smells."

"Since when is she so necia, Dolores?"

"Listen to me, Soveida, you need something. It's going to be a very long day."

"Leave her alone, Dolores. My mother, Eduvijes, she used to say, if you're hungry, you'll eat. Take the tuna away, Dolores, she isn't hungry. She doesn't want to eat. If she were hungry, she'd eat."

"Do you want frijoles, Soveida? I got some beans I can give you."

"I don't want beans, Dolores."

"Bring me some beans for my chilito, will you? Don't offer her food, Dolores, she's not hungry."

"Bread, do we have any bread, Dolores?"

"Bread? What are you, a bird, Soveida? You'll get empache, your stomach will bloat up and then the bread will clog up your guts. You don't want to do that. You won't have a movement for days. You'll have to resort to something artificial. ¡Ni lo mande Dios! No man or woman should be using tratamientos to induce something that should be natural. Look at me: an old lady. You think to yourself: has she ever used artificial means? Do I look like I would? No! Well, I have. Once. And I can tell you, it's a lot worse than empache or even childbirth. I won't go into the details, but it set me back a long time. It almost killed me. I was sick for days. I had to practically live outdoors, and it was in the winter. It should be a lesson to you. Don't mess with your body. God knows why he does such and such and why he made this or that or why this goes this way or that the other. It's not good to affect this or that with that other thing or this. Do you understand me? Don't bring her bread, Dolores. Se va tapar, she'll get plugged up. And that wouldn't be good. Not on her wedding day. You have to listen to your body. And it says it needs to eat, Soveida. Bring me a few tortillas to mop up my beans, Dolores, and sit down. You're making me dizzy with all your going back and forth. Leave the plate there. If she's hungry she'll eat. When you don't listen to your body, it gets you in trouble. If it gets angry enough, watch out! It can betray you.

"When I was a girl, en el año del oso, in the year of the bear, as my father used to say, I heard tell about one of el Señor Zertuche's nieces from Rinconcito. She came to visit her uncle for a few weeks, and met a local boy, Adán Fuentes. His father was from Agua Oscura, they'd been here for years. The poor innocent niece comes to visit and she turns the Fuentes boy's head around until he was looking the other way. He was good-looking, but a good-for-nothing. And yet all the girls were crazy about him. He was older than me—my sister Esperanza's age. Oh, he was a wild one, promising this and that to all the

Agua Oscura girls, and never keeping his word. Un vividor, your mother knows what I mean, Soveida. The niece, I've forgotten her name, she was from the rancho, a pretty girl, sweet, but stupid. What could she know about society anyway, way out there in Rinconcito, with the cows? What could she know about life, the way things were done? She was so dumb where men are concerned, she consented to go on a pickinicky."

"I think the word is picnic, Mamá."

"They went on a pickinicky in a buggy to La Sierra de las Uvas. Adán had his plans, no one else had ever refused him, why should she? Let's go for a walk, he said. So they did, but later, Mela, Melina, she came running out of the trees covered with leaves and thorns, her long blond hair flying. Her clothing was torn, and she was screaming: He wants to marry me, he wants to marry me! She was a sonsa, a fool! She thought that was what men did when they want to marry you! Poor Adán was shocked! Yes, she was a virgin and she stayed a virgin! All the other girls were loose with him, but not Melina. Adán turned around and straightened up and courted her after that, like a gentleman, and he married her! Melinda was her name. Melinda Mediera from Rinconcito. The only one who could tame Adán Fuentes! But the story doesn't end there.

"On the day of her wedding, Melinda was still pretty stupid, even though the women had talked to her the night before and told her: Just lay there, you'll get used to it. She was all dressed up in her store shoes and wedding dress, looking like an angel. She had to go to the bathroom, but she didn't want anyone to know. So she held it and held it. She didn't want people to see her dragging that dress with its train to the outhouse! She was afraid to tell anyone, least of all her new husband, that she needed to make chee. She was ashamed, as if it wasn't a natural thing. Well, maybe it wasn't in that dress! Tontita, she held it all that morning and all that afternoon and by that night she was already sick. In those days the wedding went on all day, all night, and all the next day. Well, Melinda made it to the baile, but then she was struck down. Finally, no se aguantó, she couldn't stand it, and when she went to make pipi, she couldn't go, not then, nor for several days. She was poisoned inside. Ignorant, stupid, silly girl from Rinconcito!

"So you listen to me, Soveida Dosamantes, you better eat, and you better go to the bathroom, lace or no lace. Ay, m'ija, but you don't have to go through with this. It's not too late, Soveida. You can call it off. We still have time. Eat your tuna fish, anyway. Marriage or not, you need your strength!"

"All right, Mamá, I'll eat the tuna, but I have a feeling I'll be sorry!"

"Your mamá's tuna is the best. It's one of the best things you make, Dolores, that and your cherry Jell-O peanut-butter and cottage-cheese dessert."

"Thank you, Mamá!"

"Why so quiet, Dolores? You'd think you were getting married, instead of Soveida. You look sad."

"I'm not sad, Mamá."

"It's me who should be sad. Soveida was supposed to become a nun. What happened?"

"I don't know, Mamá. It just didn't happen."

"You stopped going to early-morning Mass with me, that's what happened."

"Does anyone want another sandwich? Mamá? Soveida?"

"Do we have any pickles?"

"Pickles?"

"Pickles like in pickle?"

"Don't give me that look! I'm *not* pregnant!"

"Sssh, por favor, let's not talk about things like that, not today. Of course you're not pregnant, Soveida. What's wrong with you, Dolores? Bring your daughter some more olives and some pickles, it's her wedding day."

"First and last!"

"It has to be that way, m'ija. It's God's law. So where is he? The one who made you leave the Holy Orders behind?"

"Ivan Eloy?"

"El mismo, the one and the same."

"I don't know, Mamá. At home, I guess."

"Well, is he coming here first or are you meeting at the church?"

"I don't know. He's meeting me there, I guess. I forgot to ask him. We'll leave the dishes, Mamá."

"No, señorita, we're going to do them now, Soveida."

"Can we finish up here? I have to get ready. Where's my dress?"

"In the bathroom, Soveida."

"What is it doing in there?"

"I was steaming it!"

"What happened that it needed steaming? Was it wrinkled or what?"

"Hector closed the hall door and it fell off the hanger."

"Oh, God!"

"God had nothing to do with it, Soveida. Don't you take God's name in vain, especially on your wedding day. Do you want this marriage to be cursed?"

"So that's it, Hector leaves the dress on the floor? Where is he?"

"He's gone to work."

"Well, he better show up at Our Lady of Grace on time. He's the head usher."

"What about el arrimado, the moocher? Are you sure he's meeting you at the church?"

"I wish you wouldn't call him that, Mamá. He's got a name. Ivan Eloy! Ivan Eloy! He's my husband!"

"To be. The day isn't over yet, m'ija!"

"Do we have to start this again, Mamá? I know you don't like him."

"He's a nobody. The father's dead and the mother thinks she's Katy Jurado. They're all nobodies. He's not what you call successful. Success is not working at the Motor Vehicle Department giving people driving tests."

"He's the manager!"

"What if there's children? Can he provide for them?"

"Enough, Mamá. Please! It's Soveida's wedding day. We've been through all of this before! She's going to marry Eloy."

"Ivan Eloy."

"And there's nothing you or I can do about it, Mamá."

"She thinks she loves him. But he's the kind of man who's got chicken feet. When I was a girl, this good-looking man came to a dance at Manuel Dosamantes's barn. He was very beautiful as only some men can be. Nobody knew him. All the women were drawn to him, irregardless of age. He danced all night, first with one and then another. Oh, he was a good dancer! The band played on, if you could call it a band: Tito Tenorio on guitar, Felipe Armendariz on violin, another guitarra played by El Pelón, Manuel's bald foreman, Pilo Portera. Suddenly the lights went out and came up again. By kerosene lamp you could see the stranger dancing with the most beautiful girl in Agua Oscura, Estrella Casas. Just then, someone screamed and pointed to the stranger's feet. They were chicken's feet! Immediately the lights went off, and when they came back on again, the stranger had disappeared! Estrella was lying on the floor. There was a circular burn on the wooden floor, directly under the spot where they'd been dancing. Everyone could smell sulphur. Without a doubt, Estrella had been dancing with the devil!"

"Mamá! You always have a story for everything."

"I was there, Dolores, I remember! I've never liked chicken since then. When I get around that boy, Eloy, I smell sulphur like I did years ago at the dance!"

"He doesn't smell!"

"I can smell him even if there isn't a smell. He's a handsome boy, though, too bad for the women. If he doesn't smell like sulphur, Dolores, then he smells like semen!"

"He's a man, Mamá. He's twenty-four."

"And Soveida's barely twenty-two. He's a rooster, Dolores! He'll say he'll love her till the end of the world, and keep a woman on the side!"

"Sssh, Mamá! Here she comes."

"Don't marry Eloy, Soveida! He's got chicken's feet!"

"Mamá, what are you talking about? You don't even know him!"

"Did I ever tell you the story about the handsome stranger with the chicken feet?"

"No."

"Ay, Mamá! Please. Soveida, don't ask her!"

"There was this stranger, he was very attractive . . ."

"Ouch, be careful, Mamá, it's fastened, undo that."

"It was in the summer. Around this time of the month."

"It doesn't look bad, does it? You can't see any wrinkles, can you?"

"It looks beautiful!"

"This good-looking stranger came to a dance at Manuel Dosamantes's barn. All the girls wanted to dance with him. I did, too, and I was a little girl."

"There, that does it. Stand there, Soveida, by the window. Look at her, Mamá. Isn't she beautiful?"

"Where's your slip, Soveida? Put your legs together! I can see up to your nalgas. When she stands in the light, Dolores, you can see everything."

"Slip? Mamá, I'm not wearing a slip."

"No slip, no slip? You're getting married without a slip! Dolores, can't you see her calzones? Didn't I tell you?"

"I'm not wearing a slip, Mamá! I don't need one!"

"The wedding is off! Dolores, you tell her. She *has* to wear a slip!"

"No one cares, Mamá. No one is going to look at me the way you do, with X-ray vision in the sunlight."

"It's all right, Mamá!"

"¡Qué all right! I'll find you a slip myself!"

"Mamaaaaaa!"

"No granddaughter of mine is getting married without a slip to a man with chicken's feet in the middle of the afternoon on an empty stomach! Oralia! Oralia!! Find me a slip!"

"What next?"

"I'll be right back. I have a slip at the house. I can see your panties! It's a church wedding! What will el Padre Zernawalski think? He's a baby himself, just out of diapers. Wait for me! Ay, Oralia! I need a slip."

"What is it, Oralia?"

"Señora Dolores, es el Señor Dosamantes Junior. He wants to know if you need anything. He says he'll be home soon."

"Oralia, go and get my long slip. It's on the top drawer in the chest of drawers in my room . . ."

"Tell him to bring me a pair of panty hose, Oralia. Panti-medias, please, por favor, size medium white, and a box of tampons. Oh, and mouthwash!"

"Sí, Señorita Soveida. Ahí voy, Doña Lupe, wait for me. The first drawer—"

"What was all that about chicken feet, Dolores?"

"Don't ask, Soveida. Your grandmother's just nervous."

"Can you really see through, Dolores?"

"Well—"

"Well?"

"Yes, Soveida, you can."

"What is it, Dolores?"

"Nothing, Soveida."

"Are you crying?"

"No, I'm not crying!"

"Are you sad?"

"No, it's not that."

"What is it?"

"I'm laughing. I was thinking about your grandmother's story and about the slip and then I thought about your brother buying you a box of tampons!"

"I don't really need them. They're just security."

"You're not . . ."

"No, I'm not pregnant!"

"Promise me you won't do anything . . . if you get pregnant that you'll keep the baby."

"Okay, I promise. Now, can we get on with this wedding? Where's the veil?"

"What veil? Just kidding."

"Does it really look that bad?"

"Just cross your legs and stay in the shade. What I'm worried about is the paper plates. Mamá wouldn't listen to me. Those Dosamantes! It's either done their way or it isn't done. And the way they do things is not the easy way, it's the hard way! On purpose! Let me look at you, Soveida."

"Can you see anything?"

"Just let me look at you, Soveida. Don't say anything. God bless you, sweetheart. I want you to be happy. Like I never was. I loved your father, but sometimes love isn't enough. I hope you'll be happy. You deserve to be happy, slip or no slip! Forget about Mamá, she's an old woman."

"Wait for me, don't go, not yet . . ."

"Here she comes."

"She never gives up, does she?"

"Here, Soveida, try this on."

"What is this thing?"

"It's mine. I knew I had something."

"This is yours?"

"I have always worn a slip."

"Give it to me. There, now are you happy?"

"No, m'ija. Remember, it's not too late. You still have time."

"Oh, Mamá! Leave her alone. It's her wedding day!"

"Dolores, you stay out of this, you're not one to be talking about marriage, anyway."

"And you are?"

"Shut up, Dolores. You know I never say shut up, but shut up! Now you, bride, go stand in the sun."

"The wedding can go on now?"

"If it has to."

"It has to."

"Stand there in front of the door. It's all right now. Now come over here, so I can give you la bendición. En el nombre del Padre, del Hijo, y del Espíritu Santo. Querida Virgencita, take care of my little girl as only you, a woman, can. Today is my baby's wedding day. Make her strong. Amen. Now if I were you, Soveida, I'd get tired, good and tired, fall asleep early, and keep the slip on."

"Is that your advice, Mamá?"

"Yes and no. Which part the yes you'll have to guess, which part the no, you already know. So, that's it. The chicken man should be arriving at any moment."

"Don't ask, Soveida, don't ask!"

"I can smell the sulphur a mile away. Ay, Virgencita, what happened to my little nun?"

Powers

24

The Poor Man's Dolores Del Rio

"The poor man's Dolores Del Rio. That's what you are, Soveida," Bud Ermin said.

"You can say that again," joined in Whitey Moldon.

"Say, let me look at your hands."

"Soveida, watch out!"

"Monkey Mendoza, shut your face and leave us alone. I'll have you know I'm a certified handwriting analyst. I also read hands."

"Read hands, Whitey? You got to be kidding."

"Yeah, read hands, Monkey!"

"So, read my hands, Whitey."

"I'd rather not."

"Go on. You can read hands, read mine."

"I come in here to get some peace of mind, enjoy a drink or two from my favorite waitress, a Dolores Del Rio look-alike, and I'm saddled with you, Mendoza. Doesn't the city sanitation department have something you can work on in your off-hours?"

"Like his personality!"

"That's a good one, Bud!"

"For your information, Moldon, I work in the Purchasing Office, not the sanitation department."

"Soveida, come on over here. I want to read your hands."

"Read me first, Whitey."

"Will you leave us alone? I don't want to read your greasy mitts, Monkey."

"No way out of it, Whitey."

"I guess not, Bud."

"Give me the right hand. I said right. Christ, what the hell is this?"

"Tattoo."

"On your palm? It's gonna be pretty damn hard to read your palm if you have a tattoo the size of a pancake on top of it. What is this?"

"The agony of Christ."

"Jesus!"

"Yeah, see the thorns."

"So give me the other hand. God!"

"What is it?"

"Nothing."

"Nothing? You saw something!"

"No, I didn't. You're going to be happy and have ten kids. You'll live to be 106. Now leave me alone."

"I don't believe you, Moldon."

"Have I ever lied to you, Monkey?"

"Yes."

"I read your hands. Now leave me and Soveida alone."

"So I'm next, Whitey? What can you see?"

"You got a long life line, Soveida girl. That's for starters."

"Hell, I'm gonna live long, too, Soveida. Give me another beer, Joe. I'll drink to that!"

"How many girlfriends you got, Monkey?"

"Only three this week, Billy Jane."

"You want another girlfriend, Monkey? Buy me a drink."

"Give Billy Jane her usual, Joe. It's on me, what the hell. Aaaahhhuaahhh!"

"What the hell was that god-awful noise, Monkey?"

"My victory call."

"Well, goddammit, go yell in someone else's ear, Monkey. You scared the hell out of me."

"This is your last one, Billy Jane."

"Are you talking to me, Joe?"

"You heard me, Billy, this is it."

"It's not even five o'clock, Joe. Happy Hour hasn't even started yet. So let's get happy!"

"Where's the chips, Soveida?"

"Be right back with them, Monkey. We're setting them out. Everybody, this is my new waitress. Dedea Arenas!"

"Welcome to El Farol, name's Ermin."

"Could be sisters. You related to our Soveida?"

"No, sir, I just started this week."

"Name's Whitey. Don't call me sir."

"Yes sir, I mean, hello everybody."

"Let's get the con queso, Dedea. You hear, all of you be nice to my new waitress. This girl is going to replace me someday!"

"Aw, get on with you, Soveida! Hell, you're a career waitress from the word go. Don't give me that."

"I mean it, Bud. Just you wait."

"Howdee there. My name is Billy Jane."

"Nice to meet you."

"Stick with Soveida, honey, she'll show you the ropes. She's the best waitress in this damn town. I mean it. You are. She is, ain't she, Monkey?"

"Monkey, goddammit! Would you stop playing that tortuous Mexican love ballad. If I hear *Volver* once more, I'll go crazy."

"Where did Soveida go, Joe? I was trying to read her hand."

"Would you shut up about that, Whitey? You ain't no graphologist. You're a dog trainer. You train dogs. Here, boy. Sit up. Down, boy. Now roll over. That's what you do. That and clean up dog shit."

"Fuck yourself, Ermin."

"Where's a guy like you get off saying he can read hands? Bunch of mumble-jumble hokey-pokey."

"Give me that battered paw of yours, Bud. Come on, stretch out that liquor-clogged limb in this direction, if you can unwrap those claws from that drink of yours. Nobody's gonna take it. Let me have a look. Just what I thought."

"What's that?"

"You been lying about your age all these years, Bud. You old rascal! I got you pegged. Joe, how long you been here at El Farol?"

"Fifteen years."

"For fifteen years you've been hearing Ermin say he's fifty years old!"

"For fifteen years I've seen you two old coots carry it on and drag it out."

"Hey, Joe. I'm writing me a book."

"No kidding, Whitey? What's it about?"

"People. People and dogs. People act like animals. You have a pet that's crazy, look in the eye of the owner. Usually they're queerer than a five-legged malamute. I seen it once."

"No kidding?"

"Yeah, they're pretty queer, all right. People."

"Another drink, Joe, please."

"That's cutting it, Billy Jane."

"Just one for the road."

"That's it, Billy, you're cut, babe."

"Okay, okay. Never seen a five-legged dog."

"It's rare, Billy Jane, damn rare."

"Got any chips there, Soveida? It's five o'clock!"

"We're bringing them out as fast as we can, Monkey. Dedea's learning how to set up."

"It's about time, Bud, for you know who. What I tell you? Here he comes. I think he eats dinner here every night. Wonder how many other lives Eloisa saved with her con queso."

"Got any more chips?"

"They're coming out, Sky Hawk! It's barely five."

"Far out. I'll wait."

"What time you got there, Joe?"

"Five on the nose, Billy."

"I think I'll go to the powder room and take a leak."

"Shouldn't you be heading home, Billy? You've got enough time left to get there before your daughter comes back. If not, she's gonna call me up and I'll have to hold you here and then she'll come and get you and you know what happens after that, Billy?"

"What, Joe?"

"All hell will break loose."

"With Jean? No. Not Jean. I have to go wee-wee, Joe."

"You better get home before it gets dark, Billy. You don't want to get lost like you did last week."

"I did not get lost. What are you talking about?"

"Soveida will give you a ride when the night shift comes on. Should be pretty soon. So, are you working the late shift, Dedea?"

"Yes, sir."

"Call me Joe."

"Where's the damn chips?"

"Hold your lungs, there, Sky Hawk!"

"Just sit here, Billy. Soveida will take you home soon."

"I want to wait for Nayla. I haven't seen her since yesterday."

"Okay, so here's the chips, everybody!"

"Thanks, Soveida!"

"So, where's the night shift, Joe?"

"Should be here by now."

"Ease up there, Hawk. There should be some for everyone."

"I love the Cheezo!"

"Que-so. It's called queso."

"Kay-so?"

"He's got it, Soveida!"

"What'll it be? The usual? Coke?"

"I'll have a Seven-Up."

"One Seven-Up coming up."

"With a cherry."

"Seven-Up."

"That it, Soveida?"

"I'm ringing up my bills. Dedea's staying on to work with Pancha and Margarito. We're a bit low on the tostadas. Eloisa's going to be mad when she finds out about it. Somebody has been stealing chips back there, Joe, and I think I know who it is."

"When was the last time you ate a meal, kid?"

"Sky Hawk's the name. How do you make this dip?"

"Velveeta."

"Velveeta? This place uses plastic cheese?"

"It melts good. Oh, and there's the chile. A dab of mayonnaise, Carnation's milk."

"You use canned milk?

"I'm going to get more chips, Joe."

"Okay, Soveida."

"Hey, kid! Leave some food for everyone else. Haven't you eaten all day?"

"Velveeta? Shit! It's not Mexican, Joe!"

"Hell, it's more Mexican than you think, Hawk! Mexican, what's Mexican? You want real Mexican food, go out and buy a can of Spam and fry it up! Or get some potted meat and slap it on a tortilla. What's with your name, anyway, kid? Sky Hawk?"

"Sky Hawk's your name? Wow."

"Say it all together. SkyHawk. As in sky and hawk. SkyHawk. I soar with the Gods. What's your name? I haven't seen you here before."

"I just started working here this week. My name's Dedea."

"Get me some more napkins, Dedea."

"Sure, Soveida. Excuse me. Gotta go."

"Come on back, Dedea!"

"I'm writing a book about dogs. People and dogs, dogs and people . . ."

"That's cool, man, I like dogs. Big dogs. Little dogs. So, like, what's your plot?"

"There's no plot, kid, it's about people. People are the ones need to be trained. A dog will only react the way it's been taught to react. It's a matter of survival. If a dog snarls, it's because he's been taught to snarl. Some dogs got pedigrees to snarl. It's all in the pedigree. I got my book here. Watch that cheese, kid, I don't want no con queso on my manuscript."

"Wow! Too much! This is your title?"

"Working title."

"*Who's the Animal?* By Whitey Moldon."

"That's me."

"Yeah. Like, who's the animal? I get it!"

"There are some who might get tight in the sphincter zone about it. Can't understand it's the animals' way. We can train each other. So, who's the animal?"

"I got you there."

"Watch that cheese!"

"So, who's the animal?"

"See that Mexican guy in the corner? He don't have long to live. Any day now."

"How do you know?"

"I read hands."

"So, where were we? What's this about my hands, Whitey? I have a long life line?"

"Like I was telling you, Soveida, this is your life line. And this . . ."

"Got any more chips, miss?"

"She's not working now, kid. Wait till Dedea gets back."

"You better put the book away, Whitey. It got messed up the last time you showed it to someone. I really enjoyed reading it. Thanks for lending it to me. You've got quite a story there. Hey, you didn't know I was writing a book, too, did you?"

"Yeah, Soveida? So what's it called?"

"*The Book of Service.*"

"*The Book of Service?*"

"It's a handbook for waitresses. But really it's about life."

"I get it. Yeah."

"Okay, so what is it, Whitey? Go ahead and read my hands. Do you see my book in there?"

"This is your life line, Soveida. And this shows how many children you'll have. And this shows how many lovers, and this determines how happy . . ."

"Is that it?"

"Soveida Dosamantes. One kid, lots of love, the poor man's Dolores Del Rio."

THE BOOK OF SERVICE

CHAPTER ONE

The Service Creed

As a child, I was imbued with the idea that the purpose of life was service. Service to God. Country. Men. Not necessarily in that order, but lumped together like that. For God is a family man.

In our family, men usually came first. Then God and country. Country was last. Should be last. When you grow up in the Southwest, your state is your country. There exists no other country outside that which you know. Likewise, neighborhood is a country. As your family is a country. As your house is a country. As you are a country.

The first tenet of waitressing is service.

The dictionary defined serve as: To render assistance, to be of use.
To answer the purpose.
To go through a term of service.
To render obedience and homage.
To perform duties.
To contribute, to promote, to serve a cause.
To treat in a specified manner.
To gratify.
To mate with.
Whoever wrote this dictionary had it right.
Also called "divine service," the service of God by piety, obedience, etc.
This is where I always have trouble.
Maybe that's why I always was and always have been such a good waitress. My waitressing is connected with, some might say based, even bound, in a divine, preordained belief in individual service.
When I was a little girl, I wore white gloves and little flat pink-and-

blue hats rimmed in black net with sprigs of tiny white flowers. I wore petticoats, three layers of yellow net that flounced when I spun. I was cute, dressed up, and silent.

Except when spoken to. And even then I was barely audible. I went from room to room, running never walking, as my father Luardo used to say, getting Dolores's scarf or coat or hat and Luardo's glasses or tie.

I kept my white gloves in a small straw purse. Inside the purse was a tiny mirror, a comb, a plastic doll with blinking brown eyes, a toy lipstick, and a glow-in-the-dark rosary. I was a princess, happy, and loved.

My gloves kept me warm and elegant. They reminded me that I was a young lady and that someday I would become a woman. I would wear white gloves to proms and down the aisle to the man who vowed to serve me all his life.

Waiters wear gloves in fancy restaurants to serve wine. They are servers, too. And servants wear gloves to answer the door or phone. Duels are fought in gloves. Lives ended in gloves. Today our leaders wear invisible gloves to hide the color of blood that runs like water through their hands, while humanity disavows contact with the ill in plastic skin-colored gloves that speak of sterility, containment, and denial. Small softened white gloves are left behind on coffins, irregular crosses reassuring some, binding the living eternally to the dead.

White gloves were my training for service.

Children served their parents, and parents served their work, their family, their God. Towns served states, and states countries. Countries served themselves, no one else, and likewise almost every human life on this earth served itself, first. Some, the powerful, the rich, the lonely, the restless lover, the saint, served themselves through others, and through others, they ultimately always served themselves and that burning God within themselves that went by the name of service.

The service of the server was shorter, less strenuous and demanding than that of the other server, his or her lot better than the fool who was the server of the served.

Life was, and is, service, no matter what our station in it. Some wrestle more with service than others. It is those to whom more is given from whom more service is demanded.

25

Here's My Enemy

Ivan was late for dinner. I'd fixed his favorite meal: fish sticks, mashed potatoes, and canned peas. He never called to say he would be late. I waited until 9 p.m. and then ate without him. He wasn't coming home for dinner again.

I'd been married barely six months when he started disappearing one night a week without warning. The first time it happened was a month ago. No phone calls, no messages, no warnings. No excuses. I'd called all over town, but no one had seen him. I realized I'd overreacted and went to bed. He came in at three in the morning and climbed into bed. I pretended to be asleep. He hugged me and went to sleep as if nothing had happened. The next time he stayed out late I got angry and confronted him then and there and he jokingly told me he'd been "out with the boys."

"It's my night for myself. Why don't you go out with your friend, Lizzie, or go see your mom?"

"Just let me know ahead of time which night it's going to be so I won't cook and the food won't be sitting there all night. That's all I'm asking. It's no big deal!"

"That's right, it's no big deal. I'm going out when I want to and when I need to. I can't be calling you every minute to let you know where I am."

"And tell your mother to stop calling here during the day when she knows you're at work. Whenever I answer the phone, she sounds surprised when I tell her you're not here. Try returning her calls once in a while."

"You don't like my mother, do you, Soveida?"

"Sixty-three years old. Heart like a teenager. Lungs like a baby. Skin like a newborn."

"I get busy, okay?"

"And I'm not busy all day long answering the damn phone because your mother is calling?"

"Come on."

"No, that's not entirely true. I wake up at nine-thirty, then I have a bowl of cereal, then I watch television till noon, then I have a sandwich for lunch, then I watch my soap operas till two o'clock, and then the Dialing for Dollars Movie comes on, then I start thinking about your dinner and then I fix it. Then I wait for you until 9 p.m. and then I do the dishes and I go to bed. This isn't the kind of life I had in mind when I married you!"

"Soveida! I *wanted* you to take some time off, to rest. You've been working at El Farol since you were a teenager."

"Well, I'm bored, Ivan! I've cleaned everything there is to clean here. I've read a book every other day for the last two months, and now I'm tired of reading."

"So?"

"So! I'm going back to work. Larry wants me back. Everyone misses me, and I miss them. I'm going back to El Farol!"

"No!"

"No? I'm not a receptionist, I'm a waitress. A waitress, Ivan! Besides, we can use the extra money."

"There wouldn't be much."

"But it's *my* money! I don't like asking you for money! In fact, I hate it!"

"But I'm your husband!"

"Ivan, I'm going back to work! And why the hell can't you just call me to tell me you won't be coming home for dinner?"

That was the discussion the last time.

One night there was a special program on TV on wild African elephants. I never realized elephants were so intelligent, so sensitive, so family-oriented. I was amazed to see how deeply elephants mourned their dead family members, and how, in a pile of bones, they were able to identify and distinguish their kin. The terrific wailing noise they made as they sifted through their beloved's bones chilled and saddened me. I sat on the ugly brown couch Dolores had loaned us. The couch's dark brown wool cloth chafed and was unpleasant to the touch. The navy-blue fringed bedspread I'd put over it kept slipping off. The elephants wailed and keened. Their cries were piercing and painful. There was no doubt they suffered like humans do.

Six months married. Six months unemployed. One month unhappy. Who was this man I'd vowed to spend the rest of my life with? ¿Quién lo parió? Mamá had asked. Who gave him birth? Who brought him into the world? And now I knew why.

Ivan was twenty-four years old. He was the son of Lourdes and Cutilio Torres from Agua Oscura, New Mexico. Cutilio had recently died of a heart attack. He had been a real-estate agent, though it wasn't known until his death that he was also extremely wealthy. For years, he had been buying property all over Agua Oscura for very little money. He had an insider's track to the property and had wisely bought what now turned out to be a new subdivision and a recently renovated and thriving shopping mall. Cuti Torres had left his widow a fortune. They always lived comfortably. Cuti had his real-estate office in the shabby Sunshine Building on the east side. But their real extravagance all those years was food. Both Lourdes and Cuti loved to eat out and they did so at least four times a week.

The Torreses had moved briefly to Pico Rivera, California, to be near Lourdes's elderly mother, but after her death several years ago, they returned to Agua Oscura. It didn't seem possible that Ivan could get any better-looking, but he had. California matured him. He was tall, nearly six feet two. Long-legged, slim-hipped, with impeccable posture, Ivan Eloy Torres exuded a wild and formidable sexuality. Already at twenty, he was a seasoned lover of women, or so it was reported. I had no doubt it was true. For several years he had had mistresses from all walks of life, of all ages, and all creeds. He had been involved with a fifty-three-year-old woman for several months, but she became too possessive of him. High-busted and tall herself, with a ripe body, she was a wealthy widow who vowed she would never remarry. Ivan was already a man, and like his father, he was tuned to the world's expectations of what a man should be: a lover of women par excellence, managing the difficult as one would animals or underlings. Ivan had learned well from Cutilio Torres.

He had also learned from his mother. Lourdes Fonseca Torres had babied both father and son and had found her own distractions in life early on. Lourdes's hobby was shopping and her pastime was applying makeup.

In the spirit of Mexican women, who are unparalleled when it comes to applying stratas of makeup to their faces—Italian women have nothing over them, nor do the French or the American—Lourdes Torres eagerly constructed herself daily. She began each morning by steaming her face over a pan of boiling hot water and chamomile tea. This was followed by a gentle scrub with a mild soap called Las Tres Marías that she bought from a little shop near the old cathedral in Juárez. The owner, María Leyba, concocted the soap herself in the back room. After her morning scrub, Lourdes applied a face cream that she bought from the same shop, and let her face rest fifteen minutes while she tweezed, plucked, squeezed, pinched, rubbed, and removed anything that needed to be dealt with. Then the real artistry began as she applied various shades of makeup base to her face, to lengthen, highlight, cover up, and generally make more attractive what was already there. This was followed by adding the powdered rouge in varying shades to bring the rose to bloom. An eyelash curler helped train the disconcerting Indian eyelashes upward. Black Cleopatra eyeliner winged outward as if in salute. A careful and deliberate mascara application came next. This was repeated fifteen times. The lips were then lined in black eyebrow pencil and filled in with a lip brush with four alternating shades of lipstick and blotted with powder. The whole process took about thirty minutes.

Following her makeup routine came Lourdes's daily adventure in dressing, which took at least an hour. So, by noon, Lourdes Fonseca Torres was ready to go shopping. She ate lunch alone or with girlfriends downtown. From 1 to 5 p.m., with breaks to call her son to see how he was doing, Lourdes ranged Agua Oscura, hunting for perfect outfits or the newest lipstick or the brightest eye shadow. "Katy Jurado, that's who she looks like!" Mamá said. "Although, compared to Lourdes Torres, la Katy looks washed out, pobrecita. Las dos con pechos hasta al infierno. Both with breasts all the way to hell."

There was something overblown, larger than life, and overly dramatic about Lourdes Torres.

How could a woman like Lourdes have the time to call her son so often when she was busy with her makeup, or trying on a silk blouse, or fiddling with her 48D cup French lace bras with the underwires that pushed her solid chichis up to just under her double chin, where they rested there like a pillow of flesh? She called her breasts mi atracción, my attraction. It was mi atracción this and mi atracción that, as if she had conquered the world breasts first. Probably she had. Cuti was dead, his hands and lips and miembro poderoso, his powerful member as Lourdes called it, far removed from Lourdes's atracción, and yet the hot cocker spaniels had won her a livelihood for the rest of her life to come. Too bad she couldn't share her wealth with her only son. What Cuti had bought with all his money was navy-blue and green mascara, every shade of Mood lipstick imaginable, a weekly hair appointment with a tint every sixth week, an excellent credit rating in all the local stores, and a large chest of drawers full of red, black, buff, white, and purple brassières that held, lifted, and then glorified Lourdes Torres, someone who knew what pleased men: a well made up woman who filled out her clothes.

"You, on the other hand, Soveida, have the potential for beauty. You need a facial badly, a good pore cleanser, an astringent, an oatmeal scrub once a week, a better base, your eyebrows plucked and shaped, different eyeliner, a pinker blush, and to watch that your mustache hairs, ever so faint now, don't get dark as you age. First you can't see them, then you see them in the direct sunlight, and then it's the bleach at night. You need a good bra, a new one, at least one of each: white, black, red, buff, nude, and purple. Get one with a lift. You've got the breasts, except they're so low you can't appreciate them. I do hope that's the bra and not you. You probably only wear white bras. That's why I'm taking you shopping. Bring money. Try one of the underwire nippleless black lace French cuts. My Cuti always liked them."

I didn't want to think about Lourdes wearing her bras for Cuti. Or imagine Cuti kissing the ponderous puppies that were Lourdes's great prized possession. She and her plastered face and elongated breasts masticated upward by that lap dog of a husband who still nursed at his wife's teats until his last gasp and died in her arms at the height of lovemaking, "A death," Lourdes whispered to me, "he would have wished for. His penis was a trumpet to the heavens! It was good that last time. I will always have that to remember. I will treasure it as I do my son's birth. May these breasts, mi atracción, remain Cuti's in death as they were in life."

It's true they had remained his, for Lourdes never remarried. However, she wasn't against showing "a little glimpse into heaven," as she called it, wearing low-cut dresses that allowed her ample cleavage to greet the world.

"No woman, at any age, is too old to show she has got juice left to drown her man in ecstasy if she so wants, Soveida. You, on the other hand, are a prude, and as unexciting as a rainy Monday. You have all the potential and none of the follow-through. Your makeup, your lingerie, it's so, so—everyday. You're probably wearing white flannel panties up to your waist, what Cuti called turtleneck underwear. No scoop French lace split-crotch animal print thongs, right? Soveida. Answer me! No, you don't have to answer me. I already know."

I stared at Lourdes. All this was coming from a woman with enormous buttocks, each weighing at least fifteen pounds. She stood and adjusted the fluffy ringlets on top of her head. Hardened and lacquered spit curls turned inward toward her ears. The weight of her hair offset the heavy jewelry and mammoth bust that catapulted forward in eager presentation. Her short, bandy legs tottered in six-inch heels. She was a cartoon image of Mexican womanhood: big-breasted, large-buttocked, huge-hipped. This ideal is still promoted on television shows where famous cabaret stars, all of them with asses as wide as the television screen, in thongs the thickness of rubber bands, strut their stuff to Mexican men, who only want more of the same at home. Lourdes Torres had truly missed her calling, but she made up for it as best she could. She'd give anything to be reincarnated in the body of one of these "cab-a-rett" actresses, singing to men while waving her nalgas and pointing her chichis straight up into the air.

Lourdes Torres at sixty-three years of age was a wealthy woman by the world's standards, but she's never shared any of her wealth with us. She's still mad at Ivan for marrying me.

The more time Ivan spent away from the home we didn't make together, the more time I had to myself. I missed El Farol, the people, and my work.

I waited for what seemed a long time. I was tired, but decided I could use some company. I left Ivan a note:

Dear I.E.:
   Gone to mother's. (Mine.) Fish sticks in stove. (Ours.) Where were/are you? Did you know elephants mourn their dead? Be back soon.
   I love you!
   Soveida

I locked the door and drove my VW to Dolores's. I wanted something. Company. Family. A home. The Crescent Acres subdivision where we live is not home.

Dolores was out, so I let myself in with my old key. Dolores hadn't asked for it back.

Once again Luardo had separated from Dolores and was living at Mamá's. I didn't want to run into him. He'd insist we go out to eat and I simply didn't have the stomach for another greasy Seafarers catch sandwich. I didn't want to see Mamá either, not right then. Mamá would know that everything with Ivan wasn't right and I just didn't want to be interrogated and then prayed over by her. It would have been wonderful to see Oralia. Oralia never demanded anything of me, but always had a ready smile, a deep and fragile hug, and a hot cup of yerbabuena to soothe the frazzled nerves. But to see Oralia you had to filter through Mamá Lupita. No, it was too demanding.

Since Luardo had moved out, this time for good, he said, Dolores had begun to redecorate the way she supposedly had always wanted. Gone were Luardo's contributions to the decor: his two large oil paintings, landscapes he'd bought for $29.95 apiece at the Holiday Inn during a Starving Artists original closeout. The *Running Brook* that used to hang on the dining-room wall was gone; so were the *Autumn Woods* in the family room, and the *Blue Ghost*, a painting of an otherworldly figure—in blue—framed by red curtains, a rendering of a nightmare by one of Luardo's former secretaries. Also missing were Luardo's photographs. I could still see the outline where the frames had once hung in the hallway. Dolores's new hobby was collecting colored-glass decanters, which lined the shelf in the living room behind the picture window that faced Esperanza Street. Her silk flowers were now replaced by real ones. They were from "friends," Dolores had said, people interested in the same things, books, restaurants, and good movies, as she. In the twenty-odd years that Dolores and Luardo had been married, I never knew them to be interested in "good movies." Until recently the last movie Dolores had seen was *Ben-Hur*. She still talked about the scene in the prison where the guard opened the metal door to the dungeon only to find out that Miriam, Ben-Hur's mother, and his sister, Tirzah, had become lepers. "It's enough to chill your heart," she used to say. "If you and Hector became lepers, I would kill myself. Now, if your dad became a leper, well, that would be another thing altogether!"

This was not the house that belonged to the same Dolores I once knew. The house seemed airier, less crowded, full of color and light.

No, I couldn't call this home anymore. It was Dolores's home. I had my own home with Ivan, but that wasn't really home either. It was a temporary living space. I was still in limbo, that place where unborn or unbaptized children go to wait for the day of redemption. I, Soveida

Dosamantes Torres, was still unbaptized, a baby bride seeking heaven on earth. But it didn't seem forthcoming.

Ivan wasn't a drinker. He never really argued with me. I doubted that he would ever hit me. He was a man who displayed little emotion readily. Even when he was making love he seemed contained, holding himself back, insisting I release myself and learn to give, while he, I imagined, had the ability to go on forever. He was always able to hold his sperm, his emotions, to kingdom come, if that's what it took. We made love sometimes three and four times a day. He'd never neglected his husbandly duties. I never lacked for caresses. I wanted to start a family right away. He didn't. So I started on the pill. I'd forget to take it, doubling up when I remembered, but I haven't gotten pregnant yet.

I wrote Dolores a note and left it on the kitchen table:

Dear Dolores:
   Came to visit. No one home. Watched a special on TV about elephants, remind me to tell you about it. I like the house!
Sorry I missed you. Will call later.
   Love, Soveida

When I got back, everything was just as I'd left it. The fish sticks were now cold and soggy. I put them in the refrigerator and hastily did the dishes. Ivan would probably find food remnants on them. He abhorred my sloppy dishwashing.

I turned on the record player and listened to my favorite song four times, "The First Time Ever I Saw Your Face." Then I put on my cotton-flannel nightshirt that Oralia had made me—one size fits every woman—and climbed into bed. It was around nine-thirty. I turned off all the lights and lay there awhile.

The next thing I knew, I heard "Soveida! Are you awake? It's me."

"Ivan!"

"I'm back, baby, I'm back."

"Where were you, Ivan?" I asked.

"Hey, I got caught up. An old compa showed up at the Motor Vehicle. We went for a few beers. ¡Se me fue el tiempo!"

"You want to eat? There's fish sticks."

"I ate. Go to bed."

"I'm in bed. I've been in bed for hours. Why didn't you call me?"

"I promise, next time. Promise, promise, promise. Come on. Aren't you happy to see me?"

"Did you know, Ivan, that elephants cry? I heard them on the TV."

"What are you talking about?"

"I watched this TV special about elephants. When one of their family dies, they know. They cry. I saw them!"

"Tell me about it tomorrow, Soveida."

"I mean it."

"Come on, Soveida, it's late. I have to get up early."

"Me, too. I start work tomorrow."

"You don't have to."

"I want to."

"You moved your car?"

"I went to see Dolores, but she wasn't there. Oh, and your mom called twice and wants you to call her."

"I love you, Soveida."

"Do you, Ivan? Hey, it's late."

"So, you glad to see me or what?"

"Sing to me, Ivan! Where's your guitar? You never sing to me!"

"The Clown's Coffin is locked."

"Why do you call your truck that? It's not a coffin."

"You wouldn't understand. The guitar is safe there. It doesn't like walls."

"Why can't you call it Esmeralda or Minnie? I hate the Clown's Coffin. Sing to me, Ivan."

"Come here, baby. I love you."

In the darkness Ivan Eloy smelled of perfume, and the muskiness of a woman. No two ways about it: he was a stinking S.O.B. and he was stingy with his music. I winced as I turned over. He arched his back to fit my contour and slipped his perfect penis in.

26

The Mummy

No one, of course, had seen it. It was Larry's idea in the first place to purchase it from its owner, Cap Crenshaw. Cap was Ede Le's uncle, and he ran the Desert Museum in Agua Oscura. I was against the whole thing, as I generally was when Larry got some wild idea in his head. But I went along anyway, as witness, once again, to his madness.

A pajamaed septuagenarian, unshaven, gap-toothed, with a nose full of spider veins, Cap led us through his darkened living room and on back to the kitchen. Before getting there, we made our way through an unbelievable pile of litter and refuse. At first I thought we were in a storage room or garage as we stood in the doorway of Cap's house that afternoon. But, upon looking around, I noticed several easy chairs, tables with lamps, a footstool, as well as other signs that suggested the room had once been inhabited by people who spoke together, laughed, and speculated on the day's weather as well as their own and others' mortality.

Now lawn tools rested up against the front door, and a mildewed box spring leaned sadly against peeling wallpaper that had once proudly proclaimed gold coronets and effusive trumpets, a royal motif from a reign long gone.

Boxes of Christmas wrapping paper and old newspaper clippings were scattered about. At the far end of the room sat a small sofa, its faded burgundy cloth thinning on the armrests, several greasy throw pillows pegging the corners.

"Set down a minute, will you?" Cap suggested. "Don't you worry now, I'll find you ole Billy."

I would have preferred to stand, but Larry, in his attempt to placate the old man, motioned for us to sit. He moved aside the rusty garden tools and assorted boxes and sat on the couch. It smelled of must and old urine.

It was Ede Le who had first told him about the find. Larry couldn't believe it. How could it be that no one had discovered this mummy before? Where had it appeared? Or disappeared? Whose was it? And why did Cap Crenshaw want to sell it?

"You're going to have to ask my Uncle Cap all those questions, Mr. L.," Ede Le had said. "He's the one who knows all about its history. I heard about it first from my daddy, Johnny Ray. Daddy used to tell us kids that the head would come and chomp on us if we weren't good and all. Mind you, I never saw the damn thing, except in my mind's eye, but I had my imaginings. Never wanted to see it up close. Well, I was thinkin' about that one day. I asked my Uncle Cap what had become of the thing that caused us so much grief. He announced to me flat out that it was for sale. Seems he was liquidating his museum. Did I know anyone wanted the authentic honest-to-God real-and-true-son-of-a-bitchin' bona-fide genuine mummified head of William Bonney, alias Billy the Kid? Then I recollected to myself your interest in history, Mr. L., and so I thought I'd let you in on the information. I haven't told anyone else."

"I appreciate that, Ede Le."

"I mean, it's like keeping it in the family. El Farol is kinda like a family, wouldn't you say?"

"It's a family, all right, Ede Le."

"That's what I thought."

"Just exactly what do you know about it, Ede Le, the head, I mean?"

"Just what I heard my daddy tell, and what Uncle Cap says."

"What's that?"

"A fellow, Dominguez," Cap said in a conspiratorial tone, "he comes by the museum one day, back in the early forties. Told me in Spanish he couldn't talk inside the house, saying it was an outside thing. That way the spirits wouldn't be trapped by four walls, as he put it. So I locked up the entire shebang and walked around the museum by the ole cottonwood was there, facing the desert where Stumpy and Juan Pedrilla used to hunt rabbits, and walked through some scrub with Dominguez. He was holding this gunnysack and darting his eyes around like an animal about to pee who can't because he hears noises and it scares him.

"Then I have to walk with him a ways or else it was no go. So we walked clear down to the foothills of the Santa Marías. Señor Crenshaw, he said to me, and I says to him, what the hell you got in that sack, pendejo? What's so goddamn important you drag me nearly all the way to Santa Fe for? He opened the gunnysack. At first I thought it was an old piece of fur. Saw it from the hair side. Brownish pelt of some kind. He jostled the bag and it came up spades. I saw the eyes sewed shut with animal gut. I took a gander at the dusty-looking mug, looked at Dominguez and said, my voice barely coming out, who is he?

"Dominguez closed the bag, said how much? And I said nothing, if you don't tell me who he is. It ain't a woman, I know as much. No woman I ever saw had bristly hairs like that on its chin except my Aunt Vedril and she was part man, shoulda been a man, everyone thought. That's a man, I know a man when I see one. Who the hell is it, cabrón? Had to talk to him that way, even though we grew up together. Hell, Rudy was like a brother to me. But, anyway, he begins to tell me how he was over to the Holed Up Bar and a bunch of wild cats gets drinking. This man with them gets twisted around and Dominguez takes him outside. This old hooter is wrapped around the ole sauce llorón, the weeping willow, apologizing to Dominguez for being an Anglo, and Dominguez says that this blah-blah happens to people when they're drunk and feeling universal in a bar full of Mexicans. Okay, okay, so what happened, I says, you brought me way the hell back here to talk about fraternity? Shit! And Dominguez goes on, this ole man, Mender, Mender something as far as I could make out and Dominguez could recall, gave him the head. He'd been carrying it around with him throughout the Southwest. This guy Mender sold these medical apparatus and someone gave the head to him when they couldn't pay their bill. Now, Mender doesn't want the head anymore, it scares his wife. She tells him it's either him or him. So he sets out to get drunk and lose it, that way he won't remember what happened to it, and it'll go peaceful. But he just can't lose it, and would Dominguez take it from him. Seems Mender's gotten attached to it. He talks to it just like a rabbit's foot, but what the hell, he likes his wife, too, so he's in a bind. That's when Dominguez decides to take it on. He's still single then. When he marries Irma he thinks of me.

" 'Do you think you should be dealing in flesh this way, Dominguez? Hell, I known you all my life, Rudy,' I said.

" 'What you mean?'

" 'Selling stolen body parts.'

" 'What you mean, cabrón?'

" 'Cabrón yourself, Rudy. It's not legal.'

" 'So, what you telling me?'

" 'Hand over that head and I'll let you go.'

"We struck up a bargain. I'd keep ole Billy, he'd keep himself outa jail. But I felt sorry, me knowing Rudy all those years, and Irma and their kids, Davila and Rudy Jr., everyone calls him Tweeter, so I gave him ten dollars for his time, and a bottle of hooch I had in the cupboard."

"How do we know it's Billy the Kid?" I asked with growing uncertainty, poking Larry with a sharp elbow.

"Now, that's very curious," Cap yelled from the kitchen.

I sat on the edge of the burgundy sofa. Its springs bit into my bottom. The stench in the room was unbearable. I held my hand near my nose and smelled it whenever possible to keep from gagging. My eyes adjusted to the light, and what I saw distressed me.

Underneath the table nearest Larry, who sat comfortably on the couch, was a wad of old bloody Kleenex. Bits of paper, pairs of mud-caked shoes, and dirty dishes littered the floor, as well as pots, pans, and oily rags. I began to feel nauseous, and shifted my gaze to the table surfaces, trying to see things at eye level, to avoid that lower stratum of unimaginable filth.

On the tables sat old-fashioned lamps, brass candle holders, antique photo frames, and home accessories that appeared to be in fairly good, if not valuable, condition. Ole Crenshaw had had good taste at one time—someone had. I wondered if he lived alone, or if there was an old woman running around as well in some greasy nightgown?

I looked about uncomfortably and whispered to Larry, "This was probably a very nice place. So what happened?"

The sound of muffled footsteps came from the back of the enormous dining room and Crenshaw reappeared.

"I got it!"

Crenshaw lumbered forward, carefully lifting his large, bare, fungus-covered feet. Eventually he returned to the living room, sidestepping a massive armoire that stood at one end of the dining room, its open door revealing a jumbled mess of clothing, blankets, and a few old guns.

"Look at this. Watch it now, watch it!" Crenshaw held the gunnysack with both hands.

Larry and I looked at each other and then stood up. A shaft of light came in from one of the dining-room windows. Crenshaw held open the slightly damp gunnysack. Inside, the head was wrapped in a greasy Popeye's Fried Chicken paper bag. Something in me wanted to run away, or laugh. So I laughed. Then it was quiet.

Cap was an eerie, phantasmal figure in his baggy, stained light blue pajamas, holding the paper bag like a trophy.

I held my hand to my nose, gratefully smelling myself. God, but the old man stank!

Cap gave us his assurance, and then handed Larry a few wrinkled sheets of notebook filler paper attesting to the validity of the head's age and condition, signed by a Dr. William Connerly, M.D., Ph.D., C.P.A. Larry passed me the papers and I shook my head no, but it was too late. Larry winked to me, then handed over a number of crisp bills to Cap Crenshaw. He was now the owner of the mummified head of William Bonney, alias Billy the Kid, one of Larry's heroes.

Crenshaw held up the head by a chunk of wispy but strong blondish hair.

"Say hello to Mr—?"

"Larragoite."

"That's it, Billy Boy, say hello."

This was the mummified head Larry wanted to place in the lobby of the restaurant next to his exhibit of Southwestern minerals, dinosaur eggs, geodes, and stuffed animals, one deer, one bear, one mountain lion, and three fish.

The mummy debate lasted a heated week. I was against it from the beginning.

"Larry Larragoite, what have you done?"

"It's a historical artifact! You saw the documents yourself, Soveida."

"That old coot runs a flea market, not a museum, Larry! Besides, it smells!"

"Women and their smells. You're just as bad as Bonnie. So we'll clean it up a bit. Then I'll put it in the lobby."

"Larry, are you feeling all right? Nobody wants to see a dried-up mummy's head in the lobby of a restaurant while they're waiting for a table to eat Mexican food. Do you understand that? It's not nice. It's ugly. It smells."

"The lobby of a Mexican restaurant is exactly the place it should be displayed. Our customers like the unusual, the different. No more

serapes and straw hats for us, no more velvet paintings, or skull plant-
ers, or tacky piñatas, or gaudy paper flowers."

"It makes me sick."

"It's a clean taxidermy job, Soveida, well done. It's part of our
Southwestern past, our local history. People are fascinated with Billy
the Kid, it'll draw crowds. We'll place a feature article, advertise, make
T-shirts, maybe some stationery, change the name of the restaurant.
I never liked the name El Farol. I could change it to Billy the Kid's.
A theme restaurant, that's it!"

"How original, Larry. Frankly, I'm Billy the Kidded up to here!"

"The gang will go for it, Soveida. We'll take a vote. It'll bring in
more business."

"Nobody on the staff is going to go for it, Larry. Nobody!"

"How do you know?"

"I know."

"How do you know so much, Soveida?"

"Larry Larragoite, you're crazy!"

"I'll take a vote!"

"Nobody wants it!"

"We'll see about that, Soveida. We'll just up and take a goddamn
vote. See if anyone knows the value of history or not. This is New
Mexico and what could be more sacred than Billy the Kid's head?"

"Larry!"

"Don't cross me, Soveida."

"We'll just take a goddamn son-of-a-New-Mexican vote."

The vote was 12 to 3. Everyone except Larry, Ede Le, and Chuy
Barales, the day and night custodian, voted to keep as far away from
El Farol as possible what Barb Valentine, the night bartender, called
"that dried-up piece of human jerky."

Filed under B in Larry's filing cabinet is ole Billy, waiting for his
day of freedom. Larry loves that old thing, fondles it like Mender did,
a secret lucky rabbit's foot all his own.

27

The House on Manzanares Street

La Virgie had become the great love of Ivan Eloy's life.

My love for him was more like a bad toothache: you wanted to save the tooth, but the minute-to-minute pain was so bad you just wanted the tooth out, gone, rather than endure a deep, continual, nagging distress. It had been a beautiful tooth, too, with a decayed center no one could see. The smile was so bright.

After about a year of putting up with La Virgie, I took several suitcases to Dolores's. I announced to Ivan that I would stay there until he decided what he was going to do, and with whom. It was either me or La Virgie.

Otherwise known as la Virginia Lozano, a woman in her mid-twenties, La Virgie showed no signs of having suffered any pain, grief, hardship, or doubt—physical, spiritual, or otherwise. It was impossible to tell that she had given birth to any children, yet she was the mother of two little girls, who lived with their father. She was a woman untouched by life's anxieties, unscathed by mortality, chaos, corruption. Every pore was tight, every ounce of her alive. She was firm and beautifully victorious over any physical imperfection. She didn't need makeup, rarely wore it, and if she did, she was almost too incredible to behold. Despite her perfect human form, there were unsettling aspects of her personality. Men seemed rarely to notice them, but they drove women crazy.

At first impression La Virgie was likable, friendly, cheerful, and funny. As time went on, she became sexier, funnier, more cheerful, friendlier, and more likable to men, while growing colder, more distant, critical, and suspicious of women. La Virgie was a woman who celebrated her independence from men, while she oppressed other women. She was concerned, basically, with only herself, doing every-thing under a thin veneer of goodwill. She could be cute, she could be winsome, and she most certainly could be—and was—a bitch. The only people to see this Jekyll/Hyde transformation of hers were gen-erally other women she had already relegated to a place of inconse-quence outside her reign.

She would take a woman into seeming confidence, then turn around and sleep with either her boyfriend or her husband. Once she had become your best friend, she would set you up for something that only later you realized she had orchestrated to her benefit, all the while appearing to be a pleasant, sympathetic confidante.

I heard all this from my cousin M.J., who knew someone whose husband had become, as M.J. had said, "La Virgie's latest victim."

The move to Manzanares Street was effected two months after I had first moved to Dolores's.

Dolores insisted I go back to Ivan. "He's your husband. What are you doing here, Soveida?"

Mamá Lupita didn't say anything to me.

When I was back in my old room, it was as if I'd never left home, and in many ways I hadn't, although I was five years older and had, as Lizzie once stated, been through the marital grinder with a man I never should have married.

And yet I remembered that when I met Ivan he captivated me in some inexplicable way.

Ivan was the first person who really romanced me, sending me flowers, dropping by El Farol to give me small gifts, surprising me with mementos of his undying love, a love that at that time burned brightly, feverishly. I was flattered by all his attention.

And he was handsome, no denying that. He had a sleek, slender body, a good physique, with small feet, great legs, a full head of dark hair, small, deep-set eyes, "laughing" eyes, my cousin M.J. had pointed out to me, and well-proportioned, sensual lips.

"No denying, he had all the prerequisites: plenty of hair, good teeth, small ass."

"Settle down, M.J. What is he, a horse?"

Everyone loved Ivan: animals, children, old men, and women. He was so good with anyone under sixteen and over fifty. He was so polite and friendly, muy simpático. He was clean, too, no complaints there, a good cook as well, if you liked grease, just like Luardo. Grease was his specialty, in that he was unparalleled. Fried chicken, french fries, hash browns, fish sticks, eggs, steaks, doughnuts, anything dipped or covered in fat.

He was a neat man. His end of the closet was always organized, a paradigm of order, all his cotton undershirts folded crisply in thirds, the seams facing in, the T-shirts laid one on top of the other, the shirts completely buttoned on the hangers, the pants with a pronounced seam folded tightly sideways, his orderly shoes facing the door, the socks, darks with darks, lights with lights, the ties separated by color and design. He never smelled bad, never in fact smelled, his body had no odor that I could discern. He never got drunk. He never hit me. He was a fantastic dancer. What he lacked was a moral code. He was guiltless, blameless, and shameless when it came to women. That was all. But it was everything.

At first, after my move to Manzanares Street, Ivan and I saw each other every few days. It was strained, but we tried to meet on neutral ground. We went out to dinner, to a movie, to get frozen yogurt. Each night ended with his trying to seduce me in the car, or on the couch in my new apartment, on that same ugly itchy thing Dolores had given us when we first got married. One time Ivan drove me back to our house in Crescent Acres but I refused to get out, telling him to drive me home. He wouldn't, so I got out of the car and began walking. He caught up with me, and we ended up in bed at our old house. Later he drove me back to Manzanares Street. I didn't see or hear from him for two weeks.

The next time he called, I hung up on him, later relented and decided to go by the old house to apologize. He wasn't there. I still had the key, so I let myself in. The small house still had most of my furniture, my pots and pans. Everything seemed almost the same, although it was neater than when I'd left. In the bathroom I found four pairs of still wet panties drying on the shower-curtain rod. In the bedroom was a large vinyl suitcase full of women's clothing, size 6.

Zipping up the suitcase, I took it outside to the small yard and returned for the unknown underwear, which I put in a large grocery bag. I noticed there was a slight drizzle, with the promise of more rain. Upset, disgusted, feeling betrayed and humiliated, I gathered up all I could of my possessions, and ended up with an odd assortment of things: the dustpan, a mop, the crucifix Mamá had given me as a wedding gift, my high-school yearbook, a black garter belt Ivan held out for me on my last birthday. Then I locked myself in.

Several hours later Ivan and La Virgie returned. I was there to greet them. A fight ensued, La Virgie and I screamed at each other while Ivan looked anguished and upset.

"What are you doing here, Soveida?"

"I live here. What's *she* doing here?"

"You're not together anymore, Soveida."

"Says who?"

"Ivan."

"Yeah? So what's all my stuff doing here?"

"Why can't you let him go?"

"Just leave, Soveida, why did you come here?"

"I live here, Ivan, or have you forgotten?"

"You haven't been here for months."

"It hasn't been that long!"

"You've moved out. Just finish it, okay?"

"I'm sleeping here tonight, Ivan. You can find another place to sleep. And so can she."

"She's visiting. She's my guest!"

"Oh, yeah? Well, too bad. This is *my* house, you bitch! Just get the hell out of here. Get her out of here, Ivan!"

"He invited me here."

"Your stuff is outside."

"What? Outside? It's raining! Ivan, do something!"

"Well, you can just pick your shit up on the way out. I'm staying!"

"Soveida!"

"Get her out of here. This is *my* house!"

"Soveida, just go away!"

"I won't go away, get her out of here!"

Ivan took La Virgie away, to a motel, I found out later. He returned a long time afterwards, angry, upset, and tired. I was in bed waiting for him. We made love without talking. I faced the wall away from him and he rammed his penis into my anus, without warning. It hurt, but I didn't say anything. I grabbed the pillow, bit into it, and gritted my teeth. I was here and I was going to stay. That little bitch could just forget everything. I lay in bed crying to myself, thinking that, while it was impossible, I wanted to stay. Ivan moaned aloud next to me in his familiar, impatient way. I knew he couldn't stand my tears. He never could. He hated to see me cry, hated to see me weak, hated to see me become emotional in front of him. His usual mask was gone. Mine as well. My face was ugly, bloated, splotchy with red marks, my eyes like a tiny rodent's, my nose like an alcoholic's. I could barely breathe. I got up to go to the bathroom and to turn out the hall light. When I returned, I saw Ivan look at me with disgust. I saw that look and lay down again, next to him, unmoving. Neither of us slept. In the morning I left without saying goodbye.

After work I returned to get my clothes. La Virgie moved in that night and that was that.

Before the house on Manzanares Street, I had never really lived by myself. Until I was twenty-two I had lived with Dolores and Luardo, and for five years with Ivan. For the first time in my life I was completely alone.

THE BOOK OF SERVICE

CHAPTER TWO

Hands

A waitress has many tools: her head, her feet, her hands, her voice. A waitress's hands are crucial to her survival.

The nails should be clean, not too long, and not painted. If they are painted, go with a light-colored nail polish. No chipped Carmen Miranda gone-to-seed nails.

Rings will get in the way, usually distract, and will only get stuck with food buildup. You will spend much time cleaning slime and bluish-brownish-grayish softened food matter out of ring grooves with toothpicks, safety pins, or straight pins. So rings are out. Especially wedding, engagement, or friendship. They will only go down the drain sooner or later, and cause some kind of chafing.

28

The Story of Dresses

"Soveida, it's Mara! How am I? Fat. Did I wake you up? It's 7 a.m.
You should be up, Soveida. Listen, did you get the boxes of clothing
I sent you? I was saving all of them for when I got thinner. There's
all sizes. I can go from a size sixteen to a size eight and not worry
about having a wardrobe. I have clothes for any size I want to be, but
I've given up. I'll never lose the weight. Even if I lost the weight,
who wants a purple tie-dyed miniskirt with lacy, scalloped edges?
That's another woman there, another body. You liked them, huh? Yeah,
I know some of the clothes are out of date. Okay, so people aren't
wearing dashikis anymore, or toreador pants or animal prints, ha!
Maybe the animal prints, but I don't have many of those. There's a
lot of good clothes. How about the beige three-piece and the gray
coat? I got that suit for a job interview. It was so damn cold here I
thought I'd never get used to this weather, but I don't know, I guess
I did or have. I don't really get homesick, it's not that, but I miss
things. The food, a few people. I miss the cotton fields and the chile
fields and the farms and the heat. That suit cost me a lot of money,
but I was sure I was going to get the job. It was my first real job.
Maybe you can use the suit, it's one of those classic business ones,
they never go out of style. Hey, you liked that? It was one of my
favorites, that blue peasant dress. I wore it a lot. You've been wearing
it? The one with the low neck? I loved that dress! I bought it, God
knows when. I don't know what happens. First it's five pounds, then
ten, then fifteen, and then a new wardrobe. I have a wardrobe for
every five-pound increment. I mean it. What about the pants? You
can wear all of them, all the shorts. I hated to get rid of those shorts,
the white ones, yeah. I cut them up, pretty ragged. They were my

favorite shorts, ever. Everybody should have ugly clothes. Ugly clothes that you love and can work in. Ugly clothes when you feel ugly, too. All my clothes back then were ugly clothes. All you had were the peasant skirts, and Mexican blouses and tops, like Jane Russell, off-the-shoulder shit. That's until you got that stupid uniform. Larragoite is out of synch. He wants you in old-lady black-below-the-waist and Marilyn Monroe on top. If that isn't a man for you! Tell him to get something brighter. Black is for a funeral. No one wants to eat in a room full of people moving around in black. What about the print dress with the ruffles? That's the one I bought for Grandma Trancha's funeral. That was the first time I wore that dress. Time goes by so fast. What about the backless silk thing? Turquoise, with the little green circles? It fits? I bought it for the engagement party. Lou, not Ben. Except I'm damn glad I called the whole thing off. Just as well. I can't imagine myself ever being married to him. No, I don't know where he is. But I still have the dress, or, rather, you have the dress. Listen, if you don't want things, give them away. To Oralia, not that Oralia will wear anything but that dark rag she's worn since 1946. Are you okay? I'm okay, but Lester Jr. is either into drugs or crazy or dead, I can't remember. Yeah, I liked the green sweater. I got compliments. Wear a slip with it, it's very nubby. God, do you remember Mamá, I don't know if she ever did that to you or not, but when I'd go out, if I was wearing something new, another gray sack, she'd ask me when I got home: Who told you you looked pretty? She never wanted me to go out, but she always wanted to know who thought I looked pretty and what they'd told me, or if they'd liked my dress, or shoes, or hair. She was always interested in how people thought I looked. Maybe that's why she never told me herself. If I looked pretty, she'd say: It means you're a good girl. Did that mean that if I wasn't pretty, which I didn't think I was, I was a bad girl? Or maybe I wasn't pretty because she never told me so. Who told you you looked nice, she'd ask me, and I'd tell her. That would make her happy. That and when I wore my hair away from my face. She never told me I looked nice. I never felt I looked nice. I was too long and skinny, and then I had bumps and curves before anyone else did, and that was terrible. And I had big flat feet, and breasts. God, I had breasts. No, you didn't have breasts at that age like I did. The boys pulling and popping my bra. It drove me crazy! And they all teased me and told me I stuffed my bra with Kleenex! Yeah, I remember the time you got your first bra. The way you wore that see-through blouse to the Holy Angel picnic, who were you kidding, Soveida? Anybody could see you didn't need the bra, not then, nor a couple of years down the road. Okay, so now you have breasts! Thank God you don't have Dolores's boobs. I often wonder how she sleeps, the way the straps have cut grooves into her skin. Well, if it wasn't for me, you wouldn't have gotten that bra. You asked for a bra, you wanted a bra. So what if you didn't need a bra. Always remember I bought you your first bra. You owe me! The sweater coat was the first coat I ever bought for myself, from my first paycheck as secretary II. I thought I'd die if I had to stay at that job the rest of my life. The first week I brought home purses full of used paper. I didn't want my supervisor to know I couldn't type. It took me forever to write a letter. I used to throw paper in the bathroom, so no one ever found me out. I was a size eight then. Look, about those size sixteens, give them to someone. Chata. How's she doing? Does she still clean your place once a month? So who's Dolores's newest slave, I mean maid. Tere? Yeah, give some stuff to her. I mean, if it doesn't fit you. Or give it to the Goodwill. Did you like the long, flowered skirt? It goes with the white chenille blouse. It should be there. Yeah, there's plenty of belts, they're good to save. So, you got everything okay? That's all I wanted to know. And the T-shirts, you got the T-shirts, they're good to wear around the house, mix and match with the shorts, or jeans, there's a few good pair, those brown corduroy, the linen pedal pushers, they're back in style. And the poncho, it's good for the winter. I wore it until I got sick of it, but it was warm. It was a cold winter then. Size twelve. My first divorce. That's when I started gaining weight. I'm on a diet now. Might as well give you the clothes, you can use them. You need good clothes. You never have had good clothes. All you have is those damn black-widow uniforms. You better watch it, Soveida. It's ten pounds each divorce, a few for each love affair. I'll probably never lose the weight. I figured I might as well clean out my closet. I'll never ever be an eight again, and I was once a six! Might as well clean it all out. I saved all that stuff, it was time to get rid of it. Get yourself some new clothes. Time to grow up clotheswise, you look like an old hippie when you wear a dress. Thank God you have a job where no one cares what you wear or if your shoes are scruffy. But you need to dress up now and then, Soveida, go buy yourself something new. No more early-laid-back, gypsy-gone-to-seed look. Ivan is history, well, you're better off. Don't say anything. It's time for a change, buy yourself some new things. And don't wear yellow, it doesn't look good on you. Give the yellow dress to Chata. You need bright colors, blue, red, fuchsia. You're definitely autumn. I'm an autumn, too. When I see you next, we'll get you color-draped. It's changed my life. You say you make good money. What are you spending it on? I don't understand how your skin can be so bad, here you still have pimples. Why don't you do something about your hair? You've been wearing the same hair style for years. Oh, what the hell. Maybe you can use the clothes, maybe not. There's a lot of good things. If you can use them, fine, if not, like I said. Oralia. Chata. New slave. Goodwill. Enjoy them. Like I did. Funny how all those clothes remind you of all those times: another woman, another body. Do you remember that old quilt of Mamá's? The one she used to cover her bed with, the patchwork one, all pieced together like that. Her quilt of old clothing? Hers, mine, ours, the Dosamantes'. I used to love to look at that old quilt. She could tell me what every little piece had been, who it belonged to, what year it was that Oralia or Tía Bernardita had made the dress, or shirt. Maybe the cloth was an old tie of Papá Profe's or Luardo's pants, or Teo's baby clothes, or Pina's jumper. What happened to that quilt? I just wondered. Well, I gotta go. You're welcome. It's no big deal. I couldn't wear them anymore. I was fooling myself. Time to clean out. Too fat. Too big and ugly and fat. Did I wake you up? You sound tired. Stay up late? Hey, so how's your love life, anyway, Soveida?"

THE BOOK OF SERVICE

CHAPTER THREE

Voice

The voice of the waitress should be well modulated, not loud or overbearing.

Customers should always be greeted as soon as possible. Say hello. Be cheerful. But don't be cute. There is nothing worse than a chirpy waitress early in the morning.

The first and foremost thing is to be efficient and fast. Don't gush over a patron. Or hover.

After greeting a customer, bring a glass of water, and ask about their drink order. Even in these days of economy, I always believe in bringing water.

Allow the customer to have sufficient time to read the menu, for godsakes. Many a tip has been compromised by an eager beaver. In the morning, most people move slowly. At lunch, everyone moves quickly, and the pace slackens in the evening. Adjust your rhythm to the time of day you work.

Once sufficient time has passed, take the table's orders. Expect that one or two people will not be ready. Never become impatient. Either return, if you are busy, or wait patiently, if decision seems imminent. If possible, try to take all orders at once. This rarely happens, so just accept it, and try to coordinate your food deliveries with different order times as best you can.

Once you have taken an order, and placed it in the kitchen, go about your business quickly, getting drinks, and picking up and delivering as much as you can of the side orders: soup, salad, bread, etc. Soup and salad always come before the meal, unless otherwise requested. Out-of-placement appetizers may injure your tip rating.

With coffee orders, the rule is to continue circling with a hot pot.

When delivering, serve from the right and remove from the left. Keep an appropriate distance from your customer.

You should be courteous at all times. Will that be all? Can I get you anything else? Catsup? Mustard? Salsa? Your voice should be balanced, clear, as well as reassuring.

The voice of the waitress is reassuring, familiar.

I always say that if you can wait on tables you can do anything.

29

New Neighbors

I knew that eventually someone would move in next door to me on Manzanares Street. I hoped my new neighbor would be quiet, someone who would greet me mildly on occasion and then retreat into a similar and well-organized solitude.

I was not prepared for Rey and Gloria Jiménez and Gloria's baby daughter, Sandra.

One day, after work, I came home to find a large silver van in front of the house. Shortly after that, my landlady, Mrs. Bright, came by to tell me that a young couple with a small child were moving in. Straining for politeness, I was clearly not happy with the news.

"How old is the young child, Mrs. Bright?"

"I'm not sure, Miss Torres. She's just a little thing, but they say she's quiet."

"Who are the couple?"

"Gloria and Rey Jiménez. Mexican, like you. They seemed real nice. They're in their early twenties. I wanted to make sure you had good neighbors."

"It's been very peaceful here."

"I'm glad to hear that."

"Thank you for stopping by, Mrs. Bright. I'll be looking for my new neighbors."

"I'm on my way to a DAR meeting. Has Mr. Farney come over yet to check those appliances?"

"Not yet."

"Well, you just give him a holler. Same goes for me. Now, if you get anything for my son, Buddy, do hang on to it."

"Yes. Thank you, Mrs. Bright."

With irritation I pondered the inevitable unpleasantness: new neighbors. Why now, of all times, were new neighbors moving in? Just when I was getting used to silence.

Dinner that night consisted of leftover tuna fish, Pizza Puffs, and a glass of water from the tap. Around 6 p.m. the silver van drove up. For several hours there was noise and movement as boxes were moved into their part of the duplex. I could see them through the living-room window. Their child was about four years old, and cute. The woman was young, but very large from the waist down. Her face was indistinct; all I could see were the very pronounced buttocks that bobbed up and down as she went back and forth with armfuls from either the van or the trailer behind it, into the house.

The man was dark and somewhat older. I never did get a fix on his face, not the entire time the Jiménezes lived next to me. And yet I would come to know Rey intimately. After what I came to know of him, I was glad I hadn't ever seen his face.

Their conversation was furious and profane.

"Dammit, get me the fucking lid. I dropped it, Gloria."

"Screw you, Rey. I'm busy. Get it yourself, asshole."

"Where's Sandra? Where the hell is she? Christ, you're her fucking mother!"

"You're her father now that you're married to me, bastard. How the hell should I know where she is! You have as much responsibility for her as I do, and don't you forget it, asshole."

"Hurry up, bitch, it's getting dark."

Inside my part of the house, I leaned against my curtains and sighed. It was the first of many such sighs. I was sorry that this couple and their child had come to disrupt a way of life that up to now had been blessedly mine.

It had been a long day: Larry was driving everyone crazy with one of his new schemes, a tortilla-making machine. To make matters worse, the patio had flooded in the last rain and we were still cleaning up water. On top of everything, Eloisa had accused one of her kitchen assistants, Lencho, of stealing steaks. She'd fired him right then and there and was in a foul mood for the rest of the day. And when Eloisa Ortiz is unhappy, everyone and everything in the world is unhappy as well.

A rattling noise came from the hallway. Someone was trying to open the door that led from house number 2 to house number 1. I could hear the spinning of the outdated doorknob. This was followed by a soft but continual rapping, someone's shrill yell, a slap, and a child's overdramatic squeal of pain. After that was a loud, persistent wailing, mixed with occasional moans. These were punctuated shortly by harsh adult words. There was more profanity, more screaming, the slamming of a door, and the high screech of burning rubber down the once quiet street. The man had left and now the woman yelled incessantly to the child to shut up. The more the woman yelled, the harder the child cried.

I heard all this from my bedroom, which opened up to the hallway door, and which led, unhappily, as I now knew, to the inescapably clear and perfectly audible world of my fellow housemates.

The crying and yelling finally quieted down. I got up, put on my nightclothes, did my nightly cleaning rituals, and went to bed. Perhaps the worst was over, I thought. Not so. Rey came back around 2 a.m. I could feel the time in my bones. That deceptively quiet time so pregnant with violence. I'd come to understand that time from Luardo and Hector and then Ivan. Half asleep, I heard an argument that was taking place right next to my room, in house number 2's master bedroom:

"You're drunk!"

"And you're a fat-assed bitch."

She is, I thought. But you, there are no words for you, unspeakable shit that you are.

"Where the hell have you been, Rey?"

"None of your goddamn business."

"Fuck you!"

"Fuck you!"

"Fuck you!"

"Scoot over, or is your fat ass going to take up the whole goddamn bed?"

"Sleep in the other room, bastard!"

"Move over, bitch!"

"What do you want to do, make love? Ha! No way in hell!"

"Shit, no. You smell down there."

"Fuck you!"

"Shut up! Can't you be quiet? She'll hear you."

"I don't care who hears me, asshole."

"Shut up! If you don't care about your damn daughter, then what about the neighbor?"

"Fuck her!"

This went on for another half hour, as gradually one, then the other, tired. Finally there was silence. I lay in bed exhausted, but unable to sleep.

The next day the famous tortilla machine was installed at the restaurant. It was Larry's idea, another brainstorm. If the restaurant bought and ran its own tortilla machine, we could cut costs.

The question was: Who was going to run the tortilla machine? It took at least six people: one to check the masa, one to see it was replenished from time to time, another to check the tortilla path and see that all the tortillas were on track, and finally one or two people to grab and collect the tortillas as they came off the conveyor belt, bagging them while they were still hot, in plastic bags.

It was undetermined who exactly was going to run the machine. Hastily cast ballots were made from old white paper placemats that Larry had distributed.

> TO RUN MACHINE: PLEASE CHECK
> WAITRESSES
> KITCHEN CREW
> CHUY
> OFFICE STAFF
> NEW HELP
> OTHER

Everyone I'd talked to privately had voted OTHER. No final tabulations were available, as the night crew was still needed for a complete vote.

Larry did call for votes, but most of the time he took it upon himself to proclaim edicts that led to the Christmas vacation fiasco, the Halloween costume overthrow, and the overtime-payment rebellion.

But that was Larry, and Larry's way of working: the vote calls, the weekly restaurant meetings in the patio, where he gave his oft-repeated notes on service, his recurring pep talks and human-interest reportage:

"Okay now, who left the soap-dispenser lid up in the men's room? It cost us a package of soap when a customer knocked it off the wall accidentally. Let's look sharp in the rest rooms, guys.

"The busboys are getting a little sloppy. Excuse me, Sandra, I mean bus people. Pato, wear those collars down, and Peetie, cut that hair. Watch those low-cut blouses, Barb. This is a family restaurant, not a nightclub. Randy, good work!

"The employee of the week is Pito Leal, day cook. Let's give Pito a hand. Thanks, Pito, we love ya. Keep those tacos rolling, Pito, my man! Now, about the tortilla machine. I know everyone is worried about who's going to run it. Just to show you how simple it is, I'll start it up myself tomorrow."

My brain was tired. I hadn't slept all night as a result of all the Jiménezes' yelling. When it had settled down, I was so disgusted with the man's "you smell down there" that I wasn't myself all day.

The possibility that I would be bagging hot tortillas during lulls of serving hot food was too horrible to think about. It wasn't enough that I had to serve bar drinks and tabulate my checks and then Petra's. She had never been able to add, still couldn't add. There was no way I'd vote to run that machine. Let Larry do it himself, if he was so eager.

I'd just settled in at home after a long day's work when there was a knock at the door.

"Hi, I'm your new neighbor, Gloria."

"Welcome! You're all moved in?"

"I hope we didn't make too much noise."

"No, not really."

"You live alone? I wish I lived alone. Ever been married?"

"Sort of."

"Lucky. Oh, this is Sandra. Say hello to the lady, Sandra. Say hello!"

"Hi, Sandra!"

"You want to come over? I got some Kool-Aid."

"No, thanks, maybe some other time."

"Hey, I can hear you from our side. You can probably hear me. If I start hitting the wall, just answer me. We can talk that way, okay?"

"All right."

"If I have a problem, I'll bang on the wall. You can do the same. What's your name?"

"Soveida Dosamantes."

"Just hit the wall. I'll hear you!"

The Jiménezes lived next door to me for about two months, and during that time Gloria and Rey never stopped fighting. The late-night arguments in bed were the most horrible and unendurable of all.

Rey would pull out all the male stops and tell Gloria what he thought of her, her body, her relatives, their marriage, and remind her that Sandra wasn't his child.

Gloria, on the other hand, countered with what she knew to be his drinking problem, his foul mouth, his laziness, his lack of sexual desire for her, his inability to feel, his irresponsibility in raising a child, and the fact that Sandra was not his but a "real man's child."

Every night I covered my ears and tried to sleep. On my days off I would hear a banging noise on the hallway door, and I knew it would be Gloria standing there on the other side, wanting to make conversation.

Toward the end of our time together on Manzanares Street, Gloria brazenly began to yell to me through the walls.

"Soveida! Ssst! What are you doing? You got some Diet Coke? I got some Kool-Aid. Come on over!"

"Can't now!"

"You busy?"

"Yeah."

"What are you doing? Come on over, okay? I got some diet root beer."

One day I just couldn't evade Gloria anymore and I went over for a drink. I felt sorry for Sandra. She was always crying, not real tears, but make-believe tears, wanting attention, manipulating her two so-called parents.

"Hey, can I see your place, Soveida?"

"Someone chopped the house."

"And we got the ugly part."

"You got the big bedroom, huh?"

"And you, the living room."

"You've got the nice bathroom."

"But I like this kitchen better. Leave those things alone, Sandra. Dammit, I said leave those things alone! They're not yours. *Leave them alone!* Or I'll hit you. Do you want Mama to hit you again? There. I told you I'd hit you. Now shut up, and stop crying! You live alone?"

"Yeah, I like it."

"Do you ever want to get married again?"

"No."

"Me neither. What's that in your mouth, Sandra? What is it? A french fry? Give it to me or I'll hit you again! Now, stop crying."

"Must be an old one. I guess it was under one of the cushions."

"You eat in the living room? Sandra! Stop it! Leave the lady's things alone."

"Hi, Sandra!"

"She doesn't talk. Something's wrong with her. What's that in your hand, Sandra? Open it up or I'll hit you!"

"Memememememememe."

"That's all she says. Me Me."

"Maybe you should see a doctor, I mean, shouldn't she be talking by now? How old is she?"

"Four and a half. She's not Rey's. I'd never have a baby with him. He wouldn't be a good father. Give me your hand. I said give it to me!"

"It's popcorn!"

"I like popcorn."

"Me, too. She probably found some under the couch. I guess I better clean under there."

"She's into things. I have to hit her all the time."

"Mememememememe!"

"She don't want to talk. If she did, she would. So come on over. We don't have any furniture yet. We just got married. The furniture here is ugly. Huh? You got the best side. Hey, look, there's the door where I call you from. Maybe someday if I need you I'll call and you'll come, okay? You know, if there's trouble.

"And you, if you need me, just knock on the door, I'll know right away. That's the way we'll do it."

A week later I persuaded Ivan to move my things to the Manzanares house. It had taken me that long to get myself together to see him again, but I wanted my belongings.

By then La Virgie was living at Crescent Acres full time. M.J. told me that there was talk of marriage; that is, after the divorce. It didn't surprise me. Ivan was a man who liked marriage. He liked having someone to come home to, even if that someone wasn't someone he loved. But he seemed to love La Virgie, even if she was just using him. If they got married, it would be divine retribution.

Ivan wasn't happy about having to round up and move my possessions. As a matter of fact, he was especially unpleasant that day. He threw the boxes in the van roughly, and cursed under his breath. I knew that he felt it was a tremendous imposition, but I was determined to get my things out, once and for all. La Virgie had the decency not to be at the house when I arrived. Ivan probably didn't know where she was himself. He was on edge, and not quite himself. La Virgie already had him off-balance.

I drove my car from the old house to the new, with Ivan following behind. I lost him once and had to wait for him. He honked me onward. I knew he was mad, but I didn't care.

I think Ivan was surprised at the barren state of his house, but that didn't fluster me at all. He had set up an old foam mattress that he used when he went camping in the living room. He and La Virgie were now sleeping on that. Everything that had once belonged to me was gone, pots, pans, dishes, silverware, the kitchen table, my old couch, even a rug Dolores had given Ivan, which he now didn't want. All that remained was the butter dish.

Ivan threw my boxes and bags to the floor. He took a long look around my living room. Then he wandered to the back of the house, without so much as a word.

"That'll be it?"

"Thanks, I mean it."

"I'll be going."

"All right. Bye."

"Bye."

He was angry and I knew it. He never imagined that I'd leave him with just a butter dish. It came as a shock to both of us. Later on he liked to brag that I'd even taken the mustard and mayonnaise from the refrigerator, but that wasn't true.

I was surprised to find that after Ivan left I felt very light, almost happy.

There was a knock at the door. Gloria's greeting. I knocked back with gusto.

Before I knew what had happened, the Jiménezes moved out. It must have happened when I was at work. From that time on, the nights were silent and long, full of mercy and compassion.

After work, while I was vacuuming under my couch cushions, Buddy Bright came to the door, looking for mail. He was chubby, with thinning blond hair, and had a bad case of pink eye. So this is Buddy Bright, the landlady's son, I thought to myself, as I closed the door.

Oh no, no way I would feel sorry for him, either.

If I felt sorry for everyone I met or who somehow touched my life, where would I be? How strong would I ever become? No, it was best not to feel too sorry for anyone. Life calls for more than pity. It calls for resolve, action, love, without all the tears.

And yet I'll never forget that little girl, Sandra, with her high-pitched "Memememememememe."

How could I have stood by and listened to that violence. How?

30

Chata

Since I've known Esperanza "Chata" Vialpando her fees have slowly climbed. She began cleaning houses for fifteen dollars a day, raising that to twenty in the early 1960s and twenty-five in 1965. In the early 1970s she went to thirty dollars and has remained there ever since. Chata first began cleaning for my grandmother Doña Trancha, moving on to Dolores and Mamá Lupita. Now she's working for me.

I've never hesitated to give Chata extra money, as well as whatever canned goods and clothing I don't want or can't use. In addition to all these things, I make sure Chata always has a good lunch, usually hot and store-bought. Every three weeks we decide what we feel like eating on Cleaning Day.

It has never entered my mind to leave Chata alone to clean house, and so when she comes to clean, the two of us scrape, scour, wash, rinse, polish, and then dry everything as best we can. I'll be dressed in my usual cleaning outfit: an old pair of black running shorts and a very large, paint-flecked white T-shirt. On my head is a tattered red bandanna that has also seen better days. A pair of gouged black rubber thongs completes my outfit.

Chata, on the other hand, is meticulously dressed in a pleasant nylon shirt dress, sturdy brown walking shoes that lace up, and dark panty hose. She carries a special apron with her to all her jobs, and each third Monday morning at 9 a.m. she ceremoniously removes it from a webbed blue-and-white plastic satchel made in Hong Kong, unfolding it tenderly. I run around the house organizing the cleaning supplies, while noting, once again, that I am low on soap pads and that I need to go to the grocery store to get my 409 multipurpose cleanser as well as a new pair of rubber gloves. Chata takes this all in stride, and does miracles with a little ammonia and some rags from a plastic bag Dolores has given me containing Luardo's old softened T-shirts and torn cotton boxer shorts.

She moves with effortless concentration, efficiency, and speed. Chata works hard all morning, stopping briefly only for lunch with me around noon. Today we've selected fried chicken, and today I leave the house to pick up the chicken secure and happy in the knowledge that Chata is "at home" cleaning. There's no question of trust. None whatsoever. That in itself is very wonderful. I know I can leave Chata all day if I ever have to, even all night, and that nothing irregular will happen. Everything would be in its place, or rather the place Chata feels it belongs. Because it's Chata who orders where the knives should be stored and what system will work best in each cabinet—the glasses on the left with the plates, and the cans of food on the right with all the spices. Oh no, nothing will be broken or hidden or stolen as long as Chata is here.

I've known Chata since I was very young and Chata was a young woman, en mis meras—in my flesh, as she likes to say about herself, with everything to look forward to, including lying down next to a man for the very first time. Now we are women together, both of us dear friends, years apart yet very close.

A short, compact, flat-nosed little woman, Chata has the most incredible hands I've seen on a woman. I once saw a photograph of Pablo Picasso's hands, and his short, squat fingers seemed highly inartistic. The hands of a laborer, I thought, not the hands of a great artist. Chata's hands are like Picasso's. They are thick, no-nonsense hands adept at any task. They are hands unafraid and willing to reach out. They are hands that can as easily comfort a child as pull long, tangled clumps of dark hair out of a clogged bathroom drain. Chata's hands aren't repelled by moldy food or liquid slosh of any kind. They never balk at objects sharp or rough, warm or cold. They are hands that never recoil at soft, sick flesh, or untidy corners full of dark brown roach droppings. They're never repulsed by stoves stuck with the usual dried macaroni, or burners gummy with rivulets of grease. They are hands that never use plastic gloves. "¿Pa' qué? What for? If I use them, I can't feel anything!"

Chata's hands are no strangers to toxic matter, and continue to dare to plunge into burning water to get the job done. No poison is unfamiliar to these hands, no Drāno, no Easy-Off, no lyes, or dyes, or scalding water, or full-strength bleach, because, to Chata, to feel is everything.

"And because, Soveida, one of the best of God's inventions has to be the fingernail. You can keep the earlobes—they're useless unless you wear earrings. And the breast, well, it has its use with babies, but for an old woman like me, breasts serve no purpose that I can see. They just get in the way. The same goes for an old man's penis. It's even more useless than a breast, or, worse yet, two breasts. For all the trouble they give men—and you hear of prostate problems in old men like you hear about the weather—well, they're just in the way, you might as well just fold them up and forget about them. There are other useless body parts, I don't know what God was thinking about. I've just covered a few of the most important. But a fingernail. A fingernail! God knew what *she* was doing when she invented the fingernail. And when you think about it, God had to be a woman to invent the fingernail. That's what I say. Only a female God would invent the fingernail. What would we do without fingernails? If I had money I'd invent a cleaning tool, like a scrapy-scrapy thing, made out of fingernails. Nothing tougher. If you give me those gloves, muchacha, I can't feel my way in the dark and pick my way into the light. You know how in México they make those things out of bone, like Don Quixote figures and all kinds of stupid things, to collect dust? Well, maybe I could invent something with fingernails. If I had money, I would look into it. Just think about all those fingernail clippings that go to waste! We could start collecting them. And who knows? Maybe someday you'd see a thing called Chata's Scrapy-Scrapy for a dollar sixty-nine in aisle 5 at the Piggly Wiggly or the Jewel. That's if I had the money. Now hand me the paper towels on that shelf."

Chata is fond of cleaning metaphors. A house is as clean as an old man's ears. As clean as a widow's windows. As clean as a virgin's ombligo. Here is a woman to whom cleanliness is a state of grace, the highest virtue known to any living soul. Chata is good at cleaning, and fast, faster than anyone I've ever known, faster than any of Mamá Lupita's girls or Dolores's helpers. She's even faster than me, and that's something.

Chata worked briefly for Doña Trancha, but that experiment was short-lived. The old woman was quite blind by then and in ill health.

"Oh, I could have taken her dishes stained with eggs and her foul bathroom like an open sewer pit. What I couldn't take—and I'll tell you this, girl, don't be telling your mamá—was that old woman's stinginess. Not once, during those four months that I was with her, did she offer me lunch. I'd start at six in the morning when it was still dark and I'd finish after the sun set. This was still when I was en mis meras—in my flesh—and there was no food in between, nor was there time to eat anything, if I had brought it. One day I just looked her in that eye of hers—the other one was white, like a dead-fish eye—and I said, I'm sorry, Señora Trancha, but I'll be leaving next week, I have another job.

"Now, I didn't have any sort of job, but I had to say something. Who wants to live like a prostituta en el infierno? Oh, the old woman carried on. I walked her into her bedroom with that walker of hers and she lay down, still angry. I didn't bother telling her why I was leaving. ¿Pa' qué? Why? She was too mean to change and I just knew something else was waiting for me. I was in my flesh then. Shortly after that, your mother put your grandma kicking and screaming into the Del Valle old folks' home where she later died. I never felt guilty. Why should I? Let her yell at those people up there at the Del Valle, I said, and see if they forget her lunch!

"Pobrecita, your grandma Doña Trancha, she was a cruel old woman when she was feeling good and meaner when she was feeling bad. And she was cold. Cold like the inside of this freezer, Soveida. You broke another bottle of that carbonated water in here again. Why don't you let it cool in the icebox, naturally? You're always in a hurry, girl! Well, your grandma was cold, and I'm not saying she didn't have her reasons. She was jagged like this ice, may she rest in peace. If hell is hot, she's sure to be there for the warmth. After that, I worked with your other grandma, Mamá Lupita, but she didn't want to pay me my full due and tried to bargain me out of my time and wanted to subtract for my lunch, so I decided to move on to las americanas. They pay me what I'm worth. And they give me old furniture they don't use anymore, and their clothes, which are very nice—not the rags your grandma Mamá Lupita tried to give me. Las americanas, Soveida, they're good to me, they give bonuses for Christmas. I love my little ladies, la Señora Bixler, la Señora Williams, la Señora Pringler, and especially la Señora King-Kelley. I don't have anything against my own people, except they don't feed you or pay you what you're worth. The men run after you when their wives are gone, and try to lift up your skirts when you're hunched over cleaning out their toilet bowls, and the women, I speak from experience, don't have no pity for you if anything goes wrong. They start on how you're a mexicana and nobody from México can do anything right and how mexicanas can't be trusted and so on. And they forget they're mexicanas, too. Maybe they should look in the mirror. With them, it's all your fault, even if you don't do anything wrong. Me cansé. I got tired of working for no money and for people who don't appreciate me. You should see how la Señora Pringler loves me! She buys me Arby's every Tuesday; another gets me a whole pizza with pepperoni. There was food, Soveida, at your grandma Doña Trancha's, that wasn't it; she just didn't want to share it. Even with herself she was stingy and ate like a bird. Your mother always complains that Doña Trancha was always telling her not to eat so much and now, because of that, she always has an icebox full of food. After all these years of not eating with the mexicanas, now with the gringas I can eat.

"Ay, it's the little things. Las americanas, they give me rides to work and back. One old woman I used to work for, she was a mexicana, she made me walk to work and then back to my house, with two cars sitting in her garage. And not only that, she gave me chiles for lunch each week, with a single tortilla. These were the same chiles we used to peel for her restaurant. No, señorita, I said. I deserve more than this. Someone else hired me, I told her. Soveida Dosamantes, that's who. My new patrona. So, do you want this old ice cream or not? I'm throwing it out and also these old tamales in the back. The aluminum came off and they're covered with ice. Hand me the pan with the soapy water. Like I always say: Never work for someone who won't feed you. What they want is a dumb animal, not a person to help. If a person is stingy in their own home, imagine how they are out in the world? If they screw you in the kitchen, what will happen in the street? Just because you see their filth on the inside doesn't mean you *are* filth if you wipe it away. Just because I clean your toilet doesn't mean I'm not a woman and don't love to dance. So watch out! Don't push me! I'll get mad! Because if you're pushing me to get me mad I will. A clean house is a virtue. If you need a priestess, I'm the one. Call me, but softly. And then get out of my way unless you can keep up with me. Now you, *you* almost can keep up with me, Soveida! The others, if they get in my way, it'll be too late for them to say they're sorry unless they really mean it. I know. I was born with this extra body part most people don't have. I call it my other brain. It's this dark little nudo, this knot like a root in between my eyes that lets me know what's true and what's a lie. Sometimes I can feel it throbbing there in my head like a question mark or an exclamation point, depending on what it feels, lies or truth. It's no bigger than a frijol but very powerful. Not too many people have this extra body part. I never usually talk about it, but it just came up. My grandmother had one, too. She called it the nudo. With it, I can read people. I've dealt with them enough. Just hand me the sponge, I'm going to mop up the spilled water. What do you say we have Chinese next time?"

I love these Mondays with Chata. Talking in Spanish and laughing in no particular language. Spanish, my grandmother Lupita's favorite language. Spanish, my father's little-used language, he having grown up at a time when children were punished for speaking Spanish on the playground. Spanish, my mother Dolores's language of intimacy and need. Spanish, Doña Trancha's shrill, invective language of complaint and horror without ceasing, hard as a fist and painful as flesh doubled over, words spat and splattered on the white walls of her tiny room at the Del Valle Nursing Home, walls covered with family photos hung by Dolores, the daughter who wasn't a daughter, because no real daughter could put her own mother in a nursing home. Spanish. Once, lying with Ivan, his telling me thickly in the darkness, "Te quiero, te quiero, te quiero." I want you. I want you. I want you. In Spanish.

Cleaning up in Spanish with Chata the remnants of my other worlds: work and the deceptively quiet and desperate living of a soon-to-be-divorced woman. I am a waitress who knows what it is to serve others and a woman who knows what it is to work hard. I understand so well what it is to lift and clean up and mop and hose down that I have to stay home every third Monday to help my cleaning woman clean my house. I don't want Chata to do it alone, although she is a woman who knows what it is to be alone, to work alone. I work just as hard as my cleaning lady because I want to, because I have to.

I feel guilty when I hand Chata the Easy-Off with lye, because it's a job *no one* should have to do. When I can, I always wear gloves. I own three pair. Blue. Pink. Yellow. I don't feel it's right for Chata to burn her hands cleaning the stove, but Chata only refuses to use the gloves once again.

"I can't feel with them on, girl. And I need to feel."

I feel I am no better, no less than Chata: we are equals. Except when it comes to the stove. Or maybe because of the stove.

This was Monday's Chata. The other Chata had two children from a man named Candenacio "Candy" Limón. Chata worked every day of the week except Sunday. I've only heard about this Sunday woman; I never knew her. This was the woman who met with Candy when his wife, Sidelia, was at Mass.

Both Chatas have calloused hands that stroked and loved and offered lingering caresses; both had hands made no less beautiful by either scars or burns. Both Chatas had efficient bodies, whether working tirelessly for some americana or making passionate love to her Candy.

Chata and Candy loved each other, but he was married in the Church. Eventually he died of cancer. He was much older than Chata and it was to be expected, she said. She'd gone to Candy's funeral, but his grown children had asked her to leave. His wife, a living saint riddled with tumors, stopped Chata on the way out and pulled her over to the casket. His two wives sat side by side during the Mass, holding hands like long-lost sisters, each comforting the other. And when Sidelia, Candy's tumor-ridden widow, died that June, Chata was barred again by those middle-aged brats. She wept to herself, remembering both Candy and Sidelia at the same time, envying them their peace. Someday, she thought, she would happily join them. But for now she was "in her flesh" and there was work to be done.

Chata adjusted the radio that was tuned to XELO, Juárez, México, and then threw out the dirty water she'd collected from cleaning the freezer.

"There. That's it, Soveida. What's next? Are we doing cabinets this week or walls?"

There is peace on Chata's Monday. All is ordered. Calm. Correct. As any polite Mexican will say with great courtesy befitting something that is natural, apt, appropriate, "Es propio." It's as it should be.

Every third Monday there is a breaking of bread between two hardworking women who honor each other's work. A communion. A sacrament.

"You're a good worker, Soveida," Chata once complimented me. Coming from Chata, this is the highest honor ever given to me by a fellow worker. I'll cherish that blessing all my life.

Chata lives in a tiny two-room shack in Chiva Town, where once goats roamed freely through the streets. This squat woman with thick hands lives crowded with her two children in a place that has no kitchen, just a counter with a sink, a small stove, and a much-used refrigerator. It's she who has taught me what home really means, what comfort really is. And it's because of Chata, who shares a living/sleeping

room with her teenage daughter—her son sleeps in the alcove outside
the main room—that I have eventually come to know what happiness
can be. Chata has taught me what work is and how every woman should
continue to work, even in the worst of times, day after day, week after
week, year after year.

"Laughter is good and so are the tears," Chata says, as she reaches
for a clean rag, pulling out a pair of Luardo's softened Fruit-of-the-
Looms. "I had me my Candy and he had me. My kids know that I
love them. Manuel is a freshman at State University and Leticia's in
band at the high school. She'll graduate next year. Their daddy would
be proud, Soveida. And you, when are you going to have children?
It's never too late. Not for a woman like you, 'in your flesh,' who knows
what it is to work and to love. Because, girl, let me tell you, loving is
work! Even if you have an extra body part like I do, the little root still
can't stop suffering. Hand me the Pledge. We're almost out, Soveida.
Get some for next time, don't forget. I'm moving into the living room."

Chata on Monday. The Order. The Calm. A woman in a state of
grace.

Virtues

31

Strip Poker

On a Friday toward the end of the month, Veryl Beron presented himself to Ede Le Crenshaw, the hostess at El Farol, requesting a table in "Miss Dosamantes's section." The news traveled back to the kitchen, where I was picking up a large order of very hot sopaipillas.

"Es un güero, he's a blond," was the news. I hoped it might be Veryl Beron even if his hair was a light brown. It had been nearly a month since I'd met him at the Sudsy laundromat and we'd driven out to the river in his truck, Maybelline.

In my excitement I burned myself rather badly on the edge of the hot grease pit where the sopaipillas were being fried by Cresencio, Eloisa's new kitchen aide. I didn't want to show anyone that the news had unsettled me, so I merely winced and went on with my work. Eloisa, who was closely supervising the latest of her new—and unsatisfactory—kitchen aides, saw everything.

"¡Cuidado, mujer! What's with you? Let me look at your hand. Cresencio, bring me some lard to put on Soveida's burn, would you?"

He had been reading *The Red and the Black* by Stendhal, and that impressed me. I'd read it in high school, and still thought about it from time to time. I had just moved to a new apartment and had about eight loads of dirty laundry. At one point, between my switching from a wash to a dry, Veryl got up and dragged a large metal laundry cart around the room, picking up wet clothes from three distinct and far-flung corners of the room. He then put away his book and rounded the corner to the dryers. When he came back, he stood in the middle of the room and stared intently at the air in front of him. I'd noticed him right away. And, as he stood there pensively, I felt myself somehow drawn to him. A young couple were folding their mismatched and somewhat shabby laundry nearby. The girl was a chubby blonde in dirty white pants that trailed behind her, a soiled, ragged hem occasionally catching on her bare, calloused feet. She stuffed their clothing into a large plastic bag as the young man carefully placed a tattered pair of baggy jeans on a metal hanger he had removed from the garbage bin. Whiskered like a goat, with long, solitary, and very proud hairs on his chin and upper lip, he had pants on that were loose in the rear and a blond afro that fanned out, framing a face that seemed childishly bored. The girl's breasts dangled like sacks to mid-waist, in a hot-pink, calypso blouse. She stared at her man possessively with turquoise-lidded eyes. Then she moved to his side, putting a plump hand around him. He was tired of her, and there appeared to be little connection between them, aside from a commitment to laundry. I stared until I felt the young woman get uncomfortable. She eyed me suspiciously. The young man motioned for her to gather their possessions and with an air of confidence he sauntered out of the laundromat holding his prized jeans as she dragged the large full plastic bag behind her. My gaze shifted to an attractive dark-haired woman who was folding her clothes nearby. She picked up a man's still warm shirt from a dryer and tucked it under her chin, the shirt buttons facing away from her. She proceeded to button every last button. Turning the shirt around, she folded the shirt down on each side, bringing in first one sleeve and then another in an embrace, her arms invisibly melding into the shirt's arms, her chest into the shirt's front. It was as if she was sloughing away her own skin to get inside the skin of the shirt's owner, someone she loved. After folding the shirt in half she brought it to her nose, inhaling its fragrance. I wondered if I would ever love like that again.

Without my wanting to, my gaze kept moving back to *The Red and the Black*. He had missed everything that had taken place in the laundromat. He continued to stare into ever-darkening space. He got up abruptly and removed his clothes from the dryer. Then he began folding his cotton shirts and his brightly colored jockey shorts. By then my wash was done. When I put my clothes into a dryer he had vacated, I found a pair of dark shorts he'd left behind. With some embarrassment, I went up to him and handed him a slightly damp pair of black jockey shorts.

"Excuse me . . ."

"Yes?"

"You left these."

"I did? Sorry."

"It's all right. I—you're welcome—"

"Veryl Beron. Pleased to meet you."

"Soveida Dosamantes."

We started talking. I forgot to put more money into the dryer. Veryl's laundry was already long folded by the time I remembered. He was very patient as I finished drying my eight loads of laundry. He asked me to join him next door at Casa Fiesole for coffee.

"I don't drink coffee."

"Me, neither."

"It makes me nervous."

"Me, too."

"Coke?"

"No, it makes me nervous, too."

"Same here. Okay, forget that place."

"We could go some other place. I got a truck, an old piece of junk. Maybelline."

Veryl winked, turned away, and then looked back at me. I felt a chill. We were standing outside the Sudsy. He with several pillowcases full of shirts and shorts, and me with two plastic laundry baskets, one large duffel bag, and an armful of dresses and blouses on hangers.

We left my car in the Sudsy parking lot along with all my clothes, and drove to the river. It was around 5:30, twilight time, November. Veryl drove way out to the acequia, where few people ever go. The sun was brilliant pink, then red, then gold. I couldn't believe I was at the river with a stranger, and that my car was in town, with eight loads of laundry waiting to be put away.

There was something about Veryl, even then, that I loved. His blue eyes, with soft light brown lashes, looked straight at me. I could see a small miniature sun setting in his eyes. He talked about this place he loved, and the colors of the sunset. I sat apart from him and felt his love of nature, his love of beauty.

Suddenly, without warning, he grabbed me fiercely, brutally, and ran his lips over my face, while he clutched my breasts desperately and moaned like a small animal. I was so surprised I couldn't even respond. And then, just as suddenly, he sprang away from me and jumped out of the truck and into the darkness. After a short while he emerged, and we then drove back to the Sudsy so I could pick up my car. Both of us were afraid to speak.

It wasn't until later, alone, in the silence of my bedroom, that I realized that Veryl had been so excited that he'd gotten out of his truck and ejaculated in the darkness.

Veryl had said matter-of-factly at the end of our first encounter: "Don't be surprised if someday I turn up at the restaurant." I'd waited to hear from him that very week. By the second week I had my doubts, and by the third week I had lost all hope. Could this be Veryl, after all?

It was, and he sat under one of the tepees wearing a casual sports coat. His hair was still unruly, and there was a huge smile on his face. When he saw me he took off his dark glasses, stood up, and waved from across the room. I ducked quickly inside the little room where we tallied our bills, to get myself together. I hurriedly applied a fresh coat of lipstick. Pancha Portales was filling up a tray full of water glasses and nudged me knowingly. She hadn't missed a thing and flicked a white dishrag on my arm, a snapping reminder of her complicity.

"Pancha," I said in protest.

"Go on, your novio is waiting."

"He's not my boyfriend!"

"Oye, you forgot your water, Miss-I'm-in-love-don't-talk-to-me-now."

I approached Veryl's table shyly. "Hello, Veryl," I said, my voice trapped hollowly in the back of the throat.

"Soveida! How have you been? Busy, it seems. I didn't know this place was so popular."

"Fridays are like this. How are you, Veryl?"

"I've been sick."

"You've been sick? Are you all right? Can I get you anything?"

"I was looking at the menu. How about the enchiladas deluxe with a large water. Oh, and some tortillas on the side to mop up."

"Flour or corn?"

"Flour. See if the cook can burn them a little. I like them black."

"Veryl, are you okay? I was worried when I didn't hear from you. I thought . . ."

"I'll tell you about it when we get together this weekend. Can we? Some friends of mine are having a party Sunday night."

"Red or green chile?"

"Green."

"Will that be all?"

"I want to see you, Soveida."

"You do? Then call me at home, Veryl. We're really busy now and I can't talk. Sorry."

I got Veryl's water and then put in his order for the green enchiladas deluxe. I forgot the tortillas. Veryl reminded me about them once as I went by and I promptly forgot them again. I didn't remember the tortillas until I totaled up the bill and saw as plain as can be: side burnt flour.

"Here's your check, Veryl. I'm so sorry about the tortillas."

"No problem, Soveida. You can make them for me sometime."

Veryl tore off the receipt end of the check where I'd written: Soveida Dosamantes. 428-1175. 7–9 a.m., 3:45–5 p.m., and 10:30 p.m. on. Keep trying.

I walked him to the cash register and gave him his change. Veryl suddenly kissed me gently on the cheek before I could protest. The next thing I knew, he was waving goodbye.

Pancha's shrill voice brought me back. "Are you done with the cash register, or are you going to make love to it?"

When I turned around to look at Pancha she winked and smiled her annoyingly ingratiating bird-in-her-mouth smile.

"Who's your novio? He's pretty cute for a gringo."

That was it. From then on, Veryl became el novio—the boyfriend.

"How's your love life, Soveida?" Pancha purred while ladling sour cream on a green enchilada platter.

"I heard he's very handsome." Margarito chimed in. "But I'll have to judge for myself. So when is your novio coming back in, Soveida?"

The day Veryl came in, Larry was out until after four. He had gone to pick up a shipment of paper products. He came into the kitchen exhausted, irritated with the long wait, and annoyed that the day was nearly over.

"Soveida's got a new boyfriend. He was here today, Mr. L. He had the green deluxe. A face pretty like a girl's and long legs that go all the way to heaven. He's younger than Soveida. He's younger than you, isn't he?" Pancha turned to me, counted her tips, then set all the George Washingtons face upwards as she paused to smack her lips. "Ay, he's real cuerito, with nalgas asina, you know," and with that she made a round tight little circle.

"Get me some water, Cresencio, would you?" Larry barked. "I'm dehydrated. The bank says 112 degrees but I think it's at least 115. Bring me two large Dr Peppers and a pitcher of ice water on a tray. I'll be in my office, but don't disturb me. I've got paperwork."

"Which means he's going to take out his cot and lay down and take a nap," Pancha said loudly, within earshot of Larry's hunched, over-heated figure. "Soveida's got a new boyfriend. Did you hear me, Mr. L? Maybe she'll get married. Hey, you gonna get married, Soveida? You should. You're getting old and your body clock is twisting and turning. Ticky ticky ticky ticky. Your novio could make real pretty babies, that's what I say!"

"I'll be in my office, Pancha," Larry said, returning. "You on to-morrow?"

"Válgame Dios, you know I don't work Saturdays, Mr. L. I got me my dog races to go to in Juárez. You forget that?"

"Good. I'll see you later!"

"Chihuahua, the man's crazy! The heat's cooked his cesos. He should know when I work and when I don't work, he makes up the schedules," Pancha exclaimed. She picked up several nickel, dime, and quarter money rolls, tucked those in a huge black industrial-size purse with six compartments, one of which was reserved for her rolls, then clipped her bills with a lucky horseshoe money clip and stuffed that in her brassière. She was ready to go home. It had been a long day.

"Maybe Larragoite was saying you need to take a day off, Pancha. You're working too hard," Margarito offered.

"Yeah, that's true," Pancha said.

"Maybe you should take some time off and relax your tongue," I muttered to myself as I cleared my last few tables before going home myself.

It was no use telling Pancha to be quiet about Veryl. It would only aggravate matters. For some reason, I felt the talk about Veryl would never die out. He was too unusual for people like Pancha. Let Pancha have her speculations, the old bat, whatever they were. I knew I would never have the right answers to the wrong questions.

Late Saturday evening Veryl called as I was eating dinner, a burned baloney sandwich with mayonnaise inside a flour tortilla. He invited me again to the party on Sunday at Norma and Andy's—a young married couple who lived in the country, south of Agua Oscura.

Sunday night he picked me up in his truck. He was casually dressed in jeans, a Western shirt and boots. I felt overdressed in a brightly colored flowered summer dress belted tightly at the waist, heels and panty hose.

Norma was a short, petite blonde in her mid-thirties. She greeted Veryl with a kiss on the lips. Andy was a tall, thin, brown-haired fellow in jeans who hugged me hard. For all their friendliness, I never felt comfortable with them. The dinner took hours to prepare. I ranged through their high-ceilinged, cavernous house all night as the three friends sat in front of a silent television set, rolling joints, smoking them, and laughing at the shows they watched.

Not wanting to smoke, I wandered around, and found myself in the kitchen, staring at the dingy yellow walls and the dirty stove, wishing I were somewhere else. Not wanting to join the others in the living room, I sat for what seemed a long time at the kitchen counter, looking at the scruffy, spotted floor, and then down at my white heels. I couldn't understand why Veryl was ignoring me. At times he was warm and loving; at other times, cold and distant.

It was a mistake to have gone there, I thought. Veryl had said there was going to be a party, and yet, other than Veryl and me, no guests—except one—arrived. From the beginning I felt anxious.

After dinner, a friend of Norma and Andy's came over. I can't remember his name, but his face is sharply etched in my memory. "The Farmer," I called him. He had a farm and lived, like Norma and Andy, in the country. He had a medium build, a muscular body, and wild red hair. Curious, hungry eyes searched me out, wondering who I was, and made me wonder myself.

It was Andy who suggested we play strip poker. Norma agreed wholeheartedly. The Farmer looked at me with his mongrel's eyes, and, in turn, I looked with terror at Veryl, who sat on the porch with Norma and Andy. All of them were content, at ease, and fearless.

I didn't want to play. But Veryl agreed it was a good idea.

"Loser has to take off his or her clothes," Andy insisted.

"So give me the cards to shuffle," Norma said.

"You in?" the Farmer asked Veryl.

"Hell, yes! Come on, Soveida!"

"I don't know, Veryl."

I took a card, knowing that I couldn't refuse. Before we started, I had to ask the rules again, as I always do when I play poker: a what beats a what? But actually I'm good at cards; in fact, at any game that requires luck and will. And this was a game I just couldn't lose.

I was sweating profusely for what seemed an interminable amount of time, time spent in a strange hell. I couldn't let anyone know that I was afraid. I wasn't careless, like Norma, or flagrantly wild like Andy, or absent-minded and self-absorbed like Veryl. I played the dog-eyed man and won every single round, praying as I played. My dignity remained intact but was still slightly bruised. My only opponent was the red-haired stranger. I didn't care to reveal myself to him. He wanted to see me naked and I knew it. Naked unlike the others wanted to see me naked, naked with desire. Only we two were sober and we understood each other.

The losers, naturally, were Norma and Andy. In a flurry of cloth, they removed their clothes and ran across the lawn, a long expanse of yard filled with pecan trees. They yelled and whooped and hugged each other in the darkness. And before they returned, I got up and went into the bathroom, turned on the faucet, and patted my face with tepid water from the tap.

Take me home, Veryl, I whispered to the mirror. Take me home.

On rejoining the group, I saw that Norma and Andy were dressed, and Veryl was saying goodbye to everyone. I, too, said goodbye to a Norma I would never see again and the Andy who seemed so eager to remove his clothes.

I remember their naked flesh darting in the moonlight. The grass smelled of a fresh mowing. I remember my feeling of humid relief. I remember, too, those last long looks of the dog-eyed man following me hungrily to the door.

I blame myself. Then. And now. For knowing from the beginning that Veryl could never love me the way I wanted to be loved. Instead, I would care for him the way I wanted someone to care for me. When Veryl took me home after the party, he kissed me gently on the lips and left me, sullied, empty, bruised, and madly in love.

One night after a movie we decided to go back to his place. We held each other and attempted, that very first time, in fits and starts, to make love. I was startled and saddened by his penis as we both tugged and pushed and struggled to insert it into my vagina. It was no use. And so we lay, exhausted and angry and too sad to speak.

Veryl got up after a while and went to his closet. He brought out a box full of 8 × 10 photos of himself as Christ, tied to a wooden cross that was set up in an empty field.

"Who took these?" I asked.

"A friend."

"Is that you, Veryl?"

"Yes"—he laughed—"that's me as Christ."

Sure enough, he looked like Christ. No matter that he never believed. He was dressed in a loincloth and had a full beard.

"It was my turn," Veryl said, looking at me triumphantly.

And with that Veryl took the photos from me and put them away in a box that he took back to his closet.

I wanted to cry. About what it's hard to say. The penis or the pictures, or myself in relation to both, or Veryl's relation to himself.

Veryl, I learned, had Peyronie's disease. I first read about it in Dr. Huppler's column in the local newspaper:

> Dear Dr. Huppler:
> I think I may have Peyronie's disease. Is there a cure?
> Desperate in Des Moines

> Dear Desperate:
> Peyronie's disease affects vessels in the sheath surrounding the penis. As a result, the vessels do not fill with blood even during an erection. This causes a painful twisting. Since it always occurs during an erection, it can cause you discomfort, both physical and mental, but it is not life-threatening. The disease can be treated with radiation therapy, drugs, or surgery. You don't mention your age; however, Peyronie's disease rarely occurs in males under 45. Just relax, it may cure itself.
> Dr. Hubert Huppler, M.D.

Veryl said the problem was the result of a boating accident at Caballo Lake. He didn't go into details.

We dated for nearly a year, and one night, after trying to make love, he asked me to marry him and I said yes. I don't know why, but I felt myself bound to him, heart and soul, come what may. Veryl said everything would work out in time. I wanted to believe it. Somehow I knew things would never be normal, but it was all right. I was never used to normal.

THE BOOK OF SERVICE

CHAPTER FOUR

Costume

A waitress's dress can only be called an "outfit." You will eventually grow to hate it, be it short or long, low-cut or high-collared. The darker the color, the greater the loathing.

It helps to imagine you are an actress in a play, and that your outfit is your costume. The play will last from ten-thirty to three-thirty if you are lucky (the lunch shift), and then the costume can be retired. Forgotten.

The next day you put it on again, remembering at that very moment, not sooner, the smell. Food! Hot hamburger juice, grease, red chile, aging tomatoes. You remember that you haven't washed your outfit since last Tuesday and that yesterday you spilled iced tea and hot steaming soup on yourself.

It is important to keep your costume clean, mended, and ironed. Panty hose are a must, or at least some kind of socks, minihose, depending on skirt length or type of outfit. You need something to keep your bare feet from touching the cold, food-strewn, soggy floor, the one the customer never sees.

Bare feet on leather can be hot, uncomfortable, and sweaty, and can lead to calluses. A waitress's nightmare. You will probably develop them anyway, but it is best to do it slowly.

Wear socks or hose and you won't regret it. They may need to serve as insulation or protection. You're likely to find food on the kitchen floor someday, or water, something definitely oozy or juicy that you may have to jump over, tread carefully through, or slide by. The slosh and slop of a hard day's work. A dishwasher on the blitz, a leaky container of dripping Thousand Island dressing, spilled hot butter, mushy sour cream, all near the broken baked-potato oven.

Remember that you are an actress in a play. Although the play may constantly be changing, you will, under any circumstances, be prepared to assist your fellow actors. And because you are in character, your lines will be easy to remember.

32

A Better-Looking Mexican

One long hot Tuesday night Albert Chanowski told his life story to Barb Valentine, the night bartender. Barb in turn told it to me.

Albert was a retired symphony conductor from New York who had moved to New Mexico for his health. He was short, red-faced, and had a nose webbed with spider veins. His eyes were large and bulged like marbles. His right eye wandered off, pulled as it were by something to the side, a vision, an apparition, or an intimation of something coming around the corner from nowhere. Albert called it his fish eye.

Albert's hair was the color of a poached salmon. He had little hair left, but what was still his was stubborn and long, and he plastered it over the front of his gray scalp. Albert was unsure about his height, his weight, his penis, which was long and thin like a crooked middle finger. His asthma came on suddenly and just as quickly it left. At all times he carried with him a white plastic inhaler which he sprayed up his hairy nose and then put away in his pocket, fiddling with it as other men play with spare change.

New York had become too difficult for him, now that he was older. But sixty-two wasn't really that old: many men didn't retire until sixty-five or seventy. Besides, retirement was passé today, especially for artists. And Albert Francis Chanowski was an artist.

Albert had played in all the great halls. He was once a personal friend of Bernstein's, and a familiar face on the music scene. It had taken him years of hard work to achieve his success. Born in Brooklyn, he'd taken piano lessons as a child. That's how it all began. But Brooklyn was far away, as far away as that drink of vodka he longed for now, and as far away as that waitress, Soveida Dosamantes, who worked at El Farol Restaurant and caused his blood to boil.

The vodka helped his breathing. When he woke up that morning, he knew it was going to be a difficult day. Still hung over from drinking at El Farol the night before, he arose at 9 a.m. to pee, then returned to bed until 11, when he got a phone call from MasterCard asking him to purchase credit-card insurance for three years.

No, thanks, he had said. One year? Thank you, no.

He lay in bed for half an hour after that, twiddling and thumbing his penis while thinking about an old lover, Marie. He thought about going over to her apartment, him coming up behind her in her small kitchen as she was doing their dinner dishes, all the windows open and she squealing, "The neighbors will see. They'll see!" as he grabbed her from behind and she dropped down her pants and squealed again. Then they would go up to her bedroom and she lay on the bed with her buttocks raised up to him. And as he pumped her good and hard, because that's what she wanted, he would read the titles of some of her books on the wooden shelf that was now eye level with him: *Romancero Gitano* by Federico García Lorca, *Flowers of Evil* by Baudelaire, and others, a bunch of Europeans, some Western writers— because that was where she was from, Oregon—arty books by a plethora of famous and semifamous men and a few women. So, the little bitch liked to read, he thought. His long narrow penis filled her up nicely with its length. Marie.

She liked him. But she lied to him. She said it was okay when it wasn't. Said it was safe when it wasn't. Marie got pregnant and he told her he couldn't give her any emotional support, and not to expect anything from him; that he didn't even love her. Marie cried softly and then tried to become hard. She said to him she was all right and that she didn't expect anything from him. But she did, the bitch. So he told her he'd help with the kid. Tried to press two hundred-dollar bills into her hands the last time he saw her, but she pulled away violently and shrank into sobs. He almost admired her then.

Marie lost the baby. The fetus just stopped growing. She called him from the hospital to tell him. As a Catholic she'd named the baby Justine, because she felt it was a girl, had dreamed it would be a girl.

"Goodbye."

"Goodbye."

"Yeah, goodbye, and keep out of trouble."

"Yeah, and you, too."

"You're probably relieved."

"Yeah," he said. "You?"

"I loved the baby. To you, I was knocked up. To me, I was full of life. To you, all of it was lousy. To me, it was sacred."

"Yeah," he said, "here I was divorced and middle-aged and having kids. It just wasn't right. I mean, with my wife we kept trying to have kids, and with you it just happened, bingo! No, it wasn't right."

God, he knew he would miss her. That squeal, and her buttocks raised, her sex a flower whose fragrance he knew in the dark. Marie. It was good. The child probably would have looked like them both. Could have married that girl and her poems. But all he needed were more bills. And a woman to take care of. That's what happened to his last marriage. He had to be a father to Bernice. For twenty-five years. Until one night he just sat up in bed and said this is it. If he'd married Marie it would have been the same debt—a man taking care of a woman. He'd be bound to her by his purse strings, telling her what to do and how to do it. Both of them would be unhappy and still making love because they had to. Not that he'd have to marry Marie. She didn't even want it. But with a kid! What do you expect? The little bastard tying you down and making you owe for so many things, things you thought you were free of, because a man needs to be free—of children and their mothers—especially if those children are your own.

Sometimes the right woman came up at the wrong time. Like Marie. Or that girl, Soveida. He was in his late forties when he met Marie. Now he was too old to be lying in bed half the morning, holding himself while thinking of a woman. Dark rose with thorns.

It seemed so long since he had met her. Yet it was only six months ago. The first time he wandered into El Farol, he was looking for a drink. He just walked down the street, and before you knew it, he'd decided to move to that part of town. It was colorful and cheap, the only problem being all the Mexicans living there.

He knew he was in love the first time he saw her standing at the bar talking to Jimmy the bartender. He was in the far corner, near the restrooms, hiding by the cash register, and he could see her but she couldn't see him. A tall girl for a Mexican. Thin but full-figured. Not young. Not old. Just the right age. A woman for a guy like him who likes women of a certain age, women to whom life is sometimes a comfortable old coat, and then a thin translucent gown signaling promise and passion. A woman like Marie, relaxed in her blue pantsuit, doing the dishes, the next moment panting with real desire. Soveida Dosamantes could be that sort of woman.

The mating ritual began very slowly. For several months he went every day into El Farol to stare at her when she wasn't looking. Then the visits tapered off to four times a week. More, and it would have driven him crazy. Less, and it would have driven him crazy, too. Hell, he was already crazy. As it was, Soveida was causing his hair to fall out. And not only was his eczema acting up again, but he'd been constipated since early February. It was deep into March. Very deep.

No two ways about it, the little bitch was driving him mad, causing him torment.

"Hey, Jimmy!"

"Say, Chanowski! Coming right up. The usual?"

"Hold it, James. Let Soveida bring it to me. I'll be over in the patio. Make that the Kachina Room. Is that where she's working tonight?"

"I can fix you up, maestro."

"Let her bring it. I'm paying for the goddamn drink."

"You going to behave?"

"Hell yes! Just have her bring me my drink."

There he'd sit, legs splayed, waiting for her. Then she'd walk in with the drink order.

"Vodka and water? Oh. It's you, Albert."

"Just set it here, Soveida."

"Albert, why do you want me to bring this little drink to you all the way over here, when you know Jimmy and Barb could have helped you out?"

"I like the Kachina Room."

"Just last week you told me you hated this room."

"I like the Kachina Room."

"And if I was in the Tepee Room, you'd like it, or the Stalactite Room if I was in there. You have to cut this out, Albert."

"See, I have my money. Tip included. There you go. Simple."

"Promise?"

"Promise."

"Why don't I trust you?"

"Soveida! Soveida! Just let me kiss you!"

He tried to grab her, but she was too fast for him, years of training. And she took off.

Damn, all he wanted to do was kiss her.

But she'd disappeared, and he found himself staring into the darkness she'd left behind, like a passing vision from his personal hell.

After that last time he had to sit at the bar if he wanted to get served. It was a slow night and Soveida came up. She was expecting a drink order when, instead, he asked: "What are you? Spanish?"

"No, I'm Mexican."

"You see that woman over there? The light-skinned one. She told me she was Spanish. You're not a Mexican. I know Mexican when I see Mexican. You're Spanish!"

"My family originally came from Chihuahua. I'm Mexican."

"Well then, you're one of the better-looking Mexicans!"

Soveida walked away. It was getting busy at El Farol.

She *was* better-looking. All the Mexicans, well, all the women he'd seen, yeah, you'd see them in the streets of New York. Hell, he'd even been to Mexico City and Acapulco a few times. Those women were short, squat, big-hipped, with either long dark nose hairs or swirling, mashed leg hairs in stockings held up by rubber ties just above their hairy knees. They wore short-sleeved or sleeveless blouses with brown armpit stains and their armpit hair hung tough over their brassières. There was hair over every damn brown inch of those women's bodies—nipples, belly buttons, thighs, toes, ears—hair like a man's wildest hair. He knew those women in dark rooms, the shades pulled down. Their bushes smelled of wet fur and musty earth. It wasn't pleasant, not really, with those women. But a man gets lonely in other countries and he was curious about all those Mexican women with their big hips and hair enough for any man, whether he liked it or not. Untrained hair and dark, sometimes unruly, with the touch of water or sweat. Some men like those Mexican whores. He never did, really. No, Soveida definitely wasn't like them.

Why did she hate him, he wondered. Albert couldn't figure it out. The last time he was in El Farol he'd drunk too much, that's why.

"Where's Soveida? Where is she, Jimmy?"

"Now, Albert, you've had enough."

"I want another drink."

"That's it. You're cut off."

"Dammit, where is she?"

"Peetie, go back and get Mr. L., would you?"

"Okay, Jimmy."

"Tell him to get up here."

"He's laying down. I had to go in to get change. I saw him resting on his cot."

"Get him, Peetie."

"Okay, okay. So all right already."

"Tell him Albert's out of control."

"I am not. I need a vodka water."

"Go home, Chanowski!"

"I just want to see her. I'll just look at her and then I'll go home. I promise, that's all. I just want to see her. Dammit to hell, I can look at her!"

"That's it, you're off. Now go home, Al. You've had enough for tonight."

"I just want to touch her!"

"How many times have I told you, you can't do that."

"She doesn't love me."

"Damn right she doesn't, now get on home, Al."

"Mr. Larragoite. Well, if it isn't. And to what do I owe this honor?"

"Get to work, Peetie."

"I am at work. I'm helping Jimmy!"

"You're underage, Peetie."

"I wasn't underage last night when you asked me to help him out."

"Get to work in the kitchen, Peetie."

"I'm working here!"

"Get the hell out of here!"

"Cheeee!"

"You, too, Chanowski, time to leave."

"I love her, Larry."

"Don't we all."

"I mean it, I love her. I mean I really love her."

"Now listen to me, Albert. You just can't come in here night after night and lunge at her the way you do. This is the last time I'm going to tell you about it. Next time I'll call the police. Besides being obnoxious as hell, it's not nice. I won't tolerate it, Chanowski!"

"She's driving me crazy!"

"Go home, old man, you're soused. Cut him, Jim."

"Done already."

"I'm going. I'll be back."

"When he comes in next time, call me."

"Will do, boss."

"Fucking hornball!"

"He knocked the drink from Soveida's tray and got her all wet. Then he grabbed her and tried to kiss her when she went by. All the time he was saying, 'I'm no prize, I'm no prize!' "

"Jesus! See what love does to a man? Look at him, then look at yourself in the mirror and walk away, Jimbo! When a man has no respect for himself, there's nothing left."

Albert went home. He'd tried to reach out. Every cell was clogged. Blocked. Impacted. Soveida! All he wanted to do was talk to her. Talk to her, was that so much to ask?

She'd recoiled. She thought he was drunk. He'd only tried to kiss her. Why didn't she like him? He was a professional musician from New York. A retired symphony conductor. Respected. He was even famous in some circles. Of course, not here. No one in this out-of-the-way burg knew who he was. Except Jimmy and Barb Valentine, the other bartender. It was important to tell his story to someone. Anyone. Might as well be you.

The fucking place was devoid of culture. Frankly, that's what he liked the best. Culture bored him. Few roses among the thorns. Few flowers in the sand. He liked it that way. He was a refined man. Always had been. He didn't understand it. He was an artist. He didn't care if she was Mexican or not. He loved her!

"You know, Soveida, your people have such pretty hair!"

"What? You talking to me, Albert?"

"I said, your people have such pretty hair!"

"Excuse me, I have an order."

She didn't know his world, that was the problem. He didn't care for this place, not really, anyway. And yet the West had a way of growing on you. He could have felt comfortable here, if it weren't for all the Mexicans speaking Spanish in the street. This was the good old U.S.A., but you'd never know it. Not that many pressures here, and yet something about it, the poverty, the mess—and all those Mexicans. He felt tired, hell, retired. For good. No one was calling him back this time. He couldn't make his home here. Settle down. Die here. In the dust? Maybe do something for the people. No, he was tired. He had come to rest, and shouldn't be thinking about working anymore. The pace was different here, life was better, the people were kinder.

If only it weren't so backwards and boring. Nothing to do. Except drink and dream. No one understanding his music, the notes inside his head.

He'd have to go to Juarez. Find someone who looked like Soveida, with hair like hers, long and full. He needed to find her. That's what he'd do. Lay her out. Down. Flat. Do what he wanted to.

Then he'd be home.

33

Girls Aren't Paid to Think

Larry sometimes meant well, sometimes he didn't. His compliments had a way of backfiring, turning upside down and inside out. He liked to hire good-looking young women at the restaurant. It was simply better for business.

"Women! They're damn good to look at, but shit, you pay for it in other ways. I won't hire me a dog, Soveida, you know that," Larry said to me. "Well, there is Petra. I know Bonnie wants me to fire her. She's old, and she can't add, it's true, but she *has* been with us a long time. Women!"

Larry told me Connie had warned him never to marry, but he hadn't listened.

"But, Connie," he had protested, "I thought you were going to give me the restaurant as a wedding gift?"

"I'll give it to you, Larry, on the condition that you *don't* get married."

"And if I do get married?"

"I'll probably give it to you anyway, but don't. There are other ways to pass the time. Live your life before you tie yourself up for eternity. Marriage isn't like going to confession. With marriage, you still carry the burden of guilt around with you. I was never free when I was married."

"Is that why you married Willie LaPoint?"

"I got lonely for what I thought I was missing, but once Willie was around, I realized that what I really missed was my freedom. I'll never marry again. May hell flood over and come rushing in through the front door near the bird cages and my tropical fish, I'll never marry. White or brown or black. As long as the man's a man, I'll never marry.

There are enough people interested in me without my having to think of being married to them. I'm free to do as I please. So look around. The reality of your daily hell will sink in soon enough. Play the field, and keep your nose out of a woman's Bermuda Triangle. Willie used to call it the Gila Wilderness. But, anyway, you get the picture. Just promise me you won't lose yourself in any one person. Stay free, Larry."

"Connie, Jesus!"

"Too soon you'll be tied to them with invisible ropes. They'll want to noose you, the way those two men tried to lasso me, and all in the name of the Sacrament. What sacrament?"

But who would be interested in Larry, anyway? Skinny, bug-eyed, chicken-legged, hound-toothed, and dog-breathed, unsure of himself as well—no woman ever gave him a second look. All his life he thought he was ugly and that no one could love him. Maybe that's why he felt so insecure with women. Oh, there was always some new hostess or some new waitress or lonely customer, someone out there with an interest in the game. But it was getting tired.

"Christ, Soveida! That cocky cocker spaniel, Ivan. I could have told you it would have never worked out, but you never would have listened. You loved him. He should have known it. And yet the bastard never did. That was the tragedy."

As a matter of fact, Larry was convinced he was the damn thing in Soveida's life. The only problem was, she didn't even know it. The only goddamn son of a bitch she could ever trust. *Ever.* Her best friend. And she was *his* best friend. Forget Bonnie. Of course, she was his *real* best friend. They say your wife or husband is always supposed to be your best friend. But Bonnie was too much like Connie. Bonnie. Connie. Connie. Bonnie. And besides, Bonnie always did everything better than Larry. Skiing. Golf. Bridge. Tennis. Backgammon. Running the restaurant. Even her Spanish was better than his, and she learned it after they were married. You couldn't deny it, though, Soveida was pretty. Not young-girl pretty. Attractive, but God, how he hated that word. Sexy, even beautiful, woman-beautiful. Even more beautiful now, only different. His best friend. At least she could *think* about it. No? She wasn't interested. Not now. Not then. Not in that way. Christ, just because you're married doesn't mean your nerve ends are dead!

"Another blonde, Larry?" I asked Larry after he hired Lucille LaMont.

"You know I like blondes."

"Dark as an Indian and you want them all white."

She should have considered it, long ago. Still could. He really could have loved her. She knew him, the way he was, inside and out. But it was more than that. She had a brain, which was more than he could say about Lucille LaMont, the new hostess. She was blond, but even that was doubtful. Hell, she was so dumb he'd have to spend all his time worrying and lying and covering up and lying low. Soveida was the only one. Together, they'd built up El Farol.

"When are you going to grow up, Larry?"

"You talking to me, Soveida?"

"Yeah, you."

"Never!"

"Next time you hire someone, make sure they can add. I'm talking about Lucille LaMont. Don't be pulling these Petras on me."

"Yeah, yeah. And don't blame me for Petra. She was here before me."

"And me."

"She was here before both of us. And besides, I thought you didn't mind."

"I really don't. Only when it gets busy."

"Soveida, I won't fire her."

"You're right, Larry. Don't listen to Bonnie. Don't fire Petra. She needs this job."

"I know that. You know that."

"Yeah, I do. You're a good guy, Larry."

"And you, Miss Headwaitress, are a pain in my ever-loving butt. You are. A sweet pain, not like the others. But still a pain."

"Hey, look it, babe," he told Lucille later. "You're not paid to think, you're paid to look pretty."

But she didn't, not with all that goop on her face, her hair like platinum cotton candy. For Crissakes, she was an albino earthworm. And so why did he have a date with her after work? He'd feel like shit doing it with a lower form of life with white hair like his grandmother's.

It was Soveida who was beautiful.

"Hey, beautiful, you're the only one," he greeted me one morning.

"Yeah, yeah."

"I mean it, Soveida!"

"Really?"

"I really mean it."

"You look tired, Larry. Stay up late? Hey, I'm talking to you!"

"It's the earthworm, but that's not it."

"What earthworm? What are you talking about? I mean it, though, you really look tired. I'm worried about you."

"It's about time to open up. Another day, Soveida. So open the door. What are you waiting for, Dosamantes?"

I sometimes wondered the same thing.

THE BOOK OF SERVICE

CHAPTER FIVE

Talks with Dedea #1: Los que se presentaron

Dearest Dedea:

Men will present themselves. It's a given. Before. During. Or after work. Take everything in stride as you would a wrong order. Instead of con queso, you get guacamole. Men can be like that guacamole. A nice appetizer, a little spicy, but not a full-course meal.

Don't put too much stock in men. They will have to prove their mettle. Are they serious contenders? Many men will flirt with you. How you respond is what matters.

I have never had trouble with men bothering me at El Farol (well, except Albert Chanowski, but that's another story). I attribute this to the fact that I approach my customers in a friendly but businesslike manner. We are not here to fraternize with our clients, remember that. Nothing is sloppier or less professional than a waitress who pals around with her customers. When I am working, I work. As much as I love my customers like Bud Ermin and Whitey Moldon, Bosford and Nayla Comingly, Billy Jane and Mr. Tangee, I leave them behind when I go home. I don't socialize with them after work. I don't need to, I see them every day. They know how I am and what to expect from me, and as a result, we are friends.

Don't have any expectations of your customers. You have to allow for changes in mood and attitude. If you don't, you will soon be disappointed.

Hungry people are grouchy. People who don't know you can be rude. Those that know you can be demanding and selfish. I approach my customers with a sense of unspoken propriety and, in return, they are polite to me.

The only person who has crossed the proverbial line at work is

Albert, and he is teetering dangerously on the edge. All his life, women have catered to him. With me, he is off-guard, off-center, and to him that is very attractive. He's not a dangerous man, but he is unpleasant.

Stay away from these men. If they bother you, tell me or Larry or switch with someone who can handle and control them. Pancha understands men and how they work. Rely on her and Melina Minao. They've both been married and divorced and married and divorced and they know what to do about any number of types of men. Ignore crude and crass jokes, the hello-honey syndrome, sexist endearments.

Stay away from people who touch you. Comport yourself with dignity. You are a waitress, and what you reap you will sow.

Many will call, but few should be chosen. In time you will understand what I mean.

Men like César Fuentes will call upon you at home on an off-night. They will be drinking, as César did, for that is the only way such men can find the strength to present themselves to you. Tall, with perfect posture, he was a teacher at Agua Oscura Junior High, where he taught seventh grade. He was an older man who used to come into the restaurant. He was never my teacher, or even Hector's, but I got to know him over the years. He came in first with his wife, Vina, and then later alone. Vina got cancer of the uterus and she was confined to her bed. César was always very gentlemanly, proper, polite. He barely seemed to notice me, and I felt sorry for him.

"That's where it begins, Soveida, you better watch out!" declared Pancha Portales.

"I do feel sorry for him, a man in his early sixties, so tall and straight, without a woman to love him," I said.

"The older you get, the more you see men like César, with crippled wives, or wives who can't make love ever again because of their womb, or tubes or cervix or back. And as a result, it goes without saying, it goes. The man's penis shrinks to the size of a small thumb."

"César never told me about his wife, Pancha. How do you know about her?"

"I know these things. The gringa's got her sex cut out and still she's sick inside, Soveida. Cesarito don't get it no more. It's been that way for over fifteen years. I say he should find himself someone for companionship."

"Pancha Portales!"

"I do! He's still got huevos underneath that brown cowboy suit and *hairy legs in those Tony Lama boots, enough to put round some woman, if you just cover up his face. It's not that he's ugly, he's not. It's just that there's something hard about him. It would be like making love to your grandfather's death mask. But just get a dark room and the plaster-of-Paris look will go away."*

"Pancha!"

"I mean it, Soveida. He needs a woman and soon. The longer this goes on, the straighter his back becomes. One of these days he's just going to snap apart or turn into a statue. Híjole, he already has! What he needs is a good woman to unloosen his calzones, they're cutting off his circulation."

"Pancha!"

"When I was single, married men never interested me at all. Who wants someone else's day-old beans? Not that the single ones aren't damaged as well. When you come right down to it, give me flowers and a little romance and then go on your way, that's what I tell my men. I don't want to brag, Soveida, but I know more about men than Eloisa knows about green chile. Once you learn a few basic principles and the variations, you'll have it all down. Sometime when we're not so busy here at work I'll give you a few tips. You could use them."

I never did tell Pancha that one night César se presentó, as Mamá says—he just showed up at my door. The house was very clean, Chata had just left, and César didn't quite seem himself. He was slightly disheveled, his light brown hair flecked with white and fluffed around his ears like muffs. I made a mistake and let him in. Frankly, I can't remember what César said. He mumbled rather incoherently, and then paced around the living room apologetically, then tried to kiss me. I could smell liquor on his breath. His lips were very wet, as if he had been hypersalivating. It was then I noticed his lips for the first time. Large, slightly chapped, they were the color of calf's liver. That's when I asked him to leave. He seemed so unlike the other César. This new César seemed so infinitely sad, I wished I could have held him, but I couldn't. Just as apologetically as he came in, he left, still mumbling, moving a moist tongue around his veiny mouth. We never spoke of that night, but I have wondered all the rest of my life what possessed César, and how he could have mustered the strength of will to present himself. There was something heroic about it.

"If it weren't for his face like a cheap papier-mâché mask and those eyebrows like a chipmunk's tail," Pancha said.

"And his meaty lips," I answered.

"Yeah, I noticed them, too. If it weren't for those things, I might once have thought about it, Soveida," Pancha stated firmly.

"Pancha!"

"I mean it! A woman has her needs. But let me tell you, men like César are to be avoided. You had César, I had Juanito Tafoya. Eulalia, his wife, weighed three hundred pounds. I call those men the Ship-wrecked. They'll cling to you because they're drowning. God forbid you sleep with them, they'll spend a good ten minutes nursing at your breasts and then fall asleep. They usually snore, too. It isn't that they're not equipped, they just got too waterlogged over the years, if you know what I mean. You can't get rid of them either, they're like seaweed."

Many will call, but few should be chosen.

So avoid anyone who is drunk, Dedea, or married, and who tries to kiss you against your will.

"Type number two, Soveida: the Fake He-Man. Sylvester Stallone with a girdle. Robert Goulet with a truss. What's his name pussycat-pussycat without a meow. Now, I once went out with a gringo, yes, I did, nothing wrong in that, I was foot-free and fancy-loose. What I didn't know was that he used hair spray, and he also painted his nails with clear polish. I didn't find out about his dentures until late one night on the couch at my apartment. Well, I got him out of there faster than you can say Bionic Man. Artificial men are afraid of real women. They don't like the way we smell. They're afraid of menstrual blood. I blame their mothers. They care more about the way their fingernails look than they'll ever care about you. They're selfish in bed, too. They like to get chupados. You'll be sucking on a dead stick all night long. So forget them, Soveida."

"Pancha!"

"I mean it, if you have the time to resurrect Lazarus, go ahead and do it."

Shun men with wives who are incapacitated with female problems, have cancer, or are fat, Dedea. Steer clear of men who are rigid, tight-skinned, thin-lipped, straight-backed, unbending, have no sense of humor, and who flirt too easily and too much, especially in front of other women.

———

"Let's talk about small-penis men, Soveida. There are several types. The Small No-Can-Do and the Small Can-Do. One of my favorite honeys was a short—in height—cowboy trucker named Squirty Boysville. Where'd you think I learned to dance country, Soveida?

"A man of the land, he called himself. Well, he knew land and he knew land. Just because he had small albóndigas, little meatballs, didn't mean he couldn't simmer the soup to a boil. The man you have to look out for is not the small link sausage but the Jimmy Dean deluxe. They're usually good kissers. Period. I call them Mr. Hit-and-Miss. Give me my 5′2″ Squirty any day."

Never let down your guard, Dedea. Stay away from the ex-husbands of relatives. Evade any men with women attached. Most men have some woman or women attached. Mothers (the worst scenario). Ex-wives (very bad). Daughters (terrible). Old lovers they can't emotionally release (unbearable).

Every woman knows men on the make, whether they're drunk or, worse yet, sober, who after circling the block pause, falter, and then gather themselves up for their passionate confessions. But don't succumb!

"Soveida, have I mentioned Mr. Everything Is Business, even that? He's usually a bad tipper with a dry mouth. There's also Godzilla, into power, like that creep Albert Chango-owski. Viejo repunoso, he wants women to wait on him. What about the Love Me I'm an Artist, tall, good-looking, with long legs and quick ejaculations? Or Mr. Regular Dollar Tip. A businessman, usually wears a suit and tie. Likes to make jokes with the waitresses, everybody knows him, nobody likes him. Like sleeping with a piece of toast. After being with them awhile, they start to make you itch. That's just a few types to avoid. As they come up or out around here, Soveida, I'll point them out to you. I haven't lived in this world fifty-two years for nothing, and been married three times without learning that when I found me Fermín Fernández I'd met a Born-Again born-for-bed. He's a gentleman, to boot. But that's all I'm going to say. To me, the bedroom is sacred."

"I feel sorry for Dedea, Pancha. She's so young, and so dumb."

"She'll learn. The way we learned. I don't feel too sorry for her. I feel sorry for all the men," Pancha said. "I mean, look at them, pobrecitos, they're so helpless. Get a good look, Soveida, check them out: Larry with Bonnie his wife and all his girlfriends, it's no wonder he has a bad heart. There's Bud and Whitey, with their little-boy dreams, Jimmy the bartender with his Playboy cochinas, and Lavel Windle, the cook, with his bottle of Robitussin. He's addicted to cough medicine and Mota. Who knows what else. You name it. Pobrecitos todos, no matter what age, nationality, or color of skin. It's for us women to be strong."

"I'll never get married again, Pancha."

"Well, I don't think I could live with a man too long without us getting married. I envy you kids, today you just live together."

"It hasn't helped us."

"I didn't think so. Oooo, look, here he comes!"

"Who, Pancha?"

"César, pobre de los pobrecitos. The poor of the poor. Pero, my God! He must have found someone. He's slouching! Maybe somebody's undone those shorts!" Pancha smiled at me and I smiled back. "It wasn't me. No way!"

"Me neither."

"I don't know who it could have been, Soveida, but I'm grateful to her, whoever she was."

Remember, Dedea, many will present themselves, but few, very few should ever be chosen!

Soveida

34

A Heart of Chiseled Stone

For a week everyone at El Farol was sick. That year's flu strain had been the most virulent anyone remembered. Larry was holed up in his office the greater part of each day, making feeble appearances from time to time.

"I think we're going to have to close El Farol, Bonners," Larry wheezed.

Bonnie eventually took charge.

"Honey, we'll manage. I'm on the register. Eloisa is cooking. She says she'll take some week nights if she has to, and Sandra is all right. So are Pancha and Fermín. Everyone else is questionable. Soveida looks terrible."

"I have news for you, Bonnie, I feel worse than I look," I said, coming up behind them.

"Go home, Soveida, you need to rest. Take a few days off. Call me when you can."

"I'll be in tomorrow, Bonnie," I said without conviction.

"This is a hell of a time for everyone to get sick, the week before Thanksgiving," Larry moaned.

"You want to call Veryl to come and get you, Soveida?"

"No, I'll walk home, Bonnie."

"Walk home? Don't be ridiculous. Why don't you call Veryl?"

"He doesn't like to be interrupted while he's designing. Really, Bonnie, I'll be okay."

"Go home, Soveida! If you won't call Veryl, I'll have Chuy take you home in his truck. We'll manage here. Larry is going home, too. I'll put him in the truck with you."

Two sadder-looking passengers never graced Chuy's old truck, Gomersinda. I sat in the middle of the truck under a large pair of red dice. Larry had his eyes closed and kept pitching forward into a row of black fringe that was tacked just above the front windshield and just below a homemade altar to Our Lady of Guadalupe. At each stop sign Chuy pedaled the old brakes to a stop.

Chuy took me home first, since my house was on the way to Larry's home out in Los Nueces, on the outskirts of Agua Oscura.

Veryl and I lived in a subdivision just south of Chiva Town called El Mirasol. It had never been that spectacular or exclusive. And yet our house was large, with three spacious bedrooms and a huge back yard. We were renting it from one of my regular customers, Gilroy Gonzaga. The house was really too big for us, but the rent was reasonable. Gilroy helped us decorate it with used furniture from his shop, the Little Red Barn.

Each of the bedrooms had a different motif. One was early Juárez, with a velvet landscape painting, orange-and-turquoise paper flowers, and straw accessories; another was late college, with the usual cinderblock bookcase, with three 2 × 4's forming each shelf, and an empty bottle of jug wine dripping with hardened candle wax. The third room was full of hand-me-downs, including the old sofa that had followed me after my divorce from Ivan. The early Juárez room became the den, and the late college was Veryl's studio.

Veryl designed bathroom fixtures. He worked at home and had done so for years, periodically sending in his designs to the home office in Daytona Beach, Florida. He had moved to Florida briefly, but it wasn't to his liking. He returned to New Mexico and continued to design fixtures from home. He never discussed his work much. He called it "doodling for the big doodle." He always seemed to be busy, either in the garage, working with metal in one way or another, or molding things out of wax or clay at his drafting table in the college bedroom.

Instead of sleeping in our bed, Veryl decided that we should sleep in the living room on a bed we dragged in from the junk bedroom. If we did this, Veryl thought, we could close off most of the house, saving heat and energy. It was a horrible system.

We moved into the living room in October. By April I hoped to move back to our real bedroom. We could well afford to pay the heating bills for the entire house. But no, Veryl wanted to economize.

"Is that why you water the yard by hand instead of with the sprinkler, Veryl?" I asked. "I mean, wouldn't it be easier to get the grass wet, really wet, all at once, instead of in small patches? You don't save either time or money doing it that way."

"But, S., you do save money! I water each section very carefully and then I only have to water once a week."

"I don't know. Our grass never looks green. Why must you be so stingy with the water for the grass?"

"It's the desert, S., we don't need grass here. And besides, it saves water!"

For Veryl, it was a matter of either time or money. For me, it was always a matter of convenience. I was too busy to water by hand, too busy to bake pies, too busy to cook anything that wasn't fast and effortless.

I'd grown up on junk food. Dolores was a good cook, but she and Mamá and Oralia were never above a meal of canned corned beef or canned salmon, with a side of canned creamed corn and canned cling peaches for dessert, with small-curd cottage cheese. I loved fried Spam sandwiches or a tortilla filled with potted meat and mayonnaise. One of Mamá's favorite meals was the hamburger, and Luardo loved his fried chicken and fish sandwiches. Ivan couldn't be without his grease for longer than a day, and thrived on pork with red chile. Veryl wasn't particular when it came to food, thank God. He loved hot Mexican food with plenty of cheese. I would bring him a daily takeout plate from El Farol. I always kept flour tortillas on hand and I burned them for him whenever he wanted.

Veryl didn't drink liquor, and he didn't smoke. It was a blessing for me, because I came from a family of men who did both. Ivan hadn't been much of a drinker, but he did smoke occasionally. I never smoked much, but I did drink regularly after work, usually a Mai Tai or a frozen Margarita or a White Russian.

"You want a Black Russian today, Soveida?" Melina Minao, the Filipino bartender, would ask me. "You look like you could use one, sweetheart. Let me fix you a double. They calm the nerves."

"It'll put hair on your chest," Larry said as he walked by.

"Oh, you!" said Melina. "She's just taking a drink to table number four. Here it is, Soveida," Melina said and winked.

In many ways, Veryl was easy to be around, yet it was difficult for me to relax in my own spacious home. Could it be because our bed was in the living room, or that Veryl wouldn't allow me to water with a sprinkler attachment and what watering I could do was only permitted at night? Was it that he kept the heat set to 65 degrees in the front part of the house while the rest was freezing, especially the room where I kept my clothes, my books, all my things?

November was a cold month in Agua Oscura, and the flu was rampant. I didn't look forward to going home to a cold house where I'd have to crawl inside a bed in the center of the living room. Veryl had at least put up a curtain made out of a sheet, separating the bed from the "public" part of the room. He had only acquiesced in response to my irritation. It was embarrassing for me when people came over. Fortunately, few people ever did. Veryl was a loner and had few friends. He no longer saw Andy and Norma. His father was dead. He never spoke of his mother, Laddie Mae. Gradually, I, too, began to see little of my family.

At least El Farol was warm. When Chuy left me off in front of the house, I went inside knowing it would probably be warmer outdoors. Veryl wasn't home, nor was he in the garage. I quickly put on my long johns, a bathrobe, socks, a wool cap, and mittens and crawled into bed. Immediately I fell asleep.

"Soveida! What are you doing home so early!"

"They sent me home. I don't feel good."

"What's wrong with you?"

"I'm sick."

"With what?"

"I have the crud."

"How long have you been here?"

"I don't know. What time is it?"

"Four-thirty."

"Already? I fell asleep, Veryl. I was so tired. Where were you?"

"I had to go to the post office to mail some faucet-handle drawings."

"I'm burning up, Veryl. Feel my head. I'm just going to have to lay here."

"I better not touch you. What about dinner?"

"I don't know. Why don't you eat something? I'm not hungry."

"I'll eat the plate you brought me."

"Veryl, I forgot it. I'm sorry."

"You forgot it? Oh, all right. I'll be in my office."

I was sick nearly five days, five interminable days in a surprising hell. I couldn't relax in my own home, and certainly not in my feverish coughing-clucking-honking ugliness. I was too sick to get out of bed to do much of anything.

During the entire time of my illness, I was never a mi gusto, at my leisure, because Veryl kept bothering me to get well.

"How do you feel today, Soveida? Better?"

"I don't know yet. Let me lay here awhile and I'll let you know."

"You want some lunch?"

"I'm not hungry."

"God, Soveida, you've got to eat something. Is your coughing that bad? Do you have to bend over and hold your ribs that way?"

"Is there any soup?"

"No. Why don't you get up and fix yourself something?"

"Just leave me here, I'll be okay. I need more Kleenex, Veryl."

"Look, maybe I should sleep by myself until you get better. That way, I won't disturb you."

"It's probably a good idea, Veryl."

"I don't want to get sick, Soveida. I'll be in the back bedroom."

"Which one?"

"I'm not sure yet."

"Maybe I should move to our bedroom. We could turn up the heat and open all the doors."

"Soveida! We can't do that! No, you just stay where you are. I'll sleep in the back."

"Will you be all right, Veryl?"

"Yeah, I will. Are you feeling better?"

"No. I'm sorry I'm sick. I thought I'd be well by now. I'm just not feeling good. I think I'll go to the doctor tomorrow."

"Do you want to do that? Antibiotics aren't good for you. They stay in your system for a long time."

"I don't care, Veryl. I need something. I have to get well. I need to go back to work."

"I won't be able to drive you to the doctor's tomorrow. I have designing to do."

"I'll be fine. Thanks, anyway."

"Maybe you'll feel better tomorrow and you won't have to go to the doctor."

"Veryl, could you turn up the heat?"

"The thermostat's set at 70. I turned it up for you."

"Turn it to 75. I'm freezing."

"Maybe you should get some more blankets, Soveida."

"I think I'll just lie here, Veryl."

"Aren't you feeling better?"

After my illness I realized I'd never been ill around Veryl. Every marriage should include a trial week of a long, unpleasant, and debilitating illness, a trip to a foreign country, as well as a week sequestered with an unpleasant relative from your spouse's side of the family.

Sadly, during my illness I realized Veryl could never live up to the words he had spoken aloud: I promise to love, honor, and obey, in sickness and in health.

Veryl didn't like illness in any form. He had no mercy for anyone who wasn't in good health. He was unpleasant, and cold to me. Why? What had happened to him that bad health bred hostility in him? What had affected him so deeply that he disliked sick people? The more distant he became, the worse I felt. He treated me as if I'd asked to get sick on purpose.

I never saw Veryl ill. He'd told me that he'd been sick, when we first started dating. That's the only time he ever mentioned any illness of his to me.

When I was a little girl Dolores would rub me with warm Vicks VapoRub and then place a hot towel between my nightgown and my chest.

Oralia would come over with one of her teas and would rub my feet between her hot, thin fingers that were so strong. Sometimes Oralia sang hymns to me, like "Eres mi salvación, Jesucristo," or "Bendito, bendito." If she was feeling a bit melancholic in the way old ladies get after a long hard day, Oralia might slip in a ballad that spoke of her lost home.

Mamá would come over from time to time to tell me stories or read to me from her Bible, pushing her glasses up as they continually slid down her nose. She would bless me with Holy Water that she kept in a white plastic quart container in the cupboard.

Luardo might carry me into the living room in his arms to watch the Mickey Mouse Club from the couch, and then return me to a freshly made bed to take a long, peaceful nap, knowing that I was cared for and loved. Later, before I went to sleep for the night, he would tell me stories that he made up on the spot, about a little girl named Soveida.

Trays would be brought to me morning, noon, and night with food and drink that tasted wonderful: Jell-O, Popsicles, orange sherbert, rice pudding, 7-Up.

But my days of illness would never be the same. Even with Ivan, there was some love. He babied me and hugged me often and whispered that he loved me and told me that I would soon get well.

It was so cold and lonely in the middle of the living room on the stage the bed had become because Veryl was too cheap to raise the heat and open a few doors. He was afraid of illness and germs and of a woman who wasn't perfect and would be a burden to him in his old age. A woman whom he might have to carry for just a little while. The load was already too heavy.

During that illness I saw for the first time how sick Veryl himself was, and from that day onward, I began to get better. The antibiotics helped, but I think it was more of a turning in my own mind. And as I crawled toward the light of health, Veryl seemed relieved.

"Are you feeling better, Soveida?"

"Yes, Veryl. I feel a hundred percent better! I'm going back to work tomorrow. I called in to let them know. Larry's been sick all week, too, and half the staff."

"I'm glad. I was worried."

"Veryl, I'm better. Just leave me here. I'll rest."

"Are you sure you're better?"

"I'm sure, Veryl," I said. Sidestepping his moods took much of my energy.

The next day I returned to work. It was a long day. El Farol was packed, but I was relieved to be out of the house. Melina tried to fix me a drink after work.

"Can't. Antibiotics."

"We missed you, Soveida. You lucky girl. A week off from work! What are you, anyway, a princess?"

Hardly, I mused to myself.

When I invited the family for Thanksgiving, Veryl let me move our bed from the living room to the Juárez bedroom.

It was the first time I invited my family over. The dinner was special. Hector announced his engagement to Narada Peña, his high-school sweetheart, and they had bought the beer. Mamá and Oralia brought most of the food. I made the turkey and the dressing. Dolores made the pies and the salads. Luardo even made an unannounced visit toward the end of the dinner, but he was drunk and Mamá shooed him away. Hector got drunk and ended up having an argument with Ada. He had tried to argue with Veryl, too.

The dinner had started at two. By six, everyone was gone and Veryl and I were moving our bed back into the living room. I felt a wincing pain my in back, as though I'd pulled something, but I kept silent.

"I'm tired, Veryl. It's been a long day."

"The food was good, Soveida."

"Yes, wasn't it? But it's too bad Luardo was drunk and Mamá left early and Hector got into that fight with Ada."

"Did you turn up the heater? Someone turned up the heater."

"It wasn't me. I never touched the thermostat."

"It must have been your mother. She kept saying how cold it was."

"It is! Why don't you turn up the heater? We can afford the heating bills."

"Let's go to bed to get under the covers."

"Where are you sleeping tonight, Veryl?"

"I'm not sure yet. Maybe I'll sleep in the back tonight."

"Why can't you sleep with me? I miss you."

"No cough?"

"No cough."

"No sneezing?"

"No sneezing."

"No fever?"

"Long gone."

"You're in good health?"

"Completely healed."

"Look, you just go to bed. I have some designing to do. I'll come to bed later. Tomorrow we'll go out and do something special for our anniversary."

"Our anniversary? That's right!"

"Six months. I'll pick you up after work. We'll go out to dinner."

"We have all these leftovers."

"They can wait. I'll be there at four. We can have an early dinner and then go out for ice cream. It's a date."

"A date!"

"You better not kiss me, Soveida."

"You're hopeless, Veryl. I'm going to bed. Don't stay up late, okay? Good night!"

"Good night, S. I love you."

"Happy Thanksgiving!"

"Happy Thanksgiving."

———

When I woke up the next morning Veryl was sleeping in the den. He really must have stayed up late, because he was usually awake by this hour and had already had his breakfast.

He hadn't come to bed with me. He was afraid of getting sick. He was completely overreacting, yet he looked so peaceful on the foldout bed with a red woolen blanket over his khaki-colored sleeping bag that I loved him despite his peculiarities.

I got dressed and left Veryl a note:

Dearest Veryl:
   Happy Anniversary! See you later on. You're so special to
me. Let's pray for years of peace and love. I love you.
   Soveida

The day went by quickly. By four-thirty, Veryl hadn't picked me up. By five, I began to worry.

"I don't know where he is, Melina. He said he would be here by four."

"Men! You can never depend on 'em. Certainly not my five ex's."

"Veryl's not that way. Besides, it's our anniversary!"

"Already?"

"Six months."

"Six months! I'd tell you to call him, but once you start checking up on a man, it's the beginning of the end. Or it was for me."

"I called him already. He isn't home. Something must have happened. It isn't like Veryl not to show up. I think I'll get a cab."

"Who's calling a cab?" Larry asked.

"Me. I'm waiting for Veryl. He must have gotten tied up. Anyway, he's late. It's our anniversary."

"Just sit down and have a Coke," Larry advised. "He'll turn up."

"I'm worried. I thought I'd take a cab."

"A cab? It's only four blocks."

"Four long blocks."

"You can walk it in ten minutes."

"I just got over the flu, remember? It's cold out there."

"Okay, so let's go."

"Are you going somewhere?"

"I'm picking up some taco meat. I'll give you a ride."

"Would you, Larry?"

"Soveida, get used to it." Melina said. "That's the way men are. If

I were you, I'd just relax and have a sloe-gin fizz while you wait for lover boy. He'll turn up later than sooner."

"Women! After twenty years you just go numb," Larry mumbled as we got into his car.

"You haven't been married twenty years, Larry."

"So? I'm already numb."

"I'm worried, Larry. He's been—I don't know—strange."

"As far as I'm concerned, he was always strange. Just kidding. No, I'm not. But anyway—"

"There's Maybelline," I almost shouted.

"Maybelline?"

"His truck. He probably just got busy with work and is soldering some metal. Thanks for the ride, Larry."

The back door was locked. All the doors to the bedrooms were open and all the lights were on. The thermostat said 80.

I found Veryl in the living room. He lay on the bed with a plastic bag wrapped tightly around his head. His hair was damp. I could see beads of what had once been his breath. The humid plastic clung to his features and made his face look grotesque.

"Veryl!" I screamed. "Veryl! What have you done? Oh, Veryl!" I cried as I tried to loosen the stranglehold of rope that cut deeply into his bruised neck. I tore the bag with my fingernails and prayed for life. "Oh, Veryl," I whispered as I held him. "Why?"

He was beautiful. So beautiful. I rocked back and forth, holding him in my arms, like holding a child, crying in a little voice already strangely familiar, as if I'd already known the song.

I held him in my arms, a sorrowful Pietà, my heart chiseled in stone.

35

El panteón

Veryl was probably the only gringo suicide in all of San Pedro Cemetery. The poorer mexicanos and Mexican-Americans were buried there. If an Anglo *had* snuck in, it was someone related to a Mexican, a long-suffering spouse, a teenager who didn't speak any Spanish, or a newborn who had no choice.

Veryl had insisted that he be buried, not at St. Anselm's, up on the hill facing the Lagrimas Valley, but at San Pedro Cemetery, in the flatlands bordering Chiva Town. San Pedro's was off a street known for its espinas. The same thorns that crowded the grave of beloved Eluid, Dolores's favorite brother. It seemed fitting, then, for Veryl to be buried with hundreds of mexicanos in San Pedro's, amid the disorder and disarray that was part and parcel of that typically Mexican cemetery. It was a place full of colorful plastic flowers and paper wreaths. There was no set order to the style of headstones: Our Lady of Guadalupe and the Immaculate Heart vied for attention with the Sacred Heart of Jesus. Handmade wooden crucifixes cropped up here and there, held together with baling wire, the name of the deceased printed in crooked black letters that dripped down and slanted right, in an irregular but endearing manner. Wild Bermuda grass grew between the graves, alternating with patches of sand, and occasional weeds. That was where Veryl wanted to be buried, near the Dosamantes family, down from the Loeras, in the middle of the bright, colorful chaos of Chiva Town's dead.

He was lucky to get in, being a suicide. No funeral was held, and I was grateful. It was because of Mamá and her connections with the priests at Our Lady of Grace Church that Veryl was even buried in holy ground. The unsanctified body was still near enough to San Pedro and his giant gold-laminated keys to merit some last heavenly change of heart.

We'd once had a discussion about death, and Veryl told me that he wanted to be buried at San Pedro's in a simple wood coffin in the nude. It was easier to get Veryl in San Pedro's than to have him buried without clothes. Something akin to a camel going through the eye of a needle. Mr. Gabaldon, from Gabaldon's Mortuary, found it an odd request. When he called up Mamá to ask about it, she was shocked, and immediately requested that Veryl be buried in a dark suit with a tie. That's how I found him at Gabaldon's, where I'd gone to take a few of his things. Without telling Mamá, I had Mr. Gabaldon remove Veryl's clothing. He was finally buried naked, holding his slide rule and a prize-winning faucet handle. Mamá and I never spoke to each other about it. That way, I figured, everyone would rest peacefully.

Veryl's death had come as a great shock to me. There was something so ignominious about it, so ugly. I felt he'd cheated me, and himself. And there was finally no explaining why he'd killed himself. I was haunted by the memory of his face inside the plastic cleaning bag, which was wound tightly with rope and then duct tape. I can never forget those desperate moments of uncertainty and unforgettable terror, my fingernails and hands bloodied by the sheer force of my clawing frenzy, as I tried to remove the plastic from his face. I had nightmares of all sorts of faces, some bloodied, some damp with sweat, some cold as ice, all with closed eyes. I would wake up with my own silent scream and realize my nightmare was real. Sleep brought no respite; in fact, I was afraid to sleep, because Veryl would appear in my dreams. But it was always a double, a Veryl impersonator, or a devil disguised as Veryl, with his mannerisms and voice. There was always something amiss, incomplete. And as much as I wanted to see and talk to the Veryl I once knew, he was always out of reach, in another room, behind a filmy curtain, and my feet would be as heavy as earth, unable to move.

I began to frequent San Pedro Cemetery. Every evening after work I would gather what flowers I could in Mamá's or Oralia's or Dolores's garden and take them wrapped in a newspaper to San Pedro's. When I got there, I would empty out the previous day's flowers from the turquoise glass vase that Veryl had once given me, and fill it with water from the spigot in the center of the cemetery, taking care not to spill it as I wandered back between the fading, sun-bleached flowers to Veryl's grave.

To me there was always movement in San Pedro. The ground was never level, and was always shifting with the constant influx of the dead. After the burial, the earth on the grave was quite high. Sometimes it took years for the graves to lie flat. No one, including the two custodians, saw fit to level the earth; they let nature take its course. Eventually the earth was washed down by heat, rain, wind, and a little snow.

Veryl's grave never seemed to level out. It grieved me to see a nest of ants overtake the lower portion, without concern for the body that lay underneath, without regard for the disintegrating face below.

There was no formal burial ceremony, but Dolores, Mamá, Oralia, and I were there, and we each threw in a bit of ritual dirt. I had been to funerals at San Pedro's where everyone in attendance threw in a bit of dirt from an offered shovel, and it was a comforting gesture. At St. Anselm's, each grave was evenly spaced from its neighbor, with a metal vase atop each metal plaque. There was certainly no throwing of dirt. As a matter of fact, the grieving family and friends never saw the burial site, but offered chaste prayers in a central cement kiosk, driving off without ever knowing where the body lay.

One day on my way to San Pedro's I saw a dead dog by the side of the road. At first, the dog seemed to be merely sleeping. But then it became clear that someone had run over it and pushed it to the side of the road near a light pole. Each day the dog's carcass changed. One day it was full-bodied, seemingly asleep; the next day it was a little deflated, surrounded by a cluster of flies. The following day, it had shrunk and seemed to fold inward near the stomach. The day after that, the head lay flat against the road and the eyes were gone. And every day I drove to San Pedro's after work to see Veryl, to talk to Veryl, to take him fresh flowers.

Mamá began to complain that I was stealing all her flowers, and so I moved on to Dolores's. Oralia had few flowers left, and winter was coming on. I decided to buy plastic flowers in a store, and that took a long time, as I went through them all, wondering what would look nice in the turquoise vase, trying to remember what flowers Veryl had loved. But I couldn't.

As I stood in the checkout aisle, still trying to choose, I began to cry suddenly and without warning. When I got to the cemetery I cried in the parked car and later when I carried water across that stretch of desert to a man who never cried.

Oralia called out to me once when I was driving off, and made me stop.

"Soveida, your mamá's out of flowers, and now so is your grandmother. You're welcome to my few, but that's not what I want to say. Stop going to el panteón, Soveida. It isn't good. The spirits of the dead have a way of capturing you after a while. They want company, Soveida. They want living flesh to hold and warm hands to grasp. Pull yourself out of there, or your soul may fly away. It's restless with flight now. You need to stop those visits, because darkness calls with such a lovely voice. When my mother died, I sank into that river of earth and refused to listen to the living. That's all I have to say. Release the dead. You are living and they have moved on. What need do they have of your tears? What they want is the light of grace. No sorrow can fill the crowded earth. The dead aren't there anymore, Soveida. You're praying to ashes. That's all I wanted to say."

But I couldn't hear Oralia, or Mamá or Dolores or Lizzie. All I heard were the heavy racking sobs that came in sleep.

I went to work every day, but only halfheartedly. I couldn't eat at work or after work, and only after seeing Veryl and laying my flowers at his feet would I go home and even try. For nearly a year I refused to go out to eat with anyone, preferring to stay home evenings. What little socializing I did, I did at El Farol. But that so drained me I had nothing left for anyone else. Only that hour or so before sunset with Veryl seemed real, near a glistening San Pedro, long shadows on the cold hard ground that refused to settle.

I celebrated el Día de los Muertos with Veryl at San Pedro's, having bought a bucket of flowers for three dollars from an elderly man who sold them from his wooden cart at the entrance to the cemetery. He did a brisk business and soon his flowers were gone.

A week. Two weeks. A month. Two months. Four. Then six. Wandering through aisles looking for the right plastic flowers, the right wreath, the best ice plant to use as ground cover. Should I plant a tree, a bush, grass? Grass takes hold and is cruel. And then there are the worms.

I never missed a day beside Veryl's grave.

Until, that is, the day I crossed words with the young custodian. He had been helpful and pleasant, with his mumbled pésames, his obvious concern, helping me carry water across the cemetery to Veryl's plot, offering to weed now and then, or to water what plants there were.

Thin, but muscular, with a broad, impish face, he knew me, knew when I would be there. After a while, I found myself irritated with his cheerful hello, his ingratiating help. He offered to do work around the house, was a handyman, he said, and available. And once, when I jumped across the many graves, nearly twisting my foot, he came up to me and put his hand across my waist. The last time I saw him, he heard me coughing and offered me a drink from a flask—"medicine," he said. I declined, and with a leer he said that perhaps my husband could give me the medicine I needed.

And that was it. That was the day I stopped going to the cemetery. What grieving I had left was now to be done alone.

Oralia offered to do a limpia, a cleansing ritual, and I agreed. When Mamá was at an Altar Society meeting, I went over to her house and found Oralia in the kitchen fixing tea. She sat me down.

"I'll be done shortly, and then you follow me into the sala. I want you to stand in the middle of the room, facing east. Close your eyes and go over in your mind the many burdens you carry. As you call them up, lay each one aside, as if it were a small, heavy child. Then ask la diosita, the Guadalupe, and all the spirits of life, to come into your heart and turn these children into angels. Each one as different as the sun is from the moon. Look at these angels and thank them. They will begin to leave, one by one. If one stays longer than he or she should, ask them what they want. Listen quietly, without speaking out loud. Once they have all gone away, ask their forgiveness and then thank them again. I'll move around you, and when I come in front, with the copal, breathe in deeply, as if you were taking in new life. Then you can open your eyes. Do all this without looking at me, as if I were the wind behind you or a rumble of thunder or a bee buzzing. Stand still, but in a comfortable position, and if you get dizzy, open your eyes and focus on a spot in front of you. Not hard, but soft, as if you were gazing at mountains. The Lagrimas. After I leave you, you can lie down. I've put a blanket on the floor for you. After you rest, come into the kitchen and drink this tea. Then we'll talk."

That was the beginning of the settling of the earth. It went down, not because it chose to, but because it had to, hardened by the sun, washed clean by rain, cleared of debris and waste, sifted and then softened into soil sprouting with fine green shoots.

Dominations

36

Who Are the Waitresses?

"Now, I don't like that word, minority." Mara said. "I have never been, nor ever will be, a minority. However, if there are minorities, you, Soveida, you are a minority. Hell, you're the minority of minorities, a waitress who actually loves what she does. When are you going to quit your Sí, señor job, Soveida? You've been a goddamn waitress for how long?"

"I forget."

"Don't you want something better for yourself, Soveida? I mean, especially now. You've done your grieving-widow bit, now it's time to get on with life. Okay, so you're good at what you do. But don't you get tired of seeing all those people come and go? Blacks, Hispanics, those blondies who need jobs and aren't in school, all kinds of kids, working hard all day in that humid nest to earn a few coins so that they can go buy a six-pack and some pretzels? What about their dreams? What happens to them? Do they become lifers like that waiter Fermín you're always talking about, or that old bat, Pancha, who drives you crazy? Are they just doing something to pass the time, a summer job, a step to somewhere else, fast cash, work with friends, the only available jobs? Do they get married and raise more waitresses and construction workers and truck drivers? Not that I have a problem with that, we need janitors and elevator operators. I'm just wondering aloud, that's all. What happens to all those kids? Do they even have plans of making something of their lives, of going to school? Not that going to school means everything or anything. It means a lot, but it's not the end or even the beginning. I didn't graduate from college, and I've done good. I have my business. You didn't go to school, but you've done all right. I really don't understand *what* you want. I mean, now that Veryl's gone, you should do something for yourself. You keep saying you want to go off now and become someone. You better do something before it's too late. Maybe you'll be someone like all those people in the *National Enquirer*. First thing someone makes it big, they remember all the shit jobs they ever had, cleaning dog kennels and venetian blinds, or parking cars. Hell, you'll be able to remember when you were a waitress."

"I wonder how many of our Presidents cleaned out toilet bowls during the summer and bussed tables, Mara? And just how many of the First Ladies wiped an elderly person's ass or that cheese that forms between a baby's neck folds, answer me that?"

"That's it, Soveida. That's what I mean. Who's better off, answer me. I don't know, you don't know. What I do know is we gotta work. At something. That I know. It's better if you like what you're doing. You seem to. I don't know why. What is it you really want to do with yourself, Soveida? Working with those wiped-out, tired-horse old women and those men—pubescent, chinless wonders—delivering half-warmed tortillas and dried-out tamales? Can't be all your life will amount to, will it? I'm a businesswoman, I'm not saying I've got it made, I don't. You work with people; I work with money. Who has it better off? You spend all your time putting babies in high chairs; I work with ideas. Concepts, statistics. After all these years, what have you learned that you didn't already know before? I mean, can you tell me, Soveida, what does waitressing have to do with life. Real life?"

"You're hopeless, Mara."

"So what are you telling me, Soveida? Nothing has changed."

"Is that it?"

"Things haven't changed. They never will."

"Maybe someday they will, Mara. Then we won't have any minorities. People won't think because you're black you'll get a job cleaning offices, or because you're Latino you'll clean bathrooms, or because you're young you'll work in fast-food restaurants, or because you're old you'll sweep the hallways."

"Oh, yeah? I don't think so. As long as there is life, there'll be slaves, like Oralia and Chata, and the other one, what's her name?"

"Tere? Oh, Mara, you're wrong. They're not slaves, they're women who serve. There's a difference. You just don't get it."

"*You* just don't get it, Soveida."

"So why are you giving me a hard time, Mara?"

"That's what I do, cuz. That's what I'm best at. But I only do it for your good, remember that."

THE BOOK OF SERVICE

CHAPTER SIX

The Waitress Fugue

As a waitress you are required to be a professional public servant, one who is efficient, but not too familiar, an arbitrator and clairvoyant, a formal, not too friendly, confidante, a member of the same basic human family, the directress of order and guardian of discipline, as well as a pleasant, newfound acquaintance.

A waitress must depend on her skills as an actress, mind reader, dancer, and acrobat.

There is nothing like the great synchronized orchestration of the waitress's fugue. Otherwise known as the waitress's shift.

There is the initial organizational preparation, the revving up, and then the steady, expanding circle of contact as the rush sets in. As the demands grow greater, the worlds of the client, waitress, and cook soon intersect and transform into one intricate, complex composition.

Everyone should wait on tables. A waitress is the observer/observed sanctified by food. That happens on occasion. Great happiness ensues.

If you are a good waitress, you forget your physical self, you become a motion, color, machine, movement itself etched on the elusive, insubstantial canvas of time.

37

The Night of the Cucas

"It's Chuy's fault, that's all there is to it. Dammit!"

Chuy Barales, the elderly custodian, had sprayed the entire restaurant for cockroaches in broad daylight. As lunch wore on, cucas in all states of health streamed out of the walls, causing a terrific panic among the clientele.

"Well, it's certainly not my fault, Mr. Larragoite," Pancha said, scraping the food from a tray full of half-eaten dinner dishes. "It's your fault. You should keep up with the cucas. I told you about them last month and you said, Yeah, okay. I knew you weren't listening to me. Then Margarito found a big one in Eloisa's con queso and she swears it wasn't there when she left the kitchen. She says it jumped out in the Kachina Room. I have it figured out this way: the dumpster's in the back lot there, mero mero up to the wall. They started making babies and found their way into the Kachina Room wall. We could see them spread from room to room. Stalactite. Roadrunner. Tepee. And Turquoise. That's the way cucas are, the traveling, making-baby kind. They got to move around, see what's going on in the world. I told you, Mr. Larragoite, I told you. But you don't listen. Now look at this mess. Pato, bring me some rubber gloves! I'm up to my greñas in cuca caca. Mr. Larragoite, it wasn't Chuy's fault. Don't blame Chuy when you coulda done something about it yourself. Now it's too late."

While Pancha was bawling Larry out, Bonnie's nephew, Peetie Townsend, stood in the doorway, singing "Traveling Man," by Ricky Nelson.

"Would you shut up, Peetie?" Larry finally said with irritation. "What is this, a fifties revival? I'm trying to listen to Pancha."

"I'm finished, Mr. Larragoite," Pancha said as she scraped another nearly full dish, shaking her head in disbelief.

"Sorry, Lar."

"Don't call me Lar, Peetie."

"Bonnie calls you Lar."

"*She* can call me Lar, but you can't. Got that, Peetie? She may be your aunt, but you're *my* employee, or have you forgotten? Why are you hanging around here, anyway?"

Peetie continued standing in the doorway, humming to himself. "Hey, I'm waiting for forks."

"Okay, okay, so?" Larry snarled.

"So? I'm waiting for forks."

"So? So okay."

"Okay."

"Okay. So maybe you shouldn't wait on those forks. Can't you see that Preddie's backed up. Give him a hand with the dishes. What were you saying, Pancha?"

"It's not Chuy's fault."

"Since when are you speaking up for Chuy, Pancha?"

Pancha got a spatula and started scraping the dishes Preddie had stacked up near the overflowing dishwasher.

"Don't blame the servant for the sins of the master, Mr. Larragoite," said Fermín, as he came into the humid kitchen with a fresh tray of uneaten meals. All contaminated.

"Don't get biblical on me, Fermín. Who asked you to butt into our conversation? I was just telling Pancha that Chuy shouldn't have sprayed for cockroaches without asking my permission first. What got into him? We always spray at night. Where is he?"

"Stop yelling, Mr. Larragoite. He's in the men's room. Maybe you should go in there and apologize to him. He was upset."

"*He* was upset? What about *me*? Why should *I* apologize? Like I said, what's all this to you, anyway, Pancha? I thought you didn't like Chuy. You've been telling me all these years to fire him."

"Mr. Larragoite, please, I never told you that." Pancha was clearly upset and moved toward Fermín, who consoled her.

"Don't you lie to me, Pancha Portales," Larry said angrily. "What's gotten into you, anyway? Talking about all this brotherhood shit. Are you feeling all right?"

Pancha looked pale. The fumes from the insecticide were beginning to affect everyone. And still the entire restaurant needed to be cleaned.

"Mr. Larragoite, please don't shout at Pancha," Fermín said, while holding a wet dishrag to Pancha's forehead. "Your yelling affects morale."

"Oh, it does, does it? Listen to me, Fermín. There are changes going on around here that are too fast even for me to follow. Pancha wants me to apologize to Chuy and my own nephew is talking back to me and you, you stop staring at me, Preddie Pacheco! Damn you!"

"I'm not staring at you, Mr. Larragoite! I was looking there, there behind you, on the wall, a cuca."

Sure enough, just behind Larry on the wall was a large cuca. With what Larry sensed was spite, the cuca flung its body toward him. "Goddamn it to hell!"

Larry lunged at the cuca, swatting him with a wet dishtowel. "Shit, it got away!"

Peetie was still near the doorway, looking all goggle-eyed and at a loss. "Go bus some tables, Peetie, and take Pato with you. Shouldn't you guys be cleaning up that mess out there?" Larry asked.

"I'm allergic to bug spray, Larry!"

"Christ, how did it happen? Where's Chuy?"

"Are we still open, Mr. L.?"

"No, Jimmy, we are closed. Closed! Tell everyone to come back tomorrow. Clean and lock up."

"Albert wants to know if he can have a last round, Mr. L."

"Damn Albert! He's probably drunk already. This is no time to be dealing with him and his unrequited love—call it the hots—for Soveida." Larry ran out the kitchen and down to the bar, where Albert was sitting comfortably.

"No, Albert, you cannot stay. No, I don't know if Soveida will be coming in. I told you I don't know!" Larry turned to Jimmy. "*Get him out of here, Jimmy! Get Bud and Whitey out. We're closed, you hear me, because of the attack of the killer roaches. We're closed!*"

"Do you have to yell, Mr. Larragoite?" Fermín asked when Larry returned to the kitchen. "We could hear you all the way from here."

"Sorry, Fermín, I didn't mean to yell."

"I don't like you talking that way in front of Pancha and the young boys."

"Pancha! Shit! This is Pancha Portales we're talking about, isn't it? Waitress at El Farol? Hard-living, hardworking, hard-drinking Pancha?"

"Yes, Mr. Larragoite, that was the *old* Pancha. Now, I know you're upset, but Pancha isn't Pancha anymore."

"Upset, I'm upset?"

Everything in the kitchen stopped. Peetie and Pato left. Preddie faced the wall.

"I've been meaning to talk to you for some time now, Mr. Larragoite. The staff will not condone your profanity anymore."

"Hell!"

"I mean it, Mr. Larragoite."

"Fermín, please, it's been a long night. Where's Chuy? We need to clean up the restaurant, set up for tomorrow."

"Righteousness will not wait."

"Well then, what about this? Get the hell out of my way, Fermín Fernández!"

"Or what?"

"Fermín, please, someone call Soveida. Where is she?"

"It's her night off, Mr. L.," Pancha said, mopping her brow with the edge of her apron.

"Pancha, get her on the phone. Tell her to come down."

"She doesn't want to be disturbed, Mr. L. She has class tonight!"

"Class, what kind of class? Tell her it's an emergency. Tell her I— we—need her here."

"Everything is under control, Mr. Larragoite, or soon will be," Fermín assured Larry, halfheartedly.

"What are you doing back here, Peetie? Isn't there enough work out front?"

"I came to get the forks. Besides, the smell makes me sick."

"Fuck those forks, get back in the Kachina Room and start sweeping up roaches!"

"I will not tolerate profanity, Mr. Larragoite. Pancha, get your purse. We're leaving."

With a grand gesture, Fermín removed his waiter's apron and helped Pancha to do the same.

"Yes, Fermín. Mr. L., we'll not accept your language anymore. Or the abuse."

"Pancha Portales, don't you dare leave me now!"

"I feel sick, Larry."

"Shut up, Peetie."

"Things are not under control, Fermín! Roaches are streaming out of the walls. The lobby is a war zone. The Turquoise Room is a sea of floating brown bodies. The restaurant will lose God knows how much money, the health inspector is probably on his way, or maybe even had dinner here, and you tell me everything is under control. Have you looked in the Kachina Room? The storytellers are holding roach babies, everyone of them! We're lost! This is the last straw, dammit, where's Chuy?"

"In the bathroom, I told you, don't you ever listen, Mr. L.?"

"Out of my way, woman!"

"Don't you talk to Pancha that way, Mr. Larragoite," Fermín said, his voice raised unnaturally high.

Fermín and Pancha embraced, as Preddie turned around to stare openmouthed.

"Christ, the world is ending! Let me out of here! Give me that broom, Peetie. I'm going out there to do battle!"

"What's wrong with him, Pato?"

"You tell me, Peetie."

"Put your purse down, Pancha, we're not going anywhere anymore," Fermín said suddenly.

"But, Fermín, you told me."

"The Bible says to turn the other cheek."

"But, Fermín."

"Get the dustpan, Pancha."

"Yes, Fermín. Here I come."

Larry pushed past Pato Portales, who was no relation to Pancha, and Peetie Townsend, the two busboys.

The attack had begun around 5 p.m., just before dinner. A mass exodus followed. Larry had to herd folks into the patio, where everyone was hastily given a rain check.

Clumps of stunned and writhing roaches lay on the floor, or leapt from the moist walls, throwing their agitated bodies wherever they could. Others bounded past, feverishly driven, and under siege from none other than Chuy himself, who had exited from the men's room brandishing a large can of Roach-X in his hands.

Larry and Chuy nearly collided in the middle of the patio. Larry was flustered, angry, and now off-guard. Chuy, his head down, was abashed. There was a moment of silence.

Larry knew that it was up to him to begin the questioning. Mustering all the managerial calm he could, he cleared his throat, and accidentally blew air through his two front teeth with the sound of a rapid and watery tth, tth tth, accidentally spraying Chuy in the face with spit.

"Sorry, Chuy!"

"No, I'm sorry, Señor Lorenzo."

"How did it happen, Chuy?"

"Bueno, Señor Lorenzo. It was like this . . ."

They stood woodenly in the patio near the white wrought-iron chairs from México.

Chuy put down the Roach-X and looked Larry straight in the eye. Larry knew at this point that it was all over except the formalities. He also knew that the explanation would take some time, and that he would eventually have to sit down and just listen. Larry motioned for Chuy to get a chair from the nearest table.

Chuy looked at him once more and Larry could see Chuy's life crumble before him.

Larry studied Chuy's ashen face. All the color was gone. He looked older than his seventy-two years. He seemed exhausted, on the verge of collapse. He put out his hand to help Chuy to the chair, and, what was worse, the aged man now accepted his help.

Chuy pulled a dust-covered rag from somewhere on his person and attempted to dust the chair. Had he ever been frisked, all sorts of cleaning equipment and supplies would have emerged from his many pockets and folds: much-used and little-used rags of all types, wet, dry, oily, bathroom soap for the restrooms, matches for the lobby, a few loose screws, a tape measure, maybe a light bulb or two, as well as a pack of Red Man chewing tobacco. Chuy, also known as Juan Jesús Barales, was a walking closet of cleaning equipment.

Larry gently took the dry rag away and pulled the chair out for him. All his anger had dissipated. He motioned for Chuy to sit, and Chuy did so, ever so slowly. He was not stiff, nor was he completely limber. And yet he was in excellent physical condition, or had been, up to this moment.

For a second, Larry wondered if Chuy had had an attack of some sort. He thought perhaps that Chuy's heart had pulled in and then out and missed a beat. He knew what this was, how you had to hold on to your chair, or lie down, and summon all your courage to stay alive. He knew what it was to feel that at any moment you had a choice, whether to go or to stay, to live or to die. Had Chuy's heart momentarily stopped and then started? Would he be all right?

"Now, Chuy, just sit there and rest. I'm going to make a quick phone call. Don't move. I'll be right back," Larry called to him.

Larry called me at home, just as I was leaving for class.

"Soveida! You have to come in. We need you! We have a crisis situation here!"

"Larry, I just got home, remember? I was there all day long."

"We've had to close the restaurant, Soveida."

"What?"

"It's bad. Chuy went nuts, everyone is freaking out. Can you come in for just an hour or so? Help us settle down? I'll make it up to you."

"How, Larry? Tonight is the first night of my class."

"Class? You're taking a class, you didn't tell me."

"Culture, Tradition and Folklore in Chicano Society."

"Oh, that kind of class."

"What, you, too? I thought Hector was bad enough . . ."

"Soveida, I promise you, please, just for half an hour, you can get there for the second half."

"Larry, it's not a basketball game. I'm taking this class for credit. I've already enrolled. I'm a student! Find someone else."

"I can't, Soveida, we need you. I left Chuy sitting in the patio. I have to get back to him. He looks bad. It's pandemonium here. God, you can't imagine."

"What was that? Larry, Larry, are you all right?"

"Yes, no, I mean, it's war, Soveida. *War!* We're under siege!"

"I can't, Larry, you've got to understand. It's my first class. Larry, Larry? Are you there?"

I missed my first class. I had to see what happened to Larry and Chuy.

Something had happened to Chuy, all right, but it wasn't what I thought.

As long as I worked at El Farol, Chuy Barales had been the custodian. He had started under Connie and was still at it after all these years. He was a hard worker and extremely devoted to El Farol and the Larragoite family. Next to Connie and Larry, he was most attached to the exotic birds in the lobby. They were like his children, and he knew them all by name. It was Chuy's job to keep their cages clean and to feed them, and, of all his jobs, this was the one he most enjoyed. A slight man with a dark complexion, he was in very good shape. He said it was because he didn't have time to sit around all day at the East Side Senior Center, "como los viejitos," he said, disdainfully, "them playing dominoes or pool and talking about the days when they came over from México or how they survived the war or the bad crops or their sons dying in Vietnam or their women not talking to them or talking to them too much."

Chuy Barales was a man who knew the end of the world was near, because everything that was happening was bad and had to do with money. He often told me he didn't have time to think about getting old or dying. "Let me give you consejos, Soveida. Don't spend your time with the viejitos. All those people who sit around sucking on Tums. Those people will make you old."

Chuy never had time for the endless pool games, the penny bets, the nickel bingos, the occasional loterías. He was the only one left in a family long gone.

"I don't need the food that they serve for lunch at the Senior Center, Soveida. It's cold food, without flavor, prepared without joy for old dogs who don't know the difference."

He told me often that he would die first before he got on line with those viejitos he called "sluggish cattle at the trough," who were grateful to have anything at all to eat.

He didn't need that food for nourishment, he claimed, and he didn't need the idle chatter of those part-time friends whining about their eyes or teeth or legs or reumas or stomachs. Not that he didn't understand, and not that he didn't have the same aches. "Getting old is a part of life, Soveida. It's real. How I choose to live is what matters to me. I want to be with young people, not with a bunch of viejitos." The East Side Senior Center was just two blocks from Chuy's apartment on Trujillo Street. 509 Trujillo. #B. But it was a place he never visited. "A compadre of mine says I should go to the Center in Rosado, where all the farm workers go. But I say no. I'll never go there."

"You might like it better than the East Side Center. The Rosado Center is full of people who have worked hard all their lives in the fields and are still working hard."

"Not like the East Side viejitos, weaned on sugar and store-bought white bread. No. I won't go there, either. I don't need those people in that nursery with its baby food and its silly games and trips downtown in a van to remind me that I am still alive."

I remembered overhearing Connie tell Chuy so long ago, "Chuy, don't you ever worry. As long as I'm around, you'll have a job. Don't worry, you can always work for me."

Both Larry and Chuy sat on the edge of their seats, facing each other. They were uncomfortable, with sad, concerned expressions.

I looked into Chuy's eyes and then at Larry looking at Chuy. I knew each was thinking about the other: "Pobrecito, pobrecito, it's not long, it's not long."

When Chuy finally looked up at Larry, his eyes were slightly moist. They were filled with great tenderness and respect. I think the two would have embraced if they'd known how. How long had it been since they'd hugged or loved another man? Too long.

Larry looked at me, blinked, and motioned with his head for me to leave them alone. I got up, put on my apron, and headed toward the Kachina Room.

He cleared his throat and spoke with a firmness that immediately reassured Chuy. "Now, Chuy, I've been meaning to ask you about the tarps in the Tepee Room. I was thinking about taking the damn things down and putting up some new booths. You know, Santa Fe style, maybe a little adobe kind of thing with some howling coyotes on the side. Slap up a few ristras, and a couple of cow skulls. What do you think? You tell me."

"Bueno, Señor Lorenzo," Chuy said with authority and no small courtesy. "You know I fixed those tepees last summer and they should last a long time, if you don't mind my saying, longer than you and I will be around."

"If it's not the tepees, it's that damn bird cage in the lobby. I feel like just getting rid of it."

"Children love the pajaritos, Señor Lorenzo. Everyone does. If you'd like, I'll fix up a new cage. That way the children, the birds, everyone will be happy."

38

Ni Modo

I had carefully studied the course list. I knew I could only take one class, and it would have to be after work, early in the evening. It couldn't be on a Friday, because I needed to be available if Larry called me to fill in for the weekend rush. Monday was my day off, the day I did laundry, paid my bills, and helped Chata clean my house.

No one had classes on Sunday, my other day off. I needed at least two full days away from food, and the responsibilities of serving it. When I was at home on Sundays I ate quickly, baloney and cheese slapped in a warm tortilla, or ramen noodles, or a box of Kraft macaroni and cheese—anything I didn't have to spend a long time preparing. Mondays I ate lunch and dinner out, usually at Tapia's Stop-In and Eat, the best burritos in Agua Oscura: big homemade flour tortillas packed with beans and chile, only 85¢. $1.50 for a chicharrón burrito and $1.25 for a chile relleno one.

The class would have to be Tuesday–Thursday. I skimmed the course schedule again, reviewing the classes, and their times.

CHICANO STUDIES

BALLET FOLKLORICO FOR BEGINNERS 3–5 P.M.
  MWF
THE EMERGING CHICANA VOICE—SHEDDING THE
  LITERARY YOKE 1:30–3:00 P.M. MW
AMNESTY—STIGMA OR STIGMATA? THE WHYS AND
  WHEREFORES OF IMMIGRATION—WHO ARE WE
  TRYING TO SUPPRESS? 8:30–9:45 A.M. TT
LA FRONTERA—THE TORTILLA CURTAIN—A MEANS

OF SUSTENANCE—FOR WHOM? 11:00–1:15 A.M.
MWF

LAS MAQUILADORAS—TWIN-PLANT MANIA, ANOTHER
TAIWAN FOR THE U.S.? 5:00–6:15 P.M. TT

CULTURE, FOLKLORE AND TRADITION IN CHICANO/
CHICANA SOCIETY—A LOOK AT THE NI MODO
PHILOSOPHY 5:30—7:00 P.M. TT

CULTURAL RELEVANCE OF THE TATTOO IN THE
CHICANO/CHICANA MIND-SET 3:00–5:00 P.M. MT

ALCOHOLISM AND DRUG USE IN CHICANO FAMILIES,
BALM OF THE DISENFRANCHISED 8:00–9:15 A.M.
MWF

EDUCATING RAZA—JOHNNY CAN READ NOW, BUT
ONLY IN ENGLISH 3:00–5:00 P.M. MWT

They all sounded interesting, but only two courses were possible. It was between *Las Maquiladoras—Twin-Plant Mania, Another Taiwan for the U.S.?* or *Culture, Folklore and Tradition in Chicano/ Chicana Society—A Look at the Ni Modo Philosophy.*

J. V. Velásquez was the professor for the latter. "Staff," the other designated teacher. I would go with Velásquez. I'd never liked taking classes taught by Staff. I wanted to know from the outset that someone was really committed to the class. The unspoken-for, undelegated class was not for me. If I was going to take a course, I couldn't jump in fully unless the professor did, and I wanted the professor to be there, full of energy, ready for debate. Was J.V. male or female? I didn't know. Velásquez was a new professor, I could tell that. I'd never heard of him/her.

It wasn't the first course I'd taken at the Community College. The autumn before, I had studied typing and in the spring semester I'd learned to bowl. This time I wanted to expand.

Ivan had always talked about Chicano this, Chicano that, my brother Hector as well. I, too, wanted to learn more about my Chicana self. When I looked at the catalogue, I had no idea there were so many courses about things I was familiar with, understood, and yet wanted to know more about. For example, the alcoholism and drug use in Chicano families. I knew something about that, but I'd never really talked to anyone about it. Or views on the Amnesty program. Or life on the border. Where had I been all this time? I was moving into a new century but so up to my neck in food that I hadn't had the eyes to see what was happening around me.

Hector was amused by my signing up for a class in the Chicano Studies Department.

"You? Miss Anti-political? You were wearing wiglets and false eyelashes in the 1960s, sis. Hell, Soveida, you missed the sixties, and now you want to become Chicano. You don't know a brown beret from a green beret. What are you studying for, anyway? Aren't you busy enough at the Taco Shed? When are you going to have time between rolling enchiladas to study?"

"Look, Hector. I'm only calling you because I thought it was time. You never call me. I was making conversation. I'm taking a class. So leave it alone. What do you know, anyway? If you're such a dedicated Chicano, when are you going to learn Spanish?"

"I can speak it. Enough to get by."

"Por favor, mesero, otra cerveza."

"I don't just order beer, I talk to people."

"Juárez talk. I'll buy that, bring me that. You're a weekend Chicano at the mercado, buying up the place so you can talk about what great bargains you've gotten at someone else's expense."

"Look who's so righteous, all of a sudden. Well, you've got a maid. Let's talk about that, okay? That's what happens when you take one of those beaner classes. You get righteous all of sudden."

"Let's leave Chata out of this, please. It wouldn't hurt you to learn something about your own culture."

"I know enough already, sis. Fiesta, party, salud, amor y pesetas. Go ahead and take your class, there'll be no living with you once you've gone Brown Power."

"You're so racist against your own, Hector! You and your buddy El Gonie, that beer-guzzling, sexist-chauvinist-racist Mexican pig, talk about getting down, con safos, and all that, but you don't understand very much."

"So, you do? Leave Gonacio out of this, Miss-Kiss-My-Educated-Chicana-Butt!"

"Don't make fun of me, Hector. What do you know, anyway? Just forget I called. I only called because Dolores told me you'd become manager. So congratulations. But I gotta go. I can't talk to you anymore."

"You never do. Musta ruffled those smooth brown greased back feathers of yours again."

"I'm taking the class."

"Nobody's stopping you, Soveida."

"Why do I bother talking to you, Hector?"

"Because, esa, you're my seeester!"

I missed the first class because of the Night of the Cucas. Or, as Randy Holsum, the busboy who was majoring in biology at the State University, had said, the Revenge of the Blattidae Orthoptera. To everyone else, they were your plain, ordinary, simple American or, in this case, Mexican–American house roaches.

By the time I left El Farol (it was worse than I'd ever imagined), and made my way to the Southern New Mexico Community College, class was over and J. V. Velásquez was organizing some papers that had been left on top of his desk.

J. V. Velásquez was definitely a man.

"Mr., I mean, Dr. Velásquez?"

"Yes?"

"Dr. Velásquez, I'm sorry, I'm late for class."

"You're not late, it's over, Ms.—"

"Soveida Dosamantes."

"The class was over fifteen minutes ago, Ms. Dosamantes. I was just going through some paperwork I handed out."

"I'm so sorry, Dr. Velásquez. We had trouble at work, please forgive me. It won't happen again."

"Well, you better sit down and fill out this questionnaire."

"Questionnaire?"

"The Chicano culture questionnaire."

"All right. Thank you. Excuse me, Dr. Velásquez, do you have a pen I could borrow? God, I can't believe it, I mean, I always have a pen."

"There's a pen in your hair, Ms. Dosamantes."

"Oh yes, well, thank you. I'll just sit here and fill out the questionnaire. I'm sorry I'm keeping you. Shall I hand it in next time? I could take it home with me right now and bring it back, Dr. Velásquez."

"No, just sit there. I have some other work to do. Besides, I want unrehearsed, off-the-top-of-your-head answers."

"I understand. Excuse me. I'll just sit down."

"Certainly."

"Do you have any paper, Dr. Velásquez?"

God, I felt like a heel. I was two hours late and I had to keep Dr.

Velásquez waiting. He was very good-looking, and obviously serious about his work—if a bit full of himself, too—I could tell immediately.

The following questionnaire has been formulated by J. V. Velásquez, Ph.D., to determine an individual's knowledge of his/her Chicano culture and background. Answer each question as simply and as clearly as possible. If you should only know a detail or incidental fact about the subject, please record that on your paper.

THE CHICANO CULTURE QUIZ

Name: Soveida Dosamantes
Occupation: Waitress
Years of schooling: 12, with two classes at SNMCC
Place of birth: Agua Oscura, New Mexico
Primary language (s) at home: English, Spanish, depending on who you are talking to
Other languages: Spanish

Identify the significance or meaning of the following, to the best of your knowledge:
Cinco de Mayo (5th of May)
Dieciseis de Septiembre (16th of September)
César Chávez and the UFW
Name of at least one Chicano congressman or senator
Identify five well-known Chicano actors or performers
Name five female and male contemporary Chicano and
Chicana writers

Define and distinguish between the following:
Hispanic
Chicano
Mexicano
Mexican-American

Relate the stories of the following:
Our Lady of Guadalupe/La Morenita
La Sebastiana
La Llorona
El Coco/El Cucui

Identify cultural traditions:
Baptisms
Quinceañeras
Weddings
Anniversaries
Funerals
La Bendición

Describe your own family traditions

Last, write a brief essay on why you are taking this class. Do you consider yourself a Chicano/Chicana? If so, why? Why is it important to study this culture? Is it part of the American tapestry? Is it considered "foreign"? By whom? What is the importance of the study of all cultures, languages, traditions, folklore?

I felt dizzy. It must have been El Farol; I'd worked hard there all day, was back there again tonight. I had to leave the class, and soon. Dr. Velásquez would just have to wait.

He looked so nice in his white linen suit. You didn't often see a man in a white suit.

He looked up. I looked down. Quinceañera: the celebration of a girl's coming of age at fifteen, the ensuing celebration.

I didn't feel well, the fumes of the cuca spray. I'd be all right. Hector was right. What was I doing taking this class? And yet I guess there was something to it. I knew most of the answers, they were part of my life. But what about the others in the class? Would they know the answers if they hadn't grown up among the baptisms and weddings and funerals? Who would spread our culture in the future? Who would be making those connections? Imagine a world without gorditas or sopaipillas or piloncillo or green chile! I pulled the pen out of my hair and looked again at the Chicano Culture Quiz. I suddenly felt better.

Dr. Velásquez looked at me, somewhat awkwardly, as if I'd caught him off-guard, without all his educated defenses, and possibly without his calzones. I smiled. He looked at his papers, quickly. He'd seen me, he couldn't help it. And he saw me smiling at him. I might never get close to his perceptions of cultural realities, but, dammit, I knew who Baby Gaby, that Chicano singer, was and, in my book, that accounts for a whole hell of a lot of living. Dr. Velásquez, you want to know about the Chicano culture? Well, here I am, smelling of hard work.

I was thinking clearer now, even if I was jumping from question to question. It was more fun that way.

Ni modo: a phrase meaning that a person accepts what can't be undone; in other words, there's nothing you can do about it, let it go, accept it, might as well. Ni modo.

I looked up again at J. V. Velásquez, Ph.D. Mr. Perfectly Educated in his Perfectly Pressed White Linen Suit. He was staring at me now. No mistaking that. He's cute. I stared back. Ni modo.

THE BOOK OF SERVICE

CHAPTER SEVEN

Bras and Girdles

No girdles.

Tight, pinching underwear is a waitress's nightmare. That and ill-fitting shoes. There is nothing worse than a tight bra that grips the fleshy parts, or panties that grab—crotch-bite, I call it. Especially during a busy shift. There is nothing worse than having to keep pulling down or up or over. Stay away from lace. Lace will attack. Cotton is cool, and breathes with you.

These defensive actions could mean the difference between a dollar and a dollar-fifty tip.

Pray that when you are a waitress you are relatively young. Pray that your outfit is not too juvenile. Ever see an old woman in a red, puffy miniskirt, bird legs swaddled in tights, sagging bosom accented by white lace? Pray that you are single. You will meet many people at work, and you are bound to fall in love with at least one. If not two or more.

If you are a waitress, you have to live hard, drink hard, love hard. There is no other way.

39

Tangee's Tampico

The night Mr. Tangee died, he was sitting in his usual spot in the Turquoise Room, eating his familiar beloved Tampico steak con papas aguadas that Eloisa Ortiz, La Famosa, had lovingly prepared for him, as she had on all Friday nights past for the last fifteen years.

He had slipped in, as he was accustomed to, before the weekend crowd, sidestepping the hostess, Ede Le Crenshaw. Everything in the room was turquoise-colored, from the tiles on the floor to the table-cloths and napkins, to the small Tatung fan that stood on a painted turquoise chest facing an enormous turquoise-yarn Ojo de Dios, the eye of God fashioned by crafts-oriented hobbyists. Clippings from *New Mexico Magazine* and *Arizona Highways* on turquoise jewelry adorned the walls, as did maps identifying the location of turquoise quarries around the world, with charts of different types of turquoise and a brief history of the gem favored by the gods. But it was the Ojo that dominated the room.

Mr. Tangee sat quietly at a table for two in the farthest corner of the room.

"Good evening, Mr. Tangee. How are you?"

"Better than ever, Soveida, and you?"

"Just fine, thanks."

"That's good, very good."

"Can I get you—"

"The usual."

"Fine."

"No, change that, I'll have milk tonight."

"No iced tea?"

"I've been a bit under the weather."

"I'm sorry to hear that. One milk, coming right up."

"Oh, and no potatoes. Have to watch my cholesterol."

"No potatoes?"

"Just plain. No tortillas. Too heavy. I'm trying to eat light. Tell Eloisa to go light on the pico on my Tampico."

"Cut the chile."

"Put it on the side."

"Will that be all, Mr. Tangee?"

"Yes, thank you now, Soveida."

"Yes sir."

Everything seemed almost normal. Mr. Tangee was the only one in the Turquoise Room and I was glad, because it was a relief from working the first three rooms, especially the Tepee Room.

The children and young people usually request the Tepee Room because little tepees cover the light brown booths, highlighting the pseudo-animal-cave drawings on the sides of the tarp, giving the room a wonderful, almost magical effect. It's hard to wait on these tables, because you have to go inside each tepee and find your way around the darkened table. The big tepees (seating six to eight) are worse. It's like serving food in a narrow covered wagon, everyone grabbing for their own share in the luminescent darkness. But the people love it, as Larry always says.

The Kachina Room makes me melancholic, at every turn a scowling wooden figure under a dark, make-believe moon. And yet the Kachina Room has its charms, with a large clay storyteller on the fireplace holding impassive babies on its large angular legs and in its strange arms. It was Larry's idea to make this huge mother and to sic her on gringo land. The women love her.

"She's so primitive," I can hear from the other room, or "Look at that sweet thing," or "See that statue, can you beat that?" or "It's so Santa Fe," or "Son of a gun," or just "Hey, what the hell is that?" The last question is so common that each new waiter and waitress is versed in answering certain tourist-type questions: "What is a Kachina?" "Do roadrunners really fly?" "What's the difference between a stalactite and a stalagmite?"

It is my task, as official waitress/waiter trainer, to supply each new employee with a photocopy of such questions and answers. Bonnie dictated the questions and answers to me one day after work, and now this Q. and A. is a requirement for "educating the staff about folklore."

If you want to make money, it's best to be in the Stalactite Room or the Kachina Room; the Roadrunner Room comes in a close third. The Tepee Room is a lot of work and the tips are irregular. But if you want peace, there's usually no better place than the Turquoise Room.

Unless you've waited, you will never understand what it is to wait. It's no wonder Mara doesn't understand why I've been a waitress so long. How can she ever know about the people I've come to know and then love? How could I ever explain to her the memories of that particular time, that particular wait, with dear old Mr. Tangee?

I made my way to the kitchen, passing through the Roadrunner and Tepee Rooms. Eloisa greeted me heartily. It didn't matter that we'd both been at work for forty-five minutes already and had talked for a few minutes in the ladies' room, each of us from connected stalls.

"¿Comó estás, chula?"

"Tampico side chile, no potatoes."

"Pobrecito, he mustn't be feeling good. I've been worried, Soveida. Ever since la Señora Tangee died last year, he hasn't looked so good to me. Gray. Gray like an I-don't-know-what, that kinda gray. Gray like a nothing. Gray like a Tampico left out in the rain, no chile. Send him a bowl of my con queso and see if that doesn't put hair on his chest."

"One milk coming up."

Back in the kitchen, I poured Mr. Tangee his milk.

"Milk?" Eloisa exclaimed. "You giving Mr. T. milk? It's worse than I thought. I'll make his steak real tender, the way he likes. Flavio," Eloisa said to her cooking assistant, "give me my machaca. I need to soften me a steak, boy. We haven't got all day. He can't move, Soveida, he's glued to the floor. What kind of help is this? Flavio! Someone! ¡Píquele!"

After turning in my order, I returned to the Turquoise Room with the milk and con queso and a side of white bread. Mr. Tangee liked to dip small pieces of white bread into his con queso; tostadas were too hard to digest, he said.

He was reading a book, which was his usual pastime. I set the dishes down and caught a glimpse of the title: *Deification of the Persona in the Collected Works of T. M. Bindwell* by Urgethold Birikwin.

"Thank you, Soveida."

"You're welcome, Mr. Tangee."

The restaurant was getting busier. Pancha had a busload of Women Aglows from the Charismatic Convention, and Bonnie was working the Roadrunner Room with Fermín Fernández, long-time waiter extraordinaire, who'd jumped ship from another restaurant. He was showing her what to do. Suddenly she'd taken an interest in waiting herself, to see what she could learn that would improve service efficiency. The Tepee Room was closed for repairs. One of the tarp tepees had fallen down and it seemed that all the tarps were slightly mildewed.

In the kitchen Eloisa yelled to Flavio: "Don't pat that steak, boy, beat it. It's called tenderizing, haven't you ever done that to meat? I'm counting on you, Flavito, to beat Mr. T.'s steak, the way he likes it, tender. Pégele a ese Tampico hasta que sangre chile. Oh, you don't speak Spanish, Flavito? Shame on your mamá! What's happening to our kids? They don't speak Spanish no more! Hit it until it bleeds chile, you got it, Flavio?"

I delivered Mr. Tangee's Tampico way ahead of the fifty El Farol Specials for the fifty Women Aglows.

"What? Mi viejito, Mr. T., wait? Que se esperen esas holy-holies. Let them wait for their red chile pork rolled in tortillas de harina. Nobody can make my Mr. T. wait, not even God himself. My comadre Amanda is an Aglow, so I know they would want it this way."

Later on, after the tragedy, Eloisa blamed Flavio for everything. I blamed myself, feeling I could have done something. And yet, probably nothing could have been done. Not really. What was done was the best that could have been done. That consisted of Fermín racing into the Turquoise Room when I screamed for help upon noticing that Mr. Tangee was choking on his Tampico.

Fermín, slight as he was, courteous and gentle, pushed back the table, grabbed Mr. Tangee, and tried to Heimlich him back to life. I had been gone just a little while and, when I returned, Mr. Tangee was beginning to change color. Then his face turned purple. I screamed, dropped a tray of hot food, and Fermín and Bonnie came running in, but it was too late.

Fermín laid Mr. Tangee on the floor next to the table and prayed over him. The Aglows rushed in aghast from the Stalactite Room, where they had heard my calls for help. They quickly formed a prayer circle around Tangee and Fermín, and in strong voices said the Our Father, then sang "My Lord, Thou Callest Me." Still stunned, I burst into tears and was comforted by Fermín, who embraced me, saying, "It wasn't your fault, Soveida. He's with the Lord now."

At this point Eloisa came into the room, wiping her forearm across her beaded forehead, and cried out, her two-hundred-plus pounds moving as fast as they could to her beloved Mr. T.'s side. She screamed and then fainted over a nearby table. Several of the Aglows caught her and then attended to her, laying hands on her and speaking in tongues as Fermín now led the prayers over Brother Tangee. Someone called a priest.

Revived, Eloisa yelled above the din, "Era protestante!" But nobody cared, a priest was called anyway.

Now Larry pitched forward into the room as Bonnie looked at him mournfully. Margarito Cornudo, who had been working the Kachina Room and had stepped into the men's room just before the commotion, stumbled in to see what the noise was all about. He stood behind Pancha, who gripped the door handle. Fermín, who could see how upset she was, came up and took her hands in his. It was a sad hour.

The next day the restaurant was closed in memory of Mr. Tangee. Everyone was given the day off. Margarito did his laundry. Pancha took off to Juárez to buy meat and vanilla and to have a pedicure, and the Aglows, including Amanda, with Eloisa in attendance, dedicated the closing ceremony of their convention to Mr. Tangee and all those who die an accidental death. I stayed home crying.

Henceforth, the steak became known as Tangee's Tampico. It was Eloisa's idea. Some called it bad taste; others called it, as Eloisa did, "honoring the man, in life, not in death. And what is more sacred than food, answer me that?" Eloisa bellowed.

Eloisa got Flavio fired, and Pablito Ledesma took his place. After that, Eloisa was never too busy to tenderize herself, saying a prayer each time, "Pa' mi viejito, que descanse en paz con su esposa y con su Tampico."

"Wait a minute, Eloisa." Larry said. "Don't you have it all mixed up?"

"No, I got it right," Eloisa explained. "I honor him. I'm living, he's dead."

"So? The life part is okay, but what about the death part?"

"I believe in the afterlife, Lenchito, don't you? A que mi viejito, now he has all the Tampicos he can eat, and besides that, he's eating them with his señora. What could be more beautiful?"

And with that, Eloisa wiped her eyes.

40

Off Nights / On Nights

In the fading light, underneath the covers, and in the silence of my apartment, I felt exhausted. I'd worked too hard, too long, for too many years. Today I told Larry that I needed some time off and that I was taking a leave of absence.

My right ovary ached. I was sick of Albert and his stupid drunken passes. Perhaps working full-time and being back in school part-time was too much. And yet I wanted to continue working. But at what?

When I woke up, the reflection of my face in the mirror startled me. Two years ago my eyes began to go. That was the year Veryl killed himself. A year I'll never forget, like the year of Adrino's chicaro. So many things dated from that horrible year, and since then, it seems, nothing has ever been right.

Two years ago I cried so much I became a different person. Now what I have are distinct signs of under-eye pouching, that crepe-like skin disease. The damage was slight at first, barely perceptible, but it spread. The left eye is worse. One side or another of my body has usually been out of synch with the other.

And in the long run it was foolish. He wanted to die. Meeting me, falling in love, getting married, all of it was just a brief change of plans for him, a break to gather strength. It's even possible I hastened his end. I think at last he found someone with whom he could comfortably die. He knew I'd take care of things. When he married me, it was just a matter of time. In the beginning with Veryl, I felt full of hope. His was a face I knew I could love. No, it was more than that. His was a face I was destined to love. I loved him, and the light behind his bright blue eyes.

Sometimes the Face is a man. Sometimes the Face is a woman.

Sometimes it's nobody. Has no body. It's as ethereal and as real as a dream. I can try to describe Dolly's face or Mara's or Hector's. Ivan's I know in every pore of my body. Veryl's face is a tender memory. And to me there is no face in the world like Mamá Lupita's or Oralia's. What I saw in the mirror this morning chilled and frightened me. Behind my face were so many other faces, all of them changing before my eyes. Which one was my real face? The face that I knew I could accept and love? That's why I quit El Farol today. Maybe it's just a break to gather strength. Of course, Larry didn't understand. How could he? And how could I explain?

Larry has no feelings. All he thinks about is himself, what's good for him. El Farol is just an extension of his ego. Hell, he doesn't even like Mexican food! He has no sense of culture, and is as Anglo as they come. Larry's just as chauvinistic and selfish as everyone else who comes through El Farol, from Whitey Moldon, to Bud Ermin, to Albert Chanowski, all of them in need. In need of food, drink, and sustenance for a shaky and isolated spirit. The question was why had I put up with their needs for so long. Was I in need as well? And what did I need them for? There were other jobs in life, other paths. Was my salvation to be through Eloisa's con queso?

I was tired, empty and tired. Too tired to cry. Eventually someone would call. Larry. Or Dolly wanting me to run an errand for her. Or Luardo or Mamá with the usual question: "Why don't you come to see me anymore? You don't visit me. You don't have time for me. No one cares for me anymore." Maybe Luardo would ask me out to lunch or dinner, for something greasy, like chicken or fish.

I lay down and fell asleep on the couch, fully dressed. It had been so long since I'd slept in bra and panties. I dreamed about a woman the age of Billy Jane or Nayla. The woman came to me and told me she read palms. When I stretched my palm upward, the woman turned my palm down and placed her delicate white hand over mine. The two hands, one on top of the other, were held in space as if locked over some holy spot. The woman then removed her hand from mine. Everything faded. I woke up.

And then I remembered. I was no longer a waitress.

I never meant to quit, to walk out. The only other time I'd ever thought about it was last year during the Food Rights Battle when Larry had been in one of his moods and no one, not even Bonnie, could reason with him.

It had been an unspoken rule that the staff, including waitresses, waiters, bartenders, bus people, and all kitchen and custodial staff, were allowed to eat one free meal per shift. It was nice to finish a long shift and then eat a plate of red enchiladas in the back of the kitchen at one of the little tables set there for the staff. The food always tasted so good after you'd worked hard serving others.

Eloisa ran a tight kitchen, and you weren't allowed any steaks, but the Mexican food was hot and plentiful. There was nothing better than a bowl of fideos or a plate of tacos con chile verde after a long shift.

The staff took turns eating. Some people, like Lucille LaMont, never ate at the restaurant. But, for the most part, everyone else did. Jimmy and Barb Valentine, the bartenders, ate when their backups came in, the bus people whenever there was a lull, and the waiters and waitresses at the end of a shift. It was a system that worked well, until Larry, in his constant attempt to fix things, actually made them worse than they ever were.

"Gather round, everybody. Gather round. Work report. This will just take a minute, I know we're about ready to open. Just sit down, Fermín. You, too, Petra, somebody give Petra a seat. Pancha, Soveida. You guys, cut the noise. Jimmy, make sure that the front door is locked. Pancha Portales is fifty-four, sorry, Pancha, I mean thirty-nine, today. Let's give her a hand. Pancha's been with us for fifteen years. By the way, have you noticed a gleam in her eye that wasn't there before? Could it be love? Pancha and Fermín Fernández are now engaged and have set a date for their impending marriage! It's not too late to change your mind, Fermín! Let's hear it for the lovebirds! Okay, gang. Don't forget we have the Teachers' Association Convention next weekend. Before we go, I wanted to bring up the problem of staff meals. I've been doing some calculations and have figured out that staff meals are costing El Farol quite a bit. It's getting out of hand. I know Mom started the system, but the restaurant was smaller then. Now we have fifteen employees. That means fifteen, well, make that twelve, meals, at $6.95 on average. You figure it. I'm afraid I'm going to have to begin charging you for your meals."

"That's impossible!" Fermín called out.

"It won't work," said Pancha. "You gonna lose everybody and they gonna quit, Mr. L."

"I don't like it, Larry," I retorted.

"Well, that's just too bad. We're losing money, Soveida. Money that could be going into El Farol. I can't help it, folks, just bring your lunches."

"We want a hot lunch or dinner, Mr. Larragoite," said Joe Fierro, the bartender, who was usually silent.

"It's always my best meal," said Chuy.

"Him, it's his only meal," Pancha said about Chuy.

"You can't do this to us, Larry," I said firmly. "You can't, not after all these years. It's not fair. It's better to keep the staff happy than to save a few measly pennies. You just can't do this to us."

"Okay, now, everyone back to work. Jimmy, get the front door. I'll talk to you later, Soveida Dosamantes. It just can't be helped. Fermín, Pancha!"

"He's so damn cheap" was loudly heard as everyone glumly went back to their posts to get ready for work.

The Food Rights Battle, as it later came to be known, lasted just under two weeks. Morale was low from day one. Everyone was upset and in a foul mood. Larry overcompensated with his cheery attitude, but it was hopeless.

The day after the food pronouncement, Lavel Windle was publicly reprimanded for having fixed himself a Tampico steak in defiance. Money was taken out of Lavel's paycheck. When Larry ordered Lavel to cook him a hamburger from his own private stash, which he kept separate from what he deemed "all that lardy Mexican food," Lavel retaliated by patting and molding the pattie in his hairy armpit and then grilling it. The bus people, Pato and Sandra de la Cruz, were witnesses. Pato almost peed his pants when Lavel went out to see if Larry had enjoyed his burger.

This was followed by Sandra de la Cruz fixing a plate of tacos which she then ate in the women's restroom. Chuy found out about it, but he was afraid to tell Mr. Lorenzo, as he called him. He wanted to, but Pancha gave him a dirty look.

The Battle started on a Tuesday, and by that Friday, things were extremely heated. Grumbling could be heard from the Tepee Room to the Turquoise Room, from the bar to the kitchen. Chuy looked gaunt. On Saturday, Eloisa snuck him a bowl of fideos, which he ate in the cleaning closet. Saturday was a tense day. Everyone knew something was about to give. On Sunday, Larry came into work at the usual hour, to find his staff assembled in the patio. Seeing him, they quickly dispersed. He noticed that everyone seemed friendly toward one other, but not to him. People who before had not gotten along were now best friends. A few minutes later he saw the P Brigade—Preddie, Pato, Pito, Peetie, Petra, and Pancha—all huddling together. Larry knew that Petra and Pancha were like oil and water and that Preddie the dishwasher and Pito the night cook were both loners. What business did they all have together? Their coolness was beginning to fray his nerves.

Monday's lunch was tough. The restaurant seemed unusually busy. People didn't finish eating until almost 4 p.m. After nearly a week of tension over the damn food rights, Larry retreated to his office to listen to his Barry Manilow tapes and to take a rest. He unfolded his cot and lay down. He hadn't been feeling well lately; his heart would suddenly begin beating very fast without warning. Several times he thought he was going to pass out. It was hard when he bent over; he nearly blacked out. He welcomed the quiet of his office, as peaceful as it could be, given the last shift and his staff's behavior over one lousy meal on the job. Larry fell into a hard and unpleasant sleep.

He awoke several hours later, as if in a stupor, and lumbered out of his office into the bar. The place was empty. Checking the front door, he found it locked. A sign on it read:

CLOSED FRIDAY MARCH 10.
PRIVATE PARTY

"Where you been, Mr. Lorenzo? Come and eat, there's lots of food," said Chuy through a mouthful of food.

"What's the meaning of this sign, Chuy?"

"Don't know, Mr. Lorenzo. Talk to Soveida."

"Soveida! What's going on here?"

"You're just in time, Larry. Now, if everyone will be quiet."

"What the hell is going on, Soveida?" screeched Larry.

"We're having a party, and we closed the restaurant, Larry. Eloisa cooked the food. Everyone pitched in money, so it didn't cost you a penny. You either give us back our food or we're all going to walk out tomorrow just in time for the Teachers' Association Convention. That means everyone: waitresses, waiters, bus people, dishwashers, even Chuy."

"That's right, Mr. Lorenzo. You want some cake?"

"Now, just a minute, Soveida. Whose idea was this, anyway?"

"Does it matter? What's one small meal for all the hard work we do? We've made El Farol what it is, don't forget that. All total, everyone in this room has worked over three hundred years for you! Come on!"

"Did you have to close the restaurant?"

"Yes, we did! We mean business."

"Soveida!"

"We mean it, no food, no work. No work, no restaurant."

"No mercy, that's what you mean! Can we talk about this?"

"No! Now, come on, everybody! Dig in! Gracias a Eloisa and all the kitchen staff. Is there anything you want to say, Larry?"

"Yeah. Shit."

The staff didn't walk out the next day for the Teachers' Association Convention. Food rights returned and have continued to this day.

The Night of the Cucas had been bad, very bad, but probably the worst night I ever spent at El Farol was the night of Mr. Tangee's death. This was followed by the night Lavel freaked out in the Stalactite Room during the dinner shift.

Few people had seen it coming, although most everyone knew that Lavel was addicted to Robitussin. Between his marijuana and his Robitussin, he was constantly in a state of drug-induced euphoria.

Lavel was twenty-three, and he still lived with his mother, LaVeeta Windle, at the far end of Chiva Town, near the highway. The poorer black families in Agua Oscura lived there, along with the poorer Mexicans. Initially, there was an uneasy peace between the two ethnic groups, but over the years things improved. The blacks knew Spanish as well as any of the hometown boys, and the gangs on that side of town were comprised of both black and brown brothers. In Agua Oscura, it can truly be said that poverty brings strangers together.

Lavel was a vato loco from Chiva Town, just like any of the other bros he hung around with. He could banter back and forth with El Pato or La Sandra de la Cruz and he loved to tell dirty jokes in Spanish. Lavel and LaVeeta moved to Agua Oscura after his daddy, Holcomb Windle, was killed in a mining accident in Silver City. Those first few years LaVeeta cleaned houses, and then offices. Now she owned a window-cleaning business, the Looking Glass. A kind and gentle woman, LaVeeta Windle meant well, but she was too lenient with Lavel, although she tried to give him the best she could. Lavel worked from the age of twelve, in gas stations, in hamburger joints, settling into working in restaurants, where he moved up the food scale. No one, not even Eloisa, was comparable to Lavel when it came to cooking meat. One year he'd moved to Phoenix to apprentice with a chef there, and that confirmed his cooking talent. He was wasted at El Farol, and he knew it, but he liked the people there, and Pato, his home boy, had gotten him in with the boss. Lavel's dream was to own and run a steak house, though not necessarily in Agua Oscura. He'd like some town with "new" in the name, like New York or New Orleans. He was so tired of the old. At El Farol, he cooked the steaks as the orders came in, but there was no real creativity to that. Lavel was simply bored. Bored of being poor in Chiva Town. Bored of his tough macho gang, the Bad Bros. Bored of Agua Oscura. Bored of being Lavel Windle, bored chef.

Lavel took his first drugs at age ten. He'd tried them all, but mota and the Robi were what kept him going at work. The other stuff he used after work hours. The Robi kept him high and clean, a good buzz going strong, with no strange angels creeping round. The mota calmed and relaxed him. No Sweat Windle, that's what he was called.

"Hey, Sweat, two sirloins rare, and a Tampico well."

"No sweat, Fermín. Hey, did you hear the one about the puta in hell?"

"Get off with you, just get me my steaks!"

"Hey, Sweat, two Tampico medium and a sirloin rare, that and a side of green chile."

"No sweat, Soveida, looking clean and mean."

"So what about the puta in hell?"

"No sweat, Pato, my man, come around and I'll dish it out."

That was No Sweat until the night he freaked. It started that afternoon with his compadre Manuel and his bro Althon, all of them going full tilt on some rocks and Wild Turkey and him coming to work blasted and blown on that and a couple of bottles of wild-cherry Robi and a joint of mota he smoked out the back door. He was sneaking a toke when Eloisa cornered him.

"What's with you, Lavel? You don't look so good."

"Hey, no sweat, Elo, I'm mean and clean. I was just saying hello to the stars."

"Get inside, cochino, you and your puta jokes. Put away that cancer stick. I won't have my boys dying young."

"No sweat, Elo mamá."

"Que mamá ni que mamá! Don't you be mamáing me, Lavel. Don't think I don't know you got marijuana up your venas. Get a cup of hot water and put some of my red chile in it, that tea will fix you up. Go back to work, m'ijo, or you'll be in trouble."

He *was* in trouble. He couldn't walk, he couldn't talk, and when he felt himself moving against his will toward Eloisa, he suddenly bolted past the kitchen and into the patio near the Stalactite Room, screaming at the top of his lungs and scared out of his mind.

"Aaaaayyyyyychingaaoooooooo!"

Eloisa ran after him as fast as she could with her bad varicose legs, alerting Pato, who in turn called me. I was in the Turquoise Room. I called Fermín, who called Pancha, and they ran into the Stalactite Room, followed by Petra. Bonnie had heard Lavel scream and ran in from the office, where she was doing the books. She set off again to call the police, but Eloisa talked her out of it.

"My God, what happened? Is he crazy? I've got to call the police!"

"No, Miss Bonnie, por favor. Please don't call the policía. He'll get in trouble. Maybe this time he'll learn. M'ijo, Lavelito, are you okay?"

Pato and Preddie had tackled Lavel in the Stalactite Room and they dragged him into the kitchen in front of a few frightened customers. Lavel wore his big white fluffy chef's hat. He pulled it from his head and began to knead it desperately as he cried and cursed in Spanish. He thrashed around as Preddie laid himself across his chest. Eloisa wet a large dishrag and talked to him soothingly as she put it on his forehead.

"No te preocupes, m'ijo, you're all right. Just relax, Lavelito, mi niño, no problems. Just close your eyes and relax. Eloisa's not going to let no one or nothing hurt you. Preddie, take over the cooking. I know you can cook. Pato, let him go now, he's better. There, that's it. Now get to work, the rest of you. Pato, you and La Sandra do dishes when you can. Soveida, call his mamá, and you, Pancha Portales, put your eyes back inside your head. All of you, get back to work! Everything is okay. No one call the policía. Mrs. L., I don't mean to be hard, but you get back to work, too, he don't need no police now. Ya, ya, Lavelito, no problem."

This went on for twenty minutes. Larry returned to find Eloisa cradling Lavel just as LaVeeta Windle came in. LaVeeta was wearing a dark green jumpsuit, her cleaning outfit. She'd just come in from cleaning the First United Bank, a ten-story building everyone in Agua Oscura referred to as Higginbottom's Last Erection, Earl Higginbottom being the elderly president of the bank.

Mrs. Windle stood in shock, until Eloisa calmed her down with a look. "He's okay, Señora Windle. Just not feeling good."

"He's had a cold, Mrs. Ortiz. I told him not to come to work. He's been sick for months, but the medicine just doesn't seem to work."

"Señora, he's not that kind of sick. He's sad sick. He needs help. He's mota and drug sick."

"Lavel? Lavel? My baby?"

"Sit down, señora. Preddie, fix me a plate for La Señora Windle. Sit down, you and I are going to talk, okay? No, don't worry, he's all right now. Your m'jito is okay."

I remembered how Eloisa took control that night. How an Off Night became an On Night. How, once again, I was shown that beyond the work was the value of the person working. Lavel mattered to Eloisa. He was a soul and spirit in need, and nothing—no food orders, no demands—were more important than Lavel at that moment. In the course of the evening, Mrs. Windle summoned enough strength to help Lavel, who began to take stock of his life, and Preddie was moved up to assistant chef.

I loved my work, the people I worked for, my regulars, Bud Erwin, Whitey Moldon, Monkey Morales, the Cominglys, even Sky Hawk, who had told me, like Whitey, that I was beautiful and too good for all of them.

It was at El Farol that Veryl and I had our wedding reception, a gift from Larry, who told me the marriage would never work but that he loved me anyway.

The party was beautiful. Veryl was grateful to Larry, but shy around so many of the others. I had a local band, Johnny and the Huipiles, and the dancing went on until 2 a.m. Eloisa cooked roast beef and several turkeys. Everyone helped. Pancha brought her famous cream cheese and pineapple Jell-O salad, Petra her calabacita with corn, and Fermín his macaroni salad with ham.

Fermín led the marcha with Pancha. The traditional wedding dance wound around the patio, the two lines, male and female, looping in and out, now crossing, now making a bridge. Veryl and I were united at the end, having snaked around the dancers, both young and old. I wore a white suit, and everyone pinned dollar bills on my jacket, that marvelous custom. It was a memorable party, in the middle of summer, a star-filled night on the patio. Veryl looked very handsome in a suit. Tall, unblemished as men can be, with perfect teeth, a handsome face, a masculine body. Pancha teased me about him in the women's room.

"Cuerito, cuerito, with hips slim and full of hope . . ."

I stood in the doorway of the Turquoise Room watching Veryl dance a cumbia with Eloisa, who had him in a vise-like grip against her bosom and wouldn't let him go. He didn't know what to do, or what he was doing, but leave it to Eloisa, she was teaching him the intricacies of the rhythm: "Ta ta ta ta tatata rum ta ta ta . . . ta ta ta ta ta tatarum ta ta ta . . ."

I decided I'd go back to work the next day. I'd call Larry later and tell him I'd be back in the morning.

Try as I might to leave it, El Farol was home to me. I could no more get away from it than I could my own face.

41

Oralia's Story

AN ORAL HISTORY OF
THE ELDERLY CHICANO COMMUNITY
by Soveida Dosamantes
Chicano Studies 210 J. V. Velásquez, Ph.D.

The following interview was recorded in April 1988. The subject was Oralia Milcantos, an elderly domestic in my grandmother Lupe Dosamantes's service.

Unmarried, childless, most of her life employed first by my great-grandfather Manuel Dosamantes and then later by my grandfather Profetario Dosamantes, Oralia Milcantos represents the voice of a woman for whom the ideals of loyalty, steadfastness, and unconditional commitment are not governed by personal gain.

This way of life, assuredly, is a dying one. The fact that Miss Milcantos, of Indian and Mexican heritage, was born in the territory of New Mexico is of further interest. She is able, as a result of her heritage, to unite her worlds: a Native-American belief in animism, nature, and its attendant earth rituals—the spiritual interconnection of all life—with the world of Catholicism and its tenets of self-sacrifice, unselfishness, long-endured suffering.

Living as she does in the modern world, she still has a window on the ancestral one. She is a bridge between cultures, languages, and beliefs. She is a representative of that bygone ideal of service, a thing of the past, only now and then remembered in this highly individualistic society.

To me, Oralia Milcantos was oftentimes more family than family. More than a servant, more than a maid, more committed than a housekeeper, she was a laundress, a scrubwoman, a cook, a nurse, a dish-washer, a nanny, but never a slave.

Reticent in speaking about herself, she has often said to me many times, "My life is nothing."

This interview is a composite of several "cornerings" that took place between Miss Milcantos and myself, usually late at night, when she was tired after a long day's work. She would stop briefly, to rest, to talk to me as I recorded her, and to humor me, as she said, because it made me so happy. I was able, as an interviewer and a friend, to draw her out to speak about herself. Using a tape recorder, I tried to convince her that her life mattered and that her story needed to be told.

"It is all interconnected," she said. "Todo esto es trabajito de la vida. Everything we do, no matter how small, is part of the work of living. A ver si no me he olvidado de todo, con esta bola de los años. Let's hope I can remember things, with this confusion of the years."

Q: Where were you born?

A: In the pueblo. My father was Indian. My mother was a Mexican. It wasn't uncommon, this mestizaje, this mixture of peoples.

Q: What year was that?

A: 1900. Long before you were born, Soveida. Before your mother was a thought.

Q: How did your parents' marriage come about?

A: The usual way. [Laughter] No, no, my mother, Angélica, was born in Aguas Calientes, México. It's surprising she should have ended up in New Mexico. It was a territory then. She was hired as a servant at the age of fifteen; she moved north to Dilia, New Mexico, to work for an Anglo family there. The father was a Baptist preacher, el Reverendo LaWitt. Su esposa era muy delicada—she had tuberculosis—and there were two little blond girls. Later, they moved to Cuyamungué. The woman was dying already. My father became a laborer for the Reverendo. My parents fell in love. Both of them were young. He and my mother ran away to Nambé pueblo to live, and when the Reverendo came after her to take her back to Cuyamungué, the pueblo wouldn't let him. She was with child. There were hostilities as a result. The little blond girls were without their playmate, and the Señora eventually died. Mamá learned the way of the Indians, how to cook, how to prepare herbs. She learned how to speak the language and revere the sacredness of the culture. She lived there until my father was killed. It was a horrible thing. They found him with a bullet in his head. Ramón was his Christian name. Mamá was only in her twenties, imagine! Poor thing, so young to be a widow with a small child.

Q: You were born in the pueblo?

A: Yes, but I grew up in Agua Oscura. After my father was killed, my mamá left Nambé. She tried to return to México, but this was as far as she got. She went to work for Manuel Dosamantes.

Q: My great-grandfather?

A: He was a good man. And his wife, Elena, she was a saint.

Q: What about your early life?

A: There was no school for me, not at first. Little by little, la Señora Elena taught me to read, then she sent me to the school with the nuns: Loretto Academy. I was in school until age thirteen. My mother was the housekeeper. Since then, I've lived with the Dosamantes family. But my life is nothing. Why don't you talk to your grandmother Mamá Lupita. Her life is something. She's a saint, like Elena was.

Q: What is your relationship to Lupita Dosamantes?

A: Although I am older, she is like a mother to me, a spiritual mother. She is also like a sister, although we never speak of it. But more than all this, she is la Señora Doña, la dueña de la casa, my mistress.

Q: That sounds so submissive.

A: I don't want to offend you, Miss Soveida, but I am a servant. Your mother's silent sister. I work for her. My destiny was this family, and Mamá Lupita.

Q: You never married?

A: No.

Q: Didn't you ever love anyone?

A: Por Dios, Soveida! Well, yes, I did. Once, but he was in love with someone else.

Q: What became of the man?

A: No matter. It's late now.

The following part of the interview was gathered some nights later, when Miss Milcantos was in the kitchen, preparing food. She was not inclined to continue with the interview, but I pressed her.

Q: Do you like work?

A: This? This isn't work.

Q: What is your work?

A: The only work in life is watching people die and then dying yourself. It is an unavoidable ordeal that at a certain point transforms into the most immeasurably and exquisitely beautiful sacrament. I have seen death many times.

Q: You've made me cry.

A: I used to cry much as well. My heart was very soft. When my mother died, I was still a young woman. I cried until my eyes closed shut. When I opened my eyes, there was no place to go. So I stayed here. It was decided for me.

Q: Who decided? Couldn't you have gone to your father's or mother's family?

A: No, it didn't seem right.

Q: You became a servant to the Dosamantes family. Do you regret that life of work?

A: You keep asking me about the work. Now ask me about the laughter, the tears, the joy. Ask me about when your great-grandparents died, four years apart, or when you came into the world, in the room at the back of the house, or when Hector was born, or when the roof collapsed, or when the chickens got in the washer.

Q: What jobs have you done?

A: [Laughing heartily] Is this little box getting all of this? It's too small to keep account of so many words!

Q: Didn't you ever want to have your own home?

A: I have a little room behind the stairs.

Q: What was being a woman like in the early days?

A: We ate better, life was simpler, we weren't confused. We laughed more. Cried more. People could cry and not be ashamed. When Teo-delfiño died and was laid out in the sala, everyone took turns crying with your great-grandfather Manuel. He was a man who was not afraid to show emotion. Men were not afraid to feel deeply. We cried a lot then and then we went on with our lives. We were at peace, because then death was acceptable, not something hidden, like it is now. Today people are afraid to live and afraid to die. Which fear is worse?

Q: What else is different?

A: Families. The father and mother were respected. Families sat down to eat as one. Today everyone eats at different times in front of the television, watching news about war or silly things that don't matter and that only confuse people. Nobody prays or gives thanks for life. Or has a garden.

Q: How long have you had a garden, Oralia?

A: Since I was ten years old, and my mother gave me seed. That first year I grew chile and beans. Those seeds led to my garden now. Now I don't have as many plants, but I have herbs.

Q: Do you believe in the power of herbs?

A: Who cured your stomachaches when you were young, and your mamá's sick eyes? It was an infection that medicine from bottles couldn't cure. I made a wash with yerbabuena. That was what the eye needed. Power from the earth, and prayer. The herbs gave your grandfather that last rest before the end. They gave him the strength to die, for all of us need strength, especially then. How could I not believe in herbs?

Q: What is your philosophy of life?

A: Philosophy?

Q: What do you believe in?

A: So many things.

Q: What?

A: Will this little machine remember all this?

Q: Yes, don't be afraid.

A: It's not that.

Q: What is it?

A: Hand me the potatoes. Now the salt. Your grandmother likes my potatoes. She says I'm the only one who really knows how she likes to eat. It's probably true.

Q: Is that lard?

A: I drain it good, and give most of it to the chickens.

Q: It's all right, then?

A: I never eat this. This is what your grandmother eats. That and meat. She has to have her meat. It's not good, I tell her, but she won't listen. She grew up eating meat to become a man. She had to, someone had to keep things together. I never eat meat or chicken or fish. If I did, I'd begin to stomp my hooves or crow or fly or begin to sway when I got close to water.

Q: What is your diet?

A: Rice and vegetables. Corn and beans. Herbs. Simple things. Manzanilla.

Q: Is that why you seem so young? Is it your diet?

A: [Laughter] Oh no, I'm an old woman.

Q: You look wonderful!

A: Oh no.

Q: What advice would you give to people about how to live a long life?

A: That's a question only you would ask, Soveida.

Q: It is?

A: To live long is not necessarily a blessing for everyone. For me, it has been. I remember the day you were born. Your First Communion. I saw you get married.

Q: And divorced. You saw that, too.

A: Change and growth are no disgrace. To live long means nothing unless you are open and filled with love.

Q: What's your dream for the world?

A: Ay, Diosito! All right, little box. Listen to me good, then. My dream is for everyone to know what it is to belong, to be committed to something, someone, to know they are brother and sister and father and mother to everyone. Now turn that thing off. Call your grandmother, her potatoes are ready. I'll do the dishes, and you, you sit there and watch me. The little box is tired with so many words, so many thoughts. Let it rest. It's late.

Content: B

Presentation: C −

Grade: B −

J. V. Velásquez had written another of his red-ink comments.

Soveida:

While the subject is a resource of valuable material (historical perspective of Indio/Hispanic culture, territorial information), your focus is on purely emotional, non-analytical details of a life spent in small gestures. Where is the grand sweep? You've gotten involved, once again, with the subject and lost all objectivity. Try not to be so sentimental. Your honest emotionalism, albeit well-meaning, gets in the way of your keen observer's eye.

J. V. Velásquez, Ph.D.

THE BOOK OF SERVICE

CHAPTER EIGHT

The Tip Checklist (or How to Get a Good Tip)

A waitress should greet her customers warmly, in a polite, patient manner. If she doesn't, she's not interested in the way she should be.

Every customer should be handed a clean menu in a pleasant—not perfunctory or "here, take this—" manner. Customers like to be touched, whether they know it or not. Studies show that customers like some sort of physical contact with their server.

Don't give food advice. Stay away from statements like "Try the chimichangas," or "Avoid the beef tacos." Few people really care what a waitress thinks. What matters is how we look and act.

Learn how to pronounce the food items correctly. The word is jalapeño, not jalapeenie. Imagine calling spermatozoa spermazooie.

Many a waitress has lost tips due to the following: insufficient napkins, lost drink orders, confusion about separate checks, and missing condiments. Serving a good meal is like making love. You, too, would want the mood music and the lowered lights. Not to mention the professional, skilled foreplay.

When you think of serving food this way, you will come to learn when to "buzz" the table, and when to stay away. It's all in the timing.

Write a personal thank you on the bill. Always return the change yourself. Place change directly in the customer's hand. Don't lay it down in front of them, or to the side. Remember the element of human contact.

A waitress must establish her physical presence, never overbearing, but haunting as the most exquisite perfume. No one can refuse you a tip then.

42

Mothers, Teach Your Sons

TERM PAPER.
*Submitted to J. V. Velásquez. Ph.D.
Sociology 210, Section 14
by Soveida Dosamantes*

What homeland have our men? Born to women divided between worlds, México to the south, the United States to the north, our men were born in bondage. Robbed of their legacy by conquest, it is no wonder that on this Anniversary of Columbus's encounter with the New World we commemorate the dark history of our men and women's service.

We continue to be a generation that has never known the freedom of its ancestors. Our men have been disenfranchised since birth. They were conceived in anger and frustration and born to mothers who knew no real home, no real peace. Their fathers were the lowest of laborers; they were not men. They were animals who were expected to toil in the fields of others. They were disposable servants who only begat more broken children to perpetuate a cycle of pain and inequality and unmitigated loss.

This developed country we call the United States, this New World, founded in hopeful gain and based on material success, this battle zone of those who have and have not, this cultural mélange of people, was always out of reach for most of my family. We were the servants. We were the workers. We were never the landowners or the landlords. We were the ones who labored in the fields and in the houses. We were the ones who built whatever stands as testimony to the American Dream. Our scars prove it. We were the ones who, with our own hands and backs and souls, made this country what it is. Braceros, we were called, wetbacks, pachucos, chukes, cholos, spics, greasers, indios, and browners.

Our fathers were punished for speaking Spanish in the school yard. They were chastised for being behind in their lessons in a language that was not their own, a language that did not sound of home, shared life. Our fathers and mothers brought to those schools a meal unfamiliar to others: tortillas and beans, no sandwiches of white bread eaten in the sunlight, but dark food, tasting of earth, hard work, and clay pots, boiled over wood stoves in that one big room where many children scampered and then later slept four or more to a bed.

Our men once had a voice, and they could speak. But how long ago was that? They did not raise their charged, heavy voices to complain or belittle or reprimand anyone. Our men, now downtrodden and overburdened, and unhappy with the way things are, beat and abuse the women around them, women they feel mirror their own terror, rage, and grief.

Our men could once speak. But not with the angry words that have now become slurred and thick with saliva. Not with the mindless cries buried so deeply inside their bodies that no one can hear them.

The voices of our men are those of tragic characters in a play, unable to change their lines.

Our men once had words, words full of mercy and love, not words loosened by alcohol, or slowed by drugs, or masked by insecurity. Nor were they seemingly brave words bolstered by bravado coming from empty hearts. They were not the rancheras and corridos full of longing pierced by hopelessness and sorrow: that common despair of men lost to themselves, not knowing who they are or someday might become.

The broken voice of our men is our beginning to understand.

Macho men, from where have you come? From the sierras and mesas of our homeland, México. Let us know that this world of borders is ours, that it flows in our blood, that it is the place of our ancestors' birth, and that we are a mestizaje or mezcla, a mixture of culture and race. We are the mexicano, the Indio, the Spaniard, the Anglo, the European, the Asian, the black. We have been so combined. Who would ever know where or when our dreams leapt to life? What does it matter? Aren't we all still hungry with wanting to know the span of our breath?

In the past, our men had power, and their women couldn't speak.

When they did, it was with the Malinche voice, called the voice of the betrayer. That's where it all began. What do we know of Malinche, anyway? That she was the translator for Cortés, that she became his mistress, the mother of his children, and, in turn, the betrayer of a race, a culture. That is what men say. Malinche is Eve again, or any number of other so-called evil ones. Why must the snake have convinced the woman of eternal life? Is it because men would have us believe that the Father God created Adam and that He took Eve from that man's ribs? The first woman, we are told, came from a man. And why didn't he, instead, come out of her vagina, a small speck of holy, living juice, originating in the sex of the Mother God?

Who wrote the words that would betray all women? Men. And who allowed that betrayal? Women. Who perpetuated that betrayal? Mothers. Well-meaning, surely, who have taught their sons. Sons who bring war and death and imprisonment to the human heart. Why are the women silent? Why do they continue to fail to teach their sons?

In India, the bride burnings and torture continue for women who do not measure up or comply or please. Girls in México have no childhood, says a friend. Women in Honduras eat the leftovers in the kitchen, standing. Patriarchy, another woman says, is just one more privilege that oppresses.

Isn't it time for women to break those chains of oppression? Isn't it time for that endless cycle of self-hatred to cease?

We teach our children to be strong, we teach them self-sufficiency, we teach them independence by oppressing others, disregarding human life, by promoting waste and corruption and making sure that love includes deception and delusion.

My ex-husband was angry because one day he had to help me clean the house, saying later that he hadn't done anything that day, all he did was clean. Where, then, is the validity of women's work? Daily, uneventful, monotonous, universal work? How heavy is the burden of women who "only clean," who do it all, the picking up, the lifting, the folding, the sorting, the bending, the laying out, the cleaning, the cooking, the wiping, the child rearing, the caring for the old.

Who is the macho man but our father, our brother, our husband, our cousin, our friend? They've lost their dignity. To feel powerful, they must oppress others.

My great-grandfather Manuel Dosamantes was born in México. He felt impotent in his native land, already a land of the oppressed. He came to the United States. He became a foreman, an overseer of men, and though he loved and revered his wife, Elena, she did not have a voice. Not the way I know my voice to be.

My grandmother Mamá Lupita spoke up, but she deferred to her husband, Profetario. When she was younger she went to school with the Holy Sisters, as she called them; her father was a special man and he saw the need for education, up to a point. He thought that if she learned to sew and cook she would make a good wife. My mother, too, had no voice. Her grandmother and mother and father had all robbed her of her voice. She was a woman, not a man. Male children are treated differently. Anyone can see this. I recall seeing how my mother, Dolores, deferred to my younger brother, Hector. My father, too, treated my brother as someone special, not as a mature adult but as a magical child. My mother also allowed him his excesses (a manly thing), his tantrums (expected), his free time (we were there to pick up for him), and his own way (he's the one to carry our name).

Always women have felt that their voices didn't count, or, at least, in the way that a man's voice counted. We have been sterile despite the fecundity of our wombs. The children we bring into this world are monsters who create more monsters who would oppress and destroy and defile the generations of children they will never see.

I grew up, then, a woman in a long line of battered women.

Abuse was rampant, and it was mental, emotional, physical, spiritual, and sexual. What does it mean to live under the sexual yoke, the harness of the sexual myth, a sentence not laid down by strangers but by one's own family members? Male and female.

This yoke was fashioned by the fathers, refined by the sons, continued by their brothers, and carried into other generations by the uncles, cousins, brothers-in-law, handed down from person to person, through the ages, family to family, women partaking in the cycle, by looking the other way, in their obvious deferment to the male, assuming responsibility for both father and son, and in the seemingly loving act of "mothering."

Abuse was not uncommon among people I knew. My father's goal in life was to keep a scorecard of all the women he'd slept with. My brother's goal in life was to become the best lover of the most women. Oppressor of the oppressed. That is the Macho Man. I know him well. He is my father. My brother. My cousin. But he will not be my son.

Today what we see in the Latino families are these broken men: children of only more broken men. The women, their hands in the dishwater, call out: "M'ijo, my son, come and eat, your supper's getting cold. I ironed your shirts the way you like them. Are you going out again? Don't come home late! Be careful. Have you applied for that job yet? You got up so late! What time did you get in? I waited for you last night. What can I get you, m'ijo?"

It is women who have sadly helped to propel the myth forward, into each age, victims of their own supposed mercy. Conquered men need to conquer. Conquered women know no other way.

Our fathers, our brothers, the men in our families—we carry the burden of their remarks, their whispers, their looks. The cycle has not been broken, not yet, not even in my own lifetime.

We are maimed creatures, struggling for wholeness.

Despite this, we are survivors. We have had to be. Now, on the eve of woman's great awakening, we turn to each other and to those who would take our hands, and hold them. For too long we have been fearful, desperate creatures in the darkness, unable to see the cause of our blindness.

Soveida Dosamantes

APPENDIX A
MOTHERS, TEACH YOUR SONS
(from the Families of Survivors of Abuse handbook)

To do dishes, not only throw out the garbage.

To revere all women, not only those close to them.

To cook, do laundry, to clean up not only after themselves, but others.

To pay attention to the details of living, to do the best they can at whatever they do.

To trust women and their ability to communicate, not to laugh at emotion or any heartfelt feelings.

To talk out their grievances, not letting feelings build up until they explode.

To see women's injustices toward other women, and men's injustices toward other men, to see that this cycle stops and is not passed on through the generations.

To love and nurture children, plants, animals, all life, to see in them all existence.

To praise small comforts, delicate, fragile encounters between people that mirror truth.

To have pride in a home, a yard, a car, possessions, to keep them tended and in order.

To be considerate at all levels, with all people, sexually, emotionally, physically, spiritually.

To never take anything for granted.

To be honest, never to lie, not only to themselves but to others.

To be gentle and loving in all actions, a calm demeanor underlying strength.

To admit error and correct it.

To learn not to complain when change is not effected quickly enough.

To hold no grudges, to admit failure, to forgive.

To allow women their space and solitude to be themselves without crowding or feeling frightened or antagonistic.

To love unequivocally, and without restraint.

P. S. Dear Dr. Velásquez: I have begun working with an organization called F.O.S.A. (Family of Survivors of Abuse—Sexual, Emotional, Physical). We meet the first Monday of each month at the library at 7:30 p.m. Perhaps your other classes would be interested in attending these meetings. Would you mind letting them know? Unfortunately, many Latinos are unaware or unwilling to admit the abuse that goes on in their own families.

Sincerely, S.D.

At the next class, my paper was returned to me, with J. V. Velásquez's comments in red ink.

Dear Ms. Dosamantes:

You have an impassioned flair for words. You argue with great emotion and sensitivity, and yes, you have a feel for your topic. The idea is interesting, but it does not fully succeed. The ideas that you postulate for the continuing cycle of machismo seem old and hackneyed. Step into the present! Not all men are as you present them in this feminist diatribe. Heated feelings alone do not make your case. Your thesis is never clearly identified, you jump from idea to idea, and the whole lacks cohesion. Check your grammar, syntax, and use of the possessive. They are all awful. On top of this, you have no footnotes. This is a college class. Have you written other term papers? I suggest you study the Harbrace Handbook. *I would be happy to help you formulate an outline for your next paper. Your writing is impressive, but your scholarship leaves much to be desired.*

Content: C
Presentation: C –

J. V. Velásquez, Ph.D.

43

J.V. and the Metal Pin

Returning to school at night was difficult. Hector made fun of me. Larry felt sorry for me.

I was tired of work—the work of remembering. Before you knew it, your whole life had gone by and you were still thinking about the first person you ever really loved. Things could have gone better, everything could have been easier if it had not been for J. V. Velásquez, Ph.D. Try as I had, I couldn't get a grade above a B. I just couldn't figure out what the hell he wanted from me.

Velásquez got his undergraduate degree at Stanford University. That accounted for his Chicano aloofness. He had spent a full year studying in England and that explained his disdain for anything common. He had returned to the U.S. and received his master's degree and his doctorate from someplace Ivy League at one of the best sociology departments in the country. That explained his brilliant mind and his intellectual prowess, and his inability to understand the real world of Agua Oscura, New Mexico. To look at him—tall, thin, with a hand-some, intense face—was to be startled into understanding that culture has nothing to do with education.

J. V. Velásquez was an educated man; he had graduated magna cum laude. As Oralia often said, "For all his schooling, a monkey still has hair." Which in this case meant that Dr. J. V. Velásquez was not unlike a well-groomed, well-trained monkey. He had learned many tricks from his masters. He performed them exceedingly well, but under-neath his pressed suit, slicked-down hair, and neatly groomed mus-tache there lurked a chained, unhappy, and hungry man. Instead of ever causing any upset, J. V. Velásquez danced and danced as well as the tight space allowed. His fondest dream, if he could have ever articulated it, was to be set free. As Oralia also said, "Cada chango en su mecate, y yo con mi mecatito." Which means, "Each monkey on its little string, and I on mine." J. V. Velásquez had his as well.

He was not a popular professor. His students referred to him as "well-read, articulate, a hard grader," which meant that he was inflexible, picky, and overzealous. Spontaneity was not one of his traits. He disliked emotionalism, that much was clear. He abhorred sloppiness, which to him came in the guise of enthusiasm, candidness, and excitement for one's subject. "Rather that you research well than review human emotion. Rather that you know, not just feel."

His nickname, M.P. for Metal Pin, came about one evening after an especially dry and possibly brilliant discourse on deracination. I had whispered to Humberto Penego, another Chicano studies plebe, that if it weren't for the large metal pin up Dr. Velásquez's ass, he probably wouldn't be able to stand up as straight as he did. Humberto loved this remark and immediately adopted it. Henceforth, the handsome but bloodless Dr. V. became known as M.P. or Pin.

The greatest mission of J. V. Velásquez's life was to rise above the poverty-ridden, intellectual, and cultural void of his childhood and his family. He longed to be independent from his culture's expectations of him.

When he was nine years old, J.V., as he was called, promised himself that he would leave Agua Oscura and never return. He would make something of his life. His father, Manuel Mejía Velásquez, son of la Jorobada María Mejía, had failure written all over his furrowed face. He seemed placid enough, and his life with his wife, Clarita, was calm, but there was never any real happiness to spare. Manuel's two sons, J.V. and Tirzio, grew up without any sort of model by which to guide and illuminate their lives. As far as they both knew, life was meant only to be tolerated, not enjoyed. Clarita brought some stability and energy to their world, but she was a woman who was always sheltered in her husband's deep, dark shade.

For Manuel Mejía Velásquez, illegitimate son of Profetario Dosamantes and María Mejía, life was a litany of sorrow. He hadn't ever wished to be born into this world. If he had, he surely would never have chosen María Mejía and Profetario Dosamantes as his parents. That is why, when he was old enough, he had his name legally changed to Velásquez. Everyone in Agua Oscura knew the story of how Profe seduced his servant girl María and how he got her pregnant.

When J.V. was twelve years old, he found out his father was a bastard. It was a hard thing to learn in such an ugly way. Manuel had begun to drink and was now coming home drunk each day after work. This particular Friday night, Manuel had left work early and had gone to the Mil Recuerdos Lounge. He left around 10 p.m., quite inebriated, and drove out to St. Anselm's, the Anglo and better Mexicans' cemetery, where his father Profetario "Profe" Dosamantes was interred. The cemetery was to the west of town, and faced the Lagrimas Mountains, a vast range over six thousand feet high that encircled Agua Oscura like a crown of stone.

When Manuel finally returned from the cemetery, he banged on the door until Clarita let him in. An argument ensued and Manuel hit Clarita. When his older son, Tirzio, tried to intervene, Manuel hit him as well. J.V. huddled in the corner, watching helplessly. Manuel screamed that he was a bastard and that so were they. He then fell down to the floor, crying. J.V. ran to his room and locked himself in. Clarita's small, deep-set eyes widened and her pale face grew even paler while her upper lip showed tiny beads of sweat. She began to breathe deeply and sighed as if her heart would break. She tried to lift Manuel up from the floor, but she wasn't strong enough. He lay that way there all night. Clarita covered him with a blanket. Tirzio believed that was when the lung disease grabbed ahold of his mother, as she sat helplessly near Manuel that terrible night. Catching a bad cold, she was never the same. She wanted to die, Tirzio used to say, because she didn't want to live in shame anymore.

Everyone knew that famous story, except me.

When I took the Chicano Culture and Tradition and Folklore class with Dr. J. V. Velásquez, I had no idea that this Dr. Velásquez was the son of the ill-fated Manuel Mejía Velásquez. It wasn't until the next semester, after I had begun to date J.V. and had become as deeply involved as one could become with him, that the story of our interconnected destinies unraveled.

J.V. admitted to me that he had been attracted to me the first time he saw me in class. That was the night he had presented me with the Chicano Culture quiz. He told me I looked up at him, smiled, and then laughed at him with just enough mockery and disdain to bother him for a long time to come. He wanted to ask me why I'd looked at him that way. He wanted to get close, but somehow he couldn't. In fact, it wasn't until the next semester that he finally called me up to ask me out to dinner. He told me he wasn't the sort of person who dated his students, irregardless of circumstances. Instead of going to dinner, we ended up at El Gonie's party in honor of Hector's impending marriage to Ada.

That was the beginning of J.V.'s roller-coaster ride with the Dosamantes family, or one Dosamantes in particular.

The party was held at El Gonie's house in a low-rent subdivision called Calabazas Estates. At one time the area was used for the cultivation of an inordinate amount of squash, hence its name. Lots of beer, tamales, and tacos, the usual amount of back slapping and crude jokes in Spanish about virgins and virginity, or male sex organs and their ability to perform.

In the medium-sized living room sat all the older folks, including Mamá Lupita, who clearly disapproved of the host, Gonacio, and his *Playboy* pinup bathroom wallpaper. She believed that he was the one responsible for her grandson Hector's corruption, the one solely culpable for the child that Ada now carried in her womb.

The men all stood in the back yard by the keg of beer, drinking and laughing loudly. J.V. had worn a suit and was distressed to see the others in shorts. As it turned out, he spent half the evening talking to Mamá Lupita, who was convinced that he had once been a priest. During the party Mamá looked up at J.V. fondly and clucked to herself while she stroked her little beard. He didn't know she had plans for him.

"Dr. Velásquez, if my granddaughter Soveida hadn't married twice and wasn't now a widow, she could have become a nun. But why am I telling you, you who have known the Holy Orders."

"Señora Dosamantes, I haven't—"

"I understand. Priesthood isn't for everyone. A good-looking man like you, tall, with long legs. My husband could never have been a priest. I found that out on our wedding night. You're different. Ay, en el nombre del Padre, del Hijo. Shame on me, an old woman, for my thoughts! Have you ever been married? To a woman, I mean?"

"I'm a professor of Chicano studies at the Community College, Señora Dosamantes. And I'm single."

"Bendito sea Dios. Since my granddaughter Soveida has given up all ideas of the nunhood, it would do her good to meet someone nice. Now, if you'll excuse me. Save my spot here on the couch, next to you, would you? I have to go. To—you know. Have you seen it? Con esas cochinas encueradas with their pezones pointing in all directions. No, padrecito, better that you don't see it. You just stay right here. I'll be right back."

"I'll be here, Señora Dosamantes. Watching people dance."

"Soveida will be back soon, padre. She's helping in the kitchen. Pobrecito, you're very nice to talk to an old lady like me about México. No one around here has been to México and here they are all mexicanos. Look, there's Soveida."

"Where?"

"She's dancing over there. Ooh! The way they spin around the room makes me dizzy."

"Señora Dosamantes, are you all right?"

"I'm all right. I just got up too fast."

"They dance well together."

"They should. She taught him how to dance."

"She did?"

"That's Hector."

"Oh. I thought— I haven't met him yet."

"If you get a chance to talk to him alone, padre, it might be good. He needs to go to confession."

"Soveida's a terrific dancer!"

"She's leading him, no, now he's leading her. Ay, el arrimado, El Gonacio, he's trying to cut in. Cochino, he's already drunk and it's not even eight o'clock. Here she comes!"

J.V. and I danced around the swirling room. Mamá Lupita paused in the doorway, assessing us. Out of the corner of my eye I saw her wink to me as J.V. twirled and tumbled deeper into the darkness of his thoughts. Later I sat down with J.V. on El Gonie's old couch as J.V. adjusted the softened slipcover that had partially fallen to the floor. Slowly, tentatively, but with gentleness, he put his arm around my shoulder.

Later, when J.V. took me home, I asked him in, but he declined. He did take me into his arms and kissed me softly. We fit perfectly together. It felt so wonderful to be held that way. To be appreciated and desired, without pressure. All the pretense had dropped away. He was no longer J. V. Velásquez, Ph.D., M.P. I was no longer Miss B— Dosamantes or Miss Soveida Dosamantes Torres Beron Dosamantes. We were just a man and a woman. Two people holding each other without talking. Suddenly J.V. mumbled a goodbye and left.

Damn it, I thought, it's that metal pin again.

Thrones

44

Paralyzed People

Dolly and I sat in the intensive-care waiting room of Los Fuentes Medical Center. Luardo had had a stroke, though Dr. Wenchy said he was going to make it. His left side was paralyzed.

"You should have seen Luardo this afternoon, Soveida. He looked terrible. You know, the first paralyzed person I knew was my Tía Adelaida Santos, my mother's cousin."

Dolly settled into the dark green Naugahyde couch. The waiting room's television turned to a black-and-white movie in Spanish, XEPM, from Mexico City. The sun was setting and the blinds were turned down, but shadows filled the room. There were only four of us there at that time, Dolly and I, and two older women, one of them in a battered-looking sweat suit and dirty white running shoes. The other was younger, and wore a uniform of some kind, with a dark brown sweater and sturdy work shoes. They were dozing, and looked as if they'd been waiting in the room for many hours.

"Their mom," Dolly whispered. "Cancer of the liver." Dolly looked calm, but I knew she was genuinely concerned. Her usually perfect makeup was tear-stained and her hair was disheveled, and when that happened, she tended to talk non-stop. I was tired, and knew we would be waiting for some time. Exactly for what, I wasn't sure. And yet we were consoled by each other's presence.

"I *thought* that was him. Soveida, it's Pedro Infante! He's wearing Coke-bottle glasses, but it's him. I haven't seen this one, Soveida. Turn up the sound!"

Pedro, called Braulio Pellais in the movie, was a small-town school-teacher who goes to Mexico City to become a movie star. His name is changed to Alfredo Malvarosa, and after a series of misadventures, he falls in love with a movie star and wins the lottery.

As we watched the movie with Pedro Infante unfold before us, Dolly told me the story of Tía Adelaida.

"Mi Tía Adelaida wasn't always paralyzed, you know. Once she was over six feet tall, a big, large-boned woman. Her father, Nicasio, always said Adelaida was as strong as any of her brothers. At the time, you might have said that was a compliment. Today, no woman in her right mind wants to be strong as an ox and twice as dumb, like Nicasio's six boys. Dumb. Dumb. Dumb. Like Don Faustino's pig, Pascualita, who lived next door.

"Adelaida and her younger sister, Bernardita, grew up in a house full of men. That's where she got her strength. And whether you live with one man or eight, you need that strength, as well as endurance, pride, and a sense of humor.

"Adelaida was ten years older than Berna, as they called her, and because she was the older sister and had ovaries of steel, she liked to say, no one ever gave her a hard time. Mrs. Santos, the mother, had died birthing Bernardita. Adelaida became like a mother to everyone, including her father.

"The only one Adelaida pampered was Berna, who the others claimed was the reason for their mother's untimely death. Berna was born premature and was always ill. At age nine she developed polio. She was a thin, very ugly child with limp hair. Everyone but Adelaida thought she was an unbearable brat.

"Adelaida knew that her brothers—Memo, Nabor, Chapo, Chito, Bul, and Juan—were jealous of Berna, and she made up her mind to settle things once and for all. On her father's deathbed, she made him promise and then sign in writing that all his property would go to the two sisters. She told him that the boys, after all, could fend for themselves. Nicasio proceeded to die three days later, leaving Adelaida as executor. There was no money to be had, but the brothers were incensed. Bul was the first to leave, and soon only Chapo stayed on. Once he graduated from high school, he, too, went to seek his fortune elsewhere.

"Oh, Soveida! Look at Pedro. He's so handsome, even with those glasses. No, I never did see this movie.

"Mi Tía Adelaida was a take-charge person. When all the brothers had gone, without so much as offering to help them, she got a job as a housekeeper for Colonel Compton. He was a youthful widower of fifty, with grown children already. Tall and handsome, he had dark brown hair graying at the temples.

"Let me tell you, no one could have ever been better suited to run the Compton household. Adelaida spoke good English, she was a good cook, she was good with numbers, she was smart, she was clean, she was dependable, and she was a hard worker. She could decorate a house for a party, bake for it, and then clean up the mess. What more could Colonel Compton want?

"But things change. They always do. Like with your dad. Even with Pedro Infante. And he was so handsome! Pobrecito Pedro. Que descanse en paz. He was killed in a plane crash with his mistress.

"Mi Tía Adelaida was not a beautiful woman, she was not even good-looking, but in her soft and simple way there was something attractive about her. Yet no one ever bothered to let her know her chin hairs were too dark and long. She didn't seem to care either about them or the mustache that began to grow when she was about twenty-five. By the time she got to Colonel Compton's she was thirty years old, with more facial hair than her younger brother, Chapo. When strangers looked at the family photo album, they always thought that Adelaida was one of Nicasio's sons.

" 'If only it weren't for those chin hairs, those eyebrows, and that mustache, she might have found love,' Tía Bernardita always told me. 'She was my sister, Dolores, and little by little I found her getting quieter and softer every day. Once I found her in the kitchen crying. And then I realized why: she was in love. But with whom? And then it struck me. Of course! She was in love with Colonel Compton!'

"I think it broke my Tía Adelaida's heart, Soveida, to realize that she could never fill el coronel's life with anything more than passing service. She was the old clock ticking in the hallway, the starched lace on the living-room table. She was the one who allowed no dust, no noise, no rudeness to enter the perfect house on the perfect street.

"It was the end of an unbearably hot June when it happened. For weeks Tía Adelaida had been preparing for Colonel Compton's annual summer party, making sure all the silver was polished, that the lace tablecloths were hand-washed and ironed, and that everything was in its proper place. El coronel had told her he had a special announcement to make. Would he be retiring, Adelaida wondered? Was he leaving Agua Oscura forever?

"The day of the party was incredibly hot. The temperature was about 115 degrees in the shade. Although Adelaida had called in several others to help, the bulk of the work was hers. Around two o'clock she fell suddenly ill and stopped to rest outside in the shade of a willow tree. But then she gathered herself up and went into the house to finish cooking. She continued to work until around 5 p.m., then she left the colonel's to go home to shower. She planned to return at six to begin heating the food. She would serve the meal and then return home whenever the party was over. Breathless, slightly dizzy, with perspiration dotting the hair on her upper lip, she got into the shower, her heart pounding as the water beat down on her.

" 'The water hit me like ice and then fire,' she later told me, Soveida. She lost control of her thoughts. Her heart fluttered in her chest, and she collapsed, the cold water hitting her face. The sound of the water slapped her awake. How long had she lain there?

"Tía Bernardita found her in the bathtub, crumpled in a heap, unable to move. 'Can you get up?' Bernardita asked her. 'Are you all right?' There was no answer. Bernardita turned off the water and propped Adelaida up against the side of the bathtub, covering Adelaida's nakedness as best she could. She then ran to the neighbors for help. Three of them lifted Adelaida and laid her on her bed. One called the priest, one the doctor, and the other went personally to tell the colonel that Adelaida would not be coming to his party. That night he announced his marriage to Leniña Fuentes, daughter of the man this hospital is named for.

"Just think of it, the strong became weak and the weak became strong. After that shower Adelaida never walked again. And she never went back to el coronel's. She was paralyzed from the waist down. Well, at least the two sisters had each other. That's something, isn't it? If Bernardita ever wanted to get married, she lost her chance when Adelaida got paralyzed. Now both of them have long chin hairs and smell like dusty clothes in an attic. Promise me, Soveida, that when I am dying and too sick to speak that you'll pluck out my chin hairs for me? I promise to do the same for you. I know I'll go first, sweetheart. Just remember what I said. You know, one of these days I'm going to talk to mi Tía Adelaida woman to woman when Tía Bernardita's not around and ask her if she'd like a shave. Just to try it out. She might like it. Paralyzed? Mi Tía Adelaida? She's not paralyzed. She just can't walk. Paralyzed is your father. Now, there are paralyzed people and there are paralyzed people."

45

I'm Better

In a booth in the basement cafeteria of the Fuentes Medical Center, Dolly ordered the chef's special, a red enchildada plate with a side of beans and rice. I sipped an iced tea. The smell of food nauseated me.

"You don't look so well, Soveida," Dolly said.

"I'm just run down. I think I have a cold."

"Hospitals do that to me, and nursing homes. No matter how I feel, when I come out, I always feel worse. There's germs everywhere. I don't like hospitals. Try and keep me out of one. Just let me die at home. I can't help but think about your grandmother Trancha. It's ten years since she died, but whenever I smell a hospital, it reminds me of the Del Valle Nursing Home."

"It's been ten years already?"

"In October. Remember, she used to sit in her wheelchair behind one of the large, doily-covered armchairs, swaddled in her favorite orange-and-chartreuse lap robe, the one she knit herself. Your grandma hated the Del Valle. And in a way I don't blame her. At first she tried to make conversation with the other residents.

" 'I heard you say your name was Clavel. Are you one of the Clavels from Fairacres?' she'd say. 'Pariente de Florindo Clavel? I knew Florindo and his sister Luz María. My brother used to do some work for Don Florindo. Luz María never married. Her brother did. Luz María stayed on with Rufina and Florindo. They had six children.'

"But one day she found out that the old woman who sat next to her during mealtime being spoon-fed oatmeal and pureed vegetables was none other than her next-door neighbor for forty years, la Señora Zumaida, who was Lina's madrina. The Day of the Recognition was what she called it.

"No, your grandma never liked the Del Valle, and neither did I. I didn't want to send her there, but it was impossible to take care of her at home. She was diabetic, nearly blind, with both legs amputated above the knees. She was more than I could handle. Hector was still little then."

"How long did Grandma Trancha live there?"

"Not too long. She usually sat in the sala, the large living room/reception area. Mrs. Babette Blalock, the director of the home, thought it was more cheerful for the families to gather in there than in the residents' rooms. B.B., the staff called her behind her back. She served tea as well as hot coffee on Sundays. Her cookies were of two types: one for the hard to swallow and one for the patients with good dentures. They were terrible, Soveida. Some mash with a pecan in the middle for the diabetics, the other one with a fork mark in the middle, for patients who had trouble swallowing. I always felt so sorry for esos pobrecitos waiting for their families to come and visit. I can still hear them."

" 'My daughter should be here soon. She's probably still at Mass.'

" 'Nestor can't come today. He's out of town.'

" 'Margaret has to watch the kids and she probably won't make it over today. She doesn't have a babysitter and Facundo went fishing.'

" 'My husband doesn't have anyone to bring him out. Our niece is out of town.' "

"I remember going to see Grandma Trancha," I tell Dolores.

"You do, Soveida?"

"She always asked me who I was. La hija de Luardo, I'd say. And when I asked her how she was, she'd always say, 'I'm better,' no matter how bad she felt."

"She used to complain her stumps were sore, Soveida, because of their thinness. She could always feel bare bone on the chair seat. She lost her right leg in 1973. That was a blow. But somehow she was able to get around the house with a crutch. But when she found out in 1975 that her good leg was gangrenous and that she would lose it, too, she was never the same.

" 'The grave opened up in my own kitchen, Dolores. I'm no good to anyone now. Let me die,' she told me.

"In a way, your grandma Trancha did die then, Soveida. I had to put her in the Del Valle, there was no other way. The other residents made a life for themselves, she never could. She always stayed huddled behind some smelly old chair, staring at the door.

" 'Llévame a mi rinconcito, my corner,' she used to say. She hid behind those old gray armchairs as if she were in a little cave, in the darkest spot of the dimly lit room with drawn curtains. I guess she felt she could sit there and see everything and yet not be seen. There was a comfort in that. From her vantage point, she could be the first to see anyone enter the room and be the last to see them leave. Soon everyone knew that this was her spot, just as they knew that the area to the left of the entryway belonged to Mr. Winston, or the far-right chair, opposite the television set, was reserved for Albinita Cuarteles, and the love seat was property of Mr. and Mrs. Del Fiore.

"On Sundays the viejitos sat there from 10 a.m. to 2 p.m., talking among themselves or staring at the door or the motes of light that swirled lint in their eyes. There was a lunch break at noon. Around 2:10 p.m., the staff would wheel or walk the residents back to their rooms, telling them to pick up their feet and 'stamp the ants. That's it, stamp the ants. You pick your foot up high and put it down hard, like you're stamping an ant.'

"I used to go every Sunday. Sometimes you would go with me, and sometimes Hector. After a while I stopped taking you. The visits weren't pleasant. Every Sunday your grandma gave me her usual sermon.

" 'I didn't think you were coming, Dolores. Why should you come to see your mother? You have things to do. Me, I don't have anything to do. What can I do? My hands are so weak. Look at this, no strength. I keep going like this, opening and closing my fingers in a fist, just to keep the blood moving. I can't even walk to the bathroom. I'd have to drag myself on the floor like a snake. Little by little the coldness is creeping up from the place my legs used to be. If I could walk away from here, I would, but I can't. You've forced me to live here with these old people. Yes, I know some of them are young, but in what state? Drooling baba from their chins and them lapping it up like candy, or strapped by their heads to a wheelchair, with a plastic bag con orín hanging by its side, and oxígeno nearby just in case. And that's just the young people here. The old people—faaa! To know them the way I do is enough to make you stop believing in God. There is no God. No God that would let an old woman already maimed and weak as a baby die like this in a pit of wolves. There's a lesson to be learned in this. Don't call me Mamá, I'm nothing to you. No, I haven't used the sleeping jacket you gave me. I didn't like it, so I threw it away. And, Dolores, don't bring me any more handkerchiefs, please. Is that all you think of when you think of me? Mocos? How am I? What do you care? See esa americana vieja over there? The one with the blond wig? Her husband just died and already some old cochino slips into the old sow's room. I may be half blind with bad eyes, but my hearing is perfect. I can still remember those noises. Let me tell you, it's disgusting what goes on in here. No, I don't need any more Vicks. That? It's just a rash. It's surprising I'm not full of bedsores. You don't know the way they are around here, especially to some of us. I could tell you stories. There's a lesson to be learned. Yes, I'll see you next week. If you come. You have so many things to do. Can we go for a ride? I thought we'd go over to San Pedro Cemetery, the old part, where Eluid is buried—you probably don't have the time. I'm a bother. There's a lesson to be learned in this. If you can't take me to the cemetery, take me to my room. Just put me to bed and then you can go. Yes, yes, yes. Goodbye, goodbye.' "

"I remember Grandma's room, her bookshelf full of unwrapped boxes of handkerchiefs, baskets full of her knitting, spools of orange and bright green yarn, her favorite knitting needles, Dolores. She had the things she loved most in the world on her shelf."

"María and José. The names of her needles. José was a bit longer and María had an imperfection on one side."

"All her photographs."

"One of her parents, another of herself as a young bride, Primitivo at the gold mine, me as a baby, Lina just before she met Miguel Angel Fortuna, Mara age three, and your First Communion, Soveida."

"All the Valentine's Day, Easter, Halloween, Christmas, New Year's, and birthday cards she'd received since she'd moved to the Del Valle."

"Her room was next to the laundry room. She liked the noise. The washers going from a wash to a rinse to a spin. Sometimes she said she could count up to twelve machines going at once. I didn't like her room, it wasn't my first choice. I wanted something near the main building, down the hall from the crafts room, but that was all that was available. It wasn't that it was cheaper, either. I had to pay for extras, including soap and diapers.

"I had your grandma moved to a bigger, brighter room with a window, but she didn't like the sun that came in, or seeing the field outside the window that seemed to stretch into eternity. She asked to be returned to her small, windowless room, where she could hear the washing machines. One time she told me she imagined that she was at home at her old house, Tremolina Street, number 45, and that she was doing the wash.

"Your grandma had a little altar with a ceramic statue of Our Lady of Guadalupe. She said la Guadalupe always looked across to her in such a peaceful way, with such love and compassion, that she decided to let her stay.

" 'La Virgencita hasn't been much help, not with you, Dolores, or Lina, or the boys, most especially with Primitivo, but she's young, she'll learn. She's also of royal blood. If she was old like me, without legs, she'd have to sit down with a blanket over the place her knees should be, with a plastic pad where her thighs should have been. Her sex covered by thick clothing to hide the opening that no one cares to remember but that I have to live with every single day.

" 'Oh, but what does it matter? La Guadalupe's eyes are the last ones I'll ever see and that's that. They're beautiful soft eyes, like Lina's. I remember Lina's eyes and Lina's face and her mouth like an O screaming: Kill me, kill me. Turn off the lights and bring me my rosary. The one that glows in the dark. Primitivo. One decade. Eluid. Another. Rubén. Onesímo. Another wash. Enos. Now a rinse. Cesario. Now a spin. Lina. Number 6 is stuck. Lina. Kill me. Kill me. Kill me. All right, now. Now more footsteps. Now more noise. No more cycles. Each bead in the rosary's chain is a set of eyes. My fingers go over them with love. Closing them. In peace.'

"I hate to think of her all alone in the darkness, Soveida."

"She wasn't alone, Dolores."

"That's right. She had all those people she loved in the room with her. But hospitals are sad places with sad smells. They make me think of your grandma Trancha. In hospitals, the living are nearly dead and the dead live once again. Let's go now, your father is waiting for us."

46

Miguel Angel Fortuna

"Are you there, Soveida? It's me, Mara. I couldn't remember who I'd called. You sound different, are you all right? Hold on, I'm taking the phone to the bathroom. I can't wait, I'm dying. I gotta go. There. So, how's Luardo? You were telling me what the doctor said. Okay, it was a stroke. Well, if you want my opinion, it would have been better if he had died. He should die and get it over with."

"Mara!"

"He's not my father, he never was. He should die and he should go to hell."

"I understand your bitterness, Mara."

"When I think about the shriveled little old man Luardo has become, I wonder how he ever terrified me. All I feel for him now is pity."

"He's sick, Mara, he always has been. I'm sorry he hurt you."

"That sick little old man. I was so afraid of him."

"He's still in intensive care, but he seems better. Mamá wants to take him to her house."

"Ha! She's in her eighties and *she* wants to help *him*! Well, let her if she wants, but *you know* who'll be doing the work. It'll be whatever slave she has around at the time. Una pobrecita, some poor girl, for fifty dollars a week, if she even pays that, the stingy old woman."

"Tere. And she gets room and board."

"Christ! Well, she can always call up your mother if Tere takes off. Dolores is always good for that after he's run off all the young virgins by taking out his seventy-year-old dick and pointing it in their direction, or battered the old hens with his incessant demands. She's good after the hired caretakers, the young girls beholden to her favors, the vagabond, fly-by-night winos, have quit. If all else fails, there's your mother. All Mamá has to do is yell: Dolores, come and take care of your husband."

"Ex-husband."

"Ex, my foot! She still does his frigging laundry! Although I must admit, I never did think she'd have the strength to get a divorce. Will wonders never cease? You think it would have been the other way around."

"How are you, Mara? It's been too long."

"I've been busy. Hold on. Hey, I've always wanted to know, can you hear the flush? I've always wondered."

"You got a long cord?"

"The longest and it's too short. But I can cook, clean, pee and fuck on the phone if I want to or have to, so I guess it's long enough."

"I'll keep you posted about Luardo."

"You do that."

"We don't know what's going to happen. He'll be in the hospital some time, then I guess he'll go to Mamá's."

"Let's hope he doesn't make it there. If not, he'll take your mother, Mamá, Oralia, and the new slave to the grave with him."

"When I talk to you on the phone I can see you."

"It's a good thing you can't. I'm sitting on the pot."

"You're beautiful."

"A fat, middle-aged beauty when it doesn't matter anymore how you look."

"It matters. You get prettier all the time, Mara."

"From the neck up. Big deal."

"How's your diet?"

"Which one?"

"The latest."

"I forget. It doesn't matter. I'm still fat, with no sign of losing weight, unless I cut off a limb."

"Are you feeling okay?"

"Yes and no. I don't want to talk about it, it'll upset my ulcer."

"How's work?"

"Work is work. Hold on a minute—I got a call-waiting. All right."

"Who was it?"

"Ida. She wants me to meet her at the Lancer Club for a drink."

"I thought you gave up drinking."

"For a week, then my ulcer started acting up. I figure I'd rather be calm and in pain than anxious and upset and in pain. It's all how you look at it. Do you know what day today is?"

"August 3."

"The anniversary of my mother's death. Who ever thought being shy would kill someone?"

"What do you mean?"

"You know the story. When my father, Miguel Angel Fortuna, came up from México and was hired by Grandpa Loera to help with the crops, everything seemed to be going well, until he got my mom pregnant."

"He was married, wasn't he?"

"Hell, yes, and here my mom had never been married. Not only that, but she followed him all the way to Harlingen, Texas, and on to Idaho, and then back to Texas. Finally, she came back to Agua Oscura."

"Didn't he come back here when you were born, Mara?"

"He promised to get a divorce. Pendeja, my mom believed him! He did go back home, some little village, Tla Tla something. But he never came back for either of us."

"When did your mother get sick, Mara?"

"After I was born. Her stitches got infected. She never stopped bleeding. She didn't want to go to the doctor. Grandma Trancha said she was that way, avergonsoza, she got embarrassed easily. So my mom bled for years, until it was too late. She got cancer. Her sexual organs were like raw, bloody, rotten meat."

"Is that when they tied her to the bed?"

"They tied her to the bed with old bed sheets and they left her there. She kept begging for morphine, but Trancha and Dolores would only give it to her at the prescribed times. I remember her screams, Soveida."

"I can't believe your mom didn't do something about all the bleeding, Mara. It doesn't seem possible she just let it go."

"That's the way the Loera women are, Soveida. They abuse their own bodies in the guise of shame. It just goes to show you how stupid women are, how eternally, confoundingly stupid. Stupid with love, stupid with grief. Just plain stupid. Miguel Angel cut my mother like an overripe melon. When Lester and I went to México on a trip—our last as man and wife—I tried to find the village my father was from. Lester just couldn't understand why. I just wanted to see the place he came from, that's all. To walk the streets, to look inside the houses when it got dark, to eat the food, to wash myself clean early in the morning from water heated on a stove, and to cry with the beauty of the stars at night. I didn't want to *know* my father personally. I already knew him. But I didn't know her, and I can't forgive her for leaving me. And I can't forgive Trancha and Dolores for covering up their ears so they couldn't hear my mother screaming.

"Now I'm a fat alcoholic who has ulcers, drinking to the future, and trying to settle the past. But it comes up like the bile I try to keep down. There's this plunger noise in my throat that rises up and tries to choke me. The doctor calls it a hiatal hernia, some kind of acid. My cherry and lemon Tums have stopped working after all these years. Without warning, the acid comes up, and then it gurgles down. Sometimes I think I'm going to regurgitate my whole life on the floor. I'm afraid I won't be able to stop spitting myself up. It makes you feel like a child. Like when you shit or puke all over yourself in your sleep. Exploding like that, without warning, not being able to control yourself. When Lester and I were in the subway in Mexico City during that trip I told you about, I got diarrhea and barely made it into the women's bathroom. Just as I got into the stall I shit all over and around the john and the floor and into the next stall on some lady's white purse that was lying down there on the floor. I'm sorry, I said, trying to clean it up. Couldn't you wait? the attendant said, look what you've done. I was sick, I said, and tried to wipe up. She wouldn't let me and shooed me away. I came out of there feeling sick and awful and embarrassed like I was an old woman, worse yet, an old man, shitting all over himself and not even being allowed to clean up."

"Are you all right, Mara?"

"No and yes. Hang on—someone's calling. I'll be right back."

"Mara? Are you there?"

"It's Ida. I'm going to meet her. I gotta go, Soveida."

"Take care of yourself, Mara. Look, I'll call you, okay, if there's a change."

"Call me if Luardo dies."

"Mara!"

"May he rest in peace with his hand on his prick."

THE BOOK OF SERVICE

CHAPTER NINE

Talks with Dedea #2: The New Waitress

Dearest Dedea:
There is so much I want to say to you. When I look at you, I see myself: fifteen years old, bright and happy. I had just started working at El Farol. I was in love with myself and with all the world. I knew I could do anything, be anything I wanted. When I graduated from high school, everything seemed possible. Because I loved so much, everyone was in love with me. I mean that. I can hear you laughing now, but it's true. People began to ask for me at the restaurant. My first regular customers were two young businessmen. I called them the two combinations with iced tea. They always left me a dollar tip.

Later on, there were men who were attracted to me. Although I must say, I never really had any trouble with anyone getting fresh. Well, until Albert. I've told you about him. The retired symphony conductor. Before and after Albert, I was always treated respectfully. As long as you demand respect, you will get it. Remember that. It doesn't matter who the person is, the age or sex, or the state of inebriation. I always conducted myself well and people treated me with dignity. It's possible to work in a Mexican restaurant and be treated courteously. You're probably thinking that I'm saying two things at the same time. Well, I am. You see, sometimes we have to deal with stereotypical images of what people imagine Mexicans to be, as well as what they imagine waitresses to be. If you are attractive, like you are, and I was, you have to conduct yourself in different ways. Men will always come on to you. Most of them will be respectful, almost shy. There will be the young poets in the corner, the painters who have stepped out of their studios and are still adjusting to reality, the old men who drink in the middle of the afternoon, the lonely husbands, the macho superintendents, and the crippled dishwashers. The ones you work with every day will be the hardest to deal with. Be honest. Let them know that you care for them, as friends, and that is all. I don't advise going out with customers, although I've done it myself.

Beware of the dark stranger sitting behind the bougainvillea, or near the back wall. He'll stare at you, and although at first you may not notice him, soon he'll crawl into your heart and nest there, like an insect who will not leave you alone. He'll try to surround you with his mystery, and after a while you may find yourself breathing his delicate and strange perfume. These men are always handsome and disturbed or rich or engaged or married. They'll never commit to you, ever. Don't ever think they will. They'll want to love you, and they will, in their own way. When you want more from them, they'll run away.

I love you so much, Dedea, and I care about you. You know how I feel about your boyfriend, Gene. He doesn't appreciate you. You're always doing things for him, and he never gives you anything in return. He has never really had a permanent job. You support him, I know you do. He's always coming in here for lunch, and bringing in his friends. Dedea! He can never make you happy. So many times you've come in here crying to me about him. What about the time he went to see his ex-girlfriend in California for a week, leaving you alone? And you let him come back!

Last night I dreamed I was someone else. When I looked in the mirror, my face was different. My hair was piled up on my head and it had white streaks in it. I was from India. And I was crying. About some man. I was deeply in love with him. Although he was attracted to me, in other ways he was repulsed. He didn't like me because my skin was too dark.

Do you know what it is to love someone that way, or be loved that way? When I woke up I was so upset. I'm still upset. This letter to you is about what I see. Gene can never give you what you want. Ivan and Veryl could never give me what I wanted. These men only saw my face, not what was inside my heart.

I want peace. And the only person who can give me that is I.

So, listen to me, Dedea. You are beautiful and talented and so full of life. Sometimes when I look at you I feel blinded, burned. Oh, go ahead, laugh at me again. You are the young girl I was, but with so many more burdens. You know that I am your friend, that I will always be here or there or wherever I can be for you. You are the sister I *never had. You are grace and beauty and doubt and struggle and you are perfect the way you are. Men will want your passion and then try to run from it. Screw the familiar refrains and all those men who would have you turn your heart inside out or upside down or quietside back. You've been underwater too long, Dedea, and now it's time to breathe! I am gasping for air right now, but this breath is mine.*

Waiting is a career. I have made it mine. My mother made it hers, as did her mother before her. Dedea, you have a choice. Breathe, little sister, breathe! Only you can change this wait.

I love you.

Soveida

47

Tirzio

J.V.'s older brother, Tirzio, had two children, six-year-old Susana and a baby, Felicidad. We met them at Susana's birthday party. The rush of children preceded us as we made our way through the back gate and into the small, carefully tended yard. J.V. led me on, greeting friends along the way, but failing, as usual, to introduce me. Behind a large willow tree, J.V. greeted someone energetically. I could see strong arms reaching forward to complete an embrace, while the piñata rope was balanced in one strong, thick hand. The man behind the tree was the piñata controller, and he held the rope that allowed the piñata, the festive clay pot covered with colorful cut paper, to bob up or down, depending on the disordered, childlike, sometimes powerless swings against an invisible foe. What the children lacked in direction, they made up for in energy and unhampered joy. Some piñata maker's idyll, this piñata was pink and blue, a colorful bird wearing a small red hat. This bird was not the usual type. It was a magic bird that strained to fly in the small, hot back yard. It was a little girl's fancy, fashioned by an older woman in Juárez on a hot, steamy summer afternoon, in a shop near the old mercado. A graceful pink and blue, it wore an outlandish red hat the color of fresh blood, and sported silver-tipped wings. The bird careened up and down and sideways as a young boy amassed the strength to knock a large hole in the bird's underbelly. The children scrambled out from the shade of several small trees as candy flew about and eager bodies huddled to gather up what they could. Ripping off the scarf that was placed over his eyes, the young boy gleefully whooped that he was the one to break the piñata. "It's mine," he yelled. "The candy's mine!" The boy was led back to the piñata and once again the scarf was secured over his eyes. The crowd moved back and the piñata sliced the air. This time he was victorious and the clay gourd completely spilled its contents to the ground. In the crush of small, overheated bodies, in the midst of that sweet, cloying, earthy child sweat, his hands still red from the rope's twisting force, I first saw Tirzio Velásquez.

He was confused, and a little excited. Small beadlets of sweat formed at his temples and just beneath his nose. My thin beige summer blouse clung moistly to my breasts. Not sure if I was wearing anything underneath, Tirzio stared long and hard.

But I was, I later told him, when we sat in his van at the river and he fingered and then unloosened the strings that held the blouse together, rolling it away from me, a wave of cloth that had begun to unravel when he first saw me, and I him, at Susana's party that hot August afternoon.

Tirzio stood behind the willow tree, watching me for some time help the children find candy, now settling a small argument between a young boy and a girl. "It's because you're a boy that you want more!" the little girl wailed. "He's taking all the candy!"

Suddenly J.V. appeared. "Tirzio, this is Soveida."

"Hello."

"Soveida, this is my brother, Tirzio."

"I didn't know you had a brother, J.V. You never told me."

"He doesn't tell anyone. He's ashamed of me. Him, Mr. Big Shot College Professor. Well, I'm his brother. The nicer guy, by the way. The nicer and the happier. ¿Qué no, bro?"

"The shorter."

"The sexier. Hell, I'm better-looking than you, guy. He may be tall and thin, but he's mean. The sooner you can say goodbye to him, Soveida, the better off you'll be."

"Would you shut up, Tirzio."

"So, you're his student?"

"Not at the moment. I *was* his student."

"That was last semester. You know I don't date students."

"Cabrón! It took you half a year to ask her out. Unbelievable. But that's my brother for you. So, okay, what can I get you, Soveida? A beer, some wine? Hell, it's about time we met."

"We'll get our own beer. Thanks, anyway."

"Intellectual pendejadas, that's all you're in for. Just remember what I said, Soveida."

"Tirzio!" J.V. exclaimed.

Tirzio *was* nicer and shorter, and he became the brother I would always love. And yet a woman is not supposed to fall in love with her lover's brother. Yes, he was short, and thick. With slightly heavy thighs that were so solidly built they were like beautiful columns. His chest was large, robust; his waist boyishly thin. His head was enormous, very large in circumference, or so it seemed when I first looked at him.

Mara and I used to measure each other's heads when we were young. The tape measure was always ready to measure any head we could find, as if it could gauge the breadth and scope of each woman's or each man's trembling life. My head was considerably smaller than Mara's. Mara's head was bigger, more full of mischief, mystery, misery. That's what I used to think. Now I don't know anymore.

When I saw Tirzio's head I knew, from my reckonings and ruminations of head size and its attendant qualities of stubbornness and general intuition, that this, indeed, was a head to be reckoned with. Little did I know that I would not only come to love it, but to revere it. Silly as that sounds, it's true. Had he lived in the past, his would have been the head of a king, modeled in marble and left behind for posterity as a proud reminder of a ruler's sanctity. His dark, almost black hair was tight, coarse, and close-cropped. His clear skin seemed always tanned. When I met him he was forty-seven years old, married nearly thirty years to the same woman, Patsy.

I had been seeing J.V. for six months already when I met Tirzio. We began to go over to Tirzio's to play cards, or any number of board games. After a night of playing hearts or crazy eights, Tirzio, J.V., and I would go out for ice cream, leaving Patsy at home to watch the kids. She didn't want to go with us, and she said it was all right. I was often sandwiched between the two brothers in J.V.'s sports car, my legs straddled over the gears, as J.V. zoomed through the darkened streets of Agua Oscura. But I found myself pressing ever closer to Tirzio on those wild turns. When it first happened, I was stopped cold by the look in Tirzio's eyes. Gently and gingerly he righted me, as I pulled my skirt over my knees and primly sat back or forward as was demanded by the cramped space. It never occurred to any one of us to take Tirzio's truck on these forays. Surely the three of us would have been more comfortable, and maybe, if she had wanted to, Patsy could have joined us.

J.V., meanwhile, was oblivious to everything except the road. He was cautious by nature, but behind the wheel he was a maniac, taking turns widely, speeding as fast as he could. In the city he was simply dangerous, but once set free in the country, he was unparalleled in his relentless pursuit of speed. On stepping out of the car, he assumed his normal tone and demeanor: expectant but wary. He had a peculiar habit of wearing very dark sunglasses except in class, as if he needed the distance they allowed him. Tirzio constantly teased him about his California movie-star aloofness.

"Who are you?" Tirzio would ask. "The man with no eyes? I never know what you're thinking. Do you ever see the whites of his eyes, Soveida? Just what are you hiding, Velásquez?"

"I don't miss a thing, don't think that I do, brother. The sun is too bright for me. I like the darkness, muted colors."

"It's hard to believe, Soveida, as long as I've known him, and it's been a long time, this guy here has lived in the shade."

I looked closely at J.V. There was a Rudolph Valentino handsomeness about him, tall, cool, and removed. Most women were brought up to like these qualities in men. When I looked behind the dark-tinted glasses to where I imagined his eyes to be, I saw only a tiny reflection of myself. Had I seen J.V.'s eyes, I would have found them, for all his posing, small, flat, and frightened.

"Ay, J.V., que movie star! Well, you're not bad-looking. No way you could have turned out dog meat. Soveida, you know our dad was a handsome son of a bitch. Christ, I can't believe I said that. Well, nothing was ever truer."

"Tirzio!"

"But, anyway, as I was saying, brother, you look a lo todo shine, all Hollywood-duded up with your Ray•Bans and your Oscar de la Renta chones and whatever other labels you're wearing. A pretty boy, no denying! What do you say, Soveida?" I turned to look at Tirzio and met his dark, absolutely open and honest eyes.

When we returned from getting ice cream at the Double Chill, we were met at the door by Patsy. She took the quart of ice cream into the kitchen, where she scooped it out for us. Rocky road or German chocolate or double-mint fudge. Whatever it was, Patsy and J.V. got the big bowls, Tirzio and I the small ones.

Patsy was more than fat, she was enormous. She had a pleasant face, but you could see that she was unhappy. She and Tirzio had been sweethearts since high school and had married the year after they graduated. I imagined the two of them as they were in their youth: fresh, bright-eyed kids very much in love. Patsy was still that same young girl in her red wool sailor's dress and her blue-and-white paisley sweater with the lace trim. If only it weren't for the girth that strained and bulged underneath her little girl's clothes and her comfortable and heavy brown suede pumps, Patsy would have looked the same. I wanted to believe that Patsy and Tirzio had made out in the back of an old Rambler at the drive-in or down by the river. I wanted to imagine that they had kissed each other deeply for hours until the sides of their mouths were raw and their lips engorged and that her panties and his shorts were wet with excitement. I wanted to believe that one feverish night Patsy had decided to rip off all her clothes and throw them into the back seat while Tirzio fondled her in the front seat, his short, thick fingers up her dripping crotch.

They had both gone to Valley High School before me. I hadn't known either of them then, nor had I known J.V., who told me I never would have recognized him, anyway. But J.V. didn't concern me. What concerned me was Patsy.

Was this Patsy the same Patsy Tirzio had loved? Was this Patsy ever that Patsy? This Tirzio ever that Tirzio? And what of their current sex life?

Patsy had had a hysterectomy a year and a half ago, just after Felicidad was born. She talked about it as if it was her historical day of liberation, a red-letter day, like VE-Day.

"The only side effects," she told me on New Year's Eve in the dimly lit bathroom of the Rustlers Lounge, rubbing with her little finger the baby-doll pink lipstick she held in her hand and then lightly spreading it over her small lips, "the only side effects were this." She ran her hand over her exceedingly small breasts and her large stomach.

I assumed she meant her weight.

"Oh, and this," she said, stroking the side of her forehead. What the latter gesture meant I wasn't sure. That she'd lost the desire for sex, or that she was crazy, or that she thought too little, or too much? That was what I really wanted to know, and my speculation about Patsy and Tirzio's sex life grew with each wild turn of J.V.'s sports car. But somehow I felt I didn't have to pursue the issue. Patsy would tell me everything in good time. And she did eventually begin to confide in me. But by then I had no desire to know anything about her life with Tirzio.

Patsy should have had red hair and green eyes. She should have been a flamenco dancer in her youth. She should have had a figure to kill for. She should have been graceful and charming and once have studied painting in Italy, or traveled through Europe by herself. She was, instead, short, and increasing fussy, sometimes girlish, sometimes like an old lady. She had an overwhelming fondness for food, and talked at length, as the French do, about meals long gone, from some distant gourmet past: "Remember my Aunt Molly's sopaipillas? Remember the mole I made Christmas '86?"

Tirzio humored her. J.V. admired her. To him, Patsy was the perfect wife. A little nest hen coo-cooing delights. She recalled to him a happy little scene of domestic virtue.

"If you'd known Patsy when she was young," J.V. would say, "she was the president of Home Ec, and really thin, a little wisp. And really pretty. She still is. Don't you think she's nice, Soveida?"

"Nice, yes, she's nice," I said aloud. God forgive me, then I thought: She's as nice as furry old slippers. Nice as lace collars. Nice as a white chenille bedspread. Nice as tea and crumpets. Nice as pearl-drop earrings. Nice as a roomful of early American. Nice as yellow zinnias. Nice as lawn chairs in a small back yard. Nice as a house full of quiet children. Nice as an old man sleeping. Nice as daisies and baby's breath. Nice as faded photographs on a crocheted tablecloth on a grand piano in a sitting room where no one ever sits because Mother says it's the guest room. Nice as plastic covers on the couch in that room and the molded plastic runner to match that cuts through the center of the rug that no one ever walks over because this room is for company.

"Yes, she's nice," I found myself saying without much conviction just before 11 p.m. on New Year's Eve. We had been at the Rustlers Lounge since seven. Patsy and I had just returned from the restroom, where Patsy kept talking through the stalls as both of us sat, one bursting forth a ping of urine and then being answered by her stall mate. I was reminded of the noise cow's milk makes when it spurts into a metal pail. One teat for a toot and now another. Patsy flushed and washed and rinsed her hands and began to apply that baby-pink lipstick of hers again with her little finger as she talked about how her hysterectomy had made her tighter down there and how now when she laughs she doesn't pee anymore. Thank you, Patsy, I thought.

It was now nearly midnight and Patsy and J.V. were dancing. I sat across from Tirzio and smiled at him. He smiled back.

"Okay, everybody up!" Patsy said. "Come on, I have my Instamatic. Get up, please! First, you three stand there like you love each other. I'll take your picture. Come on, get close. Move in, Soveida, and you, too, J.V., she won't bite. Come on, Tirzio, squeeze in. Put your arm around Soveida. Closer, all of you. Okay, now look at me. Smile, Soveida, and you, J.V. What's wrong with you? Be happy! Cheese. Come on, everybody, say cheese!"

Tirzio slid his arm across my shoulder, down my back, and then to my waist. He held me the way a man can. I had my arm around him. That was it. That was all. That was enough.

Tirzio sold his nameless truck and bought a new van. He called me up at El Farol and said he'd be over to show it to me.

We drove out past the Lagrimas, toward Henderson Peak, and near the Flumes by the river. I had never been alone with Tirzio before. We got out of the van and walked along the river a ways from the van and sat on an outcropping of rocks.

Suddenly there was a clap of thunder and it began to pour. Yelling like children, we ran to the van, as large raindrops pelted us, soaking us to the skin. There was nowhere to go, no shelter but inside. Tirzio opened the sliding door and we dashed in, drenched but happy. I was wearing the blouse I'd worn to Susana's birthday party.

Tirzio touched my shoulder and said, "You were wearing this blouse when I first met you. I didn't think you were wearing underwear."

"I was. Shows how much you know."

"I don't know much," he said as he fingered the plunging V of the blouse. "I do know I want to hold you. We don't have to do anything. Just let me hold you."

I looked into his eyes. Clear water, no fear. I could swim out to sea.

Inside a humid van in the rain. Miles from nowhere. Miles from anyone. No family. No I.O.U.s. Tirzio's kisses were salty. I took off my wet blouse, skirt, and shoes. Tirzio took off all his clothes and threw them in the front of the van. He lay over me as the perspiration from his body mingled with the rainwater. We made love, he naked, me in my socks.

"You're like a schoolgirl," he said. "Look at you." He never stopped, never wanted to stop, but kept going and going and going. It was so perfect.

I had never known or loved a man like Tirzio. He should be listed in the Chicano Culture Quiz as something truly great.

A simple man, he had simple needs, and our making love was as natural as the sudden storm. It stopped just as suddenly as it began. I felt cleansed, whole again, no small wonder in that vast desert of so little rain.

THE BOOK OF SERVICE

CHAPTER TEN

Shoes

Dark shoes are best. You won't have to clean them as much, or shine them as often. Remember the mucky floors. You don't have time for white shoes. Unless you have time to clean and shine them every night, forget it. They scuff easily. Remember, there's a lot of dancing behind the scenes. "Behind you! Coming through!" The waitress call. Being stepped on is part of the dance. Avoiding other feet is part of the dance as well. Think: light, airy feet in good shoes in a defensive and offensive stance.

48

Soveida's Will

Last week Larry saw a television program about wills, and now he wants everyone at El Farol to fill one out. He says he'll pay us fifty dollars if we give him our will, have it witnessed by two people, and then store it in the safe in his office. According to Rosie Rojas, his lawyer, that's all Larry needs to make it legal. I don't think he really cares whether we have a will or not. I think he only wants to read what we've written down.

On Tuesday the wills flew out to feverish hands. The majority of the wills were submitted the day after they were distributed. The rest were turned in by Friday of that week. Everyone took to accounting their mortality as ink takes to thin parchment. As of today, only two outstanding wills remain to be turned in, mine and Pito's.

Pito Leal is the day cook, a tall, thin man with enormous hands and a tiny voice. He is a great cook, probably the best after Eloisa, the weekend night cook. Maybe by now he's even better than his mentor, since he's learned those few tips and tricks of hers that eluded him at his mother's side.

Eloisa is getting old and yet she can never get too far away from cooking. It's her life. At age fifty she tried to retire, then again at fifty-eight, and last at sixty. Now in her sixty-fourth year, she is still going strong, cooking on weekend nights, the busiest times at El Farol. Her clientele loves her sour-cream chile con queso guacamole and cilantro-filled green beef rellenos with a side of posole. Eloisa is originally from northern New Mexico. When she moved south she brought her posole, her sopa, and her natillas with her. She insisted on cooking with blue corn as well, an addition to the weekend menu that she herself adopted. Larry was in the beginning very skeptical about her innovations, but he relented one night when she served him a cinnamon-and-apple-filled empanada that thereafter became another El Farol special.

"Why haven't you stayed retired?" I asked Eloisa.

"I can't, chula. I just got used to cooking for a lot of people. I can't cook small anymore. If I don't *cook big*, I go crazy. What do you want me to do, linda, go crazy—just me and Ben with our TV dinners on our laps in front of the color TV? I got to *cook big* at least a coupla times a week. My schedule's real good now. Friday, Saturday, and Sunday I cook. The rest of the time I have my nails done, watch *The Young and the Restless* and *The Love Connection* and El Wapner. I read me my magazines, the *Star, Enquirer, The Globe*, and the other one, *The Weekly World News* with the two-headed babies, pobrecitos, and El Rey, Elvis, talking through the TV. I walk over with Ben to the Senior Center for lunch, and stay around and play lotería. On Thursdays I go with Amanda Costales to our Women Aglow meetings. What else I got to do? I got a full life. I'm too busy to die as long as I can *cook big*. Why you asking me, anyway? What would you be yourself, without this place we love so much, eh, chula?"

How could Pito not help but improve his already masterly skills under the tutelage of Eloisa, the Queen of Mexican food in Agua Oscura? The nights she cooks, the place is always crowded. Diners come back to the kitchen to greet her personally, giving her hugs over steaming metal-lined trays filled with chile, beans, rice, the water underneath bubbling, rising into the air and making Eloisa's face bead with sweat. Her pink-red cheeks are moist, her forehead is dappled with the perspiration her red bandanna cannot keep in check. With a humid hug or a tightening of the fingers, Eloisa greets her friends, extending her soft, fleshy arms over steaming trays of warmed-up food. She coos and coddles over the patrons as a mother does over a small child.

The only thing Pito never learned from Eloisa was how to extend himself to others. While he isn't cold, he isn't warm, either. Some people think he's conceited or arrogant. The truth of the matter is that he is painfully shy. What Pito Leal lacks in human solicitude, he makes up in equanimity and fairness. Eloisa yells and pushes everyone around, willy-nilly. Her outbursts are frequent and legendary. Following a tirade, she will cuddle up to the offending busboy or kitchen assistant, and soon all will be forgotten. With Pito, there are no such temperamental outbursts or scenes. He is even-tempered, thorough, consistent, fair, professional, and dull. As far back as any of us can remember, he's always been dull. Even Connie remembers him as a dull boy. She originally hired him to bus tables. One day Gambo Serenata, the cook, came to work and passed out in the lobby from drink. Connie took Pito on at the last minute.

"We were desperate and Pito begged me to let him try. Wouldn't you know it? He turned out to be a very good cook, so he stayed on in Gambo's place."

Pito is so dull no one even speculates about his life away from El Farol. It surprises me that Larry wants Pito's will. Pito has nothing to leave anyone. Nothing, at least, that I know of.

When Margarito Cornudo, the night waiter, and Pancha Portales used to get together to smoke a cigarette out by the back door on a slow night—an act forbidden by Larry—they'd discuss at length the nature of everyone's sex life. In their niggling, nicotine delusions of grandeur and haughtiness, they often entertained themselves at other people's expense. They prided themselves on being the Best Waiter and Waitress at El Farol. For that matter, in all of Agua Oscura.

Pito to them was a nonentity, a lowly "day person." He was Larry's old retainer, Connie's lackey, Bonnie's slave. He was even Eloisa's doormat.

Yes, it was true Pito had risen up in the ranks, starting off that day twenty years ago when Gambo had gotten drunk and La Famosa, as Eloisa was called, could not come in, due to a bad case of diarrhea.

"There's no ways I can come in on such short notice, Señora Consuelo. I might could have if my Ben hadn't taken me out last night to eat seafood at La Ostra Azul, a new restaurant in Juárez. I think they should change the name to the Sick Oyster, if you ask me. Like I told you, I might could have, but I can't now no ways."

"Señora Consuelo, I can cook. I really can," said Pito.

He offered himself, a lamb for slaughter, with his calm announcement.

The day of Eloisa's diarrhea and Gambo's collapse, even we waitresses had to dry dishes. Larry was ignominiously forced to put his unhappy, soft brown hands into the soapy, dirty dishwater and keep them there.

Eloisa returned to work the next day promptly at 10 a.m., made up with her usual iridescent blue eye shadow. Her wide brown eyes were rimmed in black eyeliner, making her look like a benevolent panda. They stared out cheerfully from beneath fiercely painted, slightly elevated eyebrows that winged back toward her temples.

"So, how's it going?" she chirped.

Eloisa looked crisp, clean, in a freshly pressed white peasant blouse and a long red skirt with a purple sash tied somewhere around the place her waist should have been.

"How are you feeling, Eloisa?"

"Me, Soveida? Fit as a guitarra. Oh, you mean yesterday? Yes, I was sick. Sick as a wounded, putrefying dog that has been run over and had its guts spilled out and pulled back and emptied on a hot road in summertime with cars that keep passing until the guts are smashed and sprayed and splattered like glue on the road, animal glue, que huele al infierno. Yes, híjole, it stunk to hell, I've been sick. But that was yesterday. Today I feel like a million pesos.

"When Ben took me to the Bad Lobster for my anniversary, I had no idea I would nearly die on the way back home. And it was all on account of my surf-and-turf with the lobster balls. It was either the surf that got me or the lobster balls, or perhaps the baby-clam stew. I don't know. It could have been the scallops from Ben's plate. Or the halibut finger appetizers or the salmon mousse or the hush-puppied cod bits. I really don't know.

"Whatever it was, it was later that morning after dancing all night with the mariachis at Sylvia's and after stopping at the Border Cowboy Truck Stop for an early breakfast of two poached eggs with corned-beef hash, juice, and coffee, with a side of pancakes, that the sickness came on to me. I was taking off my earrings in the bathroom when it hit me. I was in there until about 6 a.m. Ben, pobrecito, el Ben, mi Bennie, ay, he brought me a foam mattress that we keep in the truck so's I could rest in between you-knows. We finally made it out of the Border Cowboy Truck Stop. My Ben drove home like I was an eggshell princess and carried me into the house just as if I was a baby girl. He's good to me that way. Then I took me a hot bath and did me my nails. I fell asleep afterwards like I had my mouth on a teton. I was that peaceful. But just to be sure there wasn't going to be no more cod balls coming up, I called in sick. I probably coulda made it, but why push a bad bowl of baby-clam stew? I figured I should just stay home. So I watched la telly on the sofa in the living room with a hot-water bottle on my panza, just in case. Ben told me get in bed, honey, so I did. I couldn't sleep, see, my tripas had gotten too much oxygen. I did me a coupla puzzles out of my *Jumble Puzzle #215*. Then I went into the kitchen to get something to snack on and took it into the living room. Then I lay down on the couch and fell asleep while I was watching *All My Children*. Imagine! I was *that* tired. I slept normal last night after a good dinner of ribs that my Ben made me. And here I am, feeling pretty good. So what's this I hear about Pito cooking and not bad, it seems?"

That was the beginning of Pito's apprenticeship at the hands of Eloisa la Famosa. Only there wasn't really too much she could teach him, except in the department of posole and northern New Mexico foods, natillas and sopa and such. Pito was a southerner and he didn't know a chico from a moco, posole from pos'orale. In the area of northern New Mexico cooking, there was a certain amount to be learned. Pito Leal, then in his late teens, was moving early on into middle age. No one really cared how old he was, all they knew was that he could cook. He was known as Eloisa's protégé. Larry liked to say Eloisa had chosen him because he never talked back to her. The fact of the matter was —and it hurt Eloisa to admit it—his rice was better than hers. But she wouldn't admit it to anyone, and neither would he. If asked about it, no one would probably have detected much of a difference, but Eloisa knew. What she respected in Pito was that he had the grace never to let on he knew she knew and she knew he knew. Eloisa moved to nights and Pito days. Business was growing and El Farol now needed more cooks. It was only logical Pito should become one.

The matter of Lavel's hiring was another famous story. Some of the staff had vigorously opposed it. The whole matter surged up, was briefly unpleasant, and then, like everything else about El Farol, became accepted and colorful history.

"It's done all the time," Larry had said. "Is this town so goddamn small, so asshole bigoted, so ultra-fascist white bread, macaroni, and Cheez Whiz racist, with such a pea-brained distorted pick-your-nose-until-it's-raw mentality, that people can't accept a black cook in a Mexican restaurant?"

Yes, Larry thought.

Yes, thought Margarito Cornudo, who was not out of the closet yet, nor would he admit openly to anyone that he was gay. He was "artistic," he liked to say. It was Margarito who had pushed so hard for new drapes, then new booths, then a new rug. Margarito himself redesigned the menu, then the logo, and then he wrote all the radio and TV ads.

"I'm only working here to make money to go to interior-design school back East," he told Pancha Portales confidentially. "But if you ask my opinion, El Farol has no place for a Negro cook."

"I agree with you, Margarito," Pancha nodded, inhaling her beloved breath with a tight sh-sh, then exhaling the smoke, drawing it all the way from the soles of her much-worn, newly polished white nurse's shoes. "Margarito, I got to hand it to you, you've got the right ideas. You'll go far in the world. Your hands are so artistic!"

"So, let's get to work, Pancha," Margarito said.

"So, what do you think about Windle, Soveida?"

"Him? I don't know. Can he cook?"

"Chittlins maybe, or corn bread. Me, I don't like the idea of him one bit."

"Me neither."

"Give him a chance, Pancha. Maybe he'll work out."

"Like the Chinese before him? Hell, my salsa had egg foo yung in it. No, I'm worried."

"Tacos are tacos."

"That's what you say."

"Says who."

"Says me. I hope that bitch LaMont doesn't screw up our tables tonight like she did last time."

"She's better than the one before her."

"LaMont me agüite. She really gets to me."

"Her? Miss Lee Press-on-Nails. What do you expect, Margarito?"

The staff was generally very supportive of Larry.

We were willing to come in early in the morning to set up sandbags when Agua Oscura was flooded in 1975. We weren't happy about that, but we were there, side by side, stacking sandbags and sweeping water out the front door. And we made it through the Food Strike of 1983.

But this time it was too much. At least, for me. Everyone except Pito and me had handed in our wills. What could Larry gain from knowing Pito and Peetie's assets? Perhaps he had a perverse desire to see everyone stripped down to the bare essentials of mortality. What Larry really wanted was power. Only *he* would offer fifty dollars for a will, with the stipulation that it stay in his office wall safe, combination T-A-C-O-S. He'd overstepped his boundaries this time. Something else was behind all this ranting and raving.

I turned off the overhead light and wandered a crowded path back to my small, disordered bedroom at the back of the new trailer I'd bought a month ago.

When would I finish my book, I wondered. And what would I do about my will?

What would I do with my trailer? That's it! To Pito Leal, the trailer. He had that crummy little place near the restaurant. He got paid less than the other cooks, by choice. He wanted it that way. He said if he had it, he'd only spend it. He could use a trailer.

I was so tired I crawled under the sheets and closed my eyes. I had the weekend all to myself. All I wanted to do was sleep. I took the phone off the hook.

As I lay in bed I turned over thoughts of

The Last Will and Testament

of Soveida Dosamantes Torres Beron

Agua Oscura, New Mexico

In the year of our Lord

I leave

I leave

my

I leave my what?

My dreams.

49

The Career Woman's Disease

Almost every woman I know has either shriveled ovaries, blocked Fallopian tubes, or a tilted uterus. I myself have endometriosis.

Everyone I've known has had yeast infections at one time or another, that goes without saying. Most certainly vaginitis, as well as a few cases of herpes, the crabs, and every once in a while a general, malodorous draining that comes and goes, depending on what is happening in each woman's life. As far as the other myriad symptoms and sicknesses of a woman's body during the childbearing years, I know them all, understand them and sympathize with all my women friends who display these ills.

I can chart my woman's woes on a graph, either horizontally or vertically. I can easily determine what sort of illness and malaise has beset me with each male encounter.

My years with Ivan were marked by great tension and a plethora of unholy and never-ending woman's ailments. I always felt as if I'd caught something secondhand, from someone else. I had a running cold for the five years we were married, a grippe or flu I couldn't quite shake, a low-grade infection that weakened and tired me and, finally, almost totally depleted me. When I made love to him, I felt as if I was making love to all the people he'd made love to in his life. At these times I almost believed in reincarnation. He was my past, present, and eternal future. When he fell from me, never completely spent, I, too, drew away, thoroughly exhausted by that swirling game he called loving.

When we first married, I suffered greatly, not accustomed to a sexually active man. I had lubrication problems for a while. Those ceased; then I had chronic yeast infections. Those would abate; then

I'd get a bladder infection. That would let up; then I'd have cramps so badly I had to stay in bed. This pattern never changed with time, I just accepted that monthly barrage of deep-rooted discomfort. I tossed and turned so badly at night that Ivan insisted I sleep on the living-room couch.

I was swollen a week before my period, the week during, and exhausted the week following. There was one week of respite, and then it would begin again. It didn't matter what week it was, nothing stopped Ivan, who found me attractive and desirable at all times: morning, noon, or night.

I liked the idea of that, but the reality was another matter.

Maybe there is something backward and unsophisticated about me, but it was at that time of the month, when I was dog-eyed, yappy-faced, and moaning, that Ivan followed me about the most, when all I could do was put a hot pad under my lower back and lift my legs up, my feet positioned on the ground, struggling to find a comfortable position that would afford me some modicum of ease.

The second year we were married, I bled intermittently, a brownish-reddish liquid, not blood, that smelled like decaying fish. That was the year Ivan had his first long-term affair. I knew something was happening, but I didn't know with whom. He still made love to me often, placing towels underneath to keep the ooze from staining our sheets red. I was careful to clean myself, was scrupulous with my grooming, but as soon as he began to thrust himself inside me, the angry bile would spill out. That's what it was, my bile and rage. I felt dirty, and it was because of him that my sex bled.

Eventually the bleeding went away. The woman left town, never came back, and for a while Ivan was heartbroken. My body was wet then. I clung to him and he angrily pushed me away. Once, in the middle of the night, he pounced on me, driven by anger. Without any sort of interaction, without any time for the slow, rhythmic building up of passion, he took me as I cried and prayed that he would never leave me, never. I loved him so much, while he thought of someone else.

Then the yeast infection came back. I denied my needs again, lay there next to him, buoying him up, while I was drowning. My punishment was the whitish-yellow ooze of rage and anger and guilt. I wanted to leave him but I couldn't. He'd already left me and still I stayed.

I decided to have a child, but although I wasn't infertile, none was forthcoming. I felt dry inside, desiccated with the grief of my long-standing disappointment.

Ivan's girlfriends came and went. I knew them by my body's symptoms: infections, fevers, tiredness, allergies. I was never sick enough to miss work. No one really knew I was sick, except Mamá Lupita, who looked at me, then through me, and knew: "What's wrong with you, Soveida? Otra arrimada? Another one of them got close?"

Mamá knew but never confronted me at length. To do so would be to negate the Sacrament. And that's exactly what it was those two last years—the sacrament of penance.

But was I the only one suffering? Did other married women suffer as well? I thought of my Tía Teeney and Tío Adrino. Teeney was fat and Adrino was thin. Teeney liked to brag out loud when all the women were together that she and Adrino slept in different beds, and had done so for years.

"I forget how many," she would say. "Sex, you can take it or leave it. Me, thank God, I left it! If I hadn't gotten married, I would have been a dancer. Adrino doesn't like to dance, but he won't let me dance with anyone else. He's that way. So all night he'll dance with me and consecrate the penance of his dancing for the Intercession of the Holy Innocents."

I know what that is like.

I prayed Ivan would finally meet someone who would take him away. That someone was La Virgie.

When he moved out, my vaginitis finally cleared up; so did my skin. I also gained ten pounds. I had gotten too thin and was on the verge of some kind of eating disorder. I was all right for a while, until I met Veryl. I found out about endometriosis in the newspaper.

> Dear Dr. Huppler:
> My doctor tells me that I have what is called "the career woman's disease." Can you enlighten me as to what this is and what can be done about it, as I want to have children bad.
> Concerned in Connecticut

Dear Concerned:

Listen to me. My name is Soveida Dosamantes. Let me tell you what I know. Dr. Huppler can let you know all the technicalities about endometriosis. He'll call it "retrograde menstruation," telling you that, instead of flowing down through the cervix and vagina, the menstrual blood and tissue back up into the pelvic cavity and Fallopian tubes, causing infertility. He can tell you about those wild cells that cause patches and scars in the pelvic region and around the ovaries and Fallopian tubes. He'll tell you it's the result of delayed childbearing and say that maybe in some cases the tissue will emerge from the uterus and continue to grow. He'll tell you it's called the "career woman's disease." And he'll tell you—it most probably will be a he— they almost always are hes, the ones who plunge their hands inside us—he'll tell you these days many women are affected by this disease, and that sometimes the cells will break away and form clumps in other organs and, responding to the menstrual cycle, will cause monthly bleeding wherever they have settled. He can tell you everything, in only the way Dr. Huppler can, without knowing names or faces, in his cold, precise, analytical way. What he can't tell you about is the pain.

He'll tell you that if you want to stop hurting, you'll need to get pregnant or take drugs that cause you to get acne, gain weight, or grow a beard.

If you have a severe case, he may suggest someone, also probably a man, who can help you get rid of it, the pain, that is. They'll just cut it out for you. They'll remove your ovaries or uterus, no problem. But then, where will you be? Back where you were. Childless, but in the know. Dear Concerned, listen to me. For too many women, pain is a career, their sole career. I know. Our mothers have lived with it every day because they were too ashamed to admit they hurt "down there." They've masked their itches, their burns, their flows. They've said it's nothing, but the pain wouldn't go away. They'd try to forget about their curse, for that is what it is when pain goes on too long. They would say everything is fine, when it wasn't.

Every woman knows someone who has died because she was ignorant or shy or afraid. I have an aunt, Lina, who died because she was too embarrassed, too fearful, to tell anyone that long after her child came out she was still bleeding. Her stitches were undone, and while the world went on doing what it does so well, and her child, Mara, laughed and played with the other children, she oozed, bled, and then filled up with pus. Mara's father was gone by then, he'd disappeared, so Lina cried hoarsely to the white walls: "He's split me, split me, both of them have done this to me." She was raving: "Cut it off, cut it out, give me something, morphine! I'm dying, give me something!" She died, screaming for her sister, Dolores, to kill her.

Everyone knows someone to whom pain is a career. The new working woman's disease. I can tell you about it, myself, Concerned. Because when I met Veryl we came together to cement our grief. But he left me, never once having cried. Imagine that.

I wanted to have a child, but when I was ready there was no one. That six months with Veryl, I tried telling the doctor, it just didn't happen. Afraid to say, he can't, he can't, never could, I can't, I can't, never could, we can't, we can't, never would. Don't you understand? We made our career together. What career? You call this a career? Yes, I do, it's the only one I've known. It wasn't only Veryl. It was also me.

Will it stop, you ask. The pain?

This is what everyone calls living.

What about your dis-ease?

Which one?

The endometriosis?

That? That's the least of it.

So what happened?

Tirzio. Tirzio. Tirzio.

Cherubim

50

Letters from Ex's

It is late. The sounds of night surround me. I sit on my front porch holding a box of letters. I can hear cars at the end of the block. The train with its long, low mmmmm, the blast becoming louder, the MMMMM trailing itself and then becoming echo, the echo fanning out left to right as it disappears and the house shimmies as the Santa Fe moves north into night. I sort through letters. Letters from my ex's. A valid exercise and a necessary perspective, while I wonder what next to do about life. Five years after Veryl's death. The anniversary two days away. Cold day remembered. I am sick again, but never too sick to reach into the past.

Dear Soveida:
I want to bury myself deeply inside you. No one has touched me the way you have. Your hands have burned themselves into my flesh. No one has kissed me the way you have. Has anyone ever licked you in those places like that? I asked Sam, my compadre, and he said no, not without asking first. As long as I live, I will always have a taste for you.
Ivan

My Princess:
You are light and love. Together we can build our temples side by side. You know those stone statues of Egyptian pharaohs in museums? The Queen stands with her hand on the King's shoulder as they look into vast eternity. That is us.

Our linkage
manifests itself
in mountains

In cryptic annotations
of stone

We are tempered by sky
the growing darkness.

Goodbye.
J.V.

> *Mi querida Soveida:*
> *I want to hold you and stroke your beautiful face. I need to*
> *see you. When can we get together?*
> *Tirzio*

There were many other letters, some from the same people, some from others. Some made me sad, others angry, some made me thick with longing.

Then a note on a small sheet of paper.

> *Dolores:*
> *In order to go on living I have to leave. Don't expect me to*
> *come back. Don't try to find me the way you've done before.*
> *Leave people alone. It's embarrassing. Just let me live my life.*
> *Luardo*

I had no idea how it got there. It was an ugly, pitiful thing. And yet there was no getting away from its hard words.

"You're like me, Soveida," Dolores had once said. "Men are afraid of us, sweetheart. We want too much. We aren't embarrassed to ask. We aren't shy. Your father was ten thousand men to me. I never knew on any given day which man I was making love to. He prepared me for the world, for all men. For that I am grateful. He was the only man I knew until Reldon. There've been so many times since your father and I divorced that I've wanted to write him a letter. The words are there, they always are, on the tip of my tongue. Oh, but, Soveida, your father has forgotten our story. The story he tells of us isn't the story I know, the story of our life. He's confused by his illness. And I'm afraid a letter to him would confuse things. He'd think I still wanted to sleep with him when all I want to say is: Luardo, live in peace. Without tears. You who never cry."

"Were you and Luardo ever happy?"

"Occasionally. But that's not what I'm talking about, Soveida."

"Then what are you talking about?"

"You never called me Mother, now at least call me Dolly."

"We're friends now, Dolores, isn't that enough? We weren't friends for a long time. Don't be my mother today, just be my friend."

"Okay, okay. The happiness was after."

"After. When after? After you made love?"

"Escandalosa! Who said anything about making love? The happiness I'm talking about is knowing I'm whole again. Knowing I'm all right, I'll survive. I haven't loved myself for so long. All my love mistakenly went to someone else when it should have come to *me*. Nobody can love us the way we need to love ourselves. Especially for women like us."

"Women who have teeth in our sex, a cage where our mouths should be? Women who pull men down into boiling water?"

"Ay, Soveida, stop talking that way. The men in our lives, Soveida, they were charming, intelligent pendejos. Womanizers to boot, and dependent like four-week-old kittens. All suck suck suck and nothing in return. You're acting like you're crazy, Soveida, but I know you're not. You've loved. Now put everything aside, even Veryl, and get on with living!"

"Is this pep talk for me or for you, Dolores?"

"Does it matter? That's about all I have to say now, anyway. As Mamá says . . ."

"I know, I know."

"Think about it."

February 16.

Dear Soveida,

Thank you for your gift: that never-changing golden sunset. I'm sorry about dinner.

You always said Ivan gave you the Before of marriage, never the After. I never even gave you the Before.

There was no boating accident at Caballo Lake. But there was a girl named Angel. We were high-school friends, on a

*school trip. We'd gone off, just the two of us. I pulled her
down, she tried to fight me off. I pushed myself inside her.
There was no pleasure for either of us. She ran off and got a
ride back to town with some friends. We never spoke about that
night and she avoided me.*

*Angel got killed in a car accident several years later. I
couldn't make love after Angel died. Until I met you, Soveida.
If you call it making love. You deserve someone who makes you
laugh and lets you turn the furnace way up high.*

*I left a letter in the desk in the back bedroom saying that you
own Maybelline and all the accumulated crap.*

*I did love you. The timing wasn't good. But, anyway, now's
the time to go.*

Veryl

It was Veryl's last letter to me. Sometimes I wish, like Dolores, that
I could write a letter to my ex. I wondered if I could ever put his spirit
to rest.

51

Face of an Angel

"She has the face of an angel and she likes to fuck."

Hector was talking about Ada, his pregnant, soon-to-be wife. She was called Ada by those who knew she hated her name, Narada.

"It sounds too much like Nada. Nothing. And I'm something, Hector!"

"Sure you are, babes, sure you are. You're a hell of a lot."

"Damn right I'm something or someone. Call me Ada, not Nada."

It *was* Ada he was talking about, wasn't it? Or was it La Virgie, his mistress, the same La Virgie that years ago had caused the breakup of my marriage to Ivan. La Virgie hadn't aged at all. She was still seducing men. First my husband, now my brother. Ada didn't yet know about La Virgie. The wedding was only two weeks off. I made up my mind to tell Ada in case she wanted to change her mind.

"Ada, I know you don't have much time."

"Hector should be here any minute, Soveida. We're going to Juárez to get our rings."

"I don't know how to say this, Ada."

"Just say it. What is it, Soveida? Why are you all white?"

"Hector has a girlfriend."

"Yeah, me. We're getting married in two weeks. So?"

"It's not that Ada. He's got *another* girlfriend."

"Another girlfriend? What are you talking about? Another girlfriend like Another Girlfriend? Like, what do you mean?"

"I heard he's been hanging out with La Virgie Lozano."

"You're crazy, Soveida. She was Ivan's girlfriend, you got it all wrong."

"M.J. saw them together."

"Oh, M.J. Well, that explains it."

"I wanted to let you know. I've heard things."

"He's your brother, Soveida. Don't you trust him?"

"No. No, I don't. I don't want you to be hurt the way I was. La Virgie won't stop at anything. I mean it. If she has her eyes on Hector, you better watch out."

"She's an old woman."

"She's a little younger than me."

"That's what I mean. Well, look. I appreciate the concern, but me and Hector are solid. We're getting married and no two ways about it. I know La Virgie and she ain't no problem. She's going out with El Gonie, Hector's compa, that's all. We double-date. I know there's bad blood between you and La Virgie and I know why, but chill out, Soveida. Me and Hector are tight."

"Just thought I'd let you know."

"So, where is your pendejo brother, anyway? He's late! We gotta go to Juárez to get us some wedding rings. Soveida, you worry too much about the men in your family. As for Hector, from now on he's mine to worry about, okay?"

"Whatever you say, Ada."

Was Hector talking about Tere, Mamá Lupita's young maid?

I overheard him telling El Gonie, his compadre, about some woman. But it doesn't matter *who* he was talking about. He was thinking that!

I can't remember if he said "*and*" she likes to fuck or "*but*" she likes to fuck. All I know is that he said something I wasn't meant to hear to someone he shouldn't have said anything to about someone he has no business saying anything about, not that, anyway, because when he said it about her, he said it about all women.

"He's that way," Dolly says. "Your brother's *that* way, Soveida."

"*That* way? How did he get *that* way?" I ask. "Weren't you around back then, Dolores, to see that he didn't become *that way*?"

When Dolly was Dolores, boys were boys, and girls were girls. Boys wore blue and girls wore pink. Boys were snakes and snails and puppy-dog tails. Girls were sugar and spice and everything nice. That's how it was, then. Hector was in that *then*, still.

It's no surprise, then, that Hector is *that* way. Luardo had been *that* way. And my grandfather Profe, and his father, too. And his father's father. All of them. *That* way. Those Dosamantes.

———

The wedding is two weeks off. Already I feel apprehension. Hector hasn't bought the rings. He's asked me to pick something out for him and Ada, but I refused. They'd decided to go to Juárez to find something reasonably priced (his idea) and they ended up barhopping. Hector got drunk, they got into a fight, and Ada called the wedding off.

"So you talk to her, sis."

"Me? She's your fianceé. Besides, it's up to you to make up with her. Dammit, Hector, what happened? You were just supposed to buy a ring."

"Well, sis, you see, we left here around ten to beat the Saturday rush, but we got caught in it. We were so tired of sitting on the bridge for two hours we decided to go eat first. Ada wanted something cool to drink, what with her morning sickness, you know how damn hot it gets over there in Mexico, so we went into the Caverns Bar. Yeah, she likes that it looks like the inside of Carlsbad Caverns. I bought her a gardenia and she got happy. We stayed there until around five. Never ate. Finally walked down the shopping strip. I was going to go to that jewelry store by the old bridge where Mamá gets her santos charms engraved, you know the one. It was closed. Ada starts screaming that all the damn ring shops are closed and now she can't get married and here she is three months pregnant. She was getting ugly, so I suggested we relax and get a drink. What can I say? We finally went to Mundo's to eat sandwiches and got home about 3 a.m. I had to carry Ada into the apartment, she was so drunk."

"She's a pregnant woman! She can't be getting drunk. And yet you still didn't get the rings?"

"No, we didn't get the rings. Woman's been driving me nuts ever since. You know how much rings cost, anyway? I saw an ad for rings on sale for $199 at Montgomery Ward's, but shit, she don't want that, she wants at least a carat solitaire. Finally I said, if you're marrying me, you'll have to settle for any damn ring I choose. No more trips to Juarez, Ada, you're a damn alcoholic and I'm not having my baby coming out deformed because his mother is a lush. I'll get the fucking ring. Just leave me alone. Just be there at the damn church in two weeks."

"There's no hope for you, Hector."

"For me? For her! Why does she want a ring that will cost me two months' pay? Isn't it enough I told her I'd marry her? I didn't have to, you know."

"Why are you getting married, Hector?"

"You know. Ada's pregnant."

"That's no reason to get married."

"Says who? I'm doing right by her."

"But you don't love her!"

"Says who?"

"I do. Who would want to marry someone like you, anyway? You're just like Luardo."

"Shut up, Soveida. I'm nothing like him. And if you say that again, I don't want you at the wedding."

"I don't know why I bother talking to you."

"That's just what I was thinking."

"Why are you doing this?"

"You *know* why. She's pregnant, okay? With my baby, okay? Mine!"

"If you can't give Ada peace, then don't marry her, Hector. She's had enough hard times in her life. She's got no one except you. If you can't be there for her all the way, I mean it, Hector, don't get married! And whatever you do, leave La Virgie alone!"

"Shit, Soveida, you finished? How about selling me the set of rings Veryl gave you? You won't ever be using them again, will you?"

"Go to hell, Hector!"

"Sis! I do love to see you get all worked up. For your information, I already am in hell. This is what this wedding is turning out to be, one long, endless, fucking hell!"

Most weddings are a nightmare. The two of mine were. The night before I married Ivan, I was literally sick to my stomach. I didn't know if I was going to make it the next day or not. Unfortunately, I did. Both Mamá Lupita and Dolores were driving me crazy with their last-minute questions. The same thing I was now doing to Hector.

I was ill during the ceremony. Too hot in there. Too many people in the church. A strange reception, too many people kissing me on the cheek, some on the mouth, saying how happy they were for me. Ivan and I danced all night. He took my hand and led me to the center of the dance floor. A love song, "Malagueña Salerosa," words full of desire, was playing.

Ada clings to Hector like I clung to Ivan. He knows that. And he's handsome, as Luardo was at his age, with the same look of cruelty I see in photos of Papá Profe. The upturned lip, the eyes burning like coals in the darkness. The scent of earth after the rain. Lilies that rise up, potent with perfume.

You have the face of an angel.

And you've been fucked.

You who never want to become Nada.

THE BOOK OF SERVICE

CHAPTER 11

Order

The last shall be first and the first shall be last. Except when serving food. The first are always first and the last are always last. The ability to discern order requires more than normal eyesight, and intuition. It requires luck.

The order of waitressing is a holy one.

A waitress's nerves are in a state of constant attention. Attention to detail, no matter how slight: a cough, a shifting of bodies, a silence. An attention without words.

The last shall be first and the first shall be last. Except when serving food.

52

Pito's Will

"I, Agapito Leal, leave everything to God. That's the way I want it to be, Mr. Larragoite."

Pito and I were Larry's last holdouts. Everyone else had handed in their wills.

"How can you leave everything to God, Pito?" Larry asked. "God isn't a person. I mean, he's a person, but he's not human. He's dead, I mean, he's not dead, he's alive, well, in a manner of speaking, he's alive. You can't leave everything to God, Pito, and that's all there is to it. Take this seriously, would you? We're talking about leaving your *things*—touch-and-feel *things*—to *someone*, a person, a human being, someone who breathes, is alive."

Larry turned to me. "Soveida, you talk to him, he's not listening to me. Now, let me explain it to you again, Pito. Leave that lettuce alone, there's enough lettuce there to feed the entire town. Don't be chopping that. Look at me. You need a will. A will is a piece of paper that says that you know what you are doing with your life. After you die, it lets people know what you want done with your things. Your Jaguar, for example."

"I don't have a Jaguar, Mr. Larragoite. I can't have no pets in my apartment."

"It's a joke, Pito. Your bike, then. You have a bike, okay? A will gives someone—a person you want—the right to have your bike when you die. Got me so far? That person doesn't have to give the bike to the government. Or someone like Mr. Largalengua, old Long Tongue, the state senator."

"Shoot, Mr. Larragoite, it's an old bike. He can have it if he wants."

"What's he want a rusty, old, scrapped-up bike for, Pito? He's the state senator, he's got a Cadillac."

"Maybe he needs the exercise."

"Let's get back to the point of all this. You need a will and you need someone to leave your things to. Put those onions away. I'm talking to you, Pito. In your will you'll write down who gets the bike."

"I thought Largalengua got the bike."

"No, Pito, he didn't get the bike! It was just an example. Soveida! Come back here. Talk to Pito. Explain to him, would you? Stop setting the table and tell him why he needs a goddamn will. I want you to write out this will and have it to me after lunch, Pito. What kind of a restaurant is this, anyway? No sense of priorities. People eating and farting—excuse me, Petra, I didn't know you were there—carrying on, never bother time, health, property. Doesn't anybody care? Soveida, you and Pito are the only ones who haven't given me your wills. You gave me yours, Petra. I got it in the safe. Your daughter helped you, huh? Don't you think you shoulda left something to Junior, all of it going to Alicia like that? I know she helped you with the will. Okay, okay. What is it, Peetie? We need napkins? Soveida! Check the back for napkins. Look at me, Pito. Leave that Longhorn cheese alone. Someone else can grate it. I want you to know how important it is to have a will while you're alive. Because when you're dead, not having a will is going to mean hell on earth for your family. The world can't run that way: lack of concern, total disregard for what's happening, everybody looking the other way. What would happen if I died and there was no will, Pito? I'm not saying I'm going to die. Today I feel just fine. But what if I *did* die, suddenly. What then?"

"Largalengua."

"You got it! Me working so hard, and Mom before me, not to mention you guys, sorry, Petra, and Bonnie, don't forget her, and our kids, if we had any kids, don't forget them. No will equals no future. No future equals no will. You think I'm doing this for me? I got enough to worry about without thinking about you, your wills. Hey, I care. I was watching this TV program. I saw what happened to this old lady who got moved to a nursing home because her husband forgot to put her and their cat in the will. How would you like to be sent up to the Del Valle Nursing Home, Pito, just because your husband forgot to provide for you in his will?"

"I'm not married, Mr. Larragoite."

"How about the wealthy young woman who died leaving her four-year-old girl with nothing? Her kid got sent to the State Home. It didn't matter that her grandfather had left an inheritance. The stories go on and on. So, who gets the money, the cats? Pito? Who? Are you listening to me?"

"Largalengua."

"That's it, Pito. *Now*, do you see? So you just tell Soveida what you want. She'll write it all down for you. Hell, she can go into my office and type the damn thing. I mean, it's not a damn thing. Sorry, Petra. That's just a figure of speech. It's important, very important. Damn! I'm not just doing this for my health. So, what do you say, Pito? Who's going to be your beneficiary?"

"What's that, Mr. Larragoite?"

"The person who gets the cat."

"I don't have a cat, Mr. Larragoite."

"Your dog, then, your TV set, your electric blanket, your radio, hell, I don't know, your things."

"I don't have none of those, Mr. Larragoite."

"You know what I mean. Who gets your things? Clothes, furniture, papers, things like that."

"I don't get the paper."

"Not that kind of paper."

"I don't write so good."

"So, no papers. What about clothes?"

"Goodwill."

"What?"

"Goodwill gave them to me and Goodwill can take them back."

"Okay, Soveida, write that down. Soveida! Where is she? Okay, I'll write it down. Clothes: Goodwill. Papers: forget that. Furniture?"

"Goodwill."

"Okay, furniture: Goodwill. Got any photos, paintings, decorative items?"

"What?"

"Frou-frous. Things on the walls, things to look at. Junk, you got any stuff like an old pocket knife, shoes, utensils?"

"My old frying pan?"

"Goodwill?"

"Yeah."

"What about your mom, Pito? She still living?"

"Yeah. She's crazy in the head. She doesn't want my stuff."

"How about your dad?"

"He died when I was little. He's the one named me Pito. I was born during the cotton gin's pito, the eleven o'clock whistle."

"Any brothers or sisters?"

"I got one brother, Freddie, but he doesn't like me."

"You can leave things to people you don't like. They don't have to live in Agua Oscura, either. Give Freddie your old smelly socks!"

"Freddie's in a wheelchair on account of his motorcycle accident. Someone has to clean him. He hates that. He says he can't feel his pee no more. He's always drunk."

"Any other family?"

"My sister, Carmen, lives in Hachita, New Mexico. She's got her kids, and Willie, her husband. He likes to drink and she likes to eat. She works at the school cafeteria."

"Now we're getting somewhere. Okay, we'll divide up your things. Your mom, Freddie, and Carmen. Look, it's almost time to open. You can list your things, okay? Just think about it when you're back here cooking. Freddie, socks. Mom, whatever. Carmen, bike."

"She's too fat."

"Leave a blank space and go on."

"I don't know."

"Who, then? No, don't say it, Pito."

"God?"

"No, I am not going to accept that. Look, I'm giving each of you a fifty-dollar bonus to write, sign, and hand in these wills to me. Fifty dollars is worth leaving Carmen your bike, isn't it? She's got kids?"

"Oh, yeah, I forgot."

"I am not doing this for myself, Pito. I got my own family, my own priorities, and my own death. Hell, we each got our own deaths. Now, that's something nobody can take away from us. We do have a choice about all those things we cared for, worked for, sweated for. Look at yourself, Pito. You've been here since I was a kid, twenty years. How many more tacos you got coming? How many more combination plates? How many more T-bones? What happens to all the enchiladas you rolled? You going to let someone else roll them, and ladle the chile and fry those sopaipillas, their hands up to here with grease? What does it matter?"

"I don't know, Mr. Larragoite."

"Think about it, Pito. It's real important."

"Yes, sir, Mr. Larragoite."

"Jot things down."

"Yes, Mr. Larragoite."

"Donate your organs, Pito. Save a life! What happens when that little girl needs a cornea or that old man needs a pancreas? This little paper is going to make it all worth something."

"Yes, Mr. Larragoite."

"How about the Church, you want to leave them anything?"

"Nah."

"That's what I say. They got enough money. Now, I'll expect that paper in my office at checkout time, Pito. You give me the will, I'll add fifty dollars to your next paycheck. It's my way of saying thank you for that liver and thank you for that lung and thank you for that cat. Now get to work, Pito. It's time to open."

Later Pito and I went over his will again.

"I, Agapito 'Pito' Leal, leave everything to God, including my good frying pan at home."

"That's the one my grandma gave me, Soveida."

"All my pots and pans. My clothes and aprons, shoes and socks. My key chain and my bed and my chair and table. The sweater Petra made me last Christmas. And all the things I never used that everybody gave me for my birthday, all the Life Savers and handkerchiefs and the rusty copper ashtray. The bird's nest I found in the grass near the park. The things in my top drawer: string and rubber bands and paper clips. My work outfit."

"Mr. Larragoite can keep the outfit, Soveida. It belongs to El Farol. The next cook can wear it, only he better clean it. It smells like red chile and meat."

"You can't get rid of the meat smell, Pito, I've tried. Just leave it to El Farol, they can figure out what to do with the uniform, okay? I'll keep on reading.

"I, Agapito Leal . . ."

"Remember when I was real sick with pneumonia, Soveida, and you brought me food? You stayed with me that night? That's when I was the closest ever to dying. I knew what it was like to be old, like my mom, and sick, like Freddie. I was everybody I ever knew and other people I didn't know as well. I was old ladies and old men and babies. I was my dad with that hole in his throat where the cancer said hello."

"I've been that sick, too, Pito. When you're sick like that, things around you don't mean anything. They're just things."

"You called the priest, Soveida, and he prayed over me and put oil on my forehead and on my hands. After that, I felt a small little fire, a light in my heart, like a burning candle that was lit. That's why I want to leave everything to God. Okay, read me that part again."

"I, Agapito Leal, leave everything to God."

"Oh, I forgot, Soveida. I want you to have the picture I made of myself when I was in bed."

"Your retablo?"

"It's a picture of the miracle when God made me better. I want you to have it. Everything else I leave to God."

"Is that all, Pito?"

"Yes, Soveida."

"Okay, here's the last part then."

I, Agapito Leal, leave everything to God.
Signed:
Agapito "Pito" Leal
Day Cook. El Farol
Agua Oscura, New Mexico

"Add 'For forever,' Soveida."

"For forever?"

"Yeah. For forever. I like that. Okay, now read it to me again."

Signed:
Agapito "Pito" Leal
Day Cook. El Farol
Agua Oscura, New Mexico
For forever.

THE BOOK OF SERVICE

CHAPTER THIRTEEN

Meditations on Hair

"Surprising how much hair you find on plates."
—Preddie Pacheco, dishwasher

"No waitress should ever have pens or pencils stuck in her hair. It looks bad."
—Pancha Portales, night waitress

"A waitress should have her own natural god-given hair, from the moment she's born until the day she dies. Have you ever seen someone who dyes their hair day after day week after week year after year forty years down the road? A few pelitos, medio pintaditos, medio secitos, which means a root line from here to Albuquerque with a scalp as smooth as a white plucked chicken's butt. A waitress, she's a professional woman. She should never dye her hair. It looks cheap."
—Fermín Fernández, night waiter

"Hair? I don't care about hair as long as it's where it's supposed to belong. Under a hairnet. Department of Inspection Regulations."
—Larry Larragoite, manager

"I was a strawberry-blonde when I was a baby, but about age ten it started turning goose-brown. Stayed that way on into my teens. Larry knows me as a strawberry-blonde, my friends too, and my customers. What do I want to startle them for? In my mind I'm strawberry blonde."
—Bonnie McNuff Larragoite

"P.S. Soveida, I don't know why you want to write this book about waitressing anyway, but I like the idea. As I was about to say, there's a few people around here who could do 'something' about their hair. Petra Montes, for one. It looks like a blender ran amok in there. I personally think she should retire. I say, it's not only the hair, it's what's under the hair. I don't have to tell you, Soveida, she can't add worth a damn. You're the one who has to bear the brunt of her ignorance. That's all it is, plain and simple ignorance. Hair, that's the least of it! I swear, but New Mexico is backward in at least four ways, one of them being old-lady hairstyles, another being bad home-dye jobs, another being the misplaced idea that you have to keep on employing an old waitress who doesn't even comb her hair and can't add worth shit. Four? Give me a minute."

—Bonnie McNuff, assistant manager, occasional fill-in waitress

"Hair? I don't know."

—Pito Leal, day cook

"When I first started here, I didn't know what hair meant. Well, it meant I had to cut my hair. It wasn't that long, but it looked good. Now I look like a freak."

—Pato Portales, night busboy

"I feather my hair up with the hair dryer and then spray and tease it, you know, the way everyone wears it, except mine is higher than anybody else's. Hairnets are for old ladies, they flatten your hair, after you've spent all that time getting it fluffy."

—Sandra de la Cruz, day and night bus girl

"¿Hair, qué hair?"

—Chuy Barales, custodian

"There's no way I'm ever going to cut my hair. It took me too damn long to get this ponytail. My girlfriend likes it this way and so do I. If it's a matter of the hair or the job, you know what it's fucking going to be."

—Peetie Townsend, night busboy

"I've always tried to be neat and clean. My dead husband, may he rest in peace, Leopoldo, always told me, Pancha, one thing I'll say for you, *mujer*, is that you are neat and clean. Also, you have very nice legs. Nowadays, it's drugs and sloppiness. The way people go to town, in running shorts or jogging pants, *me mortifico*, I mean, what's the world coming to? Old ladies at the mall in tennis shoes, women in stretch pants that have done all the stretching that can be done around their *bolas* and *lonjas*, and those tank tops, *con las chichis sueltas*. People can say what they want about me, they probably have, Soveida, but one thing they can't say is, Pancha Portales wasn't ever not neat and clean. I tell you, Soveida, it doesn't look good to have pens stuck in your hair the way you sometimes have them. I know you talked to me already, but I still had some things to say."

  —Pancha Portales, *night waitress*

"I grew up with grease. Brylcreem, Wildroot, you know. The fifties. Elvis. The Big Bopper. I still comb it back with water, then grease it down. Hair stays neat that way. As far as women go, it doesn't matter to me as long as it's out of the way and out of the face. We're too busy around here for *greñudas*."

  —Joe Fierro, *night bartender*

"The gypsy look, that's what I like. I want my women wild, hot, and with lots of hair all jungled out like Ursula Andress in She."

  —Jimmy Lucero, *night bartender*

"What do you want to know for? Is my hair okay?"

  —Lucille LaMont, *night hostess*

"I like a man with a smooth chest. Oh, that kinda hair! Hair has nothing to do with it. A bald woman can still make good enchiladas. Huevos rancheros red, side of beans and rice. Whose order is this, anyway?"

  —Eloisa Ortiz, *weekend cook*

"So what you doing, writing a book or what? Hey, Soveida, can you lend me a ten till Tuesday? No sweat."

  —Lavel Windle, *night cook*

53

Grandmothers, Mothers, Daughters

I. Lupita

Mamá Lupita couldn't sleep. It was a rainy, impenetrably gray, slightly chilled night, como un ojo de hormiga. Like the dark eye of an ant, was how Oralia had described it. The heat was off, and Mamá's restlessness grew worse. She didn't dare turn up the floor furnaces, her gas bill was already too high. On this sullen night thick with memories, she felt crowded by spirits, haunted by the souls of her mother, Eduvijes Castillo, and her sisters, Esperanza, Soledad, and Anacita.

Mamá sat on her bed. She let down her long black hair and allowed it to breathe as it fanned her small shoulders. Wisps of white hair around her forehead circled her face like a halo. She wore a long white nightgown, sewn by Oralia from a hundred percent cotton and trimmed in antique lace that had belonged to her mother.

On her feet were floppy lamb's wool slippers, Soveida's gift to her the previous Christmas. At first Lupita had not liked the "ugly man's shoes." But one cold night she found the slippers in a dark corner of her closet, and slowly felt herself becoming attached to them, particularly on those long nights in the Blue House when Oralia had turned the heater down to 60 degrees. Now she wore them all the time in the early-morning hours when Oralia pretended to sleep for her sake.

All sorts of tactile memories came to Lupita: she felt her fingers gently brushing her mother Eduvije's thin gray hair, gossamer threads that were barely contained in the short braid that was bound and then tied, up on her mother's head. The old woman had little hair left, but she was vain enough to want it combed a certain way.

"Ay, and I used to have such long thick hair, Lupita. What happened to all of it?"

"Sit still, Mamá, don't move."

"There's little enough to gather up."

"Oh, there's enough for your trenzita, Mamá."

"That's what it is, a little braid, like a goat's whiskers, fine and very naughty. May God spare you the loss of your finest gifts—your hair and your teeth. Look at me, I have neither left. Childbearing and age have destroyed what little grace I had. Our beauty leaves us, Lupita. Someday you, too, will have hair like the cottony balls from the álamo trees."

"Ay, viejita, sit still! Let me finish up."

Mamá got up from her bed and walked around the cold room.

"Too many memories. Everything happened so long ago. And yet it seems just yesterday when Mamá told me that I, too, would grow old. Mamá was wrong in one thing. My hair isn't like hers at all, and my sisters aged a different way as well. Esperanza became fat, Soledad grew exceedingly thin and died a cadaver, unable to eat anything the last month of her life—even water made her choke. Anacita developed a skin rash and was covered from the shoulders down with scales, like a bright pink fish.

"Before our bodies' betrayal, we combed each other's long, proud hair. Esperanza's was the thickest, Soledad's had the most beautiful luster, and Anacita's was the curliest. Mine was by far the most common. And now I am the only one who has any hair left. They say hair still grows in the grave. My sisters may well have their hair and toenails, but they have little else."

Running her freezing hands over her tangled hair, Mamá absently picked up the comb that was a gift from her father, Bonifacio Castillo de Gonzales.

"It's made out of some sort of shell dyed red, a vain color for an old lady's bedroom!

"Papá told me of a dream he'd had before my birth. He was trapped in a large house. He ran from corridor to corridor, only to have every door close on him. Frantically, he lunged for one last door, barely prying it open. When he did, he fell down a pathway. It was made of braided straw that circled downward farther than he could see. On the sides of the narrow walkway were small niches that held all sorts of handicrafts: leather bags, belts, jewelry, copper pots, weavings, bright-colored handmade clothing. Papá was enthralled by the beauty of the goods. Little windows faced inward to the building's center and from time to time young women peered out of their stalls. Papá became distracted and wanted to stop and select something for his family. Suddenly the straw floor collapsed. He clung to the side, then tumbled down the crumbling passageway of grass and straw and reed. Down he went, barely holding on, sidestepping one crumbling portion and then another. At one juncture, as he was frozen in space, he stopped to admire a small comb-and-brush set with glass insets. A young woman came out from a door on the side and fixed one of the shards of glass that was loose. He put the brush-and-comb set in his pocket. As he did, he suddenly reached the ground. There, to his right, was a baby in its crib, sheltered from the wind in one of the small niches. He took the soft brush and ran it gently through the baby's hair. That child was me, his new daughter, Lupita.

"In memory of that dream, I still have the red comb-and-brush set Papá found one day while shopping at Hiram Jones's Dry Goods.

" 'It isn't as lovely as the set I gave you in my dream, Lupita, but it will do. May this gift remind you of my love.' "

"Poor papá! He never knew luxury, but worked hard every day of his life. Each night I used to soak his tired feet in salted water, then dry them off and then rub them with a little grease and wrap them in woolen socks.

"Why is it that I remember Papá's feet this drizzly night when I was thinking of women's hair? Men's feet and eyes and teeth always get in the way when I want to remember women.

"I remember rubbing cream on Soveida when she was a baby. She smelled sweet as babies smell, her sweaty hand in mine. But she grew up too fast. After she was four years old, we never had enough time together, except for those early-morning walks to and from Mass. I was grateful for this time with her. I crossed her warm forehead with the cool Holy Water. When she kissed me, her small, humid breath was a dear, persistent reminder of her innocence and purity.

"Mara's kisses to me were always dry and without love. My son, Luardo, always kisses me without spirit. Dolores kisses me dutifully and with respect. The only person who ever kisses me with any affection is Oralia. She is a little mouse woman and she kisses me with tender little mouse kisses. They are quick kisses on the cheek or long, grateful kisses to my hand. They are kisses that are kisses. I want soft kisses in my old age. I don't want kisses like my husband Profe's hard purple kisses—kisses like a slap.

" 'I know you like it little, woman, but you are my wife. You always will be . . . I don't want to hurt you, woman, but you make me,' he used to say after he'd pushed me around, used me up, and then apologized to me for *his needs.*

" 'What about the other woman? Is she your wife, too?'

" 'Damn you, whore!'

" 'Me, a whore! Look to your puta, Profetario!'

" 'I'm your husband!'

" 'In name only. Now leave me alone, I have work to do.'

" 'Come here, cabrona!'

" 'Let me go, Profe. Haven't you had enough already? Why must you drink so much? I thought you were so happy with your puta.'

" 'Damn you, woman, and damn this life of mine for having been born to Manuel Dosamantes. Damn that pinche puta Ismindalia for stealing my inheritance. Damn this earth, its dark water. And damn these hands for being afraid to take my own cursed life!'

"Oh, how he disgusted me!

"Why is it that I always come back to men's eyes or feet or hands? I want to think about women tonight. My mother's brown eyes soft with cataracts. My mother's hand on my knee, comforting me somehow. My mother's embrace—thick, rooted, her large bosom surrounding and sealing me in. Instead, I think of men. Men! No wonder the night is so long! Oralia should at least get up and join me for a cup of yerbabuena. Maybe then the welts will go down."

II. Dolly

"I don't understand how Soveida can do this, Mamá. She's so nice to her friends, she talks to them so sweetly, and to me she's so ugly."

"Ay, Dolores! Once one of my children threatened to kill me, I forget who it was. Did I listen? No, I just hit them with the broom and told them to get away from me. If you had done that to Soveida, you wouldn't have this problem now. She was indulged."

"She hates me. She loved me once. She stroked my face and called me her Dolo. She couldn't say Dolores."

"That's where you went wrong, Dolores. No mother should tolerate a child calling her by her first name. Now you're paying for your mistakes."

"She calls me Dolly now. I like the name Dolly."

"Dolly? What kind of a name is Dolly, Dolores Dosamantes? You tell me! What are you, a baby Dolly with furry eyelashes who cries real tears and wets her pants? What are you, a butterfly flitting around the room? You're sixty years old! And now you're wearing your hair loose, and in curls, hair that used to be gray. You go around with your legs uncovered, in sandalias. You wear short sleeves or no sleeves. What would your mother, Doña Trancha, say? It all began with the new name. And with the divorce. I should never have lived to see you take up with another man! To see you engaged, ay, no aguanto el dolor, to an americano. ¡Diosito! An engineer from Fort Bliss. Un desconocido. ¡No es posible! Where does he come from? Do you even know that? He's calvo. Bald, with no hope for reprieve. The color of an earthworm. I've lived too long to see my son's wife, yes, his wife, for in the eyes of God there is no divorce, engaged to a retired barbón, fello y calvo. All the hair that should be on his head is on his arms and chest. I have to tell you, it's not a good sign for the other body parts. But let's not even think about that. You'll have to deal with *that* soon enough. Praise God, I don't! May I never live to see the day you marry that bleached salute with his lower body still at attention. I don't know what you see in him. Reldon Claughbaugh! His name's like a family of insects or a seafood dish at Marisco's restaurant. ¡Ay, mi Dios! I never thought I'd live to see the day you changed your name, María Dolores Dosamantes! Such a pretty name—only to become Dolly Claughbaugh. What got into you? Soveida, say something to your mamá!"

"Dolores, Mamá's right. Are you sure this is what you want? I mean, are you sure Reldon's the one?"

"Neither of you understand. You hate me and you don't want me to be happy. But I'm happy. For the first time in my life, I'm happy! I *love* Reldon. Now leave me alone."

"Dios te salve, María, Llena eres de gracia . . ."

"Stop praying, Mamá! I'm getting married!"

III. Soveida

Dolores has always felt sorry for herself. When I was growing up, I hated her need, her pain. Now that she's happy, neither Mamá Lupita nor I recognize her. I want to wish her happiness. The same thing I want for myself.

As a child I spent so much time with her. I was an only child for many years before Hector was born. I loved to watch her dress and put on her makeup. Dolores loved to dress nicely and was proud of the way she looked. She had a lovely figure, but was modest in her taste.

I would curl her hair, wetting the ends with water from a glass I'd carried to her bureau. She sat in front of the mirror, waiting for me to attend to her. I lifted sections of her hair straight up toward the ceiling and then brought them down as I curled them around turquoise rollers. Her hair was short, bouncy, it held a curl.

I unknotted her neck when she got yet another migraine. I popped her toes when they were tight, and her knuckles whenever she wanted. I was her chiropractor, jolting, knocking, rubbing, and pushing her into place. I cleaned Dolores's rings with a straight pin or safety pin, sliding out the soft gray-brown food matter.

She had many errands for me to do and I was happy to do them. My first role of server was to my mother and her needs. Dolores was my training for service. She taught me first to ease her woman's aches, and only then tend to my own flesh. I ran her countless errands gratefully and gladly. It was only when I began to work at El Farol that I didn't have time for her continual needs anymore.

"You promised to give me a back rub, Soveida!"

"I'm tired, Dolores!"

"My toes need popping. The big toe on my right foot is killing me. Ay, my calambres! Quick, I have a cramp! Hit my leg, hit it!"

After years of kneading, punching, popping, hitting, rubbing, and rolling her in place, I was tired of it all. And yet now I would like to sit down with Dolly and roll her hair the way I used to. She used to thank me so profusely:

"Thank you, sweetheart! It looks very nice, Soveida! I mean it."

I would love to go to Mass with Mamá Lupita, listen to her small reedy voice swell to the strains of the song "Bendito":

"Bendito, bendito, bendito sea Dios . . . Los ángeles les cantan . . . Y alaban a Dios . . . Los ángeles les cantan . . . Y alaban a Dios . . ."

Grandmothers. Mothers. Daughters. All of us with a chain of absent men. Men who might have touched us. Instead, we eased each other's discomfort as best we could, as much as we were able at the time.

We heard the echoes of voices in the early hours. It's hard to say whose voices they were. It could have been the voice of Doña Trancha, a solitary old woman, with loneliness as her only friend. Or maybe it was the voice of Mamá Lupita, a lonely old woman with a sole friend, Oralia, who never slept. It might have been the voice of Dolores, who screeched to me, her only daughter, all those times when I wasn't tending to her toes, her back, or rings, or curls:

"You can be nice to your friends, but not to me. *To me.*"

Doña Trancha. Mamá Lupita. Dolores Dosamantes. Women losing their grasp. Afraid of the daughters and granddaughters they no longer know.

There, the calambre's subsided . . .

The welts have gone down . . .

Thank you, thank you, now let's go to bed . . .

If I ever have a child, I will name her Milagro. She won't be like the women I always knew: lonely, clinging, afraid. She'll be someone new. Someone to behold. Milagro. In a room crowded with other women, she will always be herself. Miracle. Loving the others. Blessing them. Wishing them peace. Milagro. Miracle.

54

El Remolino

"M'ijo, look, here's Soveida," Mamá prompted. "Soveida, just look at your daddy, how good he looks!"

I kissed Luardo on the forehead, patted his hand.

"How are you, Luardo?"

"Call him Daddy, m'ija. He's your daddy. Now I'll go see about dinner. Oralia! Tere!"

What would Mamá do if she couldn't yell for someone? I thought.

Luardo lay in his rent-a-bed. Only the best bed for him, with a button on the railing, instead of a dangling control panel. Sometimes Luardo woke up and didn't remember that he couldn't walk or that he was sick. Early on, he tried to get out of bed, but not now. He was feeble, wasted. His muscle tone had disappeared. His lips and skin were always dry, a dryness Oralia tried to remedy with her many salves. His eyes were closed. No longer the robust, handsome, light-skinned man with the full head of still-dark hair, the man so many women had loved, fought over, cried about, and cursed, Luardo was simply a man in a rented bed, trying to breathe, using all his willpower to go on.

He'd had a second stroke, though he was doing better. Or so we wanted to believe. He had gone to Hector's wedding. Argued and carried on and even got drunk. Now he couldn't talk. But suddenly he opened his eyes and tried to say something to me.

The I.V. went off. I pressed the button that regulated the flow of solution, as I had so many other times these past few weeks. His bed was set up in Mamá's dining room—closer to the heart of the house —near the kitchen, where Oralia mixed up her fomentations, her special teas and compresses. It was also near Mamá's room. When

Mamá was nervous or afraid, she ate, hovering near Oralia and her kitchen with its ordered universe.

The smell of braised flesh touching scalding water filled the air. Oralia was making a caldo from sirloin tips. She would throw out the meat and skim the broth, and then later bring it to Luardo to sip. On the stove there was a pot of yerbabuena tea that was always ready to drink. The nearby floor furnace held a pot of water in which herbs had been placed, more of Oralia's remedies, these to cleanse the air of impurities. She was a woman who knew when to attend to food, the exact moment meat should be turned, the gas lowered, the bread removed from the oven, the herbs brought in from the sun. She had told me that Luardo was very ill. "Tengo miedo," she said, her soft gray eyes watering. "He was a strong man once, but no longer. Something snapped. Like María Mejía's back. Some people are that way, especially men. You look at them and see victory, what others thought was a happy, successful life. But their hearts are like the swirling wind, without a place to rest. Como el dicho: Quien siembra vientos recoge tempestades. Who sows the wind reaps the whirlwind."

The medicines were on a table near the bed. But they were of no use. Luardo was dying. His hands were waxy, always cold, and they gripped the white sheets like claws. What little body hair he had left was wiry, dark, and defiant, like small quills. His nails had recently been cleaned and cut by Mamá, who had moved quietly and patiently from one side of the bed to the other, working one finger and then another, first with a large nail clipper, and then an old metal file that had belonged to her for over fifty years.

"The dying smell," Mamá said. "But each one smells different."

Luardo smelled of after-shave and Lysol and hand cream and fear.

The I.V. went off again. The shrill noise interrupted both prayer and reverie.

"What an ordeal," Luardo whispered to me one afternoon when he still could speak.

And then he sank into a wordless coma for several days, his organs without words to express their pain. The many pill bottles were eventually moved to make room for the essentials: clean rags, warm water.

Mamá came in to stay with him, saying interminable decades from that one dark soft rosary she'd had so many years, the one she kept in a handkerchief pinned to her underclothes. Oralia, too, came in to pray, but she had no rosary, she simply counted on her arthritic fingers, a multitude of prayers from memory: The Fifth Sorrowful Mystery. The Third Glorious Mystery. The Apostles' Creed. The Memorare. The Acts of Faith, Hope, Love.

"I knew that you and I would outlive your father," Mamá said. "Before he got ill, I knew he was in a bad way. I found him crying. I held him without saying anything, led him to his bed, and stroked his head, because that's what he needed then. He was terrified. He had seen el Angel de la Muerte, and he would never be the same. When a man's spirit has drowned in his chest, almost nothing can bring it back to life. Your father wasn't a man who ever had faith. I knew we women would once again be alone. The men in this family are weak. It started with your grandfather Profe and continued with Luardo and then Hector. Who knows what Hector's sons will be like."

Luardo's eyes opened a little, and I realized he saw me. I got close to his bed and took his hand, then squeezed it gently. Through half-closed eyes, he moved his head a little, side to side, and then feebly squeezed back.

Luardo was a multitude of men to me. All troubled. Sick. Without boundaries. Sometimes I recalled the inappropriate things Luardo had done to me: the penny arcades he'd subjected me to, the trips to Juárez to see strippers, the topless nightclub he once took Mara and me to when we were teenagers. I remembered him hurting Mara, and then me. I remembered all his women, the secretaries, the clients, the cleaning women, the neighbors, all the women who loved him, wanted to love him, Dolores and Mamá waiting up nights for him to come home, their endless tears, their humiliation, and their shame.

One time Luardo took Hector and me to a little carnival. He bought us tickets for the Ferris wheel. Hector and I clung to each other fiercely. We were so afraid we started to say the rosary. Finally we relaxed and began to enjoy the circling ride high above Agua Oscura.

"Look, there's Dad," Hector yelled. "He's so small."

"Where?" I yelled back excitedly.

"There," Hector said, "there."

"Where is he, Hector?"

"He was there. He was just there, I swear, Soveida."

I couldn't see Luardo, not then or later when we feared that he'd left us. We yelled to the Ferris wheel operator to get us down.

Only afterwards did we realize Luardo had paid not only for that first ride but for another two. He thought we would enjoy it.

We thought he had forgotten us.

But no one had forgotten him. Oralia rubbed his dry feet with Vicks, Mamá massaged his once dark hair, greasing it down with Jergens lotion until he was soft and oily like a newborn kitten, and Dolores came in evenings to read to him from the Psalms, and then held his hand, the way old lovers do, their fingers lazily laced together.

I had wanted to say so many things to Luardo, to tell him that I knew he loved me, as he knew I had loved him; that I never agreed with him, the way he lived his life; that I never wanted to be like him. Sin juicio.

And yet he was my father. The only one I'd ever have. The only one I'd ever known. He taught me what love was through his love-lessness, and what loyalty was, and yes, trust, through his lack of both. Perhaps we learn the most valuable lessons from those we've ceased to understand.

Luardo couldn't talk, so others had to talk for him. Mamá. Dolores. Oralia. What words he had for me, I never heard.

55

Lupita's Ruth

It wasn't long after Luardo's death that Mamá became very ill and took to her bed. She claimed she no longer wanted to live.

"Today I told my liver I was tired. And my lungs. Yesterday I spoke to my heart, and my brains. Before that, my bones and muscles. Last week I had a little chat with my sex. Tomorrow I'll consult with the rest of my body. Each organ separately, because they deserve that respect. Then all together, because they should know at the same time. Es propio, it's only proper.

"Maybe then my body will listen to me and understand. Once and for all: I'm tired. Toda la mujer duele. Every pore, every tuck and fold, every arruga, every inch of wrinkled skin, every hair on my head, every vein hurts. I'm an old woman, Soveida. I'm ready to die. Please accept this. And yet I don't want to die so fast I can't say goodbye to everyone the way I want. That's why I took to my bed last Friday, to work out what needs to be worked out. Two weeks' time should be enough.

"Already I feel my lungs slowing down. That's good. My sex has been numb for years, so there shouldn't be any problem there. The liver, the pancreas, they're beginning to listen. The stomach has obeyed. The brain and heart have just gotten the news. My eyes are growing weaker by the day, and my sense of taste is gone. I could just as well be eating caca as a link sausage. My hearing is still pretty good, it should go last, just before my sense of smell. I want to hear the birds outside my room, and smell your mamá's roses from my bed. Other than that, all the major organs are beginning to loosen up and float around in some kind of stew, my last posole.

"So don't get upset if I seem far away or distant, Soveida. It's just that I'm talking to God—or to myself.

"I want you to go to la Casa Azul and get my metal chest. The one under my bed. Oralia knows where the key is. Bring the chest to me and we'll go through my lists. I want to make things very clear. I want you to have the house and most of the furniture. I have some things for Dolores, and a few things for Hector. Very few. Bring me the lists tomorrow and we'll sort that out. What I want to do now is just lie here and look at you, m'ija. We can talk. We have time. I want to visit with your mamá, too. And Oralia sometime when she isn't running around making me ponches and yerbabuena and all kinds of tratamientos that are making me sick. She's out in her herb garden getting me something to help my appetite. Let her bring it to me, if it makes her feel better. It's because of her good care that I'm still alive and having to work so hard at dying. My body just doesn't want to quit, but it has to, m'ija. I'm getting so old it's disgraceful. I never wanted to live past eighty, and here I am, still taking up space. Not that great human beings shouldn't take up space. We should give them all the space they deserve and then some. I'm not a great soul or one of those precious human beings I'm talking about, so my long life has truly surprised me. But I guess my God had plans for me.

"So often I wished my mother had lived to be really old. She was so precious to me. I would have spoiled her and pampered her and dressed her up in little satin chalecos when she got cold, and put little pink bows and rosebuds in her hair. But it wasn't meant to be.

"My living had to do with your daddy. I was kept alive to help him grow to become a man and raise a family. Now I have two great-grandchildren, Michael John and Juan Miguel. It breaks my heart to think about that ugly business. The children are innocent of their father's and mother's sins, remember that, Soveida. They are blameless in the sight of God. They are not responsible for their parents' bringing them into the world. Pobrecita Tere, she was a young girl and stupid. But not as stupid as your brother, Hector, for getting her pregnant. My heart goes out to Tere and la otra, Narada. She's his one and only legal wife, just as I was Profe's one and only legal wife. But where did it get us? Everything will be resolved. I really can't worry about that now. What concerns me are the ins and outs of my tripas and the slowing down of the juices and the clumping of my blood. I want to get to the point where my orín stops and my last caca comes out like a rabbit's pellet, clean and neat. May my last pedo be odorless and slightly sweet."

"Oh, Mamá."

"Yes, that's what I want. There's nothing wrong in wanting that. When people die, they smell sweet. There's a sweetness that comes from decay. My uncle Ricardo died of cancer; he was full of it, but you never would have known it, his breath was like flowers. When he stopped breathing, the room smelled of strong perfume. But that was Ricardo.

"When I die, I want to smell of nothing, to have no smell. Bury me in my shady spot over at San Pedro's in the back there near the trees, ten rows up from the Loeras, far enough away from their craziness. All of those Loera children who died weren't meant to live. They were angels sent down by God to lead the way for Trancha. I've had no one to lead me. I guess God saw some sort of invisible sign on my forehead when I was born and decided that I would have to make my way in this world alone. Now that my time is near, I want to settle my affairs, Soveida."

"Mamá, is there anyone you want me to call? Anyone you want me to ask to come and visit you?"

"I've been thinking about that. Everyone I really need to talk to is dead or already knows what I have to say to them. My grandchildren, and their parents, they know where I am. There's just one person I need to see, and that's Mara. It doesn't matter that she's a Loera and doesn't want to see *me*, I want to see *her*. Have you told her I'm sick?"

"No, Mamá. I lost touch with her. It's been so long, I'm afraid to call her."

"I know. I know."

"I let her call me when she wants."

"She's difficult. But she has her reasons. Call her and tell her I've been thinking of her. How long has it been since we've seen her here in Agua Oscura?"

"It's been over twenty-five years, Mamá."

"Ay, that long? Too long!"

"She says she's old and fat."

"It's probably true. And yet she could never be ugly. If she is ugly, her ugliness is inside. The ugliness was thrown at her, and some of it had to stick. M'ija, do you know how Mara got her name?"

"The Hindu goddess?"

"¡Que diosa ni que diosa! The only diosa I know is la Virgen de Guadalupe."

"Well, I guess I don't know."

"No, you don't. Bring me my Bible. It's on the table. Turn to Exodus. The beginning of the book. I can see you read the Bible every day. Chapter 15. It's marked with a holy card. Now read it to me."

" 'And Moses brought Israel from the Red Sea, and they went forth into the wilderness of Sur: and they marched three days through the wilderness, and found no water. And they came into Mara, and they could not drink the waters of Mara, because they were bitter: whereupon he gave a name also agreeable to the place, calling it Mara, that is, bitterness. And the people murmured against Moses, saying: What shall we drink? But he cried out to the Lord, and he showed him a tree, which when he cast into the waters, they were turned into sweetness.' I never knew the word Mara came from the Bible."

"I didn't either, for many years, until one day I was reading the Bible, looking for Psalm 45, and the book opened to Ruth, and there it was. Somehow your Tía Lina knew about the name. Now look for Mara in the index. Read it to me."

" 'Ma'ra: A Hebrew word for bitterness; the name which Noemi called herself.' Who was Noemi, Mamá?"

"Read it. Go on."

" 'Whither thou goest, I will go, and where thou lodgest, I will lodge. Thy people shall be my people, and thy God my God.' "

"I am Noemi, and your mamá is my Ruth. Now you read, while I think about Psalm 45. It's about Victory. While you're reading about Noemi and Ruth, I'll talk to my intestines and colon. I've neglected them. I feel a weakness even as we speak."

"You sound well."

"I've allowed my voice to take what energy it needs until the end. The stronger the music, the fainter the pulse."

Dolly was Lupita's Ruth. The biblical story of the old woman Noemi, who urged her widowed daughters-in-law to stay in Moab, to return to their families and to their people, while she decided to return to Bethlehem, was Mamá Lupita's story, except with a twist. All of Dolores's relatives were dead. When Luardo died, it never occurred to her to move anywhere. As far as Mamá was concerned, she wasn't going anywhere either, except heaven. And to her, heaven wasn't considered out of town.

When Mamá became ill, Oralia tried to help her as much as she could, but Luardo's death had drained her as much as it had Mamá. As a matter of fact, Oralia felt worse than Mamá. One day she started bleeding from those secret places. She was forced to wear rags, as if she were fifteen years old again and just coming into womanhood.

Much to Lupita's surprise, Dolly asked the two women to move in with her. It would just be the three of them. Lupita. Dolly. Oralia. In that descending order.

Mamá would not consider it. Not at first, anyway. Not until the time she almost burned the house down making sopaipillas and the Fire Department had to come and hose down the kitchen and the utility room. Oralia had tried to put out the blaze with her mop water, but the fire was more serious than they realized. It was Dolly who had seen the flames and called the police, and some days later she made her offer. Until then, Lupita felt herself in her full mind or, at least, half in her mind. She hadn't been the same since Luardo had died.

All her life Dolly had done as Mamá Lupita had wished. And she had done it both grudgingly and ungrudgingly. She loved her mother-in-law more than she dared admit. Now that Mamá was dying, she finally had some say. It wasn't only what she, Dolly, had wanted. It was what the doctor wanted. It was the way it had to be.

Mamá had always thought she would die in la Casa Azul. It came as a shock to her that she might not, unless she could crawl over without Dolly's knowing. At first Mamá Lupita bitterly complained about the move. What she slowly came to realize was that she was actually relieved to be away from there. Maybe if she got some distance from la Casa Azul, she could rest her mind, her heart, and find the peace that eluded her in a house full of ghosts.

Little by little she got to like the sunny room she lay in, near the tall evergreen, and the blackbirds that flew to the evergreen and rested there, and the other little gray birds that also called that tree home when the blackbirds were gone. One day she thought she saw the gray birds transform into Juan Diego's miraculous multicolored birds, singing songs no human voice had heard, songs of a better world.

It was in that room, formerly Soveida's, the sunny little white room at the back of the house, that Mamá Lupita had her visions.

"Dolores, I know how Juan Diego felt when he saw the roses in winter. Or the Blessed Guadalupe's face on his tilma."

"Sí, Mamá, just rest."

"Now's not the time for tears, Dolores. Later. My heart is now too full of joy."

"Sí, Mamá."

"Someday you'll tell people about this day."

"Sí, Mamá."

"Don't forget."

"What, Mamá?"

"Nothing. I just wanted to make sure you were listening."

"Did you tell me something, Mamá?"

"Ssst! Listen!"

"Sí, Mamá."

"There she is again. The little white bird. I call her Dulce María. Ssshhh! Dulce María is singing to me, listen."

That was how Mamá came to the other house. Now that she was there, se había compuesto, she was more or less under control. Better, in fact, than she had been at the Blue House. But she could still be as angry and bitter at God as she was immediately following Luardo's death.

"I have a few things to tell you, Lord, and you're going to have to take time to listen. My life has not been an easy one, for the seeming comfort I have today. My house was big, but it was an unhappy house. You gave me a husband who was not what I expected. Not that I know what I expected, maybe someone who didn't hit women. Let's begin there, just for starters.

"Profe was a man who believed his way the best and his penis the most sacred. He gave me five children, three of them too many, and few hours of rest, but he was my husband. I was his one and only legal wife. You allowed all the stuff with María to happen. I wish you hadn't been so lenient, but there you have it. Ni modo. I would have preferred another way, another man. The man I married was not the man I buried. I thank you for my Soveida and my A.J. and for my Teeney. Please find my M.J. a man despite her mole. Thank you for my friend, Oralia. When she comes in with my herbal tea, I will make her sit down. There are many things I want to tell her. I want to thank her for being the only one who has loved me the way I have wanted to be loved. I will miss her mouse kisses. You and I know that she was always in love with Profe. It was evident as the callouses on her hands, or the medals around her neck. She thinks I don't know. I don't want to embarrass her. I plan to give her this medal of San José that belonged to Profe. She can put it around her neck and carry him close to her heart. She's an old woman, older than me, and still she has the pure heart of a young girl. You have been good to me in only this. You who took away so much, you who gave me a husband who hit me and then cried out, 'I didn't want to hit you, woman, remember that. You made me do it.' You gave me children when I didn't want the burden of a man's heaviness. You could have at least allowed me to become a nun, but instead you made me a woman. I could take the infidelities, the son from that woman. It is the beatings I could not sustain. Today my inventory has been a painful one. Thank you for these weeks of grace, and for allowing me to work through my forgiving. I forgive myself for not accepting Dolores as she was and is. She is dear to me, a good woman, despite her new name. You know if I had been stronger I would have left Profe, the way she left Luardo. Help me to accept el pelón Sean Connery. Reldon's a good man even if he is a gringo. He loves Dolores. He's good to me and respectful, the way any son should be, as mine never were. Remind me to tell Dolores all these things. She needs to know. Remind me to thank her and to ask her forgiveness for all those years when I never liked her or the Loeras, especially Mara.

"I pray Mara returns to see me before I die, and that when she comes to Agua Oscura her bitterness becomes sweet water.

"Remind me to ask Father Piedoso when he comes to pray over me what type of tree that was that Moses put in the bitter water. Also I want to ask him to not let Elpidia Arce lead the songs, she has a squeaky voice and it will only make me upset.

"Help me to forget that when I first met Profetario Dosamantes at his father's farm, at a dance one summer night, I fell in love with him, right there and then.

"Remind me to ask Oralia for a flyswatter and to rub my feet. I forgot to talk to them, as well as the toes. Either they're shutting down early on their own or they've simply gone to sleep. Either way, they have to stay awake a little bit longer. I'm still not so sick I can't go to the bathroom to make chee by myself. God grant me the grace of having control over my bowels until the very end. What else, Lord? Watch over my children, especially Pina. She's escandalosa and a gossip. I also think she's into the black market, selling stolen designer jeans. Thank you, Lord God of Power and Might, one thing about dying that makes me happy is that I won't have to get any more of Pina's chain letters to Saint Jude and whoever else she tries to hide her pagan beliefs behind. I'll rest peacefully in my grave just knowing the chain letters have finally stopped.

"I'll miss my A. J.'s hamburguesas and my ocean waters and my warm house shoes that Soveida gave me. Remind me to tell Soveida to bury me in the house shoes and without a tight brassière. I'll miss breathing in and out and sometimes sighing. I'll even miss la Casa Azul, and yelling across the yard to Dolores, or whoever it was that was there. I won't miss the long nights when I couldn't sleep, or the long days when I was sleepy and never allowed myself to sleep, out of guilt. May heaven be like a long beautiful nap in a room with an open window, the breeze blowing as I fall asleep. Thank you for my mother and for my youth. It was my happiest time, and Lord, if heaven is a going back, take me to the days I combed my mother's hair, my three sisters in the next room. Give me the dignity of a graceful death. Don't let me cry or drool or make smelly caca in my pants or in the bed. Shield me from my relatives who come to visit and say how good I look when I look like el demonio. I've lived a rich and full life, maybe not rich enough, but certainly full. I didn't read many books. I never went to school past the fourth grade. What else? I was a fair cook, not bad as a mother, an unhappy wife, a good Christian. I didn't hate anyone except those parts of a person that deserved to be hated. I once didn't like the Negros and the chinos and mexicanos with dark skin, and all the others like them, but I now see we are all your children, no matter the color of our skin. I've lived my life as best I could.

"I was never really sick, and I thank you for that. I lost three little angels, but you can give them back to me as easily as you took them away. And there's no reason for you not to, Lord.

"I'm very tired. You know that. So be merciful. I want to die awake. Don't let me go in my sleep.

"If I have forgotten anything, and I probably have, you know what it is and if it needs to be resolved, removed, or forgiven. And don't forget to remind me of all the reminders. Now I have to go talk to my feet. They're very cold. Amen."

56

The Wave

Mamá and I were going through an itemized list of objects and furniture from her entire house that I had found in the metal box under her bed. Her flowery handwriting detailed the year she bought or received the item, and whether it was a gift or a purchase.

"Now you read what I've written, Soveida, and I'll tell you who I want to leave it to," Mamá said. "Go on."

"The sala. The living room. The cabinet with the white marble top. 1928. A gift from Profetario."

"I want you to have it, Soveida. Dolores is into early lo que sea. I don't know what. She has the furniture of a white woman. I'm sure she doesn't want my antiques. I want you to have all the furniture in the house."

Day after day we went through every single item in her large house. It was without regret and with no apparent sadness that Mamá assigned a new owner to each object in her house.

I took off time from work to help Mamá, but I was distracted. J.V. had gone to Germany at the end of the summer and he had decided to stay on to do research. I had spoken to him several days before, and the conversation was strained. J.V. knew nothing about Tirzio and me. I wanted to tell him, but what? That I was in love with his brother? He talked only about his finding an early manuscript of *The Immigrant Lover* by the great-grandfather of Chicano writers, Elias Nelson-Chavarria. J.V. said he missed me and he promised to write. And yet I somehow felt that J.V. and I would never get back together.

My thoughts were interrupted by Mamá's voice. "Soveida, are you all right? Let's stop for now. We'll finish the living room tomorrow. Go find Oralia and tell her to lie down. I'm worried about her. The stomach teas she gives me she takes herself. She wants to die with me. Only I'm afraid she'll beat me if I'm not careful. We've never been rivals, but now I think she'll win."

Oralia wasn't in her room. I found her sitting outside on the old black metal chair with a missing back near her coffee pots full of geraniums. She was winded, her pink sunbonnet hanging down the back of her head. She suddenly looked as fragile as if she were a tiny glass doll. Her forehead and nose glistened with sweat. Her little bird's eyes were rimmed in red. She held her side. I looked down to see her thin legs drenched in dark blood.

I thought at first that she had fallen down. I immediately went to her. She begged me to kick the bloodstained earth into her herb garden. "My little plants have always loved the blood of chickens," she said hoarsely, holding back a sharp pain. I tried to lift her up, but she asked me to let her rest awhile. With a tinge of sadness she looked at her garden, and then smiled softly at its lush majesty. Then she stood up, her spine as straight as I had ever seen it, and with a dignified acceptance allowed me to take her hand as I led her into the house. Not concerned for herself, she instead asked me about Mamá. I told her she was resting, and that seemed to cheer her up.

Oralia spoke about her garden as we slowly and carefully made our way through the house to her small bedroom. She talked about how her mother had given her seeds to plant, and how happy she'd been that she still had the seeds of those seeds, "las hijas de las hijas," she said, "the daughters of the daughters. Maybe even a son or two. They were my only children, Soveida." At one point, just outside her room, she stopped and looked up at me lovingly. She told me she would miss her garden. I reassured her that she would be fine in the morning, and that soon she'd be out there again, in the glorious sun, her bonnet on her head. She shook her head no, and then asked me to water her plants later on. "They get very thirsty in the summer. I always check on them at noon and then at three in the afternoon and just after dinner when it's quiet."

I promised her I would check on them later, and she seemed relieved. Then she apologized for the blood. "Me da vergüenza. I'm embarrassed. An old woman bleeding like a girl."

I laid Oralia down and went to find Dolores. She was resting in her room, all the shades drawn. Mamá called from her room. "Soveida! ¿Qué pasó?"

I told her it was nothing, but she knew.

"Aaaaaay, la misma Dominga."

"Mamá, Dominga's dead," I said, trying vainly to console her.

"I forgot how much it hurt, mi Diosito. I thought you were done with me, that every organ was cold, numb, without feeling. But you've left me with little cells that still can cry. ¡Oralia! ¡Ay, voy! I'm coming!"

When Dr. Wenchy arrived, he announced to everyone that Oralia seemed to be feeling a bit better.

"I'll check on her in the morning. If she's worse, I'll admit her to the hospital."

"And the blood?"

"I've taken a sample. We'll check it out. Sometimes older women rupture this way. Did she seem ill before?"

"No," said Dolores.

"Yes," said Mamá, huddled near the doorway to Oralia's room.

"What is it, yes or no?"

"Yes. She's been very sick. I can tell," Mamá replied with conviction.

"What about you, Señora Dosamantes, how do you feel?"

"For a while there, I forgot I was sick and not Oralia."

Dolores saw Dr. Wenchy to the door and asked me if I wanted to stay the night.

"Yes, Dolly," I replied.

"You can sleep in Hector's old room. Mamá's in your room and Oralia's in Luardo's old room."

"Did you reach Mara, Soveida?" Mamá asked, regaining her composure.

"Mara? Who called Mara?"

"I want to see my other granddaughter, Dolores."

"I'm going to bed. I canceled my shift at the Center tomorrow. What about you, Soveida?"

"I have to work."

"Good night, Mamá," Dolores said as she moved to her bedroom.

"Come and talk with me, Soveida."

"Mamá, it's late. Go to bed," Dolores called sharply.

"*You* go to bed, Dolores."

"I am."

"The dying can sleep if they want and when they want."

"But the living can't, so good night."

"Soveida, come here! I'm worried, m'ija. Let's hold hands and pray."

I stayed with Oralia that night. She was exhausted, utterly drained of all color. Not long ago she had seemed invincible, with bright cheeks in a relatively unlined face. Only now did I realize how wrinkled she was.

She had asked for an herbal tea from her garden. Gradually her breath evened out, and after that she slept a long time. I checked the pads underneath her small form. The cotton nightgown she had sewn for herself, with her trademark erratic red hem stitches, was pulled up high. Her breasts were small and folded inward. Her pubic area was almost devoid of hair. I pulled her nightgown down, and leaned deeply into the large armchair and promptly fell asleep.

I woke up to the smell of coffee.

I found Mamá in the kitchen, putting a filter in the coffee pot.

"Mamá! What are you doing here?"

"What does it look like? Get me the milk, Soveida."

"Are you all right, Mamá?"

"Don't look at me like that, Soveida. I had a healing. I dreamed el Santo Niño de Atocha came to visit me. He took off his mud-splattered shoes, the ones he wears every night when he travels the world helping people, and he gave them to me. Suddenly the shoes weren't dirty, and they were made out of a soft white leather. When I put them on, I woke up. The message in the dream was: Get up, mujer. You need to walk in the world. If you think you're dying, forget it. After that, I had a talk with my body, asking its forgiveness for the false alarm. Then I went into Oralia's room and sat with her while you slept. Go call your mamá. I don't know where she keeps the Cremora."

"Between Mamá, Dolores, and you, Soveida, no one has ever taken care of me the way you have," Oralia said with a tremulous voice. "At last I am a lady of leisure."

As Dolly brought her a hot, steaming cup of atole to sip, I massaged Oralia's cold feet and stick-like legs with warm massage oil.

"Ayyy! I feel like a princess!"

"You are a princess, Oralia. Let me put on these warm socks."

"It's so hot outside and I'm so cold. My feet are like the snow on Sierra Blanca, and my head is like Paricutín the volcano."

The two weeks and three days of Oralia's illness passed in a peaceful, unhurried way. She moved gently from small naps to deeper sleep. We let her sleep, and she was grateful.

"I never needed more than a three hours' sleep at night. Whatever rest I needed, I got from tending to my garden. How is my garden, Soveida?" Oralia asked me.

"I water it every day, Oralia. The flowers are in bloom."

"It's as it should be, then. Es propio." She sighed. "Yes, I really am a lady of leisure."

Often Oralia would call for Mamá in her sleep. They would hold hands for hours, while Mamá said endless rosaries.

"Mamá is here. Don't you worry, Oralita. I'm not going anywhere. Have I told you how much I love you, preciosa? Te quiero mucho, mi viejita. Now sleep."

Prompted by Mamá's unabashed and open lovingness, Dolly and I came in, sheepishly at first, to tell Oralia how much we loved her, too.

Oralia died peacefully one evening in April.

Mamá had yelled to me. "¡Soveida! ¡Ven pronto! Oralia has tilted to one side. She isn't snoring like she usually does. Her pigeon coo, I call it."

Dr. Wenchy came by around 7 p.m., and Oralia slept peacefully that night. The last two days had been hard on her. She kept asking for Mamá. Mamá stayed with her most of the time, only stepping out of the room when it was absolutely necessary.

When Oralia had first gotten sick, Dolly had gone out and bought several folding cots, one for Mamá and one for the two of us when we alternated shifts in Oralia's room. When Oralia took a turn for the worse, we three slept in there, Mamá and Dolly on the cots, and I used the big armchair.

The morning after Dr. Wenchy's visit, Mamá called the Traveling Prayer Team. I called Sister Lizzie. Prayers were said in English and Spanish. Father Piedoso led the rosary and Sister Lizzie sang religious hymns in Spanish, "the peppier the better," said Mamá,

"None of those beat-your-breasts cochinadas." Mamá asked Lizzie to sing "Cucurucucu Paloma" and "La Mañanitas," both Oralia's favorites.

Around 5 p.m. that day, Oralia's breathing became labored. She breathed deeply at first, and then more shallowly, slowly, very slowly, as if a wave were rolling from shore to sea at low tide. The time between breaths lengthened. Each breath became a ripple and then a wave, reaching out to that ever-widening sea. Oralia's last breaths seemed drawn up from the soles of her wool-stockinged feet. The voices of women chanted and spoke in tongues and cried softly, a deep sad keen of both hope and desperation.

Mamá sat by Oralia's side, holding her tepid hand, saying gently, "I love you, my viejita. It's all right. Let go, let go."

Oralia's life moved on to the great unknown and floated away to God. It was beautiful to behold. The last breaths were so deep it was hard to imagine such a small body could take in so much air, so much life. Oralia's medals gleamed brightly in the afternoon sun. She had requested that the windows remain open, despite her cold feet, "so that I can fly from this room to God without trouble." As the breaths became deeper, the space in between breaths became longer and longer.

"Ay, Soveida," Mamá wept. "I should have talked to my heart earlier, m'ija. It will never be the same, it hurts so much. ¡Que la Diosita la cuide! May the Blessed Mother fold her into her arms."

Father Piedoso scattered Holy Water on Oralia and then placed the holy salt and oil on her forehead. Sister Lizzie began to sing "Amazing Grace."

"One of her favorites," said Mamá.

"How beautiful she is," said Dolly.

Dolly sat in the armchair and cried as she had never cried before, not for her mother, Doña Trancha, or for Lina or for her stillborn sister, Zoraida. Nor for Luardo.

When Dolores's children were born, Oralia was there, along with old Dr. Wenchy, holding her hand, comforting her, telling her that soon Luardo would arrive, even though he never did.

When Trancha died, it was Oralia who gave Dolores the news. Someone called from the nursing home. It was so sudden. Oralia had held her, gently, telling her that soon Luardo would come home. He didn't come home that night, or the following, or the night after that. When he did come home, he slept for several days.

It was Oralia who had first told Dolores that Luardo had died. It was Oralia who held her, as Mamá wailed and bent over the bed in grief.

Now it was Dolly who held Oralia. Hugged her as if her tears would bring her back to life.

"My kingdom has many mansions," read Father Piedoso from his prayer book.

I do hope my mansion will be on the same street as Oralia's, Mamá thought. Dear Lord of Power and Might, you can put us next door to each other. Better yet, why not put us in the same house! We're used to each other. We know each other's ways.

"What was her last name?" asked Dr. Wenchy, who had just arrived and was signing the death certificate.

"Milcantos," I said.

A thousand songs.

Seraphim

57

The Holy Tortilla

Oralia's funeral was quiet, dignified, the way Oralia would have wanted it. Mamá, Dolly, and I sat in the front pew, receiving the few people who remembered her. An old woman with very thin legs carefully walked over to our pew to give us the pésame, the condolences one gives to the family of the deceased. Her hoarse voice barely came out of her bony rib cage. Her spine seemed pressed in toward her chest, nearly settling into her stomach.

"Ay, lo siento tanto," she whispered. "Oralia was a friend."

A plump younger woman, the daughter of the emaciated old lady, came by to extend her moist hand. "Eran amigas," she said. "They were friends."

Others came up, mostly older people who knew Oralia from the 6:30 Mass at Our Lady of Grace Church and the Sacred Heart Society. Each offered a heartfelt hug, prayers, tears. It was easy to see how deeply Oralia was loved by those favored few who knew her. Last, Father Piedoso came up and gave each of us a chaste hug. He had officiated at the rosary and at the Interment.

It was a sad time, but it was hardest on Mamá, who had barely slept during the last two and a half weeks of Oralia's illness.

"Qué bueno que dormí antes, casi con los angelitos," Mamá said to me. "It's good I slept before, even if it was almost with the angels, because you and your mamá slept through most of your night shifts. Someone had to be awake. What would have happened to Oralia otherwise? The two of you stretched out snoring like there was a long tomorrow. It was important I held a watch. Now that my little viejita is gone, I'll be moving back to my room, and so will Dolores, I mean

Dolly. You can go home to your trailer, Soveida, unless of course you want to move in with us."

"No, Mamá, I don't think so. I'm going to Estancia, but after that I'll help you get your things in order."

"Estancia?"

"Estancia, New Mexico."

"Por Dios, Soveida, what business do you have in Estancia? No, señora, you have no business going out of town. Haven't you heard of the custom of not traveling for six months after a funeral? I've already covered all the mirrors in my room, and asked your mamá to take out the portable color television she put in there when I was sick. It was nice to lie in bed and watch my novelas, but there's no soap operas for me now. I'm in mourning until Christmas. It will be a cross to bear to miss my soap, *El amor y la perdición*, but keeping el luto, the tradition of mourning, is more important. I don't advise leaving town. The spirit of the dead person just might fly off with you. And just what would Oralia have to do up there in Estancia? Where is it, anyway?"

"Mamá! It's by Moriarity, and that's where Laddie Mae Beron, Veryl's mother, lives. I'm going to see her."

"Ay, no, Soveida! Veryl's been dead six years. Just let the pobrecito rest in peace without stirring up his bones. She doesn't want to see *you*. Why should you see *her*?"

"But, Mamá, there's things I want to talk to her about."

"What things? Are you going to talk to her about why her son wasn't ever like a husband to you or why he killed himself with a plastic cleaner's bag? Is that what you're going to talk about? No mother wants to talk about those things. But if you have to go, I'll go with you."

"Mamá! You don't like to travel. Besides, what about the six months' travel suspension?"

"There's an unspoken rule saying that if you have to travel to save an almighty soul, then you are dispensed."

"I don't need my soul saved, Mamá. I'm just going to see my mother-in-law."

"Ex-mother-in-law."

"I never got a chance to talk to her about Veryl and what he was like when he was young."

"Ay, m'ija, he was like any other cochino little boy picking his nose and hitting the little girls and then looking up their chones."

"Mamá! I'm going to Estancia on Monday and that's it. You stay here with Dolly. You both need to rest."

"Ay! Mi Dios, ¿porqué?"

"Here's a Kleenex, Mamá."

"Your eulogy was beautiful, Soveida. I want you to make me a copy. Also, promise me that when I die, and I will someday, just like you will, that you'll give me a eulogy as beautiful as the one you gave Oralia. Not that I deserve it, m'ija, but I am your grandmother. So, what about work?"

"I took some time off."

"I'm not sure about this trip. What about el padrecito professor? What if he comes looking for you? What do I tell him?"

"He's in Germany, Mamá, and he's not coming back for a while."

I had received a letter from J.V. in which he told me he'd decided to stay on another semester. He had been promised a substantial stipend and a job in the fall if he wanted it. He felt torn, but I'd told him to take it and that I was all right. He wanted me to come to visit him, but I knew I wouldn't. Even as my love for Tirzio grew, I knew it was a love that could never sustain itself.

Mamá chattered away. "Well, if you do go up there, and I can't stop you, promise me you'll go by Lake Arthur to see the Holy Tortilla."

"What Holy Tortilla?"

"Someone saw the face of Christ on a tortilla. They've made a shrine in their living room. Dominga's niece, Mari Luz, lives up there. She told me about it the last time she was here."

"Mamá, I won't have time! It's a quick trip."

"If you have time for esa gringa who won't talk to you, you have time for the Holy Tortilla."

"Mamá!"

"Now let me finish. If there's some medals or holy cards or anything, a little piece of dried Holy Tortilla, whatever, pick it up for me and I'll pay you later, or better yet, you can give it to me for an early Christmas. Now come over here, Soveida, so I can give you la Bendición. Dear God, take care of my Soveida. Allow the power of the Holy Tortilla to give her sustenance and strength. One more favor I ask you, in your divine mercy send me someone who sees *El amor y la perdición*, so I can get the stories from them each week. Amen."

"Mamá, I don't think I can go to Lake Arthur to see the Tortilla."

"The *Holy* Tortilla. It's on the way."

The Holy Tortilla was not on the way to Estancia. Not as any crow ever flew. As a matter of fact, it was out of the way. But it wasn't until

I was en route that I realized that the pilgrimage to both Laddie Mae Beron and the Tortilla were in somewhat different directions.

Mamá would have to wait for her sliver of Holy Tortilla a bit longer.

I decided to take the long way to Estancia. Through Tularosa, Carrizozo, and off the beaten path to see what Claunch looked like, and then on to Mountainair. When I got to Moriarity, I realized I'd taken a wrong turn. I turned around and seventeen miles later I drove through downtown Estancia.

I originally thought I might go to the newspaper office or public library to look up old annuals and clippings about Angel's accident. But then I decided to go directly to Laddie Mae's.

I stopped at a convenience store to ask directions. I had no idea where she lived or how to get there. I thought that perhaps someone in the store could help. When I called out, there was no answer, but suddenly an older man came out from a beaded curtain that led to the back of the store, and asked if I needed help. He thought I might have had car trouble and offered to call the highway patrol. I assured him that I was just inquiring about Laddie Mae Beron. Startled, he informed me that Laddie Mae had died the previous winter of pneumonia. I was shocked, but gathered myself together enough to let him know I was Veryl's widow. Introducing himself, Lufon Quinley informed me he had read about Veryl's death in the newspaper. According to Mr. Quinley, there had apparently been some dispute about Laddie Mae's will. Two versions existed. In one she had left her farm to the Cancer Society, and in the other to her niece, Mae Lu Beron. Mae Lu, I learned, was living in an Airstream trailer behind Laddie Mae's house, waiting for the estate to be settled. I asked for directions and thanked Mr. Quinley for his help.

The Beron farm consisted of an old green farmhouse and a small barn. The house had a pitched corrugated-iron roof. There was a pond nearby, with an oily film over it, and no signs of aquatic life to be seen. The land was on a rise, and had been completely overrun with weeds. The one pleasant spot was a U-shaped plot that was right in front of the house, filled with wildflowers.

Veryl never talked about his life in Estancia, or growing up on his parents' farm. I knew his father had died and that his mother, Laddie Mae, was still alive. But when holidays like Christmas and Mother's Day came around, he never mentioned either of them. Coming from a large and close family, it seemed odd to me that Veryl shared so few memories of his family life. But then I never pressed him very hard to open up to me, so saturated was I with my own family.

A great sadness enveloped me as I got out of the car and walked to the old silver trailer behind the house. The paint was peeling and the sides showed signs of rust. A leaky hose spit water over a muddy spot of ground. I sidestepped my way to the crudely fashioned front steps and knocked on the door. No answer.

Finally a woman's voice called out. "Who's there? Someone come for a treatment?"

"I'm Soveida Beron, Veryl's widow."

"Veryl's widow?"

There was no sound for a long time, as if she were getting herself together. I stood on the porch step and peered through the curtains into the disordered living room.

"Just a minute, I'm coming."

Mae Lu Beron pulled herself across the living room toward the door with difficulty, alternately dragging and then bracing her body, as if she were fighting back a torrent of water in slow motion. She stood behind the scrap-aluminum door, chain lock in place, looking me over. When she felt certain that I was harmless, she let me in. Her broad, bright, fiercely alive face looked so much like Veryl's it caught me off-guard. Her eyes were the same intense blue, and her hair was soft and clung to her face the way Veryl's had. I felt a small moan escape me. Mae Lu's cheeks were slightly red, and showed the strain of exertion. Apologetically, she asked me in, and suggested I move things off the couch so that we could sit.

"I hope you don't mind that I came over. Mr. Quinley told me that Mrs. Beron died last winter. I'm so sorry. I wish I'd known. I would have come sooner."

"You say you were married to Veryl? When was that?"

"Six years ago. We got married in Agua Oscura."

I didn't want to talk about Veryl's suicide, and yet it was why I'd come. I made small talk, telling her how Veryl and I had met.

"If I'd known you were coming over here, I'd have had you bring me some baloney and bread. But I don't have a phone. Can't afford it until the land gets settled. In the first will, Aunt Laddie Mae left the place to the Cancer Society. She signed a second will leaving me the place, but the lawyer from the Cancer Society says I influenced my aunt toward me."

"Is there anything I can do, Miss Beron?" I asked, knowing there was nothing that I could do for her or Laddie Mae, much less Veryl.

"Well, I'm doing what I can. Call me Mae Lu."

"And you can call me Soveida."

"When you first came up, I thought you were a customer. I'm a massage person. Because of my rheumatoid arthritis, I use a wooden stick. Just move that old serape. We'll just sit a bit and talk."

Mae Lu lived alone, except for occasional visits from her occasional boyfriend, Pete García, a laborer who worked in Moriarity. It was Pete who brought her food and drove her into town when she needed anything. If it weren't for Pete, she said, she didn't know what she'd do. She and Pete wanted to fix up the farm, if and when the settlement came through. Mae Lu talked about her life and I was relieved. I looked around the messy room and thought of her severe limitations, and how, despite constant pain, she was still cheerful and enthusiastic.

Mae Lu had her hopes pinned on Pete and the farm. Despite the fact he was married, they still wanted to have children. Pete was Mexican from México, Mae Lu said. He sent his wife and seven kids money. His wife, María Elena, wasn't interested in sex anymore, and Mae Lu was, so it all worked out real good for everyone. Once she got the farm in her name, she and Pete planned on bringing everyone down from Jalisco. Her Aunt Laddie Mae had never liked him. She didn't like any Mexicans, in fact, Mae Lu said.

It's a good thing we never met, then, I thought.

As if reading my thoughts, Mae Lu assured me that was how her Aunt Laddie Mae thought, and that kind of thinking had nothing to do with her. After all, she said proudly, she was nearly engaged to Pete.

I noticed Mae Lu looking at my hands, which lay folded on my lap. They felt clammy and very cold. I kept staring at Mae Lu and wondered if she had noticed. She was so similar to Veryl in coloring, and had the same soft catch in her voice.

Mae Lu asked if I'd like a hand or foot massage. I declined, but Mae Lu insisted. She would charge me nothing for the first hand.

I extended my right hand. Mae Lu proceeded to coax, caress, and uncramp unknown muscles in my hand. After a few minutes, I agreed to both the hand and the foot treatments, but only if I could pay full price.

"Okay, no problem there. I'll take Pete out to dinner. That'll be fifteen for both hands and feet. But I'll give you a five-dollar discount, you being kin."

"All right," I said as Mae Lu moved on to my left hand.

"I never knew Veryl was married until the obituary came out," Mae Lu said between kneading. "It was a surprise to me. I never expected him to marry after the accident."

"There are so many things I didn't know about Veryl," I said.

And it was true. I had lived with Veryl for six months, but I knew nothing about him, really. It was hard to believe that what little I would eventually learn would come from his only cousin, the young woman sitting on the couch, her crippled hands holding mine.

I spent most of the afternoon with Mae Lu. She finished working on my feet and I talked her into accepting twenty dollars for her work. We spoke at length about Laddie Mae, whom Mae Lu said was tighter than a fisted hand pulling back the change. The description somehow struck a familiar chord. She and Veryl had never been close.

Somehow that didn't surprise me.

The time wore on and Mae Lu's energy wore down. She asked me to tell her something about myself, and I did. With a sudden boldness that I hoped would not frighten her, I asked her to tell me about Veryl's accident. I, of course, meant his accident at Caballo Lake. She misunderstood me and began relating a story about another accident. Veryl had been driving his father's old Chevy truck. Just then, Mae Lu asked if I wanted to soak my feet. I said it wasn't necessary.

"Oh, all right," I finally agreed.

"Just let me get some water."

Mae Lu dragged herself to the kitchen and returned with a towel. She asked me to bring a dishpan full of lukewarm water into the room and set it down in front of the couch. Once my feet were in the pan, Mae Lu continued.

"Veryl swerved."

"He swerved?"

"Into an oncoming car."

"What?"

"I think he wanted to kill himself. But only the girl got killed."

"Who was she?"

"Her name was Angel."

"Angel!"

"I think he was trying to kill them both, but he ended up just killing her. He should have died in that crash, but he didn't. He broke both legs, some ribs, his collarbone. After that, he just wasn't the same. Him being my only cousin and all, you would have thought we'd be close. But he was always a loner. Just like Aunt Laddie Mae."

"Ouch!"

"It's not the stick does the hurting, it's that the areas I work on correspond to some part of your body. I just worked out some heart strain. Watch that area. There, see, it's loosening up now. You see that spatula over there on the kitchen counter? It looks like a back scratcher. Bring that here. For special people, I do backs."

Pete came by around 6 p.m. He and Mae Lu invited me to join them at the Country Kitchen. I declined, then hugged Mae Lu, promising to keep in touch.

That night I stayed at a motel in Moriarity. I slept little, thinking about Veryl. I felt a deep sadness about the confusion that was his life, but with that sadness came relief and a diminution of pain. And now he was at rest. Nothing else could be done.

The next morning I decided to visit the Holy Tortilla. I wandered through the wide, nearly empty streets of Lake Arthur. After taking a wrong turn, I called out the car window to a young man who was walking down the street, asking him for the Shrine of the Holy Tortilla. He responded courteously, letting me know I was very close.

The Shrine of the Holy Tortilla was located in a modest one-story white-stuccoed house with a small yard in front. I knocked on the door and was greeted by a teenage girl.

"Is this the Holy Tortilla?" I asked, feeling foolish.

The young woman nodded and motioned for me to enter. The living room was simple. An old green sectional couch was in one corner. To one side stood a Plexiglas-covered altar in which was placed the tortilla, the Holy Tortilla, two large votive candles flanking it.

The Tortilla was smaller than I'd imagined. I don't know what I had expected. You could see the black gas-burner grill marks on the Tortilla, which formed the image of a face, and it was definitely someone male. But it was hard to say whether the face was Christ's or any other man's with a full beard. Never mind, to the owners of the Holy Tortilla, the Tortilla was a sacred sign of God's appearance on this earth, the mark of God's grace.

But to the side of the supposed Christ image were human bite marks.

Someone hungry and in a hurry had obviously chomped down on the Tortilla before it was observed to be holy.

A middle-aged lady peered in from a door that led to other rooms. She greeted me warmly. I genuflected in front of the Holy Tortilla, and then settled into a kneeler that was in front of the altar. First I said a prayer for myself, and then for Mamá Lupita, for Oralia, for Dolly and Reldon, for Luardo, for Mae Lu and Pete, for Laddie Mae, for J.V., for Tirzio, and at the end for Veryl.

There were no mementos, no holy cards, no slivers or splinters or pictures or images to be taken home to Mamá Lupita.

Life would go on once again, with the gusto of those human teeth marks attempting to grab hold of the divine.

58

Bonnie Takes Over

Larry was afraid. Afraid to tell anyone he was afraid. Afraid of passing out, of not being able to breathe, of dying without a chance to lie down. Afraid of keeling over, knocking things off the shelves.

I knew he was afraid, but didn't know what to say. He would simply have dismissed me, as he always did.

When he lay down, all he could think about was how fast his heart was beating, and if he would ever calm down. He tried to relax by breathing deeply. Tried to distract himself by concentrating on other things. Usually his heartbeat adjusted fairly soon. Until the week before, when he had to stay home one day and Bonnie took over at the restaurant. He had told her he had to go out of town, but instead, he was home in bed. She never knew. I only found out because he asked me if I knew a good doctor.

He said he saw lightning bolts when he closed his eyes, and sometimes a tear like a torn curtain. Sometimes in the middle of the day he couldn't see at all. The tear penetrated his vision, and he'd get dizzy and nauseous. His arm hurt, but the worst thing was that he couldn't slow his heartbeat. It was fast, so fast he was afraid it would jump out of his chest and land on the floor. He should have seen a doctor. But what could the doctor do for him? Tell him to stop working? The restaurant was his life. His fucking breath, his chocolate, his sex.

There was a knock at the door.

"Lar, it's me, Soveida. They've just delivered the champagne for the party. Where do you want to put it?"

"What?"

"The champagne for Pancha and Fermín's party. In your office?"

"Oh yeah, sure. Here I come. I was just working on some bills. Let me unlock the door. What is it, Soveida?"

"The champagne. It's here. Were you resting?"

"Me? Hell, no! I feel good."

"Larry, what's wrong? You look awful."

"Hey, I'm okay. Tell Pito to put the boxes in the walk-in. I'll come with you."

"We can get it, Larry. Sit down. Are you sure you're okay?"

"Yeah, well, yeah. I feel just dandy. You sit there and I'll sit here. So, what's going on? When do you pick up the cake? I've doubled up shifts Saturday. I want to make sure we have people to set up everything with plenty of time."

"The food's covered. The beer, wine, champagne. We pick up the cake Saturday at noon."

"Got all the plates from Southwest Supply? The forks?"

"All ready."

"So, are we going to have us a party here or not?"

"I still can't believe that they're repeating their vows again and that they've asked the two of us to be honorary maid of honor and best man."

"It's only right, Soveida. We're family. So, who's fixing up the patio?"

"Margarito. We'll be closed from four to eight o'clock."

"And the priest?"

"No priest, a minister."

"Oh, I forgot they were Born Agains."

"They're not Born Agains, Larry, they're Waiting-to-be-Borns. There's a difference. They're interdenominational and tolerant."

"Who's the minister, then?"

"Brother Brath Galway from the Chapel of the Faithful Brethren. It's a satellite Christian community. Here's the invitation:

Pancha Portales Fernández and Fermín Fernández
request the honor of your presence
at a ceremony of renewal of the vows of Holy Matrimony
June 21, 1993
four o'clock in the afternoon
El Farol Mexican Restaurant
Agua Oscura, New Mexico

432

*In lieu of gifts, you may bring canned goods for the
Chapel of the Faithful Brethren's Food Pantry Fund.*

"Christ, is that all? Bonnie and I should have eloped, for all the trouble it turned out to be for us in the end."

"Are you all right, Larry? You want something to drink?"

"How about a Coke."

"Here's some water. Just sit down and relax."

"I just got a little dizzy. Didn't have breakfast."

"Everything's going to be all right."

"I didn't know if it would be or not, since you were gone all last week."

"I was off *two* days!"

"Well, we missed you here."

"I didn't think you had time to miss anyone, Larry. Fermín told me you were very busy. How's Dedea doing?"

"Not bad. Not bad at all. She's got a lot of potential. She reminds me of you when—"

"Yeah, when. In the good old days. Someday she'll take my place. Just like I took Milia's place."

"If she's going to take your place, then who's going to take mine?"

"Peetie?"

"Him? He's Bonnie's nephew, not mine. Jimmy's accused him of stealing, but I don't know. I haven't told Bonnie yet. I just hope El Farol will continue to be run by someone who knows how it should be run. Someone like yourself."

"Me?"

"You'd be perfect. At least I'd know everything was in safe hands."

"What about Bonnie?"

"Bonnie? To her, it's just business. Another one of her projects. To us, it's family. It isn't the same thing."

"You're going to be around for a long, long time, Larragoite! As for me, I wouldn't run this restaurant for the world. It's too much work."

"Hey, Soveida, speaking of wills, you were the only one who didn't give me one."

"Don't get started, Larry. I told you I wasn't giving you my will. But, for your information, I filled it out and had it witnessed by two people, and now it's in *my* safety-deposit box. No way I'm keeping it here."

"Why?"

"It's none of your damn business, that's why."

"Sometimes I think I know you, Soveida, and then I turn around and I'm looking at a stranger. I thought we were best friends."

"We are best friends. Look, it's getting late. We'll talk about this later."

"I'm only looking out for your own interests, Soveida. Go on ahead, I'll be there to check on the champagne soon."

Everything was ready for the party on Saturday except Larry, who woke up on the large wooden kitchen table, lying next to plastic bags of red chile. Next to him was a chile press where Pato was grinding the defrosted red chile into sauce. It stank to hell of chile pod. Larry tried to cough, but he couldn't even move. No sounds came out of his mouth. All he could do was lie there. I put a wet rag on his head, while everyone else stood around as if they were at a bake sale. Eloisa loosened Larry's tie and opened his shirt a little, and then someone brought some towels and put them under his head.

My mom ate that bowl of red chile the night before I was born, he thought, and here I am now on the same table, breathing in the fumes of my birth chile. Not even a bed to lie down on. I have to die in the middle of the fucking afternoon, with everybody, even the bus people, looking on.

The new dishwasher, Refugio Gandales, stared from the corner all bug-eyed, his hands full of soapy water. Chuy looked at him with his pobrecito-chingao face. Larry lay there afraid. He tried to talk, but I insisted he keep quiet.

The paramedics got to work on him as he closed his eyes again. He felt a hot, searing pain. His mother's legacy. His birth. His death. Red chile in between.

I tried to assure Larry that everything was all right, but it wasn't. Larry had had a heart attack. The doctor said he wasn't surprised, given the state of Larry's arteries. He would have to have a quadruple heart bypass as soon as he was stabilized. That left him in critical condition and in intensive care.

The anniversary party was postponed indefinitely. We hadn't prepared the food yet, and the champagne and beer were in the walk-in. The only thing we couldn't do anything about was the wedding cake, so Chuy picked it up on Saturday and everyone enjoyed it between the afternoon and evening shifts. Fermín prayed over the devil's food cake, Pancha's favorite, and said it was a party before the party.

On Friday, Bonnie took over. The following Monday afternoon, she called a meeting in the patio, just as Larry used to.

"As you know," she addressed us, "Mr. Larragoite had a heart attack and bypass surgery. His recovery looks good. He'll be in the hospital for a while, so I'll be taking over as manager.

"When Mr. Larragoite recovers a bit more, he'll be moving to the Del Valle Nursing Home for a while, where he'll get the round-the-clock care he needs.

"I want to thank you for your love, support, prayers, flowers, notes, and food. What Lar—what Mr. Larragoite—needs now is rest. He's in intensive care and can only see family members at scheduled times during the day. I know you all want to see him, but it's just not possible now.

"Several changes will be in effect as of today. First of all, I want to let you know that Petra Montes has decided to retire, effective next Friday. We wish you the best, Petra! We'll be hiring a new waitress as soon as possible. Also, as everyone knows by now, Pancha and Fermín's party has been postponed. Soveida will also be cutting her hours to go to school part-time. We wish you well, Soveida. In January, Margarito will be leaving us to go to design school. I'll be hiring a new waitress and she'll be sharing her hours with Dedea and Soveida. No, Soveida will *not* be leaving us, just shifting her hours around. I've hired a cook to replace Lavel Windle, who's moving to New Jersey. His name is Chuckie Samaniego. He used to be the chef at Sánchez's Casa de Comida. He'll be starting Monday. I'm ordering a new time-card system that should go into effect at the end of the month.

"Another thing. Instead of unlimited employee meals for those who work two shifts, we'll be limiting that to one meal a day, with a charge of three dollars per meal, to be taken out of your paychecks each pay period. And, by the way, I've decided to cancel the insurance plan we've had up to now. From now on, you're responsible for your own insurance. This includes all staff.

"As I've said, Mr. Larragoite isn't receiving any visitors now. He's much better, and he's responding to treatment.

"Are there any questions? If not, I'll be in my office. I want to thank everyone again. Without you, El Farol wouldn't be what it is today: the best Mexican restaurant in all of Agua Oscura. Thank you!"

After Bonnie's talk we all felt deflated. Larry was better, and that was good, but that was the only good news.

Lavel had been given his official notice the day after Larry's heart attack. So had Petra.

Petra was devastated, but tried to keep her spirits up. "I'm an old woman who can't add. I *should* retire. I've been a bother to all of you these years, Soveida, because I gave you all my tickets to add up. My granddaughter did give me one of those calculators chiquitos, but I do worse on them than I do with my pencil. So it's time for me to hang up my apron and spend more time knitting and making toys for my grand-kids. I deserve a rest, I guess."

Lavel wasn't so philosophical. "Goddamn meddling bitch! She never did like no black fixing her Tampicos. I'm a hell of a cook, and she knows it. She told me I had drug problems and that she wasn't going to take no more of what happened when I freaked out that one time. I told her I'd gone straight, and that my mama was proud I'd kicked the mota and Robi. I was thinking of getting my GRE, but she doesn't care one damn bit. She still thinks I'm the same person I was back then. And she accused me of stealing money from the cash register. I told her no way, I'm always at the grill. What does she think? Me, fired? Hell, I've never been fired from a cook job. And just who's going to be cooking those steaks five nights a week, just tell me? Pito has his hands full at the stove, and Eloisa's only here weekends. Just who's going to fill in as salad backup? Mrs. L., I hope Larry's feeling better, 'cause when he finds out you fired me and Petra, he's going to shit a cow. If you're the manager now, then I'm out of here. I quit!"

That was the beginning of the new order under Bonnie McNuff Larragoite, manager of El Farol Restaurant.

Later I found out Larry had written his own will.

"I, Larry Larragoite, being of sound mind and unsure body, bequeath to each of my employees $1,000.00 to do as you wish. To Soveida Dosamantes, a woman I have always loved, I leave sole ownership of El Farol Restaurant. To my beloved and bossy wife, Bonnie Larragoite, I leave my house, my property, my C.D.s, my savings bonds, my various bank accounts, and my condo in Acapulco. Dated the nineteenth day of October. In the year of doubt."

In another life, maybe Larry and I could have gotten together. If I weren't so smart and he wasn't such a smart-ass.

THE BOOK OF SERVICE

CHAPTER THIRTEEN

The Waitress's Face

The waitress's face should always be clean.

It is not necessary to wear makeup if you don't want to. A little may help you feel more attractive. It is all a state of mind. Better to have none or a little than a lot.

The makeup base should be an anti-grease formula (you will sweat).

Lipstick is fine, but don't expect it to last. It's better not to wear a dark red shade. At the end of the shift, you'll be left with two red outlined clown lips with pale centers.

Eye shadow isn't necessary. You're not going to a dance. Never wear a bright blue shade in daylight. Halloween comes once a year, but never when you're on duty.

The eyebrows should be soft, as well, not Theda Bara fierce, with swooping tips.

Don't expect to go to the bathroom unless there is a lull. You'll learn to pace your bodily functions. But don't punish yourself: for ages women haven't gone to the bathroom when we need to go.

We're always doing something for someone else besides ourselves. Don't neglect yourself. When you have your period, attend to yourself gently. All women know the book of their own bodies.

In general, moderation is the best policy.

What is the face you greet the world with then, woman?

A face that pacifies the children when they cry, soothes old men when they are sad, and appeases hungry people who want more than food. An all-giving, all-loving face that never lies.

59

Nuns

"Women don't need men to be happy," said Sister Lizzie. She dipped her straw into her gigantic frozen Margarita and then lifted it, sipping the juice from the straw's tip. I sat across from her. It was a Friday afternoon at the Holiday Inn near the end of Happy Hour.

"Not all women need to be completed in that way, Soveida. Thank the feminist God we grew up with in the sixties. If we'd grown up ten years earlier, we'd both be married with kids. Even the Church was different then. Remember? You'd see a pew filled with ten, eleven, twelve kids from the same family, the mother in the middle acting as referee. Motherhood was IT. The Be-All and End-All. That and becoming a nun. Mind you, this was Sister-bind-me-up-and-lock-me-away in a nunnery.

"Nuns were disconnected from society then. They were shunted off to cloisters where you'd see them peering from behind some metal grate. Not only couldn't they see what was happening in the world, they couldn't do anything about it. It's another era now, thank the Mother God! I never would have become a nun if I'd been born in *that* God's world. Do you want another Margarita, Soveida? I think we're going to be here awhile."

"No, Lizzie, you go ahead."

"They make a good Margarita here. I don't come here much, I usually go over to the Lion's Den by the university. The kids and I will walk there from the Newman Center for a pizza and some beer."

"It sounds like you enjoy your work, if you can call it work."

"I love being with young people. Not that we're so old, but hell, you know what I mean. With my kids, I'm back in the struggle. I marched against the Vietnam War, became a Brown Beret, and then

I joined the Revolutionary Communist Party. Now I'm a feminist lesbian nun. What greater trial is there today than to live honestly and with love in a time of plague? That's what this struggle with AIDS is all about. It's become my cause."

"You always seem to know what the struggle is and where it's happening. My struggles always seem to come too late."

"Never too late."

"Maybe you're right."

"When I'm with my kids, Soveida, the world is full of possibility. That's what my life and the ministry are all about. I never would have made it when nuns were nunish, dressed in black like spiders, and lived in religious penitentiaries making linen for the priests. Priests can make their own linen and cook their own food. The ecclesiastical Middle Ages are over. My life as a nun is in the heart of the world, not in some mausoleum with other women, praying for the pagan babies in Africa. I didn't become a nun to sit home or in church twiddling my unworked, white-starched, collared hands over a set of softened black beads. It's Nun's Lib I'm talking about."

"I remember when nuns were all covered up, Lizzie. There have been so many changes in the Church."

"Not enough. Most nuns are still barricaded behind school desks teaching or holding steaming urinals and working as nurses. We're still just glorified babysitters. Asexual nonentities. And as a result, we don't have any benefits. No retirement. No union. There are so many nuns in infirmaries, strong women who believed the Church would provide. But it just hasn't worked that way. When I go into a parish I make sure I have health insurance. Remember Sister Emilia Marie, the principal at Holy Angel?"

"She was the one with the smelly false teeth?"

"I worshipped the woman. To me, she was a saint. She used to bring me pomegranates from the nuns' garden. But she could be mean if she didn't like you. Remember when Ralphie Lerma snuck into class an hour late? Sister Emilia Marie beat the hell out of him with her map pointer. Oh, she was a tough bird. But you should see her now. To think she worked hard all her life to end up in the worst of nursing homes full of old nuns."

"She never brought me any pomegranates."

"She didn't? Well, she should have. To this day, I can't look at a pomegranate without thinking of Sister Emilia Marie."

"I never liked her."

"You never got past the teeth. Few people did, Soveida. She was a beautiful woman once you got past her mouth. She liked me, I don't know why."

"She never . . ."

"Oh, come on, Soveida! No, she never seduced me, for God's sake. That's all you heterosexual people think about—when we lost our virginity, and to whom. I was ten or eleven years old, Soveida, okay?"

"What grade was that, Lizzie?"

"Fourth. Junior Castillo used to sit behind me and grind his pencil into my back and then outline the shape of my bra with his eraser. It drove me crazy. God, how I hated him!"

"You were wearing a bra in fourth?"

"It was a 28 AA and it fit me big."

"You were crazy, mujer, crazy! I didn't get a bra until I was in sixth."

"But you needed one. I didn't need one in fourth or sixth or eighth. Yeah, I guess some things have changed. In the old days, nuns didn't need to worry about clothes; you just had your habit. Today it's panty hose and jogging shoes. Instead of teaching Catechism after school, I teach yoga in the morning and wok cooking on the weekends."

"So what happened to Sister Emilia Marie?"

"I had been thinking about going into the convent and went to the priory in Missouri to check it out. I had heard that Sister Emilia Marie wasn't very far away, in a retirement home for nuns. I took the train to see her. It was really cold. I had to walk from the bus station to the convent. It was around lunchtime. This old nun ushered me in and asked if I wanted to eat. She left, and an even older nun brought me a tray of the most delicious food I have ever eaten in my life. I don't know if it was the cold, or the walk, or the spirit in which it was given. Later the old nun took me to see Sister Emilia Marie. She was sitting in the middle of this large room, surrounded by a bunch of very old nuns. Conditions weren't good. Despite the fact that she was very frail, she stood up to greet me. She was still tall, unstooped. I liked that. Oh, Soveida! It was like coming home. A happy home in the middle of a dark night, and seeing a bright face in a room without shadows, and hearing the words: Welcome, welcome! We were so happy to see each other. I thanked her for all the pomegranates. And then she told me about her life.

"Emilia was never her name. Marie was never her name. The name she was born to was Mary Alice. Her mother's sister's name. Mary Alice wanted to become a nun; she died at age eighteen in a flu epidemic. Instead, her niece became a nun. Fulfillment of a name, many names, namesakes, someone else's dream. But she could never really become *that* Mary Alice. She didn't want to become a nun in those early years when everyone said she was going to be a nun. It's a life she never would have chosen for herself. But she had no choice. Her life was chosen for her. That's how it was for women back then. She was told she was going to become a nun, so she became a nun. In each family there was a predestined sacrificial lamb. This one becomes a nun, that one a priest. 'Do I sound hard?' she asked me. 'Child, let me tell you it took too many years for me to feel happy in these robes. I had wanted a husband; I wanted to know what it was like to be with a man. Does that surprise you? Let us talk honestly today, like two friends. Now that I am old, I can say anything I please. I can startle people if I want. I can reflect on those things that I have been a stranger to. Why not? Old age is the time to question and attempt to understand the hollow parts within oneself. My God is a God that allows questions, especially in the face of death. You will someday know what I mean, child. Tell me, have you ever slept with a man? What was it like? Did he frighten you with his strangeness, or was there joy? Not just some biological need, or some nasty unpleasantness, but the union between two people who truly love each other, in all ways. You have known that? Truly, God is great. Praise him! Perhaps in my next life I will know what ecstasy is. Now I know what the Church says about such things, but, child, couldn't it be possible, in God's grace and mercy, to continue our work of salvation—if necessary—through not one, but many lives? Does this startle you?'

"We had so little time to talk. She thanked me for my kind letter to her. And for coming 'inside this humble heart and resting there awhile. But let's not talk of impending Paradise,' she went on. 'I want to talk about life and loving. For me, Christ was my only spouse. I conjured him nightly, wishing many times he were instead flesh and blood and not that nocturnal fever that resolved itself in daylight. Tell me your stories and they will become my stories. Your lovers will become my lovers. What does it matter if they were real or not. You could tell me lies and I would love them just the same. I wouldn't know the difference. Here we are: two women, one Burning Master. One of us is old, the other young, and yet there is one sole story of loving between us. It holds no wounded future, it is not a tale obliterated by time. Have I confused you? Frightened you? Think about these things. One buried woman to another. Which brings me to my point. I understand you are thinking about entering the convent. This is what your letter said. I wish you the best. My prayers will go with you as you find your way to that great question of loving. Of service. It's getting late now. I feel myself waning. Please ring the bell and Sister Domitilia will help me to my bed. Give me a kiss, and be on your way. Thank you again, sweet child, for your indulgence. Come back if you can. Won't you now?'

"When I left, I prayed for her, Soveida, and for all nuns, for all women with bad teeth."

"So, was that when you entered the convent?"

"No, first I had boyfriends, got laid, finished college, had boyfriends, got laid, got laid some more, and then thought of going to law school. I didn't want to go to my everlasting grave like Sister Emilia Marie. How did I know then that I would just be coming into my sexuality and would meet the love of my life in a convent? If you had told me in the sixties that I'd become an activist feminist lesbian nun I would have said yeah, sure, and the Pope is a woman. I remember the first two gay nuns I met. Sister Encarnación and Sister Doris John. One of them from Chihuahua, México, and the other from Missoula, Montana. I once saw them holding hands. I didn't want to disturb them, so I quietly slipped away. Later on I saw them kiss each other deeply. At that moment I realized they were lovers and had been for a long time. It gave me peace to know that even in a place where sexuality was repressed and denied, these two women, from completely different worlds, could meet, fall in love, and find solace in each other. I didn't know that I could love another woman then. And yet I've found my greatest joy in loving in my supposed world of denial. I'm not only talking about sexuality. Loving has to do with so many other things as well. Now, I'm not saying that this way of life is perfect or forever."

"You *sound* happy."

"I'm content, Soveida. Times and God are a-changin', girl! They have to. Priests and nuns need insurance and retirement and love just like anyone else. So let's get another Margarita to celebrate the new clergy!"

"I'll have an orange juice."

"An orange juice? Sure you don't want a Margarita? So tell me, what have *you* been up to, Soveida?"

"Well . . ."

I took a sip of my orange juice. Where would I begin? J.V.? Tirzio? J.V. and Tirzio? Should I start from the beginning and go to the end?

Should I start from the end and go backwards? I couldn't say nothing. Lizzie would know something was wrong. I could never lie to Lizzie. Everything that Lizzie had said struck a chord in me. Her struggle to find love in this world was my struggle as well. Lizzie had her share of boyfriends, it was true. She had marched for the best of causes and searched for social justice and equality in public arenas. She had been a student activist at a time when it was dangerous to be one. She had delivered tons of used clothing to México and Latin America for poor families. She'd run a food pantry and once had even run for the school board and was thinking of doing it again. She was a founding board member of the Clergy with AIDS. Lizzie served the world in a way in which I didn't think I ever could.

The cocktail waitress returned with another frozen Margarita and a small glass of orange juice.

"To us," Lizzie said.

"To us," I echoed as we toasted.

Sister Lizzie's upper lip was rimmed with salt. She tapped her feet to "Earth Angel," coming from the nearby jukebox down the hall.

We sat in a little alcove off the main bar area where we could hear each other without yelling.

"Remember that one?" Lizzie said. "I sure do."

"Mamá Lupita was right, after all."

"What are you talking about, Soveida?"

"Mamá Lupita always wanted me to become a nun. She had this idea that nuns got to read books all the time and could enjoy their solitude without anyone to bother them. No torment of loving."

"Well, she was wrong there. Not everyone in the convent entered celibate or has remained celibate. And that means gay or straight. I hate the terms heterosexual and homosexual. One of these days the Church is just going to have to accept the eternal fact that it isn't good to be alone. Alone creates perverts. Pedophiles. It's not surprising we have our share of them in the Church, what with our good-old-boy mentality. These sickos have a distorted sense of sexuality. They prey on the innocent, and the worst thing is they know their superiors will cover up for them. Jesus Loving Christ! Did you know Father Richard? The new priest from Illinois? He was at Our Lady of Grace. I never liked him. I don't know why everyone always made such a fuss about him. Theologian. Studied in Rome. Spoke god-zillion languages. As far as I was concerned, he was an antisocial lump. No personality. Talked in a whisper. Couldn't connect with his own family. He had the look of a disturbed Baby Huey, remember him? He was confused, I could see that. He started molesting his altar boys and then some students in his religion class. Got away with it for a while. I just heard one of his victims came out and told the bishop. The kid was having nightmares and finally it just got to be too much. He had to tell someone. They relieved Father Richard from his duties and sent him up north to this place for sick priests. More and more you hear about this. Some fucked-up, desperately crazy priest violating young boys or girls. And all because the Pope is too damn busy living in the past. Don't talk to me about love between adults, no matter what the sexual preference, there's nothing wrong with that. Talk to me about the illness of the people who abuse children. Father Richard now has AIDS. What can you say? I used to take him groceries before he got sent away. I hated him, Soveida, for what he did, and yet I felt the Church betrayed him the way he betrayed his God.

"I thank the Mother God I'm who I am. My God is a God of possibility and Hope. She's not a never-never God. No pinched-nosed, narrow-minded old man touting salvation his way and his way only. A divine God didn't create hell to punish us for something beautiful and meaningful like sex. So when is the Church going to do something about it? I was celibate for years. I poured all my spiritual, mental, and physical juices into my life and my work. But now I want to be held. Is there something wrong with that, Soveida?"

"Have you ever suffered from loving, Lizzie?"

"What have I just been talking about, mujer? You haven't heard much I've said. So what is it? What's *really* going on with you? Are you in love?"

My sex hardened inside to the size of a small gray rock. I ached for Tirzio. Had Lizzie ever known anyone like Tirzio? Male or female? Did Lizzie know what it was to seek a man or a woman through dark prayer, swearing to God everything, save that loving? Did Lizzie know what it was to send missives in the wind, through the sky, late at night? Did she know the interminable wait of longing? Did she know how it was to welcome death after having made love? Did Lizzie know?

Each of us chooses our service.

My grandmother and mother never really broke their chain of bondage to men. So I suppose I am only one more bead in that never-ending rosary of need. I see what that love cost my grandmother. It embittered her to all men.

As for Dolly, thank Lizzie's Mother God that Dolly had the courage to finally divorce Luardo. Now she's with Reldon Claughbaugh, a man who loves her, who allows her to breathe, though she is still dependent upon him for her happiness. Lupita and Dolly are sisters in suffering who have spent most of their lives coddling men. Who ever took care of them? Not their husbands. Not their children. I'm just like them. I cry out: Tirzio! Knowing that he can never leave his wife or his two little girls or his small neat back yard to cross that great yawning night with no stars that leads to that tunnel that is my sex.

I see before me the only woman I know who is free. Truly free to love. I look at my hands on my glass and then push the glass away. I face Lizzie, my best friend, my maid of honor for husband number 1. My counselor, my confessor, my confidante for husband number 2. She is the only woman who ever really makes me laugh peals of laughter. She is the only man or woman who loves me just as I am, day or night, no matter what. She is Sister Margaret Elizabeth, my sister Lizzie, fifteen years a nun in the Order of the Sisters of the Most Holy Rapture.

I tell her in a voice almost choked with emotion: "Lizzie, I'm pregnant!"

She looks at me, beaming. Then she lifts her Margarita glass in another toast and says with great happiness: "Christ, girl, I knew it!"

At that moment I knew everything was all right, and would always be all right, because we shared the same story.

60

The Book of Faces

One day Mamá found me with a dark look on my face, the wrinkles between my eyes already too pronounced. I had settled into this expression of relentless determination without knowing it, with lines of worry, doubt, and surrender.

"Unless you stop scowling, Soveida Dosamantes, you'll get a permanent frown on your face," I heard Mamá say.

"Are you talking to me, Mamá?"

"Look at that man over there, you look like him! Don't look at the world so hard. All it does is give you a line between your eyes that night creams and oils won't erase. Lines on your face come from somewhere, from something. You see mine? Here, by the side of my mouth? That comes from gritting my teeth and trapping words I should have let go of in the first place. If I had, I wouldn't have these ditches on the side of my nose. Not to mention these lines on my forehead. Worry takes a lot from you and it gives you nothing in return. These horizontal lines like plowed fields on my forehead come from staying up too late, waiting for something terrible to happen. You worry about all sorts of things you can't say out loud, things you shouldn't even think. You worry about your husband, if he's going to come home early or late. You worry if he's drunk or sober. You worry if he'll smell of himself or a woman other than you. It's good if a man smells of himself if he smells good. Unfortunately, my father was the only man I've ever known who didn't smell. His breath was fresh, no matter if he'd been working in the fields all day. No one should inflict his smells on anyone. There's no place for uncleanliness. Even Dominga's brother and his family in the colonias and slums of México were clean. I can't say the same thing for some of our relatives. The people in the colonias lived with dead rats around the one spigot that provided water for all the colonia, in several rooms with one bathroom, really more a hole in the ground, with a bucket of water nearby that you used to flush the wastes down. I stayed with the family a few days one year when I went on a pilgrimage a la basílica de Nuestra Señora de Guadalupe. The family gave me their best bed, their only bed, while all six of them, the parents and four grown children, slept in the other room on the floor. One of the daughters worked in an office, the other was a cashier at Sanborn's in Coyoacán. One of the sons was an accountant and the other a student at UNAM. The father was a laborer. All of them were clean, hardworking people who contributed their salaries to the family. I can't imagine your cousins doing that. That just goes to show you that appearances are deceiving.

"Life is a great big face, with all the markings of our history on it. These wrinkles are my hardness and my silly worries, my lies and my unspoken words. They are the work I do and the things I left undone. Your lines, there, when you frown and look at the world as you do, say you're a person who isn't content and must always question things. It isn't an easy life you've chosen, m'ija, my Soveida. But you're the only person I never worry about. There's goodness in your face. It shows that you are capable of love.

"M'ija, we've all been taught to hide what we truly feel behind our faces. Some of us eventually wake up to see the masks our faces have become. I'm not talking about wearing makeup. I never wore much makeup. To me the greatest tool any woman can have is a little powder to cut the shine and to give your skin an even glow."

"Have you ever worn lipstick, Mamá?"

"Lipstick? ¡Ay, ni lo mande Dios! I don't want that colored lard on my lips like Lourdes Torres. She might just as well dye a bucket of Morrell lard with red food coloring. She learned the art of makeup from a clown in Chapultepec Park in México, or maybe from a dance-hall girl in Tijuana. I wouldn't want to kiss anyone with gelatin on their lips and have them leave their mark on me like a temporary tattoo. No, thank you, Soveida. All I need is a little Coty powder. Autumn Rose. I'm not one to use it like cornstarch or baby talc. I'm very light-handed with my touch, not like Doña Trancha, who in her later years was all powdered up like a mummy. Aunque la mona se vista de seda, mona se queda, Oralia would say. Even if the monkey dresses in silk, she will still be a monkey. Doña Trancha was a powdered monkey. My face is my face. With lines where lines should be, a few hairs where there shouldn't be hairs, with skin the way it should be for someone my age. We rub away, Soveida. I am exactly how I should be. Lived.

"Soveida, listen to me. I'm an old woman and I know more things that you can imagine. Some women have no connection to their face. They adorn and cover it with shades of color, with bases and hues and tints. They become a painting for the world to see. And yet it makes me feel better to see a woman badly and honestly painted up, with her eyebrows shaved or plucked entirely, her lip line inches higher than it should be, with the last traces of color like day-old stubble, than to see someone like Lourdes Torres. Lourdes covers her face with inches of putty, a dough that rises as the day goes on. Her wild animal eyes are always full of black legañas, mucus that gathers and then hardens in the corners.

"Today, m'ija, you rarely meet a woman with an open face. We're taught to shape our bodies into the molds of clothes. Your poor mamá has bra straps that cut into her shoulders. When men see her, they only think breasts. Soveida, we are more than our bodies or our breasts.

"Loss changes us. And pain. And the death of those we love. Eyes cloud over and are covered by soft cataracts. Lips are swallowed and vanish. Eyebrows and eyelashes disappear in childbirth. Age spots begin to flourish. Small moles become significant. Pores enlarge. Teeth darken, crumble, and become silver or gold twinklings in the unwelcome sea of mouths we don't care to know.

"But we are more than this change, more than this face, Soveida. We *become* our mothers, our grandmothers. And when we see people who wear their antepasados in their face, it is a relief, and a blessing to know the ancestors are near."

"I could write a book about faces." Mamá turned to Dolores. "As a matter of fact, maybe someday I will."

"Maybe someday I'll write my book, too, Dolly. It'll be about a single waitress who gets pregnant and is about to have a baby."

"Soveida! Is it true? No. Really?"

"Really, Dolly."

"Oh, sweetheart, I'm so happy for you I just *knew* something was wrong, that you were so tired, I just didn't guess. I should have known."

"She *had* that look," Mamá added. "The look of a wounded cow, half in and out of this world, one foot all the way up to her breastbone, the other dragging like a stump to the ground. You and the padrecito professor—"

"He's in Germany, Mamá."

"Ay, no. How long has he been gone?"

"It's been a while."

"Ay, no."

"I don't know when he's coming back."

"Ay, no. The baby would have been very pretty."

"Mamá! We have time to discuss everything later," Dolly interrupted. "Soveida! When? Oh, let me hug you."

"Bring my plastic bottle of Lourdes water so I can bless you and the baby. En el nombre del Padre, del Hijo, del Espíritu Santo."

"I'm a single parent, Dolly. No husband in sight."

"Does it matter, sweetheart? So am I. Why didn't you tell me, Soveida? Oh, look." She laughed through tears. "I'm crying. I need a Kleenex."

"Stop crying, Dolores, you're making me cry as well," Mamá said.

"I was afraid to tell you, Dolly. I wanted to make sure I was strong enough."

"Strong enough for what?"

"Strong enough to keep this child, strong enough to love it, and strong enough to keep going on."

"Well, we have to keep going on, there's no other way, Soveida. Ni modo. What do you think? Having a child is work, and you're used to work. It shouldn't frighten you. And in a way, you're lucky you don't have the wrong man around. Your mother and I didn't do so good, maybe you can do better."

"I'll try, Mamá, I'll try."

"We'll all try this time to get it right. Que Dios nos bendiga, m'ija."

THE BOOK OF SERVICE

CHAPTER FOURTEEN

The Passing of the Waitress Torch

Dearest Dedea:

Well, I guess this is it. The passing of the waitress torch. Milia passed it to me and I pass it to you. Don't be afraid. I'll still be running alongside of you for a while at least. Probably even longer than I myself expect. I can't imagine what I would do without El Farol. I'm proud of you and the work you've done. I've seen you grow as a waitress and as a human being. By now you know that there is more to waitressing than serving food. More to living than being fed or feeding someone yourself. More to people than what we briefly see of them in our work.

I wanted to give you a little gift. It's a copy of The Book of Service: A Handbook for Servers *that I've been working on for many years. I still don't think it's finished yet. It's taken me a long time to get my thoughts together, and longer to put them down. The handbook is about more than serving food. It's about service. What it means to serve and be served. Why is it that women's service is different from men's?*

I grew up with hardworking women. All my life I have appreciated the work they do. Here, then, is a copy of my handbook.

I wish you the best, always. I wish someone had handed me The Book of Service *when I was a young waitress. It would have saved me time, worry, and pain. Never forget who you are, and where you come from. Never forget that the work you do is important and full of lessons.*

Feel free to give me your comments and criticism. I have a feeling I'm going to be working on this handbook for a long time to come.

Your sister in work,

Soveida

61

Rain

Tirzio and I had avoided each other the way only lovers who once really desired each other could, looking away while the other comes around. I'd seen that sad and desperate face before, and Tirzio looked at me that way when we accidentally met at the grocery store. It had been weeks since I'd seen him. No calls, no notes, no explanations. Rounding a corner, I unexpectedly ran into him in the soup section, holding a can of Cream of Asparagus soup.

"Soveida!" he said with surprise.

"Tirzio," I replied, trying to remain calm.

"How are you, Soveida? I meant to call. I've been so busy."

"Me, too."

"I heard about Larry Larragoite."

"It's been a mess. How are you, Tirzio?"

"I heard from J.V. He sounds really happy."

"I know. How's Patsy?"

"She's getting ice cream."

"Oh."

"Can I call you later?"

"It's my day off. Call me after six."

"I need to talk to you."

"Me, too, Tirzio. Bye."

"Goodbye, Soveida."

Patsy was in the ice-cream section. Larry was in the hospital, hooked up to various machines. Oralia was in the ground, covered now by ants and grass. J.V. was in Germany. Little Tirzio, Jr., was struggling to come to life.

Later that night, Tirzio called to say that he was coming over.

It wasn't him I was worried about. What concerned me was the insurance Bonnie had canceled. Who would insure a woman nearly three months pregnant?

There was a hard knock at the door, but Tirzio didn't want to come inside. I suggested we go out back to the little yard he had helped me plant. The buffalo grass was patchy, but after I'd watered it faithfully for some time it seemed to be finally taking hold. I wanted a desert garden and had recently planted a desert willow, several Mexican elders, and a variety of ocotillo, cholla, agave, and yucca plants as well as a few nopals along the back to hide the ugly chain-link fence. They faced a ceramic fountain from Juárez now filled with water for the birds. It was still very hot, and would remain so until sunset. And yet it was pleasant near the back of the trailer, in the shade of a small porch that Tirzio had built for me. We sat on two blue metal lawn chairs and looked out to the small yard. It wasn't much to look at, and yet there was something reassuring about seeing so many new plants growing. A slight breeze came up, bringing a scent of earth, dry and expectant, thirsty for rain.

Tirzio seemed nervous and off-balance, which was rare for him. I asked him if he wanted something to drink. I noticed, when we briefly and awkwardly hugged on meeting, that he had a slightly sour smell, as if he had been eating watermelon some time before in the heat. Or had slept too long and arisen with a deep-seated nausea. When he brushed my cheek, I felt the harsh stubble on his face that scratched me like sandpaper. It was unusual for me to see him this way, he who had always been fresh, sweet-smelling, and full of vigor. He wore a tight shirt that seemed ill-fitting. For the first time, I saw how similar to Patsy he had become after so many years of marriage. Today he was her equal, a clumsy boy without grace, without words, afraid to stand in the front yard talking, frightened someone might see us, or, worse yet, terrified to go inside the trailer, knowing it would lead to the back bedroom.

Yet Tirzio had spent the night only once in my trailer, when Patsy and the girls went to Albuquerque for the State Fair, Patsy in the company of her two sisters and their kids.

At the back of my small closet, filled with several black-and-white waitress outfits and colorful sashes from México, from that one holy night was one lone starched man's shirt, neck size 16, neatly hung on a plastic hanger. When Tirzio was in the bathroom the morning after,

I opened the closet, moved my clothes aside, and looked worshipfully at the crisp purity of the shirt.

That was the night I cooked my only meal for Tirzio, a vegetarian mash, a tasty casserole gone ugly, full of brown rice, broccoli, and crookneck squash. He said he liked it, but I had my doubts. No matter, we hardly ate, but retired early to the back bedroom, photographs of my family enveloping us. I hardly slept all night, so happy was I, knowing nights like this were nearly impossible.

The breeze was now a little stronger, and some clouds began to appear in the sky, hinting at rain.

Neither Tirzio nor I knew where to begin. And so I began, because I had to, though in a way everything that would be said had been spoken through our silence. We were merely meeting to confirm each other's late-night prayers and hard-won resolutions.

I wish I had been able to talk to someone about Tirzio. Sister Lizzie, Mamá, Dolores, Mara, all the women I might have talked to were busy, deeply occupied with their lives. I wanted to say that I hurt, the way they had all hurt. But what good would it have done? And, besides, whatever strength I had gathered to say goodbye to Tirzio came from the power of their silent, reassuring, and unrelenting love.

My words came hard. "I'm renting my trailer, Tirzio. To Pito, from work. And I've decided to move into my grandmother's house. I'll be going to school part-time. I'm cutting back on my work hours. I want to get a B.A., and then maybe go on to graduate school."

My thoughts came quickly, as if I were trying to tell him everything at once, circling around what I really wanted to say.

"Soveida, I'm sorry I haven't called."

"I haven't called, either. Women are allowed to call. But it doesn't matter now. We're here. And besides, I don't think we were really able to talk to each other. I mean, after the night you stayed."

Tirzio looked away, and I knew the memory was painful for him.

"But that's not what I wanted to talk to you about. I love you, Tirzio, but it's not right. I just can't go on. You have Patsy and the girls, and they need you. And I need to be settled. Peaceful. Not only for myself. I'm expecting a baby, Tirzio. I haven't told you because I wanted to be complete in myself. Do you understand? I don't expect anything from you. I don't want anything. Nothing."

"Soveida! When did you find out?"

"It's been a while."

"Pregnant! I don't believe it!"

Tirzio laughed to himself incredulously like a startled young boy, wildly out of control. There was something ugly about it.

"Believe it. It's true."

"Have you told J.V.?"

"No, I haven't. Please don't laugh."

"I'm sorry. I'm nervous. What are you going to do? You're *not* going to get an abortion?"

"I *want* this baby, Tirzio."

"It'll work out. I don't know. Who knows, in a year or two, after time—maybe I can help you. Do you need money?"

"You've always told me you could never leave Patsy, Tirzio. I don't expect that. And money isn't what I want."

Tirzio avoided my eyes, returning his gaze to the majesty of the Lagrimas Mountains. He took my hand slowly and held it firmly. Then, with a deep sigh, he bent his head. We both looked at each other, and then toward the mountains. Gathering strength from stone, Tirzio quietly began to cry.

We cried together and I comforted him. I thanked God for this grace passing like a cloud. I knew I would always be the stronger. He knew it as well. We didn't say anything to each other for a while. And then I gave him a hug and thanked him in my heart for crying. I would always love him for this one moment of mercy. No matter what happened and for all time.

Tirzio sat back in the chair, and seemed smaller and more crumpled than I'd ever seen him, as if he had been folded inward. A person more confused and lost than I could ever become. He was a man who loved children, but he could not love this child. He was a person who believed in family, but not in this one.

Tirzio got up and looked out to the yard. He surveyed the new plants and said thickly, "The yard looks nice."

"I have *you* to thank," I said.

Then he held me tightly, and looked me squarely in the face. "I'm so sorry, Soveida."

"Don't be sorry, Tirzio. We have our child."

"Yes."

"I'm not going to tell J.V."

"You aren't?"

"No. It doesn't concern him."

"But he loves you."

"If he does, then he'll just have to love me and the baby. However we are. I've made up my mind. That's it. I won't kill the baby, Tirzio. I can't. Let's just say goodbye now, and go on."

"Adios, querida. May God bless you."

The yard was still, except for the growing song of the cicadas. Thunder rumbled in the distance, and lightning cracked the sky behind the Lagrimas. I could smell rain. I would sit outside and await its approach. Surely it would come and nourish the yellow and blue desert flowers in the sand, the white yucca flowers by the side of the winding road, the ocotillo's red-tipped tendrils waving to the seemingly empty sky, the nopal's sweet, blood-red fruit.

62

My Other Family

Everyone was so upset after Bonnie fired Petra and Lavel that we called a meeting and decided to go on strike. We quit early one night in protest and Bonnie was furious, firing everyone for striking. The next day the restaurant was closed. That afternoon she started calling everyone to come back to work. She promised to rehire Lavel, but he refused. Then Pito said he wouldn't come back if Lavel didn't. Finally Lavel agreed to return if Petra was rehired. Bonnie said absolutely no, no way, but everyone pressured her, so instead of waiting on tables, Petra is now a cashier. We'll see how it goes. I started classes part-time and Dedea and a new woman named Frances are taking some of my hours. Frances is a lifer. She's very good and she can add. Pancha and Fermín's party is still on hold. We're waiting for Larry to come back and be best man. I had a real good talk with Bonnie, and so did Fermín. She's settled down. I think she just overreacted. Speaking of which, Bonnie gave everybody back their wills. She said the safe was too crowded. It's just as well. We can't control our lives, how can anyone else control our deaths? Larry has some crazy ideas, but he's still my favorite boss.

Larry recovered surprisingly quickly. I went to visit him in the Del Valle Nursing Home. He was sitting up in bed. His voice was faint, but he seemed stronger. Since he'd been at the Del Valle, he'd seen a need to build a home for the crippled children who lived there, who had no other place to go. As soon as he got well, he told me, he would have a fund-raiser at El Farol. And on top of this, he and Bonnie were thinking of adopting. Was this the same Larry I knew?

I made him promise he'd rest. The home could wait until he was strong enough.

"Another thing," he announced from his bed. "We need more activities for the senior crowd. Hell, have you been up and down these hallways? I thought I'd get this arts-and-crafts thing going."

"Enough, Larragoite!" I finally said. "Promise me you'll settle down."

"Much as I can. Never thought I'd be grateful to Bonnie for sending me to this hellhole. You know, Soveida, this heart attack saved my marriage, and that's not all. It gave me back my life, if you know what I mean."

I did. Sometimes adversity has a way of healing us.

As Larry and I sat in his room in the Del Valle, the walls covered with giant "Get Well" computer posters from the staff, and cards and inspirational messages from both customers and employees, I informed him what had happened at work. He told me he had never gotten the full low-down from Bonnie.

"Petra finally has the hang of it. She's now the afternoon cashier. She's off nights and weekends. She likes it that way. Lavel's in a treatment program and he's doing well. I took a cake to work to celebrate."

"Chuy came to see me, Soveida. We both cried." He paused. "Hell, I miss you guys."

Late that night I got a call from Mara. I hadn't heard from her in years. Somehow I'd lost track of her.

"Hey, Soveida. You there? Wait a sec. Let me just get this phone cord. Shit, it's wrapped around the coffee table. That's what you get for having a cord a mile long. Are you there? I'm here."

"Mara! Where have you been? The last time I called you, I got a message saying the number was disconnected."

"It was. I dropped out."

"You dropped out, like as in the sixties 'dropped out'?"

"No, like in the nineties. I took off to México. I've lost weight. And I got engaged. His name is Roll Halwell."

"Mara, I can't believe it."

"What happened?"

"I took a shower."

"What?"

"I was drinking and you name it. One night I decided to take a shower around three o'clock in the morning. I just started screaming. Must have been in there about an hour. I don't think anyone could hear me through the water and the music I was playing. I emerged pruned out and lay on the bed, a wrinkled rag. I thought of calling you, but I was too drained. So I stayed in bed the rest of that night, thinking. I called in sick to work, and the next day I turned in my resignation. I just got tired of the way I was living. What about you? What's new?"

"God, Mara, I don't know where to begin."

I really didn't. In a phone conversation that went on for several hours Mara and I laughed, cried, and caught up with each other.

I told her about Oralia's death, about Mamá's attempt at dying, about her move in with Dolly and Reldon, and how Mamá loves to go to the dances at the Senior Center like a high-school girl. Then came the inevitable.

"So how's your love life?"

"I'm three months pregnant, Mara."

"Really?"

"Really, Mara. Please don't ask me any more. I just decided to become a single mother."

"Wow!" she exclaimed. "I better get to Agua Oscura quick before something *really* happens! So what else is new?"

"Nothing much, really."

"Maybe I'll come down sometime. You tell Mamá that I'm coming to see her."

"Why don't you tell her yourself, Mara?"

"Maybe I will."

"Well, it's about time, Mara Fortuna. It's about damn time you got your butt down here, woman. Bring Rawley . . ."

"Roll. His name is Roll."

"Bring him. I'll be the maid of honor."

"Not so fast, woman. You sound wonderful, you know it?"

"You, too. I may even run for Bazaar Queen. Get your money can ready!"

"I love you. Well, I gotta go. I mean it, I really gotta go. This damn cord is all twisted up and I can't reach the bathroom. I'll talk to you soon. Bueno, bye!"

"Bye, Mara, and thanks for calling."

"Will do! Bye!"

Fermín and Pancha were remarried one hot Saturday in late August. Larry was there, a little thinner than before, in a white suit that Preddie threatened to splash with red chile. Eloisa grabbed Larry in a huge bear hug and then set off to bring him a plate from the kitchen. Chuy led the marcha. Mamá Lupita gave la bendición. Dolly was in charge of the guest book. Sister Lizzie sang a series of songs Fermín and Pancha had selected, what Mamá later called Born-Again Pop. I was maid of honor. Larry was best man. At one point, Larry and I were standing side by side by the punch bowl, each of us drinking something non-alcoholic.

"Well, Larry," I said, "how does it feel to be back?"

"Hell, this cockroach-ridden, leaky-assed, chile-spattered, greasy-smelling pit of a restaurant is home, Soveida. What can I say?"

63

The Blue House

Monday at the Blue House. Chata was cleaning the cupboards in the kitchen. She'd arrived a little early and set immediately to work removing all Mamá's dishes from the wooden shelves. Then she laid everything out in the dining room to be cleaned. Some little-used dishes hadn't been washed in many, many years and bore signs of oily dust and a brownish wax that had settled on the surfaces. One by one Chata soaked, cleaned, and then rinsed each dish with near-boiling water that only she, after years of building up resistance, could tolerate. She hummed along with XELO as she worked, the radio not too loud, but at a volume any patrona wouldn't mind.

It was a sunny day outside, all the leaves fallen now, the trees shorn of leaves, dark brown, and dormant. A good day to clean a house, especially one that needed real work, deep work, work done with care. It was a happy day, too, for the house was being cleaned the way it should have been thirty years ago.

"Por fin I can get my hands on your mamá's mugres—all the old glass containers without lids, the rusted orange-juice cans, and the brittle cottage-cheese containers. ¡Dios mío! But those two women lived like hermits here. Let in some light, por favor, it smells of dust, Soveida. Finally I'm able to get in here and have my way with this kitchen. I refused to set foot in here more than once when your grandma asked me to come over and clean. I had to, she wouldn't let me have my way. You know how viejitas are, especially ones like Oralia: she didn't believe in covering food with Saran Wrap. And not only that, her eyesight wasn't so good—que descanse en paz—she was a saint, but I'm telling you, Soveida, she didn't use dish soap. Don't ask me what she used, I have no idea. Whatever it was, it was from a century gone by. It's a good house, big, full of enormous rooms with high ceilings. I'm glad you took out all the rugs. Now you have the hardwood floors. After the kitchen, and after all the painting you're going to do, we'll get to the floors. The floors will come last. Wait until you see how I'll make them shine!"

The kitchen already shone. The once-white cabinets took on their former gloss and the walls looked fresh, unspotted by the years' buildup of hot grease, tomato skins, stuck cucumber, and watermelon pulp. Chata could have employed her Scrapey-Scrapey on the walls, but instead she used an old, unused putty knife of Luardo's, and of course, her fingernails.

All of us, as a matter of fact, could have really used a Scrapey-Scrapey. I was settled in the large living room, cleaning the baseboards, all the furniture pushed to one side and covered over with old cream-colored sheets. Mamá had donated her old linen to the cause. "They're ugly, and besides, I can't use them any longer, not with my king-size water bed with the satin sheets. Not that I plan to use those sheets Reldon gave me for my birthday every day of the world; I have other sheets for my water bed, in all colors, with lots of flowers. Besides, I'm tired of most of my things; well, except for some of the antique furniture. But the rest of it—the dish sets, the crystal, the silver tea service—is now yours. Quiero deshacerme de mi junque. Junk, that's all it is, plain and not so very simple. Nice junk, but junk. It's passed through my hands, I enjoyed it, yes, but now it's yours. And besides, I don't have any room for a set of sterling-silver iced-tea stirrers with a matching trivet, or a pottery fish platter from the state of Michoacán. My room at your mamá's is just the way I like it. Full of light, no weight to bring me down when I finally decide to rise to heaven. Just take our lists, Soveida, and do with everything as you wish."

So Chata brought everything from the kitchen into the dining room, and I sorted through it and put it in boxes:
Battered Women's Shelter
Nuns of the Sacred Paraclete
Goodwill
Chata
Me

I would keep what I felt was a legacy of Mamá Lupita's, the christening spoons, and the John F. Kennedy plate. But what about the plate honoring Pope John Paul's visit to México? Maybe I could slip it into the Paraclete's box without Mamá knowing. The Nixon plate would go to Goodwill. From Luardo, no doubt. He had always been a staunch Republican.

I would give Chata many things, things that I didn't need, things I knew she could use. She and her kids were moving into my trailer on Fir Street. Pito had decided not to move in, saying it was too big for him, but thanks anyway. If you give it to me, Soveida, I'll just have to give it to the Goodwill. So the trailer had fallen to Chata.

Chata appreciated everything I gave her, the many packages and boxes of clothing. And yet we never spoke about these gifts. There was no need to. If she couldn't use the things I gave her, then she would give them away to someone who could. Tere now had her own low-income house, where she and Juan Miguel lived. I would gather things for her as well.

"Soveida!"

"What is it, Mamá?"

"What are you doing? Are you doing low things? Now, remember you can't be straining yourself. Leave the high things to your mamá or Chata."

"Mamá, I'm sorting dishes."

"Leave that alone and come and help me. I'm in the kitchen. I've sent Chata to the bathroom to clean while I fix lunch."

"You're fixing lunch, Mamá? But I told you I'd go out and get us some pizza."

"Pizza, ay no."

"Hamburgers?"

"Not today. I had one yesterday."

"Chinese?"

"Me afecta el MSG. It gives me, well, it gives me—you can imagine."

"Well, then, how about a sub?"

"Soveida, m'ija, I'm fixing lunch. Look, your mamá showed me how to fix her tuna fish. The secret is in the onions. You chop them finitos, finitos. Then you put in the mayonesa. I just love your mamá's tuna fish. So, where is Dolly, anyway? It's time to eat."

"She's cleaning up my room, I mean—"

"Go on, say it. She's cleaning *your* room. It *was* my room, but now it's yours."

"Will you miss the house, Mamá?"

"Will I miss it? Do you miss a cold sore, the flu, a bad case of empache, o una espina in your shoe? No, Soveida, I won't miss the house. Here, take the platter of chonoches. Remember that's what you used to call sandwiches when you were a baby? Chonoches. Take the platter—where? Where can we eat?"

"Not in the dining room, Mamá, or in the sala—all the furniture is pushed to one side."

"Not in your room, Soveida, it's not an eating place, not yet. By the way, I'm glad you chose that room for your bedroom instead of the ones on the second floor. I won't be worrying about the baby so much with him or her wandering up those stairs. Now I never would have thought of painting the room a light purple on two walls, white on the others, but I like the idea. It was too old-fashioned before, an old lady's room. Something out of el cine mejicano where the widowed abuelita lives on the rancho with a water pump and no indoor toilet. It was so dark for so long, now it's full of life and light. My great-grandchild will be happy in the purple room. I was so tired of that dark blue."

"It's still a nice color."

"Too stuck in the past. I want to see how you're going to paint the outside of the house, mixing that old navy blue with your sky blue."

"And don't forget the dusty rose, and the yellow around the doorway."

"That's how our antepasados painted their houses. A turquoise doorway there, a white banco here, pink around the windows. It's good you have an eye for color, you and that waiter, Margarito, who's helping you. No, it's not a bad house, Soveida."

"Oh, Mamá! It's a beautiful house."

"It needs work."

"Yes, but it'll get done. I want to put a skylight in the bathroom."

"Like the one over my water bed? So you can look at the stars too, eh?"

"Yes."

"I approve. Now call your mamá. Is she still mad?"

"Oh, I don't know. I guess so."

"She'll get over it. Give her a few days. What about Mara?"

"She was upset, too, Mamá."

"Every time they talk on the phone they start yelling at each other. Your mamá still hasn't let go of much. She hasn't forgiven herself for Lina, or Luardo. I keep telling her it wasn't her fault."

"Mara thinks so."

"Well, she'll eventually have to let it go, Soveida. She has to. Or it will kill her. It's as simple as that."

"I wish they wouldn't fight so much."

"That's what people do who never talk. It's a beginning, anyway, don't you see? They either need to talk some more, or not at all and just forgive. With them, I think they need to talk. Although, Virgen Santa, I don't want to be in the same room when they do talk."

"Mara was sad, Mamá. I mean, about breaking up with Roll."

"She's a woman who shouldn't ever marry again. Just live with the next one, I told her."

"Mamá!"

"Yes I did. It's true. If it works out for la Señora Borrego y el Señor Baca, our neighbors, how you kids say it, 'shacking up,' then Mara Fortuna, I told her, it can work out for you."

"Were you happy to talk to Mara, Mamá? She sounded so good to me."

"What a question! Does chile have seeds? Go call your mamá. She might be sad or mad, I don't care. Either way, she has to eat. I didn't go through all this trouble for my girls to go hungry. Not today of all days, cleaning day. Call Chata and ask her to bring chairs to the garden. We'll eat out there with Oralia."

"It might be cold, Mamá."

"I already went outside to check. I stood in the sun there by Oralia's herbs, to the side of her roses, near the walkway between the two houses. It was so warm I got sleepy. You better bring a hat, Soveida, I don't want the baby to get sunburned. Did I ever tell you the story about the pregnant woman who stayed out most of the day in 115 degree heat picking chile in July? No? Well, I'll tell it to you later. Dolly! Chata! ¡Vengan a comer! Now take the platter and don't drop it. Look at the bread, whole wheat for you. I've cut it the way your mamá does, in little triangles with a colored sword in the middle with an olive. Do you know how hard it is to find those little swords, Diosito! I bought this lunch with my own money, I'll have you know. Come back for the iced tea and then the hard-boiled eggs."

"Hard-boiled eggs?"

"I know how much you like eggs, m'ija. Ay, Dolly! There you are. Take this chilito out, and then come back for the frijoles."

"Beans and chile with tuna-fish sandwiches, Mamá?"

"Ya, Dolly! You be quiet now. Just eat what you want. If you don't

like it, you don't have to eat it. Like I say, if you're hungry, you'll eat.
Dolly, you know I have to have my chilito, and besides, Chata me
hizo unas tortillas. They're hot and big and they fold good. That's the
sign of a good tortilla. It's a mix-it-up lunch. A whatever-we-have-and-
it's-all-good-but-it-may-not-go-with-anything-else kind of meal. Mi
favorito."

"All right, Mamá."

"Don't all right me, Dolly Loera! And just because you're so necia,
I'm going to make *you* say grace. Look at your daughter, there in the
sun, she's going to have a baby, and if that doesn't make you happy,
I don't know what will. Although Soveida does look a little chiriska, a
little messy. I wish she would throw away those old rubber sandals of
hers, they're dangerous. She could fall on the new tile in the bathroom."

"She only wears them to clean floors, Mamá, that's what she says."

"That's more sensible. She can't be running around in shortes and
that ugly T-shirt with the paint anymore. Now, if *only* she would start
wearing a slip. Why aren't you wearing an apron, Dolly?"

"I don't like them, Mamá."

"You do if you work with me. Ask Chata to give me one of my aprons.
As a matter of fact, where *are* my aprons? Soveida! Where are my
aprons, the ones Oralia made me?"

"She says to look under ME, Mamá."

"ME?"

"In the box that has ME on the front. Here, I'll get them. Is this
what you want, Mamá?"

"Okay, one for you, Dolly, and one for Soveida. ¿Chata? ¿Dónde
está Chata?"

"Sí, Señora Dosamantes?"

"Tenga, Chata, un delantal."

"Señora Dosamantes, I have my own apron."

"Outside, everyone. Woman. Man. I guess we're all men here. And
child. ¡A comer! Like I was telling Soveida, everything will work out.
With Tere. With Mara. With you name anything else. It always does.
One way or another. One time or another. It's all in the way we do
things, Dolly. Like your onions in the tuna fish. Finitos. Finitos. Ni
modo."

Acknowledgments

My thanks to Rubén Darío Sálaz, who believed in me so completely, after knowing me for so little time, who believed I could write this book, who felt I was able, when I doubted it myself.

Thanks to Rudolfo and Patricia Anaya, dear friends, and to my compañeras y compañeros in spirit: Sandra Cisneros, Gary Soto, Ana Castillo, Sandra Benítez, Julia Alvarez, Ben Sáenz, Terry Tempest Williams, Michael Shay, and Eleanor Broh-Kahn.

My gratitude to Rudy Tellez and Tenaya Torres Tellez, amigos del corazón, for so many acts of thoughtfulness and care these past years.

A thank-you as well to my sisters, Margo Chávez-Charles and Faride Conway, and the unborn one. A lo dado no se le da fin.

Thank you to the "Apostelletes": Kathy Gallegos Austin, Grace Tejada Cataldo, Joanna Romero Lucero, and Joann Biel Burns—sisters all, for always reminding me of laughter's healing grace. MHS Forever!

I am grateful to all my teachers who became friends: Michael Graves, Bill Alford, Hershel Zohn, Tony Hillerman, Joe Forsythe, Paul Moore, John Hadsell, Tom Erhard, Keith Wilson, Mrs. Lick and Miss Margaret Hill.

A special thanks is due to the University of Houston Drama Department, whose support and generosity to me has been invaluable in allowing me to work on this book, and to those people in that world, Dr. Sidney Berger, Chris Woods, Roxanne Collins, Sandy Havens, as well as all my students who have taught me so well.

Thanks as well to Dr. Bill Bridges, as well as all my colleagues and students in the English Department at New Mexico State University.

My gratitude to that special woman in my life: Constance "Conita" Gale, who has taught me the meaning of the word "sister."

Thanks are also due to the many people who have helped at the Other House. And to my good neighbors, who have nourished and supported me these many years: Bob Reeves, Jim Mealy, and Ofelia Carrillo, a dear and lovely lady and a great cook.

Thank you to all those who supported me these years of legal uncertainty. You gave more than you will ever know. Estoy eternamente agradecida.

My eternal thanks to Celia Fountain, who honored me in letting me sweep her kitchen, and to Arthur Fountain, her husband, whose rendition of "Hello, Dolly" will forever be etched in my heart. And in memory of those great ladies of Las Cruces whose ideals of service are known far and wide, and with whom it was my privilege to serve: Katherine "Katy" Griggs Meek Camuñez, and Magdalena "Maggie" Gamboa.

My dear uncle, Eddie T. Chávez, a painter, was the first artist in my life. Through his example, I have come to understand dedication and devotion to one's artistic work. Thanks as well to my dear aunt, Amelia "Mela" Banegas Chávez, a strong, honest, and loving woman whose life has been a blessing to us, her family.

My gratitude to those in the spirit world, including my mother, Delfina Rede Faver Chávez, whose seed is sown. La Reina de Las Cruces, formidable, fierce, forgiving, she has taught me what true service is.

Thanks are due to my publishers and to my editor, John Glusman, from Farrar, Straus and Giroux, my "acting coach" par excellence, a talented and kind man, who was willing to go inside the whale, and lay hands on the sperm sacs. Thank you, John, for always asking the right questions, and for inspiring me to do my deepest, bravest work.

My agent, Susan Bergholz, has been light to me and hope; she has empowered me with her belief in the power of women's work. She is a friend unlike any other I have ever known. Thank you, Susan.

There is no way to thank my husband, Daniel Zolinsky, for his unflagging support and love these many years. He has been an inspiration to me in ways he doesn't know—for the careful thoroughness of his creative work, his high standards of professionalism, and his sense of justice. You have uplifted, challenged, and blessed my work. Gracias, mi amor.

I am grateful to Our Lady of Guadalupe, who has sustained and blessed me these years, la Diosita incomparable.

Thanks also to the gesticulating, reprimanding old man in Albuquerque who let me know, in clear pantomime, and in no uncertain terms, that women are not supposed to write such books.

Thanks to all my patient readers who asked me over the years what I was working on and always told me that they were still waiting.

It is for you—the old, the young, the healing, the withholding, the frightened, the brave—that this book was written.

Denise Chávez
Las Cruces, New Mexico